THE LAST TALLYHO

THE
LAST TALLYHO

A NOVEL BY *Richard L. Newhafer*

G. P. Putnam's Sons
New York

This book is for

Lt. Cortney Anderson	Lt. Danny Musetti
Lt. Bob Black	LCDR Dan Potter
Commander Charlie Crommelin	Lt. Jeff Stillman
Lt. Dick Davis	Ensign Gene Ryan
Lt. Woody McVay	Lt. Joe Kanevsky

and all the others who lived and went down
under the golden wings. . . .

THE LAST TALLYHO

I

August, 1943

This night is for the young.

On a steep hillside overlooking the city of San Diego is the El Cortez Hotel.

In one respect the El Cortez differs from the other hotels throughout the land in this war year of 1943. It is the jumping-off place for the men who go to fight the Pacific war. The bright young pennies enter here and fall into the chute of the slot machine of war. When they return, if they do, they are no longer bright and shining, and they do not sing very much either.

Crowning the El Cortez is the Sky Room, a dimly lighted room containing a circular bar. The young men who come here to say good-bye to their way of life stare out through the glass walls at the city spread below them. Flickering lights rim the harbor and outline the dark shapes of the ships lying patiently at anchor. Soon now the ships will be sailing, cutting white contrails through the water as they head out past Point Loma for the far Pacific. White sands stretch at Tarawa and Kwajalein, and the skies are blue over Wake and Truk and Marcus.

Elsewhere across the land, walking the lonely night streets or perhaps sitting on a sweep of hill overlooking a river valley, the young men and their girls look across other tables and their hands touch as they seek the unfamiliar words to say good-bye.

Yet in the air is an urgency that says, "Let's get going. Let's get moving because time is running out. Tomorrow the ships are sailing, and some of us will not be coming home again." The tinkle of ice in the glasses and the loud, forced laughter say, "There are lands far

9]

from here that I have read about, and now I must journey west to see them. But there is a bill attached to the prospectus, a bill that calls for a payment which may be more than I care to pay."

So reason the young men this August night. For they are young and in their youth move forward eagerly to battle.

The sound of laughter is loud in the Sky Room of the El Cortez. Two young men sit at the bar, considering themselves in the glass wall of the room. They are fliers; witness the gold wings over the left breast pockets.

"We leave in the morning, Bates." The speaker is tall, wide-shouldered, handsome in a reckless fashion. A lock of dark hair hangs down over one eye. He is talking more to himself than to Bates. Bates knows full well they are leaving in the morning.

The burly Bates answers, idly rubbing a finger down the beaded whiskey glass he holds in his hand. "Oh four hundred."

"On a lousy tanker. An oiler. A hell of a way for a fighter pilot to go to war."

Bates smiles. "Why the hurry? You got a death wish or something?"

"Six days on a lousy oiler," repeated the slim man whose name was Dick Marriner.

"Six days. Six weeks," said Bates. "What difference? The war will still be there."

"Yeah," said Marriner. He threw down his drink in a long swallow. "Let's get out of here. This place is dying."

Bates chuckled softly. "You're jumpy tonight, boy. A man would think you don't really want to go to war."

Marriner did not answer because he had, for some time, been thinking that exact thing. He wondered what it was that had changed in him in the short period of time since he had left carrier qualifications. He knew he was not a coward, and he possessed great confidence in his flying ability. But somehow his scale of values had undergone a change since he had married a month ago. He had not suddenly become imbued with a sense of responsibility, because Marriner was not a man to live in fear of tomorrow. But an almost indefinable caution had entered his mind, and now he was not sure that the long journey across the western sea was exactly what he would choose at this particular time of his life if he had anything at all to say about it.

Marriner's life had been a series of successes ever since he could

[10

remember. Whatever he had set his hand to had usually turned out not just well but excellently. He was a superb athlete and in his nineteenth year had been runner-up in the National Amateur Golf Championship. If he exhibited a "don't give a damn" attitude, it was due only to his natural high spirits. Those who knew Dick Marriner best summed up the man when they said, "No matter what old Dick does, he'll always land on his feet."

Now Bates was watching him, a smile crinkling the corners of his eyes. "Thinking about a wife, maybe?"

"Maybe," answered Marriner and wondered why he should feel guilty. Why shouldn't a man think about his wife at a time like this?

"No offense meant," Bates said. "I'd be thinking of her too. She's a hell of a good-looking woman, Dick."

"Thanks," said Marriner.

"But so goddam far away tonight." Bates was watching the entrance to the room. Marriner saw his eyes widen in appreciation. "Jesus," Bates whispered.

Marriner looked and saw a leggy blond girl coming toward the bar. She wore a gabardine suit and her hair fell in waves to her shoulders. Her profile was toward Marriner, and he caught his breath as he almost whispered his wife's name. Then the girl turned, and he saw flashing green eyes, and his breath went out in a long sigh.

"Christ," said Bates, "but I could use some of that."

"Who couldn't?" Marriner agreed. He was remembering the few short days they had had together. Could it be this thing that had been bothering him might be loneliness? He looked at Bates. "She looks like my wife."

Bates nodded. "I noticed."

The girl took a seat at the bar. She spoke to the bartender. "A Daiquiri, please."

"Yours or mine?" Bates asked.

"Does it matter?"

"Hell yes!" Bates laughed. "It's our last night. You sick or something?"

"You take her then." Marriner could not get the picture of his wife out of his mind.

Bates sighed. "Listen, Dick. No one is asking you to violate an oath or whatever you've made. You're going away tomorrow, maybe forever. If you want to go out with a memory tonight, that's all right with me. Christ knows when you'll be back again."

11]

Marriner studied the girl, the blond hair falling softly. He could smell the fragrance of it. He noticed the slim, handsome legs with the ridiculous shoes. Watching her, he felt a familiar stirring in his groin, and he turned to Bates.

"Let's talk to her."

They took their drinks and moved down the bar. Marriner sat next to the girl.

"May we buy you a drink?" he said.

"Thank you, no. I'm . . . waiting for someone."

It was a familiar reply, and yet she seemed unsure of herself. Not a regular at this sort of thing. Not regular at all.

"All of us are waiting for someone," Marriner said.

The girl didn't answer.

"I'm Dick Marriner." He gestured toward Bates. "Ensign Terrence Bates."

The girl looked at Bates and nodded.

"You're pilots," she said.

"We're fliers," Bates said. "Later on we will become pilots if we live long enough. The terms are not synonymous."

"Oh?" the girl asked. "You're going to flying school? Where?"

"Very far from here, I'm afraid." Bates smiled.

The girl looked at Marriner, puzzled.

Bates said, "I speak of school at twenty thousand feet, where the classrooms are soft clouds and the penalty for flunking the exam is insupportable."

The girl looked at Marriner again. "What's he talking about? Where is this school of yours?"

"In the sky above Wake Island," Bates went on, "or perhaps Midway if they are stupid enough to come back there again."

"Excuse my friend," Marriner said. "It's our last night, and we're celebrating."

He reached for her hand, and she let him take it. Marriner suddenly had to tell this girl a thing that at the moment seemed of great importance to him.

"You look like my wife," he said.

She frowned for an instant and then laughed softly. "If that was meant to be a pass, it certainly is a novel approach."

"I seem to be doing things backward tonight."

Her eyes softened, and he felt a pressure from her fingers. "I take

[12

it as a compliment because I think your wife must be very beautiful."
She smiled then and added, "And my name is Ann Saunders."

"Hello, Ann Saunders," said Marriner, and in that moment his loneliness departed.

In a penthouse high above Park Avenue a slender young man stands by a window looking out over the spectacle of New York at night. Behind him in the spacious apartment he can hear the muted strains of an orchestra which his family has hired to play for this, his going-away party. If he turned, he could watch the formally dressed friends toasting his good health and fortune and expressing the wish they too might be making the trip with him. He is fully aware that none of them has any desire whatsoever to make this particular trip with him. He has admitted to himself that he is quite fed up with his existence. The question that worries his mind this August night concerns his ability to look into the bright face of danger.

He is twenty-three years old, and ever since he can remember he has been afraid of physical damage of any kind. He does not think that this in itself is indicative of cowardice. It would be preposterous to enjoy the prospect of breaking a leg. He possesses a fine physique and wonderful coordination, and he compiled an enviable record in flight training. It was not until he had pinned on the gold wings that he had realized that the wings were all he had bargained for. Not the danger. Not the finality of combat. Not the sense of duty and responsibility. None of these things had been part of his plan.

Maxwell Winston III is beginning to learn some of the basic truths of soldiering. War is not a stirring parade set to martial music and splendid uniforms and bright accouterments. War actually begins where the glamour runs out and suddenly there is a harsh reality to face, the fact that war is nothing more noble than a joust with Death.

It is this that occupies Maxwell Winston's mind this August night as he watches his mother come across the room and onto the balcony. She is still slender with immaculate gray hair and a fine figure.

"Max darling," she smiled, "are you enjoying yourself?"

"Of course, Mother. It's a wonderful party."

"Why aren't you in with your friends? Barbara is looking all over for you."

Winston shook his head. "They're not my friends, Mother. They're yours and Dad's. And Barbara is always looking for someone. Whether it's me or someone else."

13]

His mother looked pained. "What's the matter with you tonight, Maxwell?"

"Nothing's wrong, Mother. I'm tired, I guess."

"Out here all alone. Why don't I send Barbara out here? She might help you with your . . . thinking?"

"I don't think Barbara can help me, Mother. Nobody can."

"Nonsense. Your father had a talk with Barbara's family tonight."

"What the hell for?"

"Well . . . about you and Barbara."

"Oh for Christ's sake, Mother. This isn't the Middle Ages. I don't need anyone to speak for me. What the hell is the matter with you and Dad?"

"Maxwell." His mother's tone was wounded. "That is no way to talk about your parents."

Winston sighed. "I'm sorry, Mother. Truly sorry. Sorry for so many things that I can't do a damn thing about." He kissed her lightly on the forehead. "You and Dad have done the best you know how. Somehow I'm afraid it wasn't good enough. And the failure was not in you. It was in me."

"What in the world are you talking about, Maxwell?"

"Just that I don't think I can measure up, Mother. Can you understand that?"

"It's all gibberish to me. You wait right here. I'm going to send Barbara out." His mother smiled brightly and disappeared. Winston turned back to the glittering blaze of lights spread across the horizon. He asked himself if he truly rejoiced to be leaving all this. He could not answer himself in honesty because he knew that it was only the way he wished he felt. There was a great uncertainty in his mind as to his ability to match himself against other men.

God, let me measure up, he prayed.

A few hundred miles west of Park Avenue lies an unimpressive town soiled by the blackened smokestacks of the great nearby steel mills. It is not a pleasant place, and no one grows up here without acquiring a thorough knowledge of the seamy side of life.

At the end of one street is a neat frame house. It is the home of Steve Stepik. Stepik is twenty-four years old this August evening, and tomorrow he leaves to report to San Diego for transportation to a port named "Fray." Fray is a code name for Honolulu or more ac-

[14

curately, Pearl Harbor, where replacement pilots are sent for assignment to a carrier air group.

Steve Stepik is a big man, heavily muscled, but with gentle eyes and possessed of a kind of dogged persistence that helped to make him an All-American tackle at the University of Pittsburgh. He is a good flier although one instructor noted in his logbook that he might be better off flying the big patrol planes than snorting around the sky in the cramped cockpit of a fighter plane. This may have been due to his size or it may have been due to his methodical manner and his hesitancy to act quickly, sometimes even rashly, as good fighter pilots do. In a war, however, a man fights where he is told. Stepik has been provided an F6F Hellcat fighter plane with which to fight in the skies over the Pacific Ocean. He is satisfied with this, and he knows he will fight well. He is leaving his wife and child, the two things that mean most to him in the world, but he is leaving with a sure knowledge that he will be coming back. Death and injury are something that can happen only to another man. As a matter of fact, could he but know it, this belief has been held by practically every man who ever fought. Were this warming belief not indigenous to fighting men, there would be no one around to fight the battles.

Now Steve Stepik is saying farewell to his wife in the best manner he knows, and behind the hoarse breathing there is a prayer that another son might come of this. He buries his head in his wife's hair, and then in the final convulsive moment, he thinks perhaps he has died.

Steve Stepik will know such a moment again under an alien sky.

In Peoria, Illinois, a young man sits in a room he has called his own for all the twenty years of his life. Downstairs in the living room his father and mother sit in silence, wondering why on this, his last night, they can find nothing appropriate to say to him. Tomorrow a train takes him westward to something he has never known before, and now he sits alone on his bed.

His name is Cortney Anders. He is a slender young man with curly blond hair and eyes of a startling blue. His appearance is not out of the ordinary unless you notice his hands, which are long and powerful. As yet Cortney knows only the basics of bank and skid, of power dive and chandelle, of Immelmann turn and carrier-landing technique. The tricks of his trade he will master in the near future as he

15]

discovers what it is like to kill a man. Then he will learn to his amazement that he revels in the wild, surging joy of combat, and so he will become, in his time, a legend in the sky.

He does not realize this now but the truth is there, written on his personal record which is kept meticulously with the records of countless other fighting men who are about to learn something about the Keeper of those records. But tonight he wonders why he cannot talk to his parents when he actually has so much to tell them.

Forty-five minutes from Tokyo, south around the curve of the great bay, the Yokosuka Naval Station lies in rolling country. Atop the highest hill rests the Officers' Club, a large rambling building overlooking the berths where the giant cranes unload and load the cargoes of war. Compared to similar clubs in the United States, it is a subdued place because the men who come there lack the buoyant enthusiasm of American officers.

On this August day in 1943 a lone figure sits at a desk in the small lobby off the entrance to the club penning a letter. He is not a young man, and he has been engaged in fighting wars and battles for his Emperor for eleven years. He wears the wings of a pilot and the insignia of a Commander in the Imperial Navy. His name is Isoku Yamota, and he is a ranking ace in the Naval Air Arm. In foreign skies he has proven his worth by shooting down sixty-four enemy planes. He is a man who has studied and learned his job methodically and well.

War is a business to him, sometimes boring, sometimes exciting, sometimes distasteful. He is not sure of the right or wrong of the politics of war. He tries not to think of questions that he cannot answer.

At this moment he is writing a letter to his wife in Niigata, a small city on the western shore of Japan. His writing is precise, the intricate and beautiful letters flying from the tip of his pen. He fights in the sky with a similar precise application.

Commander Yamota feels a great tenderness well within him as he writes. He also feels a flush of pride as he tells his wife he has been made Commander of the First Imperial Air Group. He smiles softly as he compares the young men under his command with their son Ito.

The fighting is of no import to him because he has fought too long. He finds no cause to hate the enemy even though, he tells his wife,

[16

it appears his young men hate with abandon. He recalls to her memory a certain Professor Hardy who visited them at their home before the war. Hardy was not a man to inspire hate, and Yamota cannot see how he could be different from all the other Americans. However, he admits, if hating is necessary for victory then he is glad his young men hate, because victory will bring him home again and that is all he lives for.

The pen flies gracefully as he begs to be remembered to their son. Finally he tells her to believe with all her heart that he will be coming home again, and he promises that while she waits for him and loves him, he will not die.

How can Commander Yamota know that he, too, has a destiny to fulfill some thousands of miles from Yokosuka? What strange interweaving of fate has married his destiny with that of Marriner, Bates, Stepik, Anders and Winston.

You have made your promise, Commander Yamota. It remains to be seen whether or not you can keep it.

The dawn is breaking, and from the hills lying east of San Diego fingers of sunlight raise the curtain on another day.

Dick Marriner lifts his head from a pillow and looks at the girl beside him. In this moment of waking there is a remorse in Marriner as he thinks again of his wife, Julie. He realizes now that he regrets he must leave today.

Quietly he moves into the next room where Bates is sprawled on a couch, snoring stentoriously.

He jostles Bates' shoulder. "Get up, hero. Time to go."

Bates rubs his eyes. "Go where? Where the hell we going?"

"To war, Batesy. We're going to war."

Bates grunts and climbs off the couch. He walks to the bureau and takes a drink out of a half-empty whiskey bottle. He shakes his head and looks at Marriner.

"How was it?"

Marriner shrugs. "Okay. It was okay." He starts to put on his tie as Bates takes another drink.

"If that's all it meant you might have given her to me," Bates said grumpily.

"What am I supposed to do? Write a book about it?"

Bates picks up his tie from the floor. "Does anything mean anything to you?"

17]

Marriner speaks quietly. "Yeah. Something means a great deal to me. Only now I think it's too late."

Bates finishes with his tie. "You could have called, you know."

Marriner nods. He shrugs into his coat. "Goddamn it, Bates, I wanted to. But I honest-to-God didn't know what to say to her. I didn't know if I was glad or sorry I got married, and I didn't like the idea of being tied down to one woman and all that. I wasn't grown up enough, I guess."

"Ah," murmurs Bates. "Now we have touched on the heart of the matter. Admitting it, I think that now you really have grown up. If you hurry, I believe you might find a telephone before we go to San Pedro."

"Why is it, Batesy, that a man never knows what he's got until he is about to lose it?"

But when Marriner called Julie long distance the phone rang and rang. There was no answer.

[18

II

September, 1943

Captain Sam Balta, USN, was forty-four years old and had spent twenty-five years of his life in the Naval service. In view of this he considered the four stripes he wore as his just reward for services rendered. Sam Balta was a tall, stringy man, his face a chiseled rock of hard angles and clefts. In his speech he still retained the twang of the Texas he had left so many years ago to enlist in the Navy as an apprentice seaman.

Balta was an easygoing man until aroused, and it was not until he had tired of the Navy's procrastination and proclivity for doing things in quadruplicate and then losing all four copies that he had become impatient and had started to make things happen his way. A year after his enlistment he had taken the entrance examinations for the Naval Academy and had placed in the top one percent of the examinees. He had entered Annapolis in 1919 and four years later graduated with honors. He had learned his trade well, and later when he realized the battleship was destined to be replaced by the aircraft carrier as the fighting core of the Navy, he had applied for flight training and had earned his wings at Pensacola in the days when only the young and the valiant cared to try their luck in an—as yet —unconquered sky.

Now Sam Balta could look back and count many things that had influenced his remarkably successful career. But he was an honest man and so admitted to himself, if to no one else, that his marriage had contributed as much as anything. Marian Bowman, when he had married her, had been beautiful, nineteen, and the daughter of Admiral Bowman, Vice Chief of Naval Operations. It has never been proved that having a vice admiral for a father-in-law is detrimental to a naval career.

When the Japanese had bombed Pearl Harbor, Sam had been an Air Group Commander aboard the carrier *Yorktown*. He had become one of the foremost aviators in the early days of the fighting. But he had been an old man as pilots went and so his combat days necessarily had been numbered. Finally he had been sent stateside and assigned to a desk in Washington. Sam quietly spoke to his father-in-law and asked for help. The Admiral had been long retired, but somehow admirals never lose their lines of influence in the antiquated and musty halls of the Navy Department. Sam's orders to command the *Concord* had been forthcoming.

Now, in the September sunlight, Sam Balta guided his giant ship over the waters of the central Pacific. Course zero five zero. Destination Pearl Harbor or, more accurately, Berth 27, Ford Island.

The *Concord* was a new ship, 27,000 tons of fighting man-of-war. She carried one hundred operational aircraft on her flight deck and on her hangar deck below. Twenty-eight hundred men manned her, lived on her, cursed her and in time came to love her. When her giant screws turned up full power she split the seas with her massive prow at speeds in excess of twenty-five knots.

The responsibility that went with the command of the *Concord* was an awesome thing, but Sam Balta welcomed it because he was a man who bore responsibility well. Throughout the fleet the *Concord* was known as a "taut" ship, an accolade not lightly bestowed. True, some admirals had been known to prefer to fly their flags aboard other carriers. This may have been because Sam Balta was not a man to mince words, and senior admirals, as a rule, do not take kindly to criticism from four-stripers. Balta looked, and was, tough, but like so many tough men he had a heart as soft as a baby's cheek. He possessed a fiercely protective attitude toward every one of his men, so that if one man could become a father to twenty-eight hundred war-weary sailors, then Sam Balta had set some sort of record in paternity.

He was standing on the inner bridge watching the play of sunlight on the water and the occasional flying fish that darted like a streak of silver across the wave-tops and disappeared again beneath the sea. Balta was irritated today, irritated and jumpy. He considered cursing his superiors in Washington, which is a thing all Navy officers do at one time or another, but abandoned the thought.

[20

He turned to the Officer of the Deck and growled, "MacNamara, where the hell are we?"

MacNamara quickly consulted a notebook. "Two three zero, two hundred miles from Pearl, sir."

Balta thought about this a moment. "I want to send a message."

An enlisted man with a message pad materialized at his side. Balta glared at him. "Rogers, take this for ComFairHawaii. To Admiral Delacrois. Priority. Mission completed. ETA Pearl 0700 Uncle. Hope my replacement group ready. Much work to be done WesPac. Sign it Hornblower."

Hornblower was his code name, and Balta knew the message was unnecessary. His air group had been due for replacement for weeks now. His pilots had flown long and hard, and now they were tired and their efficiency was declining. The pilots believed that only a certain amount of luck was apportioned to each flier, and when that was gone only the foolhardy or stupid insisted on defying the inexorable odds of war. As a flying man himself, Balta had a working knowledge of the odds and knew them to be undeviating and inflexible.

In addition, he had to go back only fourteen months and remember the time of his own trial. His only son had been a cadet at Pensacola. On Sam Junior's last flight before graduation, a formation-flying check, an errant oil tank cover had torn loose in the wind at eight thousand feet over Saufley Field. When the available supply of the precious black fluid had been wastefully expended, the engine had frozen, and young Sam had tried to effect an emergency deadstick landing in a small field near Whiting. He might have completed this precise and demanding maneuver successfully had not the stream of oil, whipping wildly in the slipstream, obscured his vision through the windscreen. As it was, Sam Junior undershot his intended landing area by some two hundred feet and flew into a power line at one hundred and ten miles an hour, cartwheeling his plane and killing himself in a blinding flash of flame and scattered debris. No one had to explain to Captain Balta the mathematical intricacies that governed the thinking of a flying man.

Now Balta pulled an old crusty pipe out of his pocket and rammed it into a corner of his mouth. He regarded MacNamara with something akin to derision. Balta had an intolerance for what he referred to bluntly as "lard asses."

"MacNamara," he said, "why don't you go on a diet?"

21]

"Why," stammered the young lieutenant, "I . . . I hadn't thought of it, sir."

"No," said Balta, "you probably haven't. Look here, MacNamara. Have you ever considered what would happen if this ship were sunk?"

"Well . . . no sir. I can't say that I have."

"No," said the Captain, "you probably haven't. Why should you? They certainly don't teach you to expect such things back there at that ninety-day college they sent you to. Sometimes I wonder how our country got so fortunate. Just imagine finding young men who can learn in ninety days everything it took me four years to learn." Balta shook his head solemnly. "It certainly does beat hell out of me. Well, I will tell you, MacNamara. If this ship got sunk, the first thing we would do would be to shut all the watertight doors. Right?"

"Right, sir."

"Good," said Balta. "You're on the ball, MacNamara. So suppose you were down on the number three deck sleeping or whatever you do down there. You'd have to get up to the hangar deck through those closing steel doors, wouldn't you? I've been wondering, Mac-Namara, if you realize the difficulty you might encounter with that lard ass of yours when you had to squeeze through one of those closing doors. You might very well get stuck and the door wouldn't close, which would imperil the ship, to say nothing of yourself. Think about this, MacNamara."

MacNamara nodded, not quite sure whether the Old Man was ribbing him or not. Sometimes it was hard to tell about the Captain. He never laughed and kidded with the ship's officers the way he did with the fliers. Not that he was a rough skipper. He just seemed, well, more attuned to the pilots. MacNamara thought maybe the Captain resented the fact that he had to stand here on this bridge and watch other men fly off over the horizon to do the fighting.

As the young officer backed away in confusion Balta felt a stirring of pity for MacNamara, who would never know what it was like to meet another man in mortal combat. He would never thrill to the heavy shudder of the engine as the propeller turned over and caught hold and the entire flight deck shuddered to the roaring. He would not feel the fierce pride that came with leading other men into combat. He would never know how it was to come down out of the landing circle and into the groove, the cockpit open and the wind drying the sweat on your forehead as you poked your head out to

[22

catch the first glimpse of the landing-signal officer with his two brightly colored flags; then sliding up past the ninety and into the final as the flight deck lined up straight through the windshield and you waited for the signal officer to draw his right arm across his neck in the "cut" signal that would send you sweeping swiftly and surely down onto the deck and into the wires where the sharp and jolting stop would tell you you had come home again. MacNamara would never know these things, thought Balta, because he was one of a great contingent who considered the war as a sort of postgraduate college course. Because he did not actively fight in it, because he remained on the ship when the planes flew away to battle, MacNamara had not become familiar with the war in the sense that the men who actively participated became familiar. It was this unfamiliarity that Balta tried to dispel in his junior officers because he felt deeply that every man had a personal stake in the fight, and if he could not himself kill the enemy, he must at least engage in the battle vicariously.

Balta's thoughts were interrupted as a yeoman approached and handed him a dispatch. "From CincPacFleet, sir."

Balta read the message, and a smile creased his hard face:

COMMANDER IN CHIEF PACIFIC FLEET
TO: HORNBLOWER
1. CAG TWO satisfactorily passed readiness inspection this date. Standing by to relieve your weary chickens.

Now Balta knew his air group would be on their way home within a few days. This, he thought, was one of the few times that war became pleasant. He turned to the OD.

"Pass the word for CAG to report to my sea cabin."

CAG was the appellation ascribed to the commander of the carrier's air group and derived from the naval custom of referring to commanding officers not by name and rank but by the name of the command. Thus, if Commander of the 7th Fleet was being piped aboard, the bullhorn voice would announce throughout the ship, "Seventh Fleet," and not "Vice Admiral So and So."

Aboard the Concord the Captain had two sets of quarters, his sea cabin and his in-port quarters. While underway, Balta invariably used his sea cabin, a small, compact room and head just off the bridge. It was not a room designed for comfort. It held only a bed, a desk, two chairs, a washbasin and a closet. On the desk Balta

23]

kept a picture of his wife with a small snapshot of his son in flight gear stuffed into a corner of Marian's photograph. The only other thing to attract attention in the spartan room was a silver ashtray on the desk, notable, if for no other reason, because it was so highly polished and shone so brightly under the desk lamp. The ashtray was engraved:

TO LIEUTENANT COMMANDER SAM BALTA USN
US NAVAL GUNNERY MEET
NAS NORTH ISLAND
SEPT 6-9, 1938

Balta had shot a ninety-four percent during the meet, a phenomenal score in the days before expertly boresighted guns. He was extremely proud of the ashtray and never used it for ashes.

Balta entered the cabin and threw his baseball cap on the bed. He turned as Barry Wheeler came into the room.

"Don't you ever knock?" Balta growled.

Commander Barry Wheeler was a big, blunt, yet soft-spoken man of thirty-eight years, with short-cropped hair and an easy smile. Wheeler was unshakable; Balta had never seen anything discomfort him in the least. He had been in Balta's air group on the *Saratoga*, and Balta knew him for a courageous man and excellent leader of men. Wheeler, although he did not know it, had already been selected by the highest brass in Washington as one of a small, select group of outstanding younger officers for whom admiral's stars had already been reserved. No little credit for this was due to the fitness reports Sam Balta had written on him. Wheeler in turn was a rabid Balta fan, having flown wing on Sam when odds of forty-to-one were considered normal.

The Captain waved to a chair. "Everything shipshape?" he asked without particular interest.

Wheeler sat down. "No complaints."

"Unusual."

"Okay then. Things stink. My boys are worn to the bone. There's no fun in the war anymore."

Balta raised his eyebrows. "You are of the opinion then that you've had a sufficiency of war?"

Wheeler knew Balta too well. "Are you asking this as my commanding officer or the guy whose ass I saved at Midway?"

[24

"I thought *I* saved *your* ass."

Wheeler concentrated. "Let me see. If I remember correctly, they came out of the sun. At the time your head was securely up and locked, a position most unbecoming to an air group commander. It was only my amazing reflexes and superb gunnery skill that kept them from scratching the old CAG."

"Hmmmm. Did I remember to thank you?"

"You gave me a Navy Cross."

"Ah yes," said Balta, "the Navy Cross. It is my one regret that I never got a Navy Cross."

Wheeler put his feet up on the desk. "You're doing all right."

Balta looked at Wheeler's hard, competent face and for a moment wondered if his own son might have turned out like this. Abruptly he said, "You're going all the way, Barry." He meant all the way to an admiral's stars.

Wheeler turned this over in his mind. He took a pipe remarkably like the Captain's out of his shirt pocket and sucked on it meditatively.

"You know, Sam, I wonder if it's worth it."

"I know what you mean. But it makes no difference. You'll go all the way anyhow. You know why?"

"Sure," said Wheeler. "Because I'm the best-looking CAG in the fleet."

"Because you're a professional, that's why. We don't have enough of them. Kids out of colleges and high schools who think this goddam war is a big homecoming game of some kind. They spend more time wondering what they're going to do when they get out than they do about winning the war. Amateurs. All of them."

"They fight as well as anyone else, Sam. Bleed about the same way too."

"You know what I mean."

"I know what you mean, but I'm not so sure I agree with you. Give them time, Sam. For Christ's sake, give them time to learn. Everyone hasn't got your dedication."

"You striking for another Navy Cross?"

"I've got that sufficiency you were talking about. Incidentally, just what the hell *were* you talking about?"

There were many things Sam Balta would have liked to say to Barry Wheeler. He wanted to thank him for the splendid job he had done with the carrier's air group, resulting perforce in a record that graced Sam's fitness report and hence assured him of future promotion. He wanted to say thank you, Barry, for your courage and your selflessness and your great ability to lead other men into battle.

Instead Balta grinned and said, "You're going home, Barry."

He waited for the reaction. Wheeler leaned back and fastened his gaze on the ceiling. "Oh?" he murmured.

Sam leaned forward. "Did you hear what I said? You're going home. You're being relieved."

Wheeler finally lowered his glance. He brushed a piece of lint off his tie. "I know it, Sam," he said.

"What!" Balta bellowed. "I just found out myself. How the hell did you know?"

"The dispatch came in," Wheeler said, "and while the operator was copying it down he spoke to the messenger. The messenger mentioned it to the flight deck crew on his way to the bridge. The flight deck crew dropped the word to the garbage detail who in turn relayed it to the mess cooks. Mess cooks are forever gabbing, and they told it to the stewards. I happened to be having a cup of coffee in the wardroom when a steward came to fill my cup. I knew it as soon as you did."

"I'll be damned," said Balta. "I guess I'll have to do something about the security on this ship."

"You could court-martial the garbage detail."

"Yeah. Well, you don't look like you're busting with joy about it."

"I am, Sam. Inside I am. Inside I want to laugh or yell or maybe cry. But it's tempered with something else." Wheeler studied a shaft of sunlight which filtered through the open porthole onto the wall, a bright ribbon against the gray metal. "I keep wondering what the hell I am going to do when I get back. Where can they put me? I'm no good at giving speeches, and I'm damned if I'll go out and sell war bonds. Where do they put old horses, Sam?"

"You don't *have* to go home."

Wheeler laughed softly. "No, I don't *have* to go home, do I? But I think I will. Did you watch my last few landings?"

Balta nodded. "Not your best."

"An understatement, Sam. A cadet could do better. I don't have to tell you how a man knows when he's had enough. The reflexes go, the eyes get tired. The hands start to shake, and you don't eat so good anymore. You dream at night where before you never dreamt

[26

at all. And the dreams are crazy and mixed up, and all of them have to do with violence of some sort. And you begin to forget things. Little things. Yesterday I came aboard without my flaps. Forgot all about them. If I'd taken a quarter-inch of throttle off, I'd have spun in. And finally, worst of all, you begin to distrust the only thing you have to live with. Your airplane. You hear noises that aren't there and feel things happening that aren't happening, and pretty soon you begin to be afraid of the airplane, and when that happens you have only a little time left if you keep on going."

Balta knew and understood. He cleared his throat. "My operations officer—Deering. He's due for orders. Maybe you could . . ."

Wheeler shook his head. "No thanks, Sam. I'd make a lousy Ops officer. I'll go back and go out to pasture. Maybe later on I'll get another air group." He smiled. "When the dreams stop, maybe."

"Well," said Balta, "the war will last long enough. It may last forever. Maybe your kid will run an air group, Barry. How is he, anyway?"

"Fine, Sam. Just fine. He asks for you in his letters. You're his favorite fly-boy. Drop him a line when you can. He's got a birthday coming up the eleventh of next month. Eleven years old."

Balta nodded. "I'll do that. It must be great to be eleven years old."

They were silent then for a moment as each man remembered his own childhood.

"Barry," said Balta. "What do you know about Air Group Two?"

"I know they're due to relieve us. I also know their group commander was killed a couple of weeks back. Flew into a target cable on gunnery practice."

"That all you know?"

Wheeler looked uncomfortable. "Not all, no."

Balta watched him closely. "You hear who was taking over the group?"

"Yeah. I heard."

"I guess it's no secret," Balta said. He waited for Wheeler to speak, and when nothing was forthcoming he made an impatient gesture with his pipe. "Well for Christ's sake, say something."

Wheeler shrugged. "What do you want me to say?"

Balta spoke softly and evenly, lending his words a particular vehemence. "Bob Crowley flew wing on you the first day at Midway. He was your wingman, and that's all you have to say to me?"

"Things were mixed up that day. Everyone got screwed up."

27]

Balta mimicked Wheeler. "Everyone got screwed up. Balls! Crowley turned his ass and ran away!"

"Crowley was shot all to hell," Wheeler said.

"Yeah," Balta said almost eagerly. "But was he shot all to hell *before* or *after* he ran?"

"We were jumped about the time he turned for home. He could have been hit then."

"Balls!" Balta said. "He made three radio transmissions after you were jumped. He didn't get hit till he was damn near back to the carrier. They saw him run and went after him. Caught him alone and shot him all to hell. You know damn well that's what happened."

"I gave you a written report. You signed it and passed it along, so you went for it."

"Yeah," Balta said disgustedly. "And now it's coming back to haunt me. I should have court-martialed Crowley. Instead I go along with you and give him a medal. So now BuPers sends him back to me. In *command of my air group!*"

"You're shouting, Sam," Wheeler said.

"Damn right I'm shouting. We're trying to fight a war out here with a handful of carriers and half the pilots needed to man them. We're fighting without bases and without a hell of a good hope of getting any. If they think we can win a war on hope and propaganda, they'll damn well soon find out we can't. So what do they do? They send me a coward to lead my air group. *My* air group!"

Wheeler sat up, an almost angry frown on his face. "Goddammit, Sam. Don't tell *me* about it. I don't know if Crowley's a coward or not, and I don't know anything about his air group. They're just like any other air group, I suppose. Some of them will piss in their pants the first time out, and some of them may cry at night for their mothers. Others have before them. Some of them will go to glory, and Crowley will have to write the letters home, and so whether or not he is a coward I still pity the poor bastard because he's on your ship and he starts with two strikes against him." Wheeler waited a moment. "You could be doing Crowley an injustice, you know."

"If I am, I'll be the first to apologize."

Wheeler chuckled. "I can see you apologizing."

Balta got to his feet and walked to the porthole. The sunlight laid bare the tiredness on his face and accentuated the heavy circles under his eyes.

"I feel so goddam futile sometimes, Barry," he said. "Like I'm

[28

playing God up here on this bridge. All I can do is watch and wonder and give orders without ever knowing if I'm doing the right thing, and if I'm not, what kind of particular hell is going to wait for me when I'm finished. I don't like being in a position to destroy other men's dreams and hopes even if I do so under the impression that what I'm doing is the right thing. It's a goddam crime to ask a man to send another man out to die."

"You have my sympathy," Wheeler said softly, "if that's what you want to hear."

"No," said Balta. "No, that is not what I want to hear. I'm tired of losers. I'd like to hear that my new air group has not one goddam soul in it who has anything to lose, that every man of them is homeless, rootless, loveless, and possessed of some ferocity or other that will make him some sort of methodical madman in the sky, impervious to pain and loss and loneliness. That is what I'd like to hear. Then maybe I could sleep better at night."

"Well," Wheeler said, and he said this only because he knew Balta better than any living man, "I can't see where your sleep at night is going to affect the outcome of this war one way or the other. Let's face it, Sam. You're making excuses already and your air group isn't even aboard yet. That's a hell of a note."

Balta looked at Wheeler, a sort of puzzlement in his eyes.

"I can't dispute that," he said. "How would *you* feel, Barry?"

Wheeler reached over on the desk and helped himself to a generous portion of tobacco from the Captain's humidor. He tamped the tobacco in slowly, lit the pipe and took a long pull.

"Good tobacco," he said.

"Marian sends it to me," Balta muttered.

"I'm a commander, Sam. I never had a command higher than an air group, and I'm not sure I want one. Not when I see what it's doing to you."

Balta interrupted. "It's not doing a damn thing to me except to ruin my digestion."

Wheeler shook his head. "You say you feel like God up there on your bridge. Balls, my dear Captain. I think you're off the track and I'll tell you why. You're not God and what the hell ever made you think you were? You're just a hunk of skin and bones standing on a bridge, and the only difference between you and some kid who takes off from that flight deck is a matter of a few years and the insignia on the collar. His is a gold bar and yours is an eagle. You're just like everyone else on this ship and when you talk about shouldering responsibilities that don't belong to you, you're like a kid throwing daggers at the moon. When it's all been said and the figures are added up, you'll find that there's no directive from the Navy Department that designates your responsibility for any man living or dying aboard this ship. Christ, Sam, they shouldered the responsibility for their own future when they signed up for this war. You're only a guy who gets saluted around here."

"Do you have any more advice for me, Commander?" Balta asked sarcastically.

"Yeah. Take that crown of thorns off your head and relax. If you dropped dead right now this war would go right on."

Balta considered Wheeler's words. Then he walked over to the desk and studied the pictures of his wife and dead son. He nodded and turned back to Wheeler.

"Why the hell can't my junior officers talk to me the way you do?"

"You'd crucify them."

"Of course I would. And it's not a suggestion to be lightly disregarded."

Wheeler laughed softly. "They love you, Sam. Every one of them from the bottom deck to the superstructure. They curse you and damn you, and every one of them loves you."

Balta was twirling a dial on a small safe set into the bulkhead above the desk. "I'm going to miss hell out of you, Barry."

"You'll get by," Wheeler said dryly.

"I intend to. I expect to remain in this war until the last gun has sounded."

Wheeler clapped his hands. "Bravo. But don't strain too hard, Sam. It might rub off on some people who have no such intentions whatsoever."

"Like my new air group commander, maybe?"

Wheeler frowned and spoke earnestly. "Sam, promise me one thing. Just one. Give Crowley the benefit of the doubt. Give him a chance."

Balta straightened up with a bottle of whiskey in his hand. He nodded to Wheeler. "He'll have his chance. That I promise you, Barry."

Balta set the bottle on the desk and placed two water glasses next to it. "Old Grand-Dad," he said proudly.

"It's against Navy regs, Captain."

[30

"Of course it is. Real whiskey, I mean. This is medicinal whiskey."

"It's different?" Wheeler asked.

"Sure it's different. This is medicine and is to be imbibed only when something is wrong with you."

"And what's wrong with you?" asked Wheeler as Balta poured the tumblers full.

"I'm thirsty."

Wheeler lifted his glass in a toast. "One for the road, Sam."

They touched glasses as Balta said, "A long, hard, lousy road and may God send me the men who can walk it."

After Wheeler had gone, the Captain refilled his glass and put the whiskey back in his safe. He sat down at his desk and from a top drawer drew a worn and wrinkled photograph. It was a group picture of his fighter squadron taken just before the Battle of Midway.

Although only fifteen months had passed since Midway, that battle was already becoming recognized for what it was—the most important naval battle that would be fought in the Pacific war.

Balta scanned the photograph and tried to remember individual faces and names. Where had they gone, those who came back? Did they fly today on some other captain's carrier? Had they had their bellyful of war or did they still know that hot urge to fight that the truly great combat fliers know? He saw Wheeler's face grinning up at him and next to Wheeler, Crowley. Balta frowned as the memory of Crowley intruded on his recollections. He put the picture down and took a drink of whiskey. He sat back and for a moment remembered how it had been.

June 3, 1942: Seven hundred miles southwest of Midway Island, the most advanced American position in the Pacific since the fall of Wake, a lumbering PBY Catalina flying boat based at the island was flying a somnolent routine patrol. The late afternoon sun bounced off the water, and the plane's windshield was an expanse of blinding light. The pilot changed course a few degrees to avoid the sun's rays, and as he did so, he saw far in the distance a minor variation in the great ocean's monotonous expanse. He turned toward the almost invisible tracings on the horizon and alerted his crew.

It was almost dusk when the sighting report from the *Catalina* reached the *Yorktown,* steaming one hundred miles northeast of Midway. The Japanese had expected the American carriers to be

31]

far to the north. They could not know that their secret code had been broken and that an American force of three large carriers was lurking behind Midway.

Balta remembered that afternoon and the sudden, harsh blaring of the bullhorn followed by the voice on the loudspeaker echoing through the ship.

"All pilots man your ready rooms. All pilots man your ready rooms."

They had been anxious to launch, but the Admiral decided to wait until the following morning to allow the situation to develop. It was too near dark to risk an encounter with the enemy. Besides, we had another trump up our sleeve. From Midway Island Army B-17s and Navy PBYs launched with the dark and headed for the enemy force. Their range was far beyond that of the carrier-based F4F Wildcat fighters.

Dawn of June 4, and Balta was briefing his pilots in the ready room. They were new men, most of them, because the Battle of the Coral Sea the previous month had thinned the already slender ranks of Navy fliers. A scout plane made a sighting report and informed the American force that the enemy was heading into the wind, preparing to launch their aircraft. All available aircraft from Midway were airborne. The carriers were still too far away to launch their planes.

Two hours to wait now, and Balta and his men fidgeted. Balta called Wheeler aside and spoke confidentially.

"I'm putting the greenest man on your wing, Barry. Take care of him."

"They're almost all green, Skipper." Wheeler laughed. "Which one?"

"Crowley. He's got a good flight jacket, but this is his first time in a fight."

Wheeler nodded, and Balta began to lecture the pilots on the advisability of staying in two plane sections. Chances of survival were approximately quadrupled if a man did not stray from his section leader.

Over the ship's intercom the bridge relayed the latest reports from the Midway based aircraft. Two hundred Japanese bombers had roared in with a fighter escort. American island-based fighters consisting of twenty-five antiquated Brewster Buffaloes intercepted the enemy Zeros twenty miles from Midway. The Japanese bombers made a mess of the island, and less than half of the American aircraft returned to base after the fight.

The ready room was still as the reports filtered in. It was not yet nine o'clock in the morning. Now the Captain's voice came over the loudspeaker.

"This is the Captain speaking. One word to all pilots in today's operations. You will make every effort to reach the enemy carriers. This is your primary objective regardless of circumstances that might arise when once airborne. The carriers are your target. Get them and get them good. That is all, except good luck to all of you and God be with you."

Balta watched the young faces settle into lines of grim determination. The laughing banter and joking were gone from the ready room as every man inspected his flight and survival gear.

"Remember," Balta told them, "you are not bomber pilots. The orders you just heard were for the others. Your job will be to stay with the bombers until we make contact with the enemy. Then it will be your job and mine to engage the enemy fighters and shoot every sonofabitch out of the sky. Our bombers can't afford to miss their target, and it's up to us to see to it that they have a minimum of interference. This is another way of saying that if your ammunition is gone and your gas is low, you still have another thing to do as long as an enemy fighter remains to contest our presence. I am not ordering you to ram him, but I trust you will know where your duty lies when the time comes."

At 0945 General Quarters sounded. "Pilots, man your planes. Pilots, man your planes."

Then the mad rush to the flight deck and the struggle into the parachute harness and the starting of the engines. That is the way the fighter pilots went to battle. They ran all the way.

Later nobody would remember the details of the launching and the rendezvous or of the vector information coming to them from the *Yorktown*. But not a man who survived would ever forget the meeting with the enemy, and Sam Balta's voice leaping across the sky, strong and calm and confident.

"Tallyho. Tallyho. Bogies dead ahead. High."

They saw the enemy then. The Zeros were above them and trying to get in position for an attack on the bombers. But the Zeros

33]

would have to come through Sam Balta and his young men before they would find range to open fire on the sluggish SBDs and TBDs in the American formation.

A massive formation of the enemy loomed up at Balta, coming in from his starboard and slightly astern. He and Wheeler were leading their two four-plane divisions when Balta sang out, "Break right."

There were eighteen of the Japanese, and now Balta held the stick far over, his foot jammed the rudder, and he banged the throttle all the way forward on the quadrant. The Wildcat fighter screamed into a vertical bank, and Balta tightened his stomach muscles involuntarily against the strain of the "g" forces. His eyes flicked to the rearview mirror, and he saw Wheeler's division sweeping in behind him. Then he was nose-on to the enemy, and he opened fire.

He hit the lead plane of the enemy formation with his first burst and saw the propeller of the Zero shred itself into splinters of steel that glinted in the sun as they spun away at incredible speeds. The Zero shuddered and then disintegrated. Then the eight Americans were in the middle of the fight.

Two Zeros were on Balta's tail and closing when he saw Barry Wheeler come up from below and blast one of them into a swirl of flame. As Wheeler broke off and turned away, Balta saw three other Zeros come down in a split-S on Wheeler's rear. It was then that he watched incredulously as Wheeler's wingman suddenly broke off from Wheeler and went into a steep, almost vertical dive. Balta pulled up and over onto his side in a chandelle, and he saw Crowley pull out of the dive and skim the wave-tops, taking up a course that would lead him back to the American task force.

"God damn him," muttered Balta. "God damn that miserable sonofabitch."

He had no time to watch Crowley further, however, because another enemy section was crawling up from his rear, and he heard the thump of their cannon. He roared up into the first half of a loop and then, rolling out on top, he flew straight and level for a few seconds before he slapped the stick over, rolled onto his back and saw the Zeros in a vertical climb. He yanked the stick back and the horizon flashed past his windshield, and he was streaking down to meet them. He had regained the advantage, and he pressed the firing button and blew two Zeros into nothingness, leaving only a spattering of debris tumbling slowly down the sky. Wheeler came in after the two remaining planes, and he and his section leader got them as the

[34

Zeros tried to head for the deck and safety. Balta wheeled around in a wide, lazy circle as the other Wildcats joined up on him. They could hear the excited voices of the bomber pilots relating the successful attack on the enemy carriers as Wheeler slid into position off Balta's port side.

"What happened to Scarlet Two-Two?" Watching over his shoulder, Balta could see Wheeler speak into his hand mike.

"I don't know. His message came in garbled. Maybe he was hit."

"Yeah," answered Balta. "Maybe he was. Well, let's head for home. My ammo is gone."

Around them the remaining American fighters joined up and they flew home together that way, those who were coming back. Down on the unfriendly waters various patches of oil and a few still-smoking fragments of debris littered the calm surface. Friend and enemy alike had perished in the meeting, and of the Americans who went forth to stop the enemy that afternoon, fully half did not return. But four enemy carriers went to the bottom before nightfall.

Balta finished off the last of the whiskey in his glass and looked again at the picture on his desk. He remembered landing back aboard the *Yorktown,* and learning Crowley was down in sick bay. The flight surgeon told him that Crowley had received a serious wound, a jagged rip down his side that would not prove fatal but would take him out of action for a while.

Exhausted, Balta merely grunted, "That's too goddam bad, isn't it? What did they hit him with?"

"The metal of the plane tore into him. He bled a lot. I can't understand how he managed to fly all the way back, considering the amount of blood he lost."

Balta fixed the doctor with a level glance. "Maybe he didn't start to lose the blood till he was almost back here, Doc."

The doctor flushed when he realized the import of Balta's words. "Maybe," he said uncomfortably, "but we'll never know, will we?"

"No. We'll never know, Doc."

But the doubt had remained in Balta's mind, and it would do so until another occasion presented itself to prove or disprove the facts.

That evening, just before sundown, the enemy made a last desperate effort. With their carriers gone, the Zeros had no place to land, no home to go back to. What had been probably the last launch from the Jap carriers found the *Yorktown* sailing sluggishly due to hits

35]

sustained during the day's operations. Having nowhere else to go the enemy pilots decided they might as well die here as in some forgotten and lonely space of ocean over the horizon. They pressed home a suicidally determined attack, and two torpedoes found the *Yorktown*. .

Two days later, while she was under tow toward Pearl Harbor, a Japanese sub wrote the last chapter for the *Yorktown,* and she went down bravely and with all flags flying.

Balta was tired now of remembering, and he put the picture back in the drawer, to remain there until the time came when he felt the need to remember again. He wondered for the last time this night what had happened to the men who had come back that day. And he wondered whether the men who would comprise his new air group would be able to fill the giant footsteps of the men who had gone before.

Again he whispered his prayer. "God. Let me have men who can walk this terrible road."

III

October, 1943

Ford Island is a flat, ugly piece of land set in the middle of Pearl Harbor, surrounded by cranes and unbecoming iron structures used to load and off-load ships. It looks like a handful of debris tossed carelessly into a garbage pail. There is a strip of cement runway bisecting the island and offering a ready access to the nerve center that is Pearl Harbor.

In 1943 Ford Island was the reporting place for all the fortunate young men who were about to be granted the privilege of traveling ten thousand miles from their homes to engage in a sportive effort in a sky they had never heard of for a prize which could not by any stretch of the imagination be bettered, their lives.

At Ford Island the young men, tired and dirty after spending six to ten days aboard a slow LST or an oiler, shuffled to a long counter on the second deck of a grim, camouflaged building fronting on the harbor. A sign on the building designated it as Building 22, but it was much more than this to the young men. In many instances it meant life or death to one man or another, for in this building they received their assignments.

The yeoman behind the long counter had seen hundreds of these faces file past him in the last seven months. He prided himself on his ability to read character from the faces, and he would have been surprised at how many times he had been right. Henry assigned replacement pilots to air groups which had returned from the forward area with depleted rosters. He did not like to think of his job in this manner, and so he thought of his duties in the light of refilling wardroom chairs.

37]

Now he raised his eyes to the young officer standing before him. A good-looking bastard, he thought. Bet he was a real hot-shot on the corner on Saturday night. Looks tired now, though. And a little bewildered. Hasn't got used to the wings yet. Well, he'll learn. The flier pushed his orders across the counter.

Henry looked up. "Maxwell Winston the *Third?*"

The officer frowned. "That's right. Do you mind?"

"It's all right with me," Henry replied. "If you can stand it, I can stand it."

"Who the hell are you talking to!" Maxwell Winston's eyes flashed.

Henry, who was tired of blustering young ensigns, looked down at the orders in his hand. "Maxwell Winston the *Third*. That's what it says here. Typographical error maybe?" Henry had gone through this so many times he had no trouble maintaining an expression of angelic innocence. A boot ensign and he wants to know who do I think I'm talking to. Fer crissake, I'm talking to a boot ensign that's who I'm talking to. It sure God isn't Nimitz or Bull Halsey.

Maxwell Winston was himself in a foul mood, and he had every right to be. He had sailed from the port of San Pedro and sixty-four hours and 800 miles later he had adequately demonstrated to himself and to the officers, men and passengers aboard the oiler APO 22 that he was ill equipped to engage in a war.

At midnight the third day out of San Pedro the radar operator of the APO 22 had picked up an unidentified blip on his scope, bearing zero four zero relative, distance twenty miles. The radar operator reported his blip to the duty officer who in turn followed the Captain's standing orders and sounded General Quarters.

General Quarters aboard a ship in wartime is an experience that does not lessen with familiarity. A horn blares through every corner of the ship, sounding with a surging, redundant cacophony. When Maxwell Winston III heard it he bolted upright in his bunk where he had been blissfully dreaming of his rich Aunt Martha and the extent of her estate, of which he was the principal beneficiary. Winston banged his head on the overhead and cursed heartily as he pulled on his pants, shirt, shoes and life jacket. There was trouble above, and since trouble was something he had had little to do with in his lifetime, he felt a strange weakness in his legs. The other men in his bunkroom were already on their way, and since Winston sud-

[38

denly was terrified of being alone he rushed out into the corridor and headed for his GQ station.

The GQ station for the passengers, all aviators, was in a relatively clear area of the afterdeck, directly below the bridge, for in case of action the Captain did not want his passengers getting in the crew's way. This seemed a reasonable precaution because his passengers, collectively, could not have done much more damage to an enemy than to shout obscenities at them.

Winston, the last to arrive, could see nothing in the stygian blackness. But he could hear the muted whispers of the other men, and he moved against a bulkhead to wait until his eyes became accustomed to the darkness. His heart thumped almost painfully, and he was dimly aware that somewhere out in the night were other men determined to kill him. Even more terrifying was the realization that he was surrounded by total strangers, none of whom could conceivably give a good goddam about his welfare.

In the darkness there was only the creaking of the ship's timbers and now and then the stifled sound of a cough or the clearing of a throat. Winston tried to calm the heavy beating of his heart. He took several deep breaths and expelled them slowly.

A voice whispered in the blackness. "What the hell you suppose it is?"

Another voice answered. "Submarine, probably."

A man coughed gently, almost apologetically, and there was the slight scuffing of feet as someone changed position.

A third voice. "It's got to be a sub. No surface ships this far east."

Winston strained to see out over the black water. His eyes were becoming accustomed to the darkness, and he could see, dimly, the outlines of the ship and the vague shapes of the men around him. He wanted desperately to say something humorous, make some witty riposte that would bring a grudging admiration from the other men, but no words came to his mind.

From the bridge above a voice sounded. "Unidentified ship bearing zero nine zero relative. Distance eight miles."

Quiet again and the only sounds were the creaking of the ship's joints and the soft wash of water along the sides of the APO 22. Winston felt the need to go to the toilet. He tried to smile to himself, but even in the darkness, unseen, the smile felt twisted and false. The clouds parted for a brief instant and a wash of moonlight hit the deck.

39]

He saw the man standing next to him, one of the ship's officers, a big, heavily bearded man with dark hair peppered with gray at the temples. The man's smile was a flash of white in the night as the moon disappeared behind the overcast.

"You'll get used to it," he told Winston softly.

"That's a matter of opinion," Winston answered and heard the man laugh.

"Probably a friendly," he said in a louder voice, and there was an unmistakable note of authority in his voice. Winston admired the calm, easy assurance.

"Don't they have IFF gear aboard?"

"Sometimes it's inoperative. Other times the weather or the sea return can foul things up. You can't count on the thing."

"Not a hell of a lot out here you *can* count on, if you ask me."

"It won't amount to anything," the man next to Winston said. "We have these bogies nearly every night from here on in to Pearl."

"What the hell do you do if it *is* a Jap?" a voice asked.

"Pray," the man answered. "Then swim."

"Eight hundred miles?"

"More or less."

"You ever been sunk?"

There was a silence while the ship's officer remembered.

"Twice," he said. "Once out here and once in the Atlantic."

"Jesus."

"Your luck is running thin, mister," a voice said.

"It's something I don't recommend. It isn't the water that kills you. It's the oil and the fire."

"Jesus."

Winston's throat felt raw. He swallowed and pressed his forehead on the cold metal.

The ship's officer spoke again. "No need to sweat it. This is more a precaution than anything else. They don't often come this far east."

In the dim half-light Winston saw one of the men move to the railing of the ship. The figure peered into the darkness, and Winston could see the sudden tensing as the man whispered loudly, "For Christ's sake. Oh for Christ's sake. Look! A torpedo. Goddammit, a torpedo!"

There was a rush for the railing. Winston tried to follow but his legs wouldn't function. He felt the weakness around his knees and something else he could not define at the moment.

[40

"Where?" a voice asked hoarsely.

"Out there. I saw it. I saw a wake."

Winston was gripped by an overpowering fear as he heard the terrified cry of the man by the rail. A torpedo brought only one thing to his mind, a fiery, suffocating, oil-covered patch of ocean with himself dying in the center of it.

"Easy now," a voice said. "There's no wake out there."

"I saw it. Heading straight for the ship."

Moments passed, and the men waited. The voice from the bridge came to them faintly. "Bogie now one six zero relative. Eleven miles."

"They're passing on our starboard. Inbound for Diego," said the ship's officer.

Then a voice heavy with relief said, "Well, if you saw a wake, the fucking thing missed us."

"Missed us a fucking mile," agreed another voice.

A man chuckled. "A whale, maybe."

"Or moonlight. The moon was out for a second."

Winston, aware that he was not going to die, tried to join in with a joking sally, tried to become more intimate with these men with whom he had just braved the ultimate danger, but before he could speak a shameful awareness came to him.

My God! He had soiled himself. He could not believe the ugliness. He moved back from the group still clustered at the railing. He had to get away, but he could not leave his GQ station before Secure.

The men moved back now and formed a group near Winston. He pressed back against the bulkhead, but he knew there was no place for him to hide his shame. The hell with GQ. He had to get to his quarters and get rid of the awful evidence.

One of the men sniffed the night air. "Jesus," he said. "Somebody shit."

Someone laughed. "It's happened before."

"Somebody scared around here?"

"Wheeewww."

Winston moved through the blackout curtains and eased past the darkened hatchway. He hurried down the dimly lit corridor to his bunkroom, knowing GQ would be over soon and the other men would be returning. In near panic he came to his cabin. He carefully removed his pants and shorts and made a distasteful bundle. What now? The shower? Not a chance; the water was turned off during GQ. He took a towel from the rack and rubbed himself dry and clean.

41]

The stench in the room was overpowering as he quickly donned another pair of trousers and tied the bundle into a knot. He left the room and headed for the passageway just as GQ ended. He was rounding a corner when he bumped into a heavy figure. Winston stepped back guiltily, hiding the damning bundle behind him. But he could not hide the smell. The big man looked at him, and a smile tugged at the corners of his mouth.

"Not that way. Out the other way. Take it to the fo'c'sle deck."

Winston's face flamed and he turned back toward the fo'c'sle. He moved silently onto the deck and quickly hurled the bundle out into the night. Then he rested his arms on the guardrail and wept in his humiliation.

Later, when he returned to his quarters, the big man was lying on his bunk reading. The man's name was Stepik, and during the time they had been roommates Stepik had made no move to ingratiate himself with Winston. He was a quiet man, and if Winston had to live with anyone he supposed he accepted Stepik as well as the next man.

Now Stepik lowered his book and nodded noncommittally to Winston. Winston looked almost angrily for a sign of amusement, but he could find none. Suddenly he found himself grinning.

"Christ, but I made a mess of that, didn't I?"

Stepik smiled easily and closed his book. "I felt the same way." Winston knew he was lying, but he was grateful.

"I thought I'd do better. I honestly did." He shook his head. "It's a hell of a note."

"It could have been any one of them. They were all scared."

Winston looked at Stepik. "You mean you won't say anything?"

"Why should I?"

"Well . . . thanks, Stepik. I appreciate it."

"The name is Steve."

"Okay, Steve. Mine's Max."

Stepik nodded. "Don't let this get you down. Everyone reacts in his own way the first time danger comes to him. It won't happen to you that way again. Believe me."

"It didn't happen to you. Or the others."

Stepik rubbed his jaw reflectively and now there was a hint of laughter back of his eyes. "I think perhaps I've led a somewhat different life than you, Max. I had my danger and my trouble when I was just a kid. Take my word for it. The next time it will get easier."

[42

Winston watched Stepik pick up his book again, and realized he very much wanted Stepik to be his friend.

"You flying fighters?" he asked.

"Hellcats," Stepik said.

"I am too. Maybe if we tried we could make sure we'd get the same outfit. I mean, with all the replacements coming in they must need a good many pilots for the few squadrons out here."

Stepik had already perceived the difficulties underlying Winston's deficiencies. Stepik had no ax to grind. He had come to this war with no great dreams of glory; he had come because he had a wife and son, and because he realized he owed a debt to his country. This was all. But now he saw in Winston something he had feared long years ago before he had become assured of his own self. He saw a man who needed something strong and certain to hang on to because he was in the grip of circumstances alien to anything he had known before.

Now in the building on Ford Island, Henry tapped his pencil against his teeth and wondered if he ought to screw this good-looking young man standing before him. It was entirely within his power to do so.

"Is it agreeable to you," he said, "if I assign you to Air Group Two?"

He was surprised when Winston frowned and asked, "You only need one?"

"*I* don't need *any*. Fighting Two needs pilots."

"Well," Winston hesitated an instant, "could we possibly go together?" He gestured to the large-boned man standing next in line.

"Well, Fighting Six and Fighting Eight both need pilots. I'm afraid we'll have to parcel you out."

Neither Fighting Six nor Fighting Eight had any pressing need for pilots, due mainly to the fact that Six was presently stationed in Norfolk, Virginia, and Eight was reforming at Santa Rosa, California.

"Look," said Winston, aware that he was demeaning himself, "Ensign Stepik and I are friends. We'd like to go together if it can be arranged." His expression said "please" to Henry, and Henry was suddenly ashamed. What the hell, he thought. This guy is going out where I will never go and will do things far beyond anything I will ever do in this war. He shouldn't have to ask me for favors.

Then the big man stepped forward and pushed his orders across

43]

the counter. His voice was exceptionally gentle for such a powerful man.

"It would be appreciated, you understand."

Henry read the orders and grinned at Stepik. "Stephen Stepik." He closed his eyes and concentrated and then looked again at Stepik.

"Steve Stepik. All-American, Pittsburgh. '40. Right?"

Stepik smiled and nodded. "That's right."

"You recovered the fumble Stanski bobbled behind his own goal in the Syracuse game. Beat us seven nothing. Right?"

"You went to Syracuse?"

"For a while. I saw you play twice."

Stepik laughed softly. "I was younger then."

Henry consulted a chart on a desk behind him containing rosters of the fighter squadrons in the area. "You anxious to get out there, sir?"

"Let's just say we're ready," answered Stepik.

Henry stamped the two sets of orders and handed them to the two officers. "Fighting Two. They're out at Barbers Point. This isn't official yet, but you'll be going out on the *Concord*. That may be good and that may be bad."

"How's that?" asked Winston.

"Well," said Henry, "the captain of the *Concord* is Sam Balta. That's good. Balta is the eagerest captain out here. He loves to fight. That may be bad, depending on how you bleed. The *Concord* is a new ship, spanking new and that's good. It will shortly be heading west and that's bad. You'll have an opportunity to win a variety of medals and that's good. Then of course you may die and that's bad unless you have a death wish." Henry finished his speech, of which he was inordinately fond, and said sincerely, "I wish you the best of luck, gentlemen, both of you, and I really mean it."

The two officers shook hands with him, and Winston asked, "How do we get out to Barbers Point?"

"You can catch a bus in fifteen minutes outside this building. One stop at the Marine field at Ewa, then to Barbers Point."

Henry watched the two men walk away, and he felt an inadequacy when he remembered where they were going. He looked at the roster of Fighting Two again and noted that there were three vacancies left to be filled.

"The next three in a group," he said. He accepted the orders and spoke to the three men before him. "Marriner, Bates and Anders. All

[44

for Fighting Two at Barbers Point. Catch the bus in fifteen minutes." He stamped the orders. "And good luck to all of you."

Barbers Point Naval Air Station was situated at the western tip of Oahu, far enough from the mountains to avoid the low-hanging clouds that invariably smothered the mountaintops during the midday hours. Thus it was usually CAVU weather, ceiling and visibility unlimited, permitting around-the-clock flight operations. Two giant runways crisscrossed and ran almost into the water surrounding the field on three sides. Row upon row of fighters, bombers and torpedo planes studded the parking ramps and filled the hangars. But there were not nearly enough planes and fewer pilots. An airplane could be assembled in far less time than it took to assemble a pilot. The human factor had proved to be far less pliable than the metal one.

Fighting Squadron Two was located in the first hangar near the flight line. The offices on the second deck were totally inadequate for their intended function. Since the office space was intended to affect the paper work attendant to running a Navy organization, no one really gave it a second thought. It was there, and that was all. In Fighting Two it would have been difficult to find one man who was the least bit interested in paper work. A fighter pilot supposes he has been born for one reason and only one—to hurl himself around the sky in a manner impossible to imitate by anyone except another of his own breed.

The bus from Ford Island drew up before Fighting Two's hangar and disembarked the occupants who were met by an enlisted man in dungarees. He regarded them with an expression of benevolent pity.

"This way, gentlemen," he said sorrowfully. "The Skipper will see you on the upper deck."

As they climbed the ladder to the second deck the enlisted man, who identified himself as Chief Machinist's Mate Leary, maintained a running discourse on squadron idiosyncrasies.

"Everybody in this outfit goes to work at 0700. It don't really seem sensible, but I'm only an enlisted man. I take orders. You will too. Around here we only do one thing. That's fly. Nothing else is important. Skipper don't care how you look or if your eyes are bleeding in the morning or if you stink of rotgut, as long as your job is done and the planes keep flying. We quit work when flying is done for the day unless we night-fly, in which case we work until everybody is

45]

so goddam tired they can't see straight. No doubt about it. This outfit is the best damn fighter squadron in the fleet."

They walked down a long passageway and turned in to a large, cluttered room whose walls were covered with maps and navigational data. Five slovenly pilots in stained flight suits reposed in chairs and on a battered sofa. Leary observed the lounging fliers with a grin.

"I got the new boys. The Skipper busy?"

He was answered with a variety of yawns and unintelligible mutterings. Finally one tired-looking man opened an eye. "Leary"—he yawned—"you know damn well the Skipper is busy. He's always busy. Everyone in this squadron is always busy. That's why we're all so tired. But he's never too busy to welcome the new boys." He eyed the newcomers with a squint. "Hello, new boys." Then he shook his head, as though some great catastrophe was in the offing. "So young," he murmured, "so very young. Take them in, Leary."

Leary knocked on a door at the far end of the room, and a voice bellowed, "Come in goddam it." And so Marriner, Bates, Anders, Winston and Stepik entered the office and met the man who would take them into war.

Lieutenant Commander Harry Hill, skipper of Fighting Two, was pouring a three-finger shot of whiskey into a tumbler on his desk. He did not look up until he had finished and had carefully recapped the bottle and replaced it in his desk drawer. Then he rose to his feet, a tall man with sandy hair who gave forth an aura of quiet determination and inflexibility.

"Your orders please," he said. He read the names on each set of orders, then shook hands with the men.

Marriner watched him closely, remembering the stories he had heard about Hill back in flight-training days. Hill's was a name known to every Navy pilot, fledgling or veteran. His exploits were legendary in ground school training, and he was credited with devising the now standard defensive weaving maneuver in aerial combat. The "Hill Weave" was an integral part of every flying cadet's training.

Harry Hill was a born leader, and like so many similar men, he disclaimed it. He had been flying fighter planes for seven years, and he possessed the flair and the color to attain high renown and stature in the Naval establishment. But the desire for high rank and responsibility was foreign to him. He wanted to be a good squadron com-

[46

mander, and if he was considered that and nothing else, it was enough for Harry Hill.

He took a swallow of his drink. "What you gentlemen see me doing is absolutely taboo in this squadron. I am drinking on duty, and I am drinking in the middle of the afternoon. Both of these are reprehensible things, and I trust none of you will try to emulate me. If you do, I will naturally be forced to have your asses. The reason I am drinking at this ridiculous time of day is because I am the commanding officer of this squadron, and I have been flying these airplanes since all of you were in grammar school. I need no more training. You do. Therefore none of you will drink in the afternoon while you are in this squadron.

"You come to me secure in the knowledge that you have learned all there is to know about flying a fighter plane. This is preposterous. You know absolutely nothing about flying a fighter plane. All you know how to do is land and take off. But you will learn, young men. Oh yes, you will learn, if I have to leave strips of your asses out there on the runway."

Hill came from behind his desk and picked up a large shield from a table. He held it up so the newcomers could see a figure emblazoned on the polished mahogany device. It was a snarling cat, claws poised for attack, spitting in anger at a formation of Japanese Zeros.

"This is our squadron insignia," Hill said. "It has been and will continue to be the most respected insignia in the Pacific fleet. Good men have died under that insignia, and unfortunately more good men will follow them."

He laid the shield down and returned to his desk. Taking another swallow of his drink, he sat back in his chair and relaxed.

"When you were assigned to this squadron you became one of the chosen few. You will now proceed to live up to what is expected of you. What is expected of you is that each and every one of you will become the best damn fighter pilot in the United States Navy. This may sound like a contradiction of sorts, and as a matter of fact it is. It is impossible and impractical for any of you to become the best fighter pilot in the United States Navy. *I* happen to be the best fighter pilot in the Navy. Remember that. And remember one other thing. You are out here for one purpose only. Nothing else. Someone back in the States who knows less than nothing about what is going on out here may have told you that you have come out here to catch the

47]

torch that has been thrown to you from faltering hands. Or they may have told you that you are to carry the honor and glory of the Navy as best as you are able until the last blue and gold pennant sinks beneath the seas. All information such as this is horseshit, gentlemen. Nothing but horseshit.

"You have but one purpose, and that is to destroy enemy airplanes in the air and on the ground. You have become nothing more and nothing less than the operator of a flying gun platform. You will aim and fly that platform in such manner that you will destroy any enemy plane with which you come into contact. Keep it that simple, and you may all live to become aces. Now, are there any questions?"

"Yes sir," said Marriner. "When do we fly?"

"Ah," said Hill, a note of approval in his voice. "How old are you, Marriner?"

"Twenty-four, sir."

Hill studied Marriner a moment. "A good age. I was twenty-four once. A long time ago it seems. You're eager to fly, eh? Good. We need the eager ones in this squadron. When do you want to fly, Marriner?"

"Right now," said Marriner.

"Me too, sir," chimed in Cortney Anders.

Hill looked at each of the new men in turn. He apparently liked what he saw because he grinned broadly and bellowed, "Remson."

The sleepy pilot who had pitied them in the outer room appeared in the doorway. "Yeah, Skipper?"

"Remson, get these men issued their flight gear. Right now. You can sleep later. They want to fly. Get that? They really want to fly."

Remson lounged in the doorway and looked with favor on the new officers. "It's about time they sent us some people who know what they're out here for. Welcome aboard, gentlemen."

"Get going, Remson," Hill said.

Remson turned and went out, muttering an unintelligible order to follow him. As the others turned to go, Hill spoke. "Men, I like your attitude. Because I like your attitude I am going to start you out by demonstrating how little you know about fighter planes. Does that please you?"

Five eager faces beamed, and five voices in chorus said, "It sure does, Skipper."

"Fine. Then after you draw your flight gear, Lieutenant Remson will give you a lecture on field rules and regulations. I realize this

[48

will bore you, but the Admiral does not approve of mid-air collisions however innocent they may be. After the lecture you will take off in a plane assigned to you, and you will climb to twenty thousand feet directly over this field. When you arrive there at exactly 1600 you will find that I will be waiting for you. In any order you may choose among yourselves, you will attack me. In case any of you don't know how to initiate an attack, just growl and make noises like a tiger and try to get on my tail. After each fight I will climb back to twenty thousand feet and take on the next man. You may employ any means, ruses or tricks you think you have up your sleeves. Your orders are to get on my tail and stick there if you can. I will tell you on the radio when the fight is over. To the man or men who beat me, a happenstance I seriously doubt, I will generously donate a fifth of Old Overholt rye whiskey. Of course, you will not drink this whiskey in the afternoons. If that is all, gentlemen, you may go. I will read your orders now and memorize your names because we will be together for a long time and through some very trying experiences. See you at twenty thousand in an hour."

As Hill so rightly guessed, there was not much in the records of his new men that surprised him. The Maxwell kid was twenty-three years old, which figured, and the "Third" that was tacked on to his name meant something in the social and high financial world in New York, but he was neither arrogant nor subservient. In fact he was nothing as yet and could go one way or the other. He had an enviable record in flight training, and that wouldn't hurt him. Hill nodded his head and read on.

Stepik, Stephen. Twenty-four. Married. One kid. Pittsburgh, Pa. He, too, had a name behind him. All-American tackle. University of Pittsburgh. Built for it too. Sturdy, likable, dependable. Good solid material, Harry Hill thought. They can't all be fireballs or young millionaires. Again he liked what he had read.

Anders was the youngest, Hill noticed. Only twenty. From Peoria, Illinois. Probably never left home until he left for training. But he had those blue, blue eyes. Hard as steel, soft as sky. Why do all young men with wings have blue eyes? This wasn't a new question, and it hadn't been thought up by Hill. Do you need blue eyes to fly an airplane? No, but the fighter pilots said that ninety-five percent of the live ones have blue eyes. . . .

Bates and Marriner . . . Hill was deliberately dispensing with reading them in order, now that he had the facts. Hell, he didn't need

49]

any facts about those two. Not really. His eye noted with something less than interest that they had trained in Chicago. . . .

Four days earlier, Hill would have been totally disinterested in a darkened corner of the Blackhawk Bar on Randolph Street in Chicago but Dick Marriner would have shared a moment of near panic had he been there. Marriner would have seen a golden girl, deeply tanned, with soft waves of blond hair falling to her shoulders. When she smiles her white teeth are a streak against the brown of her face. She has had too much to drink, and as the whiskey assumes a sour taste in her mouth she is abruptly afraid of the thing she is about to do. She has been asking herself wherein she has failed, and in the asking she has turned to the whiskey for comfort because she has found no answer. Now as she reflects on the short month she has been married, her eyes are sad.

She considers herself fortunate to have been married to a man with whom she had fallen completely in love. She is not a girl who loves easily although she has given herself to other men in her time. But that was before she met her husband. Before the whirlwind courtship, before the dizzying round of gay parties and the talk of the flying men, before the solemn knowledge had come to her that she had found the reason for her life.

When Julie Simmons had met Dick Marriner at a party at the Glenview Officers' Club, she had watched with a detached amusement as he made his play for her. Then suddenly, for Julie, it had no longer been play, and she had found herself falling in love with the handsome flier who carried a world of lightness and gaiety in his eyes. Marriner had been making his carrier qualification landings on the Wolverine, and his time at Glenview was necessarily short. Julie knew this and deliberately tried to make herself realize that this thing could not last and that soon he would be gone. So she laughed with him, and they held hands on the moonlit shore of Lake Michigan as Marriner spoke of himself and this place to which he was traveling.

Julie knew men, and she knew that Dick Marriner was not at all sure of his invulnerability in this sky to which he was going. He was trying to build a wall of security about himself and in doing so was attempting to disassociate himself from humanity by defying convention and by assuming a mantle of self-sufficiency. Julie saw this and understood. She saw he was a man who would never be weak

[50

but who needed to understand that his doubts were the same as those every human being must live with.

Three days after their first meeting they had been married by a justice of the peace in Cook County. Dick had three weeks' leave before reporting to San Diego, and so they had laughed and loved and spent long hours getting to know each other. But there had been something more seriously wrong with Dick Marriner. Something that Julie could not put a name to.

Dick had been gone almost a month now and since the day he had left there had not been a letter or a telegram or a phone call. Where had she failed? What had she done? At first she had been angry, but that soon passed, and then came the worry. When even that had passed, she knew with a weary resignation that this had been too good to last, and she had been a fool. Then the hurt had come and with it the bitterness.

But where had she failed? The sense of loss had emptied her of tears, and tonight she finds herself in this bar and sitting across from a man she has just met. She tries, but she cannot remember his name as she watches him now through the thick pall of smoke that hangs heavily in the room. She can see the three full stripes of a Commander and the gold wings on the breast.

Why must he be a flier? she wonders. They all look so strong and self-reliant, so alike. He was a big man with short-cropped hair. The wrinkles around his eyes reminded her of Dick, and she stifled a quick flash of guilt.

"Who was that girl who introduced us?" His voice was heavy, masculine.

"I thought she was a friend of yours."

He laughed. "I never saw her before in my life. Maybe I looked lonely."

"Maybe you are," Julie said.

He nodded, and his eyes fell to Julie's hand where she wore Dick Marriner's ring.

"Your husband?" he asked.

"Dead," Julie said, and the lie slipped out before she knew she had spoken. She tried to call it back then, but the hurt was too much so she let the lie hang there.

He looked up. "I'm sorry."

Now the lies poured out, tripping over themselves. "He was a Navy flier too. He was killed in the Pacific."

51]

He nodded his head in pity. "Where?" he asked.

For a moment she sought an answer. Then it came to her. "Midway," she said. "It was at Midway."

"I was there."

"We'd only been married three weeks when he left." And she left unspoken the knowledge that he had gone with a kiss and a tender word, and she had not heard from him or of him since that time.

The man was uncomfortable. He lit a cigarette, making a production of it.

Oh God, I'm sorry, thought Julie. Not for my lie or because I am sitting here with a man who means less than nothing to me. I am sorry because it is terrible to lose something when you don't know why. What did I do? I gave him all I had. But now I have nothing.

"I don't even know your name," Julie said aloud.

"Crowley. Bob Crowley. And yours?"

"Julie Simmons," she answered, not even aware that it was her maiden name.

"You're very beautiful, Julie," he said.

"My husband thought so," Julie said and then after a moment added, "for a little while, anyway."

He ordered another round of drinks and then another and another. They danced, and for a time Julie forgot her loss.

It was late when they left the Blackhawk, and Julie had drunk herself sober. She was tired, and the thought of the lonely apartment appalled her. Suddenly she was terrified of being alone.

"I'll take you home," Crowley said as they stood on Wabash Avenue under the shadows of the El platform. "I'll call a cab."

"No," Julie said. "I don't want to go home. Not now."

Crowley looked at her intently, trying to fathom her meaning.

"Will you come with me?" he said gently.

Julie barely heard him speak. She did not care what happened as long as she did not have to be alone. She nodded, and he beckoned a passing cab.

Twenty minutes later Crowley was signing the register at a dingy collection of cottages on the northern outskirts of the city.

The night clerk yawned. "Luggage?" he asked.

"Out in the car," Crowley replied. "I'll take care of it."

"Suit yourself." The clerk rubbed a dirty hand across his eyes and returned to his chair. Crowley turned and looked at Julie.

[52

"This way," he said, taking her hand and moving toward the door.

The room was a dull gray, and the carpets were worn and scruffed. A washbasin in the corner of the room was stained under a dirty mirror, and a large bed stood against the far wall. Julie caught a glimpse of herself in the mirror, and the dirt blurred her image until all she could see was the whiteness of her smile.

Later Julie would remember many things concerning this particular night. She would remember her stifled gasp as Crowley peeled off his shirt and she saw the livid scar stretching down his side, the twisted, seamed ridge of tortured flesh standing out against the pale whiteness of his body. It ran from just under his right arm down and disappeared below his belt line.

"My God," she breathed. "What is that?"

"A memento from the Japs." He smiled. He looked down at it and rubbed his palm along the scar. "They hit me in the cockpit with a fifty-caliber. The cockpit tore inward, and I was in the way."

She could not take her eyes away from the scar. Could this happen to Dick? Would his body be ripped by a fifty-caliber like Crowley's? Would his blood run and the pain sear him and she unable to help him, to lay gentle hands on his hurt?

"Where?" she asked.

He did not at first understand. "Where? Oh. Midway. It happened at Midway. I told you I was there."

"And now you're going back. I didn't know they made you go back."

"They don't," he said. "Not always. I asked to go back. I'm leaving tomorrow." He looked at her and laughed self-consciously. "It's hard to believe, isn't it? That a man would ask to go back again, I mean."

"Why did you?"

He considered this a moment. "Suppose I told you it was because I am a professional, and this is the way I make my living."

"I wouldn't believe you. It wouldn't be the truth."

"And you'd be right," he said. "It wouldn't. I'm going back because I have to find something out."

He waited, but Julie said nothing. Then he said, "I've got to know if I'm a coward. One way or another I've got to know."

"You didn't find out before?"

"In a way I did, and what I learned was distasteful. I'm going back to prove to myself that I was wrong."

53]

"Then I wish you luck," Julie murmured. "A great deal of it because I think you will need it out there."

Crowley nodded and said nothing. He sat on the edge of the bed and stripped down to his shorts. Julie pointed at the scar again.

"That could happen twice."

"It could," Crowley said. "Or something worse. But whatever it is it can't be as bad as the other. The wondering." He didn't want to talk any longer about his scar or where he was going, so he stood and lit a cigarette. He offered one to Julie, but she shook her head and lay back on the bed. She felt sorry for Crowley because he had so little to hang on to. They were so much alike. Neither knew the cause of the failure, and each was seeking an answer. The only difference was that Crowley had to go across the world to seek his answer while Julie could only wait and wonder and hurt.

Now Crowley came to the bed again. He watched Julie as she looked up at him, her eyes puzzled.

"You're thinking of him," he said. "Your husband."

"In a way," Julie admitted, "you remind me of him. Maybe it's just because you're both fliers. Are all fliers alike?"

"No. I wish they were. Then we could all be brave heroes and none of us would have problems." He said it lightly, but she knew he meant it.

"I feel sorry for you," she said.

"No," he said roughly. "That's not what I want you to feel. I don't need pity."

"No? What is it you need then?"

He lay next to her and kissed her on the mouth. Julie lay impassively, her hand resting lightly on his shoulder. As he drew back she looked at him, and he saw the pity in her eyes.

"It's no good, is it?" he said.

"No," Julie said. "It's no good, and I'm sorry. Truly I am." She saw him blow his breath slowly through his teeth, and she said, "My husband. He's not really dead. I lied."

"I thought so. The ring gave you away. They don't wear them after their husbands are gone for good. None of them do."

She reached up and drew his head down to her breast. She sensed his lips on her breasts, but she felt no response beyond pity for this lonely man who had a greater fight coming up than any she would ever know. They lay there quietly, not speaking, and Julie suddenly hoped that somewhere, somehow, some other woman might be able

[54

to give this small portion of affection to Dick when the day would come when he needed it. Was it too much to ask, this thing that Crowley wanted tonight? She had given it before with no sense of shame. Because it was no good for her, did that mean it could not be good for him? It was all she had to give, and since it apparently meant so little to Dick, why should it not be given to a man who tonight, at least, desired it?

She waited in the silence of the room. Her hand gently rubbed the muscles along the back of Crowley's shoulders. For a short while she almost wished her passions would mount, but as suddenly as she wished so, she knew it would not be. Dick Marriner had left her life as abruptly as he had entered it, and the emptiness she had inherited was hers alone now.

She could feel Crowley's heart beating against her hand as she rubbed his back. He had so damnably little to take with him. A wave of pity almost choked her, and she said softly, "Bob?"

He stirred in her arms. "Yes, Julie?"

"You can if you want to." She hesitated a moment. "It will be all right."

He turned and propped himself on an elbow, staring down into her upturned face. He said nothing, merely nodded. He bent down to her.

His arms encircle her, and they are hard and eager. She hears him mumble thickly, deep in his throat. His kisses become less gentle, and still she cannot arouse a response within her. But it will not be necessary, she thinks. All that is necessary is that he be satisfied. She waits.

And waits.

Now Crowley is twisting and turning on the bed beside her. She sees his forehead beaded with sweat, his features twisted in desperation. She turns to him and rubs her hand gently along the scar, an overwhelming sorrow in her for this man.

"What is it?" she asks softly. "What's the matter?"

"I don't know," he moans. "God damn it, I don't know." The tears are wet on his face.

"That's all right," Julie whispers. "Is it always like this?"

"Not always. Sometimes . . . sometimes it's all right."

"It's all right," Julie whispers again, not wanting to add to this man's shame. "It would have meant nothing anyway. Try to sleep now."

55]

Later sleep comes, and Julie cries out in her dreams for Marriner. Crowley does not hear because he is having dreams of his own, and they are unhappy dreams. When Julie wakes before dawn, she lies in bed and knows she is alone again despite the heavy form beside her. Will she always be alone, and if so, is there an answer to it?

"Ready to growl like a tiger?" Bates demanded. The five men were in the squadron ready room, slipping into the parachute harnesses and buckling the straps. The parachute packs were installed in the airplanes, and the pilots wore only the light straps of the harness. They had spent fifteen minutes earnestly devising various techniques which were intended to teach Harry Hill that he too had something left to learn in the sky. Remson had finished a laconic lecture on the inadvisability of taxiing against traffic and had suggested that none of them attempt to enter the landing pattern unless their wheels were down and locked. Now he was leaving them with one last word of advice.

"Give it all you've got. Someday you'll realize how fortunate you are to learn from Harry Hill. He'll beat your asses up there today, but he'll do it for a damn good reason. He doesn't want you ever to forget that no matter how good you think you are, somewhere, someday, in some piece of sky you'll meet another man just as good if not better. When that day comes it will be the man who respects his adversary the most who will make the fewest mistakes. That man will fly away alive. Hill wants that man to be you. So try hard and learn quick. Time is short. Good luck."

"Let's ante up a pot," suggested Winston after Remson had gone. "Whoever beats the Skipper takes it all."

"Might as well save the wear and tear on your bills," said Bates. "Nobody is going to beat Harry Hill."

Anders smiled and said quietly, "You're right, Bates. But I intend to let him know he's been in a fight."

"I think you will, Anders. I think you will give him a hell of a fight." Marriner's voice held no hint of sarcasm.

"That's what we're here for," Stepik said softly.

"I'll go along with that, Steve," said Marriner. "What the hell. It's all fun, and I'm beginning to like this war better than I figured."

"We won't be doing any fighting at all if we don't get off our asses," said Bates.

[56

They headed for the flight line in the warm Hawaiian sunshine, five new friends on their way to twenty thousand feet where they would receive primary instruction in the art of remaining alive in the sky.

Three hours later two meetings took place aboard the Barbers Point Naval Air Station. One was in the office of the Skipper of Fighting Two. The other took place in a barracks room in the Bachelor Officers' Quarters where five chastened young men gathered ruefully to discuss a recent debacle at twenty thousand feet.

"Jesus Christ," Bates whispered reverently, "that bastard shot me down in sixty seconds. Let me start the damn fight on his tail too. What the hell did he do? I looked around and couldn't see him and then all of a sudden there he was, smack on my ass with his nose sticking three feet under my tail. I want to know how the hell he did it."

"I imagine we'll learn soon enough," said Stepik. "He drew me into a tight turn and spun me out before I ever got started." He looked at Winston. "How about you, Max?"

"I think I ought to go back to Corpus Christi and start all over again. I honestly don't know what he did, but whatever it was it worked."

"I have an answer," said Marriner. "Hill is a fighter pilot."

"And what are we?" asked Bates.

"We are pilots who will learn to be fighter pilots in time. Except maybe Cortney here. He may be quite a bit ahead of his time." Marriner smiled at Anders. "You almost beat him, Cort."

"No," said Anders slowly, "I didn't almost beat him, but a break here or there or a mistake and I might have been lucky. But I don't think Hill makes many mistakes in the air."

"I know why he beat all of us," Marriner said. "At least I think I do."

Stepik watched Marriner closely. A perceptive man, Stepik knew that both Marriner and Anders could teach him things he would need to know in order to survive. Stepik had a knowledge of his limitations which is the second best thing a fighter pilot possesses, the first being love for his airplane.

"Why, Dick?" he asked.

"You remember in primary training? We all wondered why they

57]

made us learn snap-rolls and slow-rolls. We knew we would never need that sort of a maneuver in a fight. You're helpless in one of them. Why do you think we had to learn them?"

"Familiarity," Anders said.

Marriner nodded. "Right. And that's what Hill has that makes him great. The seat of his pants tells him what's going on. He doesn't have to stop and figure out what the position of his plane is, if he's upside down or right side up, if he's nearly stalling or about to go into a high-speed spin. While you and I and the rest of us are trying to decide what the hell our next move ought to be, Hill is making it automatically. I guess you'd say he was a part of the airplane, and we're just sort of interlopers, somebody coming along for the ride."

"I think you've got it, Dick," said Winston. "But we'll get the same way."

"You're damn right," said Bates, "and I'm glad that bastard Hill is going to be up front when we go in. I don't think he makes any mistakes in the air."

While this was taking place in the BOQ, Hill and Remson were sprawled in chairs in Hill's office, sipping whiskey. Hill had his shoes off and his feet propped up on the desk. Remson's eyes were closed. There was a comfortable silence in the room.

"You make out the flight schedule for tomorrow?" Hill asked.

Remson, his eyes still closed, reached out a hand and groped until it found the whiskey bottle. "Don't I every day?"

"Got the new boys on a gunnery hop?"

"Naturally. Want me to take them out?"

"I'll do it myself."

"My, my. The Skipper is getting eager."

"Just for that you can fly the tow plane."

"Wait a minute." Remson sat up with a pained expression. "Tow planes are for boot ensigns."

Hill laughed. "Do you want to become a boot ensign? That can be arranged too."

"Okay, okay. I'll fly the damn tow plane. They'll probably overshoot, miss the target and clobber the hell out of me."

"You're getting fifty percent flight pay. It's about time you earned it."

"You josh me, Skipper. I've got a DFC."

"Have I congratulated you?"

[58

"No, but it's all right. I'm modest, and adulation only embarrasses me. Tell me about the dogfights."

"They're all good. Very good. Anders and Marriner damn near beat me. But all of them are good, Hank. Better than we were at that stage. I'm happy about the whole thing. Marriner may be a great one. Maybe they all will. They love to fly, and that's the big thing. You don't love this business, then you're facing disaster."

There was another silence until Remson reached into his pocket and placed a dollar bill on the table. "Make you a bet."

"You already owe me thirty dollars. Pay up."

"Later. Make another bet now."

Hill appeared to give deep thought to the subject. Finally he said, "Fort Shafter?"

Remson nodded. "Where else?"

Hill handed the dollar bill back to Remson. "It's foolish to bet on a sure thing. Let's take the new boys along."

"I was about to suggest that very thing," yawned Remson.

IV

October, 1943

Hill drove the canvas-covered carryall up to the gates of Fort Shafter. He mentioned his name to the sentry, and they were admitted with no more than a cursory inspection.

During the long ride from Barbers Point, Hill and Remson had explained the function of the Women's Air Raid Defense Service. The girls at Shafter operated radar and radio gear for the area's defense warning system. There was some doubt in high places that the cost of the defense system was justified. A Japanese attack on Pearl Harbor in 1943 was more than a little improbable. But the cost might have been quadrupled, and still it would have found justification in the eyes of the pilots who didn't care a damn for the defense system but considered the WARDS an integral part of the war effort.

Hill drove slowly down a darkened street, peering at the rows of blacked-out buildings.

"Like a cemetery around here. Where the hell is that place, Hank?"

"Up at the top of the next hill. Who's throwing the party?"

"I don't know," answered Hill. "I think it's being given for the new admiral."

"Didn't know we had one. Who is he?"

"I don't know. Replaced ComFairHawaii, I guess."

Hill started to drive up a climbing, winding road as Winston said, "How did we get invited anyway?"

Remson chuckled in the darkness. "Because our revered skipper is something of a social lion in these parts."

Hill pulled in to the curb before a long, low-slung building. From behind the blackout curtains they could hear the sound of music and the muted babble of voices.

"Follow me, gentlemen," Hill said.

As they walked toward the entrance Marriner lagged behind and wondered what he was doing here. Was he deliberately rubbing a wound just to remind himself it was there? Was he afraid to admit that Julie had spoiled other women for him or was this refusal to believe that a change had occurred in him and in his thinking a sign of his immaturity?

The party was being held in a tremendous room under a ceiling festooned with balloons and papier-mâché figures. A long bar stretched the entire length of one side of the hall, and before it groups of officers stood clustered in heated conversation. It was mostly flying talk, as could be determined by the bits of dialogue which rose above the babble of voices.

"He shot sixty-three percent on overheads this afternoon. The bastard is uncanny."

"Eight cuts in a row this afternoon, without a wave-off. Beat that if you can."

"I haven't had a wave-off in three years."

"You lie like an Air Force pilot."

"You may insult my mother, my sister, my wife. But never dare to call me an Air Force pilot."

"Well, Jack, I'll tell you one thing. When I meet my first Jap I intend to pull an Immelmann turn on the bastard and shoot him down with the first burst."

"You make about as much sense as a whore in church. You try an Immelmann on a Zero and I'll practice walking slow behind you. Because that's what I'll be doing when I take your body home. Black armband and all."

A waiter came past Marriner and the others, and they took drinks from the tray. Hill lifted his glass.

"Tallyho."

The others made a gesture of salute in return. The drinks were warm in their stomachs, and even Remson seemed to come alive.

"I wonder," Remson said, "where we should start this safari?"

"Over at the bar?" suggested Bates. "I usually begin at the bar. I lie better at bars."

Hill spoke. "I'm looking for someone. Meet you at the bar later."

Hill moved off to be swallowed in the crowd, and Remson led

61]

them to the bar where four bartenders strove to satisfy the seemingly insatiable thirsts of the fliers. At the far end of the hall a four-piece orchestra played to a packed dance floor.

Minutes passed, then, past Remson's shoulder, Winston saw Hill escorting three girls across the room toward them. Unconsciously he straightened his tie. Remson, following his glance, whistled in appreciation.

"War is hell, isn't it, gentlemen?"

Hill made the presentations.

"You girls know Hank Remson. These neophytes are Max Winston, Cortney Anders, Terrence Bates and Dick Marriner. Men, meet Doris Dowling, Helen Stoddard and Ann Murphy." Hill stepped back, looking very pleased with himself. He turned to Remson. "How did I do?"

"Not well at all. There are only three of them."

"I did not have the benefit of reconnaissance."

Bates started to move toward Doris, only to stop when he noticed she was looking straight at Winston.

Winston flushed, and to cover his discomfort, asked, almost plaintively, "Would you care to dance?"

Doris smiled. "Did they teach you to ask that way at the deb balls?"

Winston frowned and Hill laughed, "I gave them a rundown on you. What's wrong with Park Avenue, Doris?"

"Not a damn thing." She smiled as she took Winston's arm and moved toward the dance floor.

Hill sighed as he watched them go. Doris was a true beauty. Tonight she wore a light gray gabardine suit and an open-necked shirt of soft white silk which emphasized the way she was tanned by the sun. Her copper hair hung lazily to her shoulders. Doris Dowling walked the island of Oahu as though it belonged to her. She played golf and tennis well enough to hold her own with the men, and she could outswim most of the young pilots who courted her. Hill wondered sometimes at her almost too bright laughter, but he knew that he would envy the man who won her love.

Bates spoke to Ann Murphy, a girl with a piquant face and a spattering of freckles. "Since you already know everything there is to know about me, I suppose you are falling in love?"

"Is there another way? You're irresistible."

"I agree with you, Ann. Shall we dance?"

[62

Anders said to Helen Stoddard, "I'm not very good at this sort of thing, but I'll try if you'd like."

Helen looked as though she couldn't care less one way or another. "Anything you say," she told Anders.

As Hill ordered another round of drinks Marriner noticed a man watching them from farther down the bar. He was a full Commander, a tall man with the ubiquitous crew-cut. As the man finished his drink and came toward them, Remson saw him approaching.

"Ah," he murmured to Hill. "The new CAG approaches."

Hill turned his head to watch the new man. But when Hill spoke to him, his voice was coldly impersonal.

"Hello, Crowley. I read your dispatch orders today."

Crowley's eyes swept over Remson and Marriner and then held on Hill. He gestured toward Marriner.

"One of your pilots?"

Hill nodded. "Dick Marriner. Reported aboard today. Did damn well up there too. Nearly had my ass."

"I thought that was impossible," Crowley said, and Marriner was surprised at the sarcasm in his voice.

There was something unpleasant here that Marriner did not understand. This wasn't the light badinage the pilots used to rib each other. Something between Crowley and Hill smoldered.

"You're right," Hill agreed with a smile. He turned to Marriner. "Marriner, meet Commander Crowley, our new air group commander."

Crowley nodded perfunctorily. "I'll want to see a progress report on your squadron, Hill," he said and his voice was colder, if anything.

"They're waiting for you. Any time."

"Tomorrow morning then."

"Make it the afternoon. I'm leading a gunnery hop in the morning."

"I prefer the morning. Ten hundred."

"Suit yourself, Crowley. The reports are in my desk. I'll leave it open for you. I'll be at fifteen thousand feet at ten hundred."

A slow flush appeared on Crowley's neck.

"If you've got a flight schedule tomorrow what are you doing out here tonight?" Crowley said in a low voice.

Remson spoke laconically. "What are you now, a house mother?"

63]

Crowley's voice rose and the officers nearby looked toward him. "You keep out of this, Lieutenant." He deliberately accentuated the rank.

"As you say, Commander," Remson replied.

"Are you in the habit, Mr. Hill, of taking a night on the town when you have an operating schedule the following day?"

Hill smiled coldly at the CAG. "We have an operating schedule every goddam day of the year, Crowley. Let me worry about it."

"You're straining too hard, Commander," said Remson softly. "It doesn't become you."

There was silence now around the little group, and the CAG's face was bitter. "God damn you, Hill. What are you trying to do?"

"Trying to keep you from making an ass out of yourself."

"You're in hack, Hill," said Crowley. "Go back to your quarters."

Hill shook his head slowly. "Crowley, go away. I don't know if you're drunk or not. Maybe you're gnawing on a bone from a long time ago. I've forgotten Midway, if that's what you're worrying about," he said very gently. "But go away, Crowley."

Marriner looked questioningly at Remson.

"The Skipper and Commander Crowley flew together at Midway."

"I'm warning you, Hill," Crowley muttered.

Hill thrust his face against Crowley's. "Balls," he said. "You will never warn me about anything. Understand that. I'm in your air group because that's where I've been sent, although why the hell they gave you the group I'll never know. But don't come roaring in here and try to assume command by virtue of that goddam silver leaf on your collar. You need more than that to lead an air group, Crowley. Your rank doesn't mean a damn thing to me. And remember something—" Hill's eyes moved deliberately down to the ribbons below Crowley's wings. "We've got medals in the outfit too."

Crowley's face was congested, and he started to grab Hill by the arm as he turned back to the bar. Marriner moved quickly, taking Crowley's wrist and holding the arm down by the air group commander's side. Hill wheeled around at the slight scuffling, and Remson moved smoothly between the two men. He spoke gently to Hill.

"Not here, Skipper. What the hell. The Captain is over there."

"Okay." Hill relaxed and turned back to his drink. "Tell the air group commander we'll talk about this later."

[64

"I'll be interested in the results of your gunnery hop tomorrow," Crowley said and stalked away.

"They'll be in your office at twelve hundred," Hill said to his retreating back. Then he clapped Marriner on the back. "Good work. I think you'll do to take along."

"What the hell was it all about, Skipper?" Marriner asked.

"I knew Crowley a long time ago. For some reason he thinks I'm a threat to his command of the air group. But that isn't the real trouble. The real trouble is that Crowley is trying too hard to prove something to himself. I know what it is, and that's what he resents."

"Am I supposed to understand any of this?" Marriner demanded.

Hill looked at Remson and laughed. "You are supposed only to do justice to this fine whiskey. Then we will look for girls, girls, girls."

A few feet from the bar two men sat in a booth and watched Hill and his men.

"That's a hell of a way to start out," said Sam Balta, a scowl on his face.

Barry Wheeler shrugged. "Hill doesn't bend easily."

"What, for Christ's sake, was Crowley trying to prove?"

"He's confused. He thinks everyone who was at Midway is running around whispering behind his back. That sort of thing can make a man mighty foolish at times."

"I have a feeling Crowley is going to be nothing but trouble."

"Sam," Wheeler said, "you want a first-rate air group. Crowley evidently wants the same thing. What's eating you?"

"If Crowley thinks he can wipe away that day at Midway by hard-nosing my air group he's got another think coming."

"It's not your air group," Wheeler reminded him bluntly. "It's Crowley's. You promised to give him a chance. Remember?"

Balta growled an inaudible comment and ordered another drink.

Wheeler watched the dance floor for a time before he spoke. "Heard anything about my orders yet?"

"Hmmm?"

"Don't play coy, Captain. You know what I mean. They should have been here already."

"I thought maybe you'd changed your mind," said Balta.

"I haven't changed my mind and I don't intend to. Have you got those orders pigeonholed in your desk?"

"Why would I do a thing like that?"

"You'd do anything you felt like."

"It's against regulations," Balta protested.

"Look, Sam. Crowley has relieved me. There's nothing more for me to do out here."

"Okay," Balta sighed. "I'll look in my desk tomorrow. Maybe I misplaced them under the impression they were old blotters or something."

"I wouldn't be surprised if you did," Wheeler said and grinned.

Winston held Doris' hand as they walked along the garden path. They had danced well together, feeling no need for words to fill the intervals of silence. As the party grew older and louder other pilots had begun butting in on Winston until he had asked Doris if she would like to walk outside.

"Want to sit for a while?" she asked now, pointing to a small bench off the path.

"If you do," Winston said. He took out a handkerchief and dusted off the seat before she sat down.

"Thank you," she said. She looked at him with a small smile on her lips. "That sort of thing is unexpected around here."

"What?"

"The handkerchief. Cleaning the bench." She laughed. "Max, I bet the mothers on Park Avenue simply loved you."

Winston answered seriously. "I always got along with the mothers and sisters. But I didn't do too well with the girls, I'm afraid."

Doris took a cigarette from a gold case, and Winston held a lighter to it. "Did Harry tell you anything about me?" she asked.

"No. Not a thing, damn him."

"I like Harry Hill," she said.

"Everybody does. I think it's because he can do things so well and still he doesn't make you feel inadequate."

"I don't think you'll ever be inadequate, Max."

He smiled ruefully. "You don't know me, Doris. I have a long way to go before I even know myself, I'm afraid."

"I've heard it before, Max," she said softly. "I've heard it from other young men who come out here, not sure of themselves even as they get ready to go out and do things that other men could never hope to do." She looked up at Winston.

"We'll see, Doris," he said.

[66

"You make it sound like a conspiracy. The 'we' part, I mean."

"Maybe I mean it that way."

She was surprised and made no effort to conceal it. "You might not say that, Max, if you knew me better. I don't know much about your kind of life, and I'm not sure I'd like it if I did."

"Why? Because my mother has her picture on the society page every other day? Listen, Doris, pity my mother, don't envy her. She has nothing else to do but get her picture in the paper. It gives her a reason for living, and it makes her feel she's of some importance to people outside her own family. She and my father live in a little world, and I was glad to get away from it."

"You'll be glad to get back to it. Everyone leaves something behind that they have to go back to."

He shook his head. "I tried to leave very little of real value."

"Let's walk," she said.

They strolled slowly, and he could smell the fragrance of her hair. He wanted to know more about her, and he knew he wanted to see this girl again.

He looked at her as she spoke. "I hear you thinking, Max Winston. Why did you come tonight?"

"Curiosity, I guess. I didn't know I'd meet you. I'd have had a reason then."

They halted on a terrace. Below them they could see the landscape sweep down and merge with the indistinct outlines of Honolulu.

"Someday they'll lift the blackout," Doris said. "Come here when they do, Max. You never saw such beauty in your life."

"Let's make it a date."

"We'll see," she said, "after you know more about me and I know more about you."

She held another cigarette for a light. As he held the flame she looked into his eyes, her mouth serious.

"Max, never trust your eyes. They don't tell you enough. What do you see when you look at me?"

"A beautiful girl."

"I'm a bitch, Max," she said abruptly. "Believe me."

"I prefer not to."

"Oh, I admit I'm trying to be better. But it takes time, and I don't know how much of that I have coming."

He couldn't tell if she was being serious or not. He said, "At the risk of appearing stupid, I don't believe you."

67]

She turned away from him and smoked in silence a moment. Finally she said, "Do you want to sleep with me tonight? Is that why you came out here?"

He was momentarily angered. "God damn it, no. Well, maybe before I talked to you."

He heard the sound of her laughter. "Don't be angry. I'm not insulted. Good heavens, you don't think I'm a virgin, do you?"

"I hadn't really given it any thought. No, I suppose you're not. How the hell did we get on this subject anyway?"

"You just said you didn't want to sleep with me."

"I did not. I said I didn't come out here for that." He realized she was laughing at him. "But now that I'm here it's a different matter."

"We will, Max. But not tonight. Maybe not for a lot of nights."

"I don't understand you, Doris. Am I dumb or something?"

"You're sweet," she said. She took his face between her hands and gently pressed his lips to her own. "I will tell you something, Maxwell Winston the Third. I know all about you and to crack an old saw, you are a maiden girl's delight. Money, social position, young and"—she paused a second—"did anyone ever tell you you were very handsome?"

"Thousands of people," he said.

"Well, there you are. I don't want you to misunderstand. I may set out to get you, Max, and when I do I won't give you time to come up for air. I'll use every trick in the book and I don't think you know much about the book I'm speaking of."

"What's all this got to do with sleeping with me?"

He liked the sound of her laugh. "Don't you know that a girl always plays hard to get? It's the only way."

"Traditional?"

"When the subject is rich, young and good-looking."

"You're giving me a superiority complex."

Suddenly serious, she said, "Maybe that's what you need, Max. Maybe I can be good for you after all."

They began walking again along the graveled path. Without plan, Doris' hand joined Winston's.

"Do you love flying, Max?" she said. "The way Harry Hill does, I mean. He seems to live for it."

"I don't know," Winston said. "I want to love it because I stand a better chance of staying alive if I do. But I'm not sure of myself. I don't think I'm colorful enough."

[68

"What's that got to do with it?"

"I'm not sure of that either. It seems the good ones like Hill or Remson all are. Laconic, don't give a damn, laughing all the time, and they don't seem to care a great deal whether they survive or not."

"But they do, Max. They do." Her voice was gentle. He felt a sudden pressure from her hand.

"Maybe," he said. "I think I'll learn from them. And from the others too. You met Marriner, remember?"

"He looks something like you. Wilder maybe. He looks like he's mad at something, like a little boy who lost his popsicle."

"He's good at this business, Doris. He and Anders are very good. I'm sure of it although we haven't flown together yet except for a few minutes this afternoon when we went up to meet Hill. Whatever it is they've got, I want some of it."

"Max, Max, Max," she breathed, "stop demeaning yourself. You've got everything they have."

He stopped suddenly and halted, turning to face her.

"I've been telling myself that ever since I left New York. My father told me something when I left. It was the first time I could remember when he ever found it hard to find words. Words came quite easily to him."

She waited silently while he remembered.

"He told me, 'Son, I have given you everything I could. All your life you have wanted for nothing. But I haven't been able to give you what you'll need where you're going. I suppose it's because I don't have it within me to give. If it is within you, you'll know it when the time comes. I think it is. Remember this though. No one out there will give you a damn thing. You'll have to make it on your own, and you'll find that survival is a lonely and personal responsibility. I pray you'll measure up, not only because I love you but because when you do, it will make me a little less a failure myself.' "

"He doesn't sound like a failure to me," Doris said.

"I don't think so either. He's been a good father. But his world died a long time ago, and he lives a life that has to be dusted off every so often or it'll be forgotten in time."

She did not speak for several moments. "Are you afraid, Max?" she said finally.

"Anything can happen out here, I suppose."

"The idea of dying doesn't disturb you?"

"Of course it does. It always will. But I want something to cover

69]

up the fear. That's what Marriner and Anders seem to have. Bates too. You haven't met Stepik, but you will. I'm sorry he didn't come along tonight."

"You're fond of this Stepik?"

"More than that. I think he's going to be very important to me."

"Don't let anyone become too important or too close, Max. I know this much."

He smiled. "Not even a maiden girl?"

"Maiden girl, hell," she laughed. "You'd be shocked at what I've done with my life."

"Then shock me."

"I will, but not tonight. It's been too nice. I'll save the gory details for later."

"We'd better be getting back to the others," he said. "They've still got a curfew on this island."

They turned and started walking toward the building, where the sounds of the party had grown louder and more raucous.

There was laughter in her voice as she said, "The others have probably disappeared by now. That is, if I know Hill and Remson."

"Disappeared?" he said. "Where?"

"Into the sack. The bed. The pads, Max darling. Beds are lonely places for the men out here, and this is something most of them can't tolerate. They'll get up before dawn and sneak out past the monitors at the doors and the guard at the gate will look the other way when they drive past."

Remson and Marriner were more than a little drunk when Winston and Doris joined them at a table near the bar. Winston held her chair while Doris seated herself.

"My," said Remson, "we finally found us a gentleman, Doris."

"About time," she said. "I was getting tired of sitting myself down. Where are your sex-maniac friends?"

"Acting like sex maniacs," answered Remson.

"Leaving you two to canvass the joint?"

Remson gestured at Marriner. "I have been spending my time trying to keep this young tiger from clobbering the air group commander."

"What for?" asked Winston.

Marriner's face was a study in concentration. "It just seemed like a good idea," he said.

[70

"He doesn't realize that ensigns don't clobber commanders unless they want to go to the bastille," Remson explained.

"I still think it's a good idea," said Marriner. "He gave the Skipper a hard time in front of the whole goddam party." Marriner looked at Doris. "Excuse the language, ma'am."

"Ma'am accepts the apology." Doris smiled. "Where is Harry, anyway?"

"Gone with the wind," answered Remson. "He will appear on the flight line tomorrow, satiated, bleary-eyed and bemoaning the fact that he has become an old man."

"He'll never be old," said Marriner. He concentrated a moment. "Who the hell are we talking about?"

"We're talking about your skipper," Doris said, and turned to Remson. "I'll tell you something about Harry. He'll sleep tonight with a girl whose name he won't even remember tomorrow. It's a game with him, and he plays it joyfully. I don't think there will ever be any hard feelings or recriminations when Harry is finished. Hill always leaves people laughing. When he's gone they'll find the world a little duller, and every one of them will be looking forward to the day he'll come back again."

"Well," said Remson, "I think I'd rather have a beautiful girl say that about me than get a Navy Cross."

"How about Anders?" Winston asked.

Marriner lit a cigarette with some difficulty. "He and Bates will be back in the morning." With mock incredulity he added, "That crud Crowley was going to throw the Skipper in hack. The bastard. Excuse me, ma'am. I think I will walk over and clobber the sonofabitch. Excuse me, ma'am."

Marriner started to get up, but Remson placed a restraining hand on his arm. "Not yet, young tiger. Wait till we're leaving if you must. I warn you, the bastille is drafty at Barbers Point."

Winston ordered another round of drinks, and Remson began a lengthy discourse concerning Harry Hill's probable activities at that exact moment. Marriner sat quietly, his eyes becoming more clouded as the time went by, until finally he tipped his chair over backward and sprawled on the floor.

"I think maybe you all ought to go home," Doris said. "Before the Shore Patrol comes after you. Who's driving?"

"I am," Winston announced firmly.

71]

"Come on," Doris said, "I'll walk you to the car."

Winston rose, and he and Doris left the room while Marriner fumbled some bills onto the table for the waiter.

"Got one thing to do yet," he said thickly to Remson. "On the way out."

"Then let's get moving," said Remson, helping Marriner to his feet.

On the way out, Marriner stopped to take a ferocious swing at an unsuspecting lieutenant standing at the bar about fifteen feet away from Crowley. The astounded lieutenant flew through the air and landed in a heap in a corner.

"There, goddammit," Marriner said, blowing on his knuckles.

"An admirable blow," Remson conceded. "But you hit the wrong man."

"Admiral who?" asked Marriner.

"It makes no difference, I guess. Whoever he was he probably deserved it. Come to think of it, he had a mean mouth. Let's get out of here."

"I enjoyed it, Doris," Winston said, "more than I can say."

"Me too, Max. Call me tomorrow?"

"Six o'clock?"

She nodded and kissed him, a long, gentle kiss.

"Be on your guard, Max Winston," she murmured. "I fight dirty."

[72

V

October, 1943

Many things happen in a war of which the great majority of the populace never hears. On October 11, 1943, an event took place off the coast of Oahu, Territory of Hawaii, that is logged in no record book and was never released to the press and wire services. It is remembered only by the men who lived through the war, so that if you listen carefully where flying men gather today, you may still get the story second hand or if you are lucky even first hand.

At 0730 on that day a certain Lieutenant Flagler reported for duty to the ready room of Patrol Squadron 24, a PBY outfit located at Kaneohe Naval Air Station on the windward side of Oahu.

Flagler was an earnest young man, twenty-four years old and quite proud of the nine hundred hours recorded in his logbook. He approached the operations desk and asked the yeoman on duty, "What's in store for a man with my name, Carson?"

"For a change, sir, you have a patrol in Area Baker."

"I'm good and goddam tired of Area Baker."

"I agree, sir. This is a lousy war. Too many Area Bakers if you ask me."

Area Baker was a stretch of water approximately seventy miles long lying between the island of Oahu and the island of Kauai to the west. The military importance of the area was negligible, but because it was used as a gunnery training space, large amphibious patrol bombers flew patrol, in case of emergency landings in the water by the fighter planes. The sea was usually angry, but even when it was calm, eddying currents raced to and fro making the surface a poor bet for forced landings. In addition there were sharks

73]

in the waters, and they had been known to attack humans. There are people of vast nautical experience who will tell you that a shark will never attack a human being. There are others who say that the best defense against a shark is to rap him smartly on the nose. Both of these statements are ridiculous. The best defense against a shark is to get out of the water, because a man who decides to fight a shark with his fist has the same chance of survival as a drowning man who is given artificial respiration without being taken out of the lake.

Flagler went to the weather hut where he met his co-pilot, and together they checked the weather. Assured of perfect flying conditions, they repaired to the flight line to inspect the airplane, an antiquated prewar relic whose hull had taken such a beating for so long that its entire length was a patchwork of repair scars. Flagler grimaced with distaste as he inspected Number Six and reminded himself to consider carefully before allowing Hardy any practice landings today. When he had decided that Number Six was as seaworthy and airworthy as she would ever be, he went to the officers' mess for coffee. He had not the faintest premonition that today would be a day he would remember as long as he lived.

At the same moment that Flagler entered the officers' mess, Ensigns Anders, Marriner, Bates, Winston and Stepik walked into Fighting Squadron Two's hangar. With the exception of Stepik, none of them felt worth a damn. They climbed to the second deck and entered the operations room. The rest of the squadron was not flying, and the entire operations area had the gay, convivial atmosphere of a funeral parlor. Lending color to the atmosphere, Remson's supine form lay stretched out on a battered sofa. He sat up with a loud groan.

"Good morning, men. I feel awful."

"Good morning, sir," said Marriner. "You are not alone."

Remson nodded. "So be it." He got to his feet with a great deal of effort and gestured toward a blackboard at the far end of the room. "With your permission, gentlemen, we will now conduct a skull session."

The officers took seats facing the blackboard, and Remson carefully drew a rude caricature of an airplane. Trailing from its after section was a long line on the end of which was a rectangular object.

"We are going out today to shoot holes into this target." He made an X on the target. "It is roughly thirty feet long and eight feet high, and it is made of some sort of material that is receptive to fifty-caliber shells. So don't worry about hitting the target and damaging it. This

[74

target will be towed by an airplane flown by myself. I will fly at one hundred and fifty knots so you can figure out your lead angle from that information. I will maintain an altitude of fifteen thousand feet, and I shall not deviate more than a few feet from it. So you can make your initial turn based on that information. We will make only overhead runs. From what I have just told you, Ensign Marriner, what deductions have you made?"

"Well, sir," said Marriner, "I suggest we assume position ahead of the target at approximately one o'clock. That means that by looking back over our left shoulders we should just barely be able to see the target tow plane. From that position we start a slow but reasonably steep banked turn to the left. We maintain control of the plane in such manner as to arrive over a spot just forward of the tow plane in approximately an inverted position. From this upside down position we will continue on through into a split-S, pulling our noses through until they pick up the towed target. We will hold on the target until it hits a position on our sights indicating it is in the proper position for a ninety-degree deflection shot. Then we open fire, making certain our guns are charged and off safe and that we do not open fire from a distance greater than that called for in the boresighting instructions of the guns. In this case I believe nine hundred feet."

Remson looked at Marriner with something akin to awe. "Mr. Marriner, for a young man who drank half the booze on Oahu last night, you amaze me. As a matter of purely impersonal curiosity, do you think you will hit this target this morning?"

Marriner answered in a matter-of-fact voice. "I believe, Mr. Remson, that I will shoot fifty percent or better."

Remson nodded. "If you do, Mr. Marriner, I believe you may well earn a division in this squadron while you are still an ensign." He erased the markings on the board. "You will not have full ammo loads. You will have one hundred fifty rounds in each gun so don't waste bullets. Don't shoot until you think you're in too close. Then wait a second longer and you'll probably have the right range. Try to watch the Skipper. Do what he does, and you'll be all right. One more thing."

Remson drew up a chair and leaned forward, speaking in a confidential voice. "Our esteemed air group commander, Commander Crowley, will be anxious to learn the results of this hop. He is hoping someone dopes off or at the very least that our gunnery scores are terrible. Crowley hates the Skipper's guts. Never mind why. The point is, we can't let the Skipper down. Crowley would just plainly love to climb all over his back after last night."

"I still don't know what the hell was going on," said Marriner.

"It's not important that you do," said Remson. "You probably will before you're out here a hell of a lot longer. Just remember to keep on your toes and shoot straight. Okay? Then let's get out and ground check the planes."

While the gunnery flight was ground checking airplanes on the flight line at Barbers Point, Lt. Flagler was warming up his engines on the ramp at Kaneohe. He could see out past the harbor entrance. The swells were more active now. A wind was building, and though this in itself was not important, Flagler had intended to give Hardy some practice landings. A choppy or heavy sea would preclude this, and God knew Hardy needed them. Flagler drew his attention back to the engine gauges and spoke aside to Hardy.

"Get taxi clearance."

"Kaneohe tower from Navy Six," intoned Hardy. "Taxi for one."

"Navy Six cleared for immediate taxi and takeoff. There is no other traffic. Your wind 170, ten knots."

"Roger from Navy Six."

Flagler poured power to the twin engines, and the lumbering PBY moved down the waterway toward the takeoff area.

At Barbers Point, Lt. Commander Harry Hill checked his parachute harness as he stood in front of his F6F Hellcat. He looked down the flight line and gave a thumbs-up signal to the other pilots already in their planes. He received in turn a thumbs-up from each of them. Then he climbed into his cockpit, and the plane captain scrambled up on the wing and helped buckle him in.

Out on the runway Remson sat in his plane while the target crew fastened the tow line to the underside of his aircraft. Several hundred feet down the runway the target lay along the side of the take-off strip. The mech moved out in front of Remson and gave him the all-clear signal. Remson nodded, stepped hard on his brakes and pushed the throttle all the way forward. The engine came to life, winding up into a full-throated roar as the streamers flew from the madly spinning propeller. The tail of the plane tried to rise, reacting to the pull of the prop, and Remson, standing hard on the brakes, had to exert strength to hold the stick back in his lap and thus keep the tail on the ground. When it seemed the plane would burst into

[76

motion despite his efforts, Remson gave a last quick glance at the tachometer and took off. He felt the jerk as the target abruptly left the ground, and he eased the stick back into his gut and flipped up the wheel lever. Remson was airborne with his target at the same instant that Flagler, on the other side of the island, took up a heading for Area Baker.

A minute after Remson became airborne Hill sped down the runway and took off. He was followed by the others who swung in toward him as he circled and effected a rendezvous. The planes then swung west in close formation and followed Remson out to sea.

In the Barbers Point tower the duty tower operator, Radioman Second Class Andrews, made a notation on his log to the effect that a VF-2 gunnery flight, flight leader Hill, had departed Barbers Point at exactly 1000 hours, destination Area Baker, purpose live gunnery practice.

Lt. Flagler was heading for an area adjacent to Area Baker. He knew enough not to fly directly under the gunnery range for he had no intention of dodging fifty-caliber shells during a routine operational training flight. He trimmed up the lumbering PBY, and when he was satisfied the airplane was flying straight and level, he turned the controls over to Hardy and settled back to watch the young ensign control the plane. The flight was scheduled to last for three hours, and three hours was a long time to cross back and forth between Oahu and Kauai with nothing more exciting to watch than the endless succession of choppy seas below. He told Hardy to maintain an even five thousand feet. Flagler then allowed his attention to wander, and he was soon reliving the past evening when he had had inordinately good luck with a half Japanese waitress whose name was Missy Sing. While Ensign Hardy cursed Bureau Number 105436 for a faithless and obstinate bitch and vainly tried to keep the altimeter needle on 5,000 feet, Lt. Flagler drifted off into an erotic résumé of the passionate hour and a half he had spent with Missy Sing. He was remembering the delightful curve of her belly as Hardy guided Number Six just north of Barbers Point and headed out over the waters adjacent to Area Baker.

Fifteen thousand feet above Flagler, Harry Hill looked back over his shoulder and watched with approval as the other five planes of his flight held in perfectly aligned formation.

Hill called Remson on the radio. "Boxcar Bunny from Boxcar Leader, what is your position?"

77]

Remson, flying along five thousand feet below Hill, searched the sky above him diligently. He had long ago learned not to stare at any fixed spot in the sky, not to funnel his vision even to a particular area but to let his gaze rove across the vast expanse of sky so that he would more easily pick out the minute specks that would be Hill and the others. In a short time he made out the formation.

"Boxcar Leader from Bunny. You are ten o'clock high from me."

Anders, flying tight on Hill, spotted the tow plane first. "I've got him Boxcar. This is Boxcar Two."

"You've got the lead," said Hill. "Take us down."

Anders tapped his head, then slid his plane under Hill's and banked away. He swept down in a wide, diving arc, and the six planes sped past the slower flying tow plane. Remson waved to them as they passed.

"Let's see you riddle this target."

Anders led the formation up, climbing in a steep angle of attack until once again they had reached 20,000 feet. Now Anders flew forward of the tow plane until, looking back over his left shoulder, he could barely see Remson's aircraft. At this distance he could not see the target twisting slowly at the end of the tow line some 900 feet behind Remson's plane.

Anders was now assured he had the proper position to commence his overhead run. He waggled his wings twice, a signal to the planes behind him that he was peeling off, then started a gentle turn to the left, his head craned to watch over his shoulder at the tow plane. It was in this initial step in the run that the success or failure of the maneuver was insured. Watching carefully in order to control the degree of his bank, he slowly swung a hundred and eighty degrees, maintaining a precise 20,000 feet as he did so. Remson's plane was closer now, and Anders could see the tiny white banner that was the target. As he approached a position almost directly above Remson's plane, Anders was in a bank so steep that he was almost inverted. Now he rolled completely over on his back and let the nose of the plane accede to the force of gravity and drop on through the horizon and down until it pointed straight at the white-capped waves almost four miles below. As he began the roaring dive toward the ocean he saw the white banner enter the outside ring on his gunsight. So far so good. The airspeed was building rapidly, and the plane began to buffet from the increased speed. He centered the target banner ninety

[78

mills from the middle of his sights and eased back gently on the stick, pulling the nose forward to keep the target stationary in his sights.

When the target filled approximately one-third of the entire gunsight, he assumed he was 900 feet from the target and at the perfect firing distance since the guns were boresighted, or aimed in the wings, to converge at that distance. Now Anders gently pressed the firing button on the forward side of the control stick with quick, sporadic pressures from the middle finger of his right hand. The tracers burst through the air, and though it appeared he had undershot and the tracers had fallen short of the target, Anders knew that tracers, if properly fired, always appear to fall short of the intended target. He swept by the target in a vertical dive with a grunt of satisfaction. He knew he had hit the banner. He pulled back harder on the stick and shut his eyes as the "g" forces pressed him down into his seat and the plane's nose rose toward the horizon and then up into a steep climb as he headed back for his approach position.

One after the other the five other planes of the flight peeled off, made their carefully calculated approaches to the roll-over point, dropped their noses through the horizon and onto the target five thousand feet below them. The runs were all good with one exception. Perhaps excited, perhaps doubtful of his ability to control the two thousand horsepower under his fingers, Winston misjudged his roll-over point. He came over onto his back far too soon, and so he found himself in a screaming dive toward the tow line long before the target had even come into view on his gunsight. In fact he couldn't even see the target, and he was heading for a collision with the tow cable. At the last possible moment he wrenched the stick hard to the left, turning the plane on its axis and missing the metal tow cable by a matter of three or four feet. He did not fire a shot at the target in his first run.

Winston's difficulties were unnoticed by the others in the flight although Hill spotted the gyrations of Winston's plane as it went past the target cable, and shook his head. But then Anders initiated the same pattern again, and the planes made their second passes.

Watching from his position as tail-end Charlie, the last plane in the formation, Winston could see the patterns flown by the other planes, and he knew that the passes they were making were good ones and that when the hop was over each of the others could expect to find numerous holes in the target left by the colored shells of his guns. Each plane had an assigned color on its shells, and Winston was suddenly afraid he would be shamed when no holes with his color were found in the target. He determined on this run to adjust for the obvious miscalculations of the last. Hill added his comment as he called on the radio.

"Boxcar Six from Leader. Hold off on your roll-over. You are coming down too steep to hit the target."

"Roger from Six," replied Winston and determined to be far too shallow rather than too steep a second time.

Lt. Flagler and Ensign Hardy were flying at five thousand feet, two miles outboard of the gunnery area and approximately halfway between Oahu and Kauai. Flagler was trying not to notice Hardy's ineffectual efforts to maintain a consistent altimeter reading. Hardy was one of those fliers who found it impossible to keep the nose of the plane on the horizon. As Flagler shook his head in exasperation and directed his gaze out the window of the PBY he could see, high above, the streamers of contrail from the wings of the fighter planes pulling out of their gunnery runs. For a split second Flagler felt an envy for all fighter pilots. Then his loyalty to the big boats returned, and he reminded himself he had a toilet, a kitchen well stocked with goodies, a bunk should he care to nap and that no one, in all probability, would ever shoot at him in anger. In this surmise he was very nearly wrong.

Winston jockeyed for position to start his next run. He watched Stepik, in front of him, peel off and swing around into the inverted position. Then he recharged his guns and turned his gunsight to full bright. He rolled a small amount of back rudder tab and started his initial turn.

In his cockpit Remson leaned forward and dropped the ashes from his cigarette into the knee pocket of his flight suit. This was contrary to safety directives, but there are only so many places in a cockpit in which to deposit ashes. Then he squirmed back in his seat with a bored sigh and prepared to watch Winston make his next run. On Remson's knee was a chart board with the plane numbers and names of each of the other pilots. It was part of his job to make comments on the runs as observed from his position. Remson kept his eyes fixed on Winston's plane, and as Winston passed directly overhead he made a quick notation.

"Second pass. Flew too far before rolling inverted. Will shoot shallow. Sucked behind."

Winston had overcorrected for his first mistake, and now he would

[80

be far behind the target and would be unable to bring his guns to bear.

Winston was sweating in the cockpit, and his hands were slippery on the stick as he rolled completely over and committed himself to his run.

Screaming straight down at nearly four hundred miles an hour, Winston saw the target slide across his sights. Now he realized he was far out of range, and the target was getting away from him. Determined that he would not waste another pass, he yanked savagely back on the stick to pull his nose up and keep it on the rapidly passing target. It was a stupid maneuver in an airplane traveling at a rate of speed at which any abrupt maneuver caused a violent aerodynamic reaction. In Winston's case his savage handling of back stick caused his elevators to assume position for a steep climb when actually the plane was in a vertical dive. The plane tried to accept the commands being forced upon it and almost succeeded. The nose came up and drew a little ahead of the target banner, but at the same time the plane was losing aerodynamic efficiency. The clean flow of air over the control surfaces was gone, and the aircraft was, in effect, "mushing" through the sky in a semi-flying condition. Winston was unaware of this, so when he found the target within his gunsight he opened fire, holding his finger on the firing button in the hope that if he shot enough bullets into the air at least some of them would hit the target. He did better than he expected.

He missed the target, but his shells flew over it and found Remson's plane, which was on a direct line with the banner. In the instant that he flashed past the target Winston saw with a horrified clarity a piece of the underside of Remson's plane fly off.

Winston shut his eyes and groaned.

Remson was aware something had happened to his plane although he had no idea that he had been fired at. Thus when he heard a dull thunk somewhere behind him, he immediately checked his engine instruments, thinking perhaps some minor part of the engine had come loose in the wind and clattered against the side of the plane as it tore off.

Remson had no way of knowing that three of the shells from Winston's guns had struck his plane. One had blasted through the tail assembly doing only minor damage to the horizontal stabilizer. The second had harmlessly buried itself in a wing root on the starboard side of the plane. However, the third passed directly

81]

under Remson's seat and hit in the engine area, puncturing the hydraulic tank, and this shell was anything but harmless. As his eyes followed the instruments Remson immediately became aware of this state of affairs although he still had no idea how it had come about. He reacted instantaneously.

"Boxcar Leader from Boxcar Bunny. I blew a hydraulic line someplace. My pressure is dropping." Remson's voice was no more excited than if he had been acknowledging an order to take a hot bath.

Hill replied immediately. "Roger, Hank. I have you in sight. We're coming down." Hill wheeled over in a steep dive and screamed downwards. He was not as yet alarmed. A drop in hydraulic pressure did not necessarily mean an emergency. Such thinking on Hill's part was abruptly negated when Remson's voice burst over the radio, still calm but carrying now an edge of apprehension.

"This is Hank. Hydraulic pressure zero. Smoke in the cockpit. I'm heading for the deck." The others saw the target banner float free of Remson's plane as he tugged the tow handle and sent his plane toward the water in a steep glide.

In the Barbers Point operations tower, Radioman Second Class Andrews had picked up the voices on the gunnery radio channel. He listened intently while he experienced a hollow sensation in the pit of his stomach. He picked up a telephone and dialed the number of the Operations Duty Officer.

"This is Andrews in the tower. Emergency with Boxcar flight in Area Baker. Hydraulic failure and smoke in the cockpit."

"Roger. Keep us informed." The duty officer hung up and barked at his assistant, "Larson, check Area Baker. What do we have out there?" As Larson moved quickly to a map on the wall studded with small tacks representing the position of various aircraft in the Hawaiian area, the duty officer spoke heatedly into the phone to a variety of persons. He alerted Air-Sea Rescue, which made ready to launch an amphibious plane upon further orders. He notified the duty officer of Commander Fleet Air Hawaii, the admiral in charge of area flight operations. He notified the radar operator situated in a shack on the outskirts of the airfield and last but not least he notified the squadron from which the ailing plane came.

When the call came through to Fighting Two there was no one in the office except the air group commander. Crowley let out a curse and headed for the tower on the double. As he ran he wasn't sure if he was worried about Remson or if he was experiencing a secret satisfaction that the loudmouthed Harry Hill had got his flight into a jam.

Lt. Flagler became aware of the emergency when Hill switched his radio to the emergency channel and sent out the flier's song of distress, a call that clears the air waves of all other transmissions, bar none, that tells anyone listening that a man is in trouble in the air and you'd better goddam not garble up this particular radio frequency for any reason whatsoever.

"Mayday! Mayday! Mayday!" Hill's voice rang out loud and clear, and a hundred hearts skipped a beat in the skies above Pearl Harbor as this airborne S.O.S. sounded. Planes from as far as two hundred miles away immediately changed course for Area Baker as Hill's voice continued.

"Emergency in Area Baker. Emergency in Area Baker. Coordinates Easy Victor 6473. I say again, Easy Victor 6473."

Lt. Flagler consulted the map on his lap and surmised he was only a few miles from the scene. He notified Barbers Point tower on the emergency channel.

"Barbers tower from Navy Six, my present position Area Baker. Coordinates Easy Victor 6260. I am four zero miles, bearing two nine five true from you. Heading for scene of emergency. Six out."

Hill, Marriner and the others flew formation off to one side of Remson. It was exasperating to be able to do absolutely nothing. They could see Remson, his head bent forward as he tried desperately to find the source of the smoke filling his cockpit. He was loath to open the canopy until it became unbearable in the cockpit. The whipping wind could conceivably fan the flames if only he could find the goddam flames. His altitude was now 10,000 feet.

ComFairHawaii's duty officer entered the Admiral's paneled office and reported the emergency. The Admiral pointed to a radio receiver on a table. "Get me that damn emergency channel."

Rear Admiral Reginald Delacrois, known to his seniors and subordinates alike as "Frog," was forty-eight years old although he looked at least ten years older. But his body was lean and strong, and humor lay just under the hard surface demanded by two stars and the braided hat.

There was absolutely nothing the Admiral could do about Remson's predicament because he had no transmitting facilities. All he could do was listen and mutter unheard encouragements to the pilots far out at sea.

In his cockpit Remson realized with a weary resignation that he was going to have to land in the water. He might attempt to glide the plane to shore, but the heavy, billowing smoke in the cockpit discouraged this. He also could open the canopy and bail out, but there is an insecurity in trusting your life to a parachute that has been packed by someone you do not know and whose diligence is a matter of conjecture.

"Boxcar Leader from Bunny. Skipper, I'm going to put her in the drink."

"Roger," Hill answered. "Boxcar Six, climb to altitude and contact Air-Sea Rescue on emergency channel. Report our position and remain at altitude. Turn your IFF on." Winston peeled off and climbed to fifteen thousand feet where he initiated his call.

Now that he knew Remson was going in the drink the enormity of his mistake burst upon Winston's mind. He had shot down his own squadron mate. What would they do to him? Court-martial? Stripped of rank? Dishonorable discharge? When he had seen the debris fly from Remson's undercarriage he had hoped for the best, had prayed that he had not hit a vital spot. Now he knew that he had not been that lucky. So dimly in his mind that it was no more than a faint tracing on his imagination lurked another and more shameful thought. Perhaps Remson did not know that he had been hit by Winston's fire. And even if he did, there was a chance that Remson would not survive the water landing. These abasing thoughts squirmed in the back of Winston's brain.

Remson whistled soundlessly as he made his preparations. He felt that with any degree of luck he could handle the situation. Ditching was not an inordinately difficult process if undertaken with skill and judgment.

Now he jettisoned his cockpit canopy and the wind whipped into his face, tearing off his flight helmet. It also dispelled most of the smoke, and his visibility cleared. He pulled his flap handle but the flaps did not move. Stupid bastard, he thought, of course the flaps won't move. Your main hydraulic pressure is gone. Because the few knots that the flaps would decrease his landing speed might mean the difference between life and death, he spent precious moments pumping them down by emergency pressure.

His altitude was four thousand feet as he tightened his seat belt and the shoulder straps which would hold him hard against the back of the seat and prevent his plunging forward into the instrument panel when he hit the water. He pulled them until they bit into his shoulders.

He maintained a steady 130 knots as he banked into a gentle, gliding turn. He estimated the wind direction from the white streamers of the waves and lined up directly into it. He might have elected to land cross-wind, in the trough of the waves, but either way the gamble remained. Hell, Remson figured, either way I've got a fifty-fifty chance.

He eased back on the stick and the airspeed needle dropped to 110 knots . . . 100 . . . 90.

In his office, Admiral Delacrois stood intent by the radio as Hill's dispassionate voice came through, reminding all hands in the Hawaiian area that a man was battling for his life in Area Baker. The Admiral looked up as a tall figure came through the door without knocking.

"Sit down, Sam," he said. "Emergency out in Baker. Fighting Two."

"That's one of mine," Balta said simply.

Hill's voice came over the radio, "Hank. How's your visibility?"

"Perfect, Skipper." Remson's voice was unhurried, confident.

Hill again. "Lower the seat all the way to the floor."

"Will do," answered Remson.

Sam Balta looked at the Admiral. "That's Harry Hill out there. He'll do what has to be done for the other pilot."

Delacrois nodded and turned the radio louder.

The time was now for Hank Remson. The plane slid down toward the wave-tops, and Remson's eyes narrowed as he watched the airspeed indicator. Eighty-five knots now and falling . . . 80 . . . 75. All of his skill was martialed now in this moment of crisis. Twenty-five hundred hours in the air, forty combat missions, a year of flight training. He was skimming the wave-tops.

Remson eased back on the stick, and the needle fluttered past 70 knots. The plane shuddered and stalled. It fell the last few feet and plunged into the water.

It was not Hank Remson's fault that his shoulder straps broke. The traitorous bit of fabric was frayed far down under the seat where it joined the airframe and where an inspector would not bother to check. Remson had braced himself but to no avail. The force of the plane hitting the water at 68 knots was sufficient to burst the straps, and Remson was hurtled forward in the cockpit. He did not have time even to curse before his head crashed into the gunsight, knocking it aside, and on into the reinforced windshield. As consciousness left him, Remson fumbled with and released the catch on his safety belt.

Marriner saw the plane hit in a giant burst of spray, and he watched as it nosed under and slid beneath the water. He dropped his flaps and flew low and slow over the scene of the crash. Hill and the others followed him as Marriner's voice rang out.

"He's out. He got out!"

Lt. Flagler heard Marriner's transmission. In the same instant he saw Remson's body in the water.

"This is Navy Six," he called. "Peter Baker Yoke. I have the pilot in sight."

In Delacrois's office the two men breathed, "Thank God."

Marriner circled and flew back over Remson. He was only ten feet above the water and the spray from the washing waves spattered his windshield.

"This is Marriner. He's unconscious." Marriner could see Remson's body floating inertly, supported by the inflated Mae West.

Hill knew the danger of the heaving seas to an unconscious man. "Navy Six," he called. "There isn't much time. It's up to you."

Flagler made a low pass over Remson, and only then did he become aware of the condition of the sea below him. He frowned as he expertly judged the height and speed of the waves. Flagler had other responsibilities besides Hank Remson. He had five other men in Navy Six in addition to the plane itself. He turned and made another low pass over the downed pilot. The waves heaved and boiled beneath him, and he remembered the thin and patched hull of Number Six.

"What the hell you waiting for?" Hill called. "That man is drowning down there."

Flagler did not answer. He had a problem but no answer for it.

Marriner bit off a curse. "Navy Six. What is the delay?"

Flagler decided to make another low pass, hoping that somehow the winds would die in the next few seconds and the waters would subside.

Flagler's hands were sweating on the control wheel as he turned and stared into Hardy's eyes. Strange, he thought, that I should look to an ineffectual man like Hardy at a time like this. He was

[86

hoping Hardy would tell him what to do, but the co-pilot only pointed out the window of the plane on Flagler's side. An F6F was flying just off the wing tip, the pilot pointing vehemently at the water.

Flagler made up his mind.

"This is Navy Six. I cannot land. The water is too rough." He looked at Hardy from the corner of his eye, but Hardy was staring ahead, his mouth a grim line. God damn it, thought Flagler, I never asked for a command.

Miles away Sam Balta heard and his face whitened. "What?" he roared at Delacrois. "He can't *what?*"

Delacrois frowned. "He's got a plane and crew to think about, Sam."

Balta started to swear but stopped as Marriner's voice came over the radio.

"Navy Six from Boxcar Three." Marriner's voice was angry. "I tell you this, you white-livered sonofabitch. You land and pick that pilot up or I swear I'll shoot you out of the sky."

Hill's voice broke in: "If he misses, I won't."

Flagler was a good pilot, but he had never been in combat and death was unfamiliar to him. He turned back toward Oahu.

"Navy Six," he called. "Air-Sea Rescue is on the way. Also a crash boat from Barbers Point." He hesitated a moment. "I've got five men aboard this plane."

Marriner reversed his course as he spoke into his mike. "Once more, Navy Six. That's all. Then you burn."

Marriner came in from behind the PBY and switched on his gunsight and gun switches. As he raced up on the patrol plane he deliberately moved the pip on the gunsight a little ahead and to the right of Flagler's plane. Then Marriner held the firing button down in a long, sustained burst. The shells blasted past the PBY and threw up a mountain of spray directly in front of it. As Marriner flashed by, Hill opened fire from the other side, and Flagler would always remember the thunderous *pom-pom-pom-pom* of the shells. He looked over his shoulder and saw three more Hellcats above preparing to peel off and come down at him.

"Are you turning back, Navy Six?" Marriner called. "Next time I won't miss."

Just as Bates, Anders and Stepik were peeling off, Flagler threw the control column hard left and banked back toward the scene of the crash.

"Barbers tower from Navy Six. I am returning to scene of crash."

Marriner swung his plane alongside the PBY. "You are fucking able right you are, Navy Six."

Tower Operator Andrews grimaced at this violation of radio procedure. For the first time he noticed Commander Crowley standing beside him and wondered at the smile on Crowley's face. It seemed a strange time to be smiling.

Sam Balta relaxed his grip on the edge of the Admiral's desk and managed a smile.

"Your PBY made a wise decision, Frog," he said.

Frog Delacrois was upset. Nothing like this had happened to him in twenty-eight years of naval service.

"God damn it to hell," he roared. "What kind of a sonofabitching thing is this?" He glared at Sam Balta in red-faced anger. "I'll court-martial every one of them. Send them to Portsmouth. I don't believe it. In *my* area. In MY goddam area they threaten to shoot down one of our own planes. Who the hell do they think they're fighting anyway? Patrol Squadron 24? I'll have their balls for this. Watch me, Sam. I'll string them up by the balls so help me. A civil war in MY area."

"Nothing happened, Frog," Balta reminded him.

"No, but something will. Turn that damn radio up. What happened to the pilot in the drink?" As quickly as his anger had flared, so it subsided.

Flagler experienced far less difficulty than he expected. He set the big plane down cross-wind into a trough in the waves and made a surprisingly good landing. This might have been because he knew now that he had no alternative. He was fully convinced that if he made a bad landing and cracked up his own plane, those wild men all around him in the sky would certainly strafe him in the water until he was dead.

He gunned the engines and taxied the plane slowly up to the floating figure. Two enlisted men in the rear of the plane opened the hatch and reached down and hauled Remson in. Flagler told Hardy to hold the plane steady and went aft to the open hatch. The crewmen were kneeling beside the inert body.

"He don't look good, sir," one of them said softly.

Remson's face was deathly pale as his body lay sprawled on the deck. His head lay to the right and rested almost parallel with his right shoulder. Flagler unconsciously tried to force his own neck into

[88

a like position and found it impossible. He knelt by the body and felt for a pulse. The wrist under his fingers was cold, and there was no pulse beat at all. Flagler overcame a distaste and ran his palm along the side of Remson's neck. His eyes shadowed as he looked up at the crewmen.

"No," he said. "No. He doesn't look good at all."

He got slowly to his feet and then abruptly turned and went back to the cockpit.

"How is he?" Hardy asked.

"He isn't," Flagler replied, sitting down in his seat again. "Turn her into the wind and hold her there." He picked up his radio mike.

"This is Navy Six. We have recovered the . . . body . . . the neck was broken and the man is dead," continued Flagler. "We are returning to Barbers Point."

Harry Hill was the only man who really knew a sense of personal loss at Remson's death. Hill was remembering many things that the others had yet to experience. The warmth of a fight shared which is a thing a man never forgets. Nights in the wardroom and the laughter and the good drinks together. Hill owed his life more than once to Hank Remson, and now he would never be able to repay. The others felt little more than regret that a man they had known briefly had died.

The flight rendezvoused and headed back for Barbers Point. Hill had made his farewell to Remson, and now he called on the radio, "Close up Boxcar flight. This hop isn't over yet. Look sharp coming into the break."

They moved in tight, and that is the way they came back to Barbers. Tower Operator Andrews watched them come, six fighters with inches between their wing tips as they swept into the break like a single plane. Then Andrews became aware of the nagging ring of his telephone. He lifted the instrument and listened briefly.

"It's for you, sir," he said to Commander Crowley who stood at his side. "Admiral Delacrois."

Crowley took the phone. "Yes sir, Admiral. Commander Crowley."

"Crowley," came the grating voice, "you're aware of what has happened?"

"Yes, sir. I've been in the tower."

"Safe a place as any with that bunch of maniacs you've got running loose. Is Hill leading that flight?"

"He is, sir."

"Your Fighting Two has set naval aviation back about ten years. You understand this, Crowley?"

"Yes, sir. I will take action, I assure you."

"You will like hell. You will bring Hill to my office at 0900 tomorrow morning. Understood?"

"Of course, sir," said Crowley.

"0900 then," the Admiral said and hung up.

Delacrois looked at Balta. "Too damn bad, Sam. About the boy who died, I mean." He added grimly, "I'll take care of the others."

Balta, standing by a window, regarded him sourly. "Why?" he demanded.

"Why?" Delacrois's voice rose. "Why? For Christ's sake, Sam, I can't have my fighter pilots going around shooting down my patrol pilots. I never heard of such a goddam thing. I don't care what the provocation was."

"You would if it had been you down in that water."

"You've got something to say, Sam, say it."

"Well, Admiral, I'll tell you. I'm only a captain, and you can tell me to shut up if you want to. But those boys up there today, they're my boys. They'll be going out soon, and they'll be doing things you and I would be doing if we were younger. Their chances won't be too good because people like you and me have seen to it that we have to fight this war from the ass end. But they'll do the best they can. There won't be enough like them out there, not nearly enough like them. They'll need something inside them that I'm not sure you and I would have under like circumstances. No sir. There won't be enough like them out there for the job that has to be done. You mean to tell me you're going to throw the book at men whose futures are as dim as theirs?"

"They almost started a civil war out there today."

"All they did was see to it that the pilot of the PBY performed his duty. Look at it that way, Frog."

"I can't ignore it. You know that, Sam."

"No. But you can cloud it up. Nobody can keep a thing like this a secret, but if you make an example of these men everyone on the island will know as much about it as we do. Go easy and maybe it will pass."

Delacrois snorted. "You should have been a lawyer."

[90

"I agree," smiled Balta. "That's why I request permission to be present tomorrow at this drumhead court you're holding."

"Drumhead court!" exploded Delacrois. "What the hell are you talking about?"

"That's what it will amount to," Balta said, "unless I'm there."

"Okay, Sam." The Admiral sighed. "You be here tomorrow morning at 0900. I'll tell you this. If your pilots can come up with a plausible excuse I may not crucify them. Okay?"

"I've already given you one."

"But they haven't." Delacrois picked up his hat. "Let's go and get a drink. I want to tell you about my third star."

"You've only got two."

"Right now. But I also have big ears. I'll tell you all about it."

They stopped at the desk of the Admiral's aide in the outer room. "Thomas," Delacrois said, "contact Air-Sea Rescue and tell them I want that area searched before dark. I want them to find anything that is left of the plane that went down this afternoon." He looked at Balta. "Maybe," he said with a frown, "we can find out why that airplane failed us."

Hill and Marriner were sorting out Remson's gear when Winston knocked on the door.

"Come on in, Max," said Hill. "We're pulling an inventory on Hank's gear."

"I'd like to talk to you for a minute, Skipper." Winston was plainly ill at ease.

"Go ahead," said Hill.

Winston hesitated and looked at Marriner.

"I'll be back later," Marriner said.

Suddenly Winston knew he wanted Marriner to hear this. "No. You stay if you will, Dick. You ought to hear this too."

Hill put down a shirt he was packing and looked quizzically at Winston.

"You sound like it's serious business, Max."

"It is serious, sir." He took a breath. "I shot Remson down this afternoon. I made a lousy pass. Got sucked back and fired anyway. I saw a piece of his plane fly off." He looked at the floor. "I killed him, Skipper, God help me."

Hill and Marriner watched Winston expressionlessly. Hill put a match to a cigarette and inhaled slowly.

91]

"Sit down, Max," Hill said.

Winston looked at them hopelessly. "I wasn't sure. I mean, I thought maybe the hydraulic leak might just have happened. I wasn't going to say anything. But later I knew I couldn't do it." He buried his face in his hands. "My God, Skipper, you can't kill a man and then just shut up about it."

"No," Hill said quietly, "I don't suppose you can."

Marriner walked over and took a cigarette from Hill's pack. "What makes you so sure you shot Remson down, Max?" he asked.

"I told you. I saw a piece fly off the underside."

"Hell," said Marriner, "that could have been a scrap of the wheel-housing. The wind could have torn it loose."

"Thanks, Dick. But I knew I got sucked on the run. I was shooting almost level with the tow plane. It had to be me."

"Not yet," said Marriner. "I made a lousy pass too. It could have been me. I was way shallow and held my fire too long."

"I'll tell you both something," Hill broke in. "When a hydraulic line breaks, the chances always are that a fire will result. That's what happened to Remson today. Maybe you both shot at him. Maybe we all made lousy passes, and we all shot at him. Remson had been shot at before. Many times. He would have said something."

"He didn't know," Winston said. "But I shot him. I killed him. I'm the one who doped off today, and I guess I deserve anything they can do to me."

"They may have to do it to me too," Bates said from the doorway. "I've been listening in on these confessions, and although they touch me deeply I have to tell you all that I too made a lousy pass today. Rolled over way too late, over-corrected on the pullout and fell short."

Winston said in a choked voice, "You guys. You goddam guys . . ."

"Let me tell you something, Max," Hill said gently. "It took guts to come here to tell me you killed my best friend." He looked at Marriner and Bates. "That goes for you men too. In a way I'm beginning to love all of you. Let me say that I sincerely believe that all three of you have grown up today. It takes a man to do what you've done. All of you. And I'll tell you something else. I'm damned proud to be your Skipper. Now get dressed, and we'll go over to the club.

[92

This incident is closed except for tomorrow morning when I will beard the Admiral in his den."

Hill was wrong in one respect. The incident was not closed.

At 1847 that afternoon, Crash Boat Four from Air-Sea Rescue arrived at the scene of the crash. It was nearly dark when they found the only remnant of the airplane. It was the hydraulic tank with a hole in the upper half. Because the lower half retained its watertight integrity the tank floated lopsidedly in the water, the rent made by Winston's bullet several inches above the sea. They fished it out and headed for port.

Chief Petty Officer Lennihan examined the tank with a practiced eye. He had been a gunnery expert for eleven years. Lennihan could recognize a shell hole in a piece of metal as well as the next man.

VI

October, 1943

It was not yet eight o'clock in the morning and already the sun was warm in the eastern sky. A soft breeze wafted from the tangled profusion of the garden, carrying with it the fragrance of bush honeysuckle and gardenia. Doris Dowling sipped her breakfast coffee and buttered a final sliver of toast.

"What time did Bates leave?" she asked Ann Murphy, who lay stretched out on the sun deck.

"I love Saturday mornings." Ann rolled over on her stomach. "He left at six o'clock. Swearing like a madman because I woke him up."

Doris laughed. "I liked him. Talk about being uncomplicated."

"Bates is complicated enough," Ann disagreed. "In bed, anyway. I like him too. He's like an old shoe."

"I wouldn't tell him that if I were you." Doris chuckled.

"How about you? Your Max looks like a movie star. A movie star with money and the Winston name. Is he married?"

"Not yet," Doris said, and smiled.

Ann sat up. "Do I detect something in your tone, dear? Like a design, maybe?"

"This is no design. This is an expedition," Doris admitted.

"You're really serious?"

"I am. I felt like someone else last night. Someone I always wanted to meet. I think he did that for me."

"He didn't stay with you?"

Doris shook her head. "No, he didn't stay. It wasn't time for it."

They were silent for a time. Doris lit a cigarette and leaned back in her chair, letting the sunlight warm her face.

[94

Finally Ann said, "How does Max feel about this?"

"I have no idea," Doris admitted. "He's just growing up, I think. I may have to be a bitch."

"Explain, please," Ann said.

"I'm twenty-four years old, Ann, and I'm really a lot older than that. It's time I found what I wanted and set out to get it. I think what I want is Max Winston. How to get him is another thing."

"Well," Ann said, "you could hold his hand and say, 'Max dear, will you do me the extraordinary honor of becoming my husband?' "

"I doubt if he'd buy that."

"I'll try it on Bates and let you know. If Bates won't listen I'll try it on Dick Marriner."

"You do that."

"Are you going to sleep with him?" Ann asked.

"Of course," said Doris. "He knows I'm no virgin."

"You're not a pushover either. As far as I know you've only been with one man the whole time you've been out here."

Doris nodded. "You're right, Ann. There's only been one. It's been enough. He's been kind and sweet and generous. I have no regrets that he isn't a young man anymore. I was tired of young men when I came here."

Ann sat up and hugged her knees.

"Where did you come from, Doris? You never talk about anything."

"I try to forget, Ann, but it doesn't work. Don't ever try to pretend you're something you're not. Do the best you can with what you have inside of you. Maybe it isn't enough, at least in my case, but I'm learning to get along with it."

"I'd settle delightedly," Ann said, "for the same things you have."

Doris smiled and refilled her coffee cup.

"It isn't a background I'd recommend."

They sat there on the sun deck while Doris spoke of her youth and the roads that had led her to Oahu in the middle of a war. As Doris talked she was surprised to find that some pieces of her life no longer belonged to her. They seemed to belong to another girl who had died a long time ago.

There was the memory of the run-down cold water flat on Chicago's South Side, a dirty, soot-stained tenement under the Elevated platform on 63rd Street near the Tower Theater. The sun never shone on the street because the wooden timbers of the El

95]

shut out all but a few strands of light that filtered through the twisted ties on the tracks. The drunks, the winos, the hoodlums and bums stood quietly in the dark doorways or lay sprawled in the gutter, empty bottles clasped in grimy hands. At night there were the sounds of loud laughter and cursing and often the wail of a police siren.

The first smells Doris remembered were of unwashed flesh and garbage, fragrances she would not forget all her life. In the autumn, when the leaves were burned in the gutters, she would walk for hours along the broken streets trying to trade one odor for another.

Doris' father had died before she was born. She knew him only from a worn photograph pasted above the kitchen sink in the flat. He had been a city fireman, a big, cheerful-looking man. Her mother seldom talked about him, and when she did it was with bitterness.

"He never gave me a chance," she would sob on nights when she had undertaken her second bottle of wine. "Or you either, my little girl. It's a blessing he left us anything at all."

Anything at all wasn't enough. Doris' mother had to work during the day in a cleaning establishment next to the Illinois Central Railroad. When Doris was ten years old she helped out on Saturdays for a wage of twenty-five cents.

By the time she was fourteen, Doris had matured. She was a beautiful young woman with golden skin and lovely gray eyes under her copper hair. And she had a mouth that smiled easily. Doris was learning that there was no sense in tantalizing one's brain with mere dreams. She defied her mother and from the money she had earned in the cleaner's, bought herself a new Sunday dress and started attending the Catholic Church at Mt. Carmel. Doris never felt any surge of faith, and she did not intend to practice the religion actively, but she enjoyed the quiet Sunday mornings, the clean people in bright clothes and the sense of peace and beauty in the church. Every Sunday she would sit in the back pew, a white hat on her head, and watch the people trooping up the aisle to communion. It made her feel part of something, and for a little while she was less lonely than she had been.

In her fifteenth year her mother married a bartender who worked in a saloon in Hyde Park. He was an old man and bald, though heavy black hairs curled around his ears and nostrils and down the backs of his wrists. He never drank on duty, but when he came home at night from his afternoon shift he and Doris' mother would sit by the open window, taking advantage of the slight breeze that barely

[96

parted the dirty curtains, and would drink three or four bottles of wine. Doris rarely stayed around because the talk became too intimate and the language vile. He would start to tease Doris, playfully pinching her and rubbing his big, hairy hands on her body.

The day of her high school graduation came. Doris' mother did not attend, claiming she had no proper clothes to wear and would not think of embarrassing her daughter. In reality her mother was sick with a hangover, on this day as on most others. So Doris had graduated alone, lovely in a white dress she had bought herself. She was easily the most beautiful girl in the graduating class, and she would have been a fool to deny it.

The party after the graduation bored her. The young men were flushed and sweaty, and they looked at Doris as though taking bites out of her. Someone dumped a bottle of whiskey in the punch bowl, and when matters began to get out of hand, Doris slipped out the back door and walked home alone, across the park under the stars.

Her stepfather was sitting in the kitchen when she came in. He was wearing only his undershirt and a pair of underdrawers. Doris looked at the hair on his matted chest and growing along his shoulders and across his back. A gorilla.

"Where's Mother?"

"Your mother had to work late at the shop." He poured a glass of wine from a half-filled bottle on the table and shoved it over to her. "Have a drink."

"I don't like it."

"Go on. It won't hurt you." He took a long pull from the neck of the bottle.

"I don't want any," she said.

He looked at her, his bloodshot eyes mean under his black brows. "I said take a drink." His voice was flat.

"And I said no." Doris started to leave the kitchen but he jumped to his feet and grabbed her arm, swinging her around to face him. She flinched at his breath.

"You do what I say, goddamn you. Who d'you think you are?" He held the wine to her lips. Frightened now, she shook her head.

He placed the wine back on the table and then viciously whipped his hand across Doris' face. She gasped and tears flooded in her eyes.

"You want more?" he muttered. "I'll slap you till your head's blue. Take this." He forced the wine into her mouth. "That's better. Now you just sit your sweet little ass down here, and we'll finish this bot-

97]

tle and maybe another one. Just you and your old dad, eh?" He laughed drunkenly and patted her thigh.

He forced Doris to drink with him until both bottles were gone. By that time her head was lying on the table, and she was stone drunk. Dimly she heard her stepfather talking to himself.

"Goddam little whore. Built like a brick shithouse. No sense all that talent goin' to waste."

He staggered to his feet and picked Doris up bodily, slinging her over his shoulder like a sack of wheat. Doris mumbled in protest as he lunged into the bedroom and dumped her on the bed. She felt his rough hands pawing at her dress and then pulling on her underpants. She tried to push him away, but her arms felt leaden, and she couldn't move them.

He was breathing heavily as he unbuttoned his pants and fell on her. She tried to squirm aside, but his heavy weight pinned her to the bed. She could smell the wine on him and stale perspiration. She knew she was going to be sick.

He was about to enter her, his breath heaving, and he was horribly ready, when her mother flung open the door to the room.

"Jesus Christ!" she screamed. "With my own daughter!"

Her mother nearly tore the stepfather's head off with a flatiron and then proceeded to beat the semiconscious Doris almost to death with a curtain rod. Doris left home that same night.

She saw her mother one more time, more than two years later. She came back to say good-bye when the woman was dying. Her mother died half-drunk, lying in a soiled bed. Even in that sorry setting some part of her death reached out to Doris. Her mother gave a small half-smile of regret, as if she were saying, "I didn't know I was going to die just yet." Then she seemed to shrink and shrivel on the damp pillow until finally she died.

Four years later Doris stood by the window in the Drake Hotel and looked down at the rich expanse of Chicago's Gold Coast. The hot summer wind rustled the trees lining Lake Shore Drive, and on the beaches the people thronged in tiny dark clusters.

On one of the beds, clad only in shorts, a middle-aged man lay with an iced drink in his hand. He was watching Doris with a great appreciation. No longer was she the little girl from the South Side who knew too much of dirt and filth. Now she was an immaculately groomed young woman, poised and possessed of great beauty. She turned to the man.

[98

"Charles, you don't know what you're talking about."

He chuckled and sat up on the bed. "I'm thirty years older than you are. Why wouldn't I know what I'm talking about?"

"Marriage." She spoke the word incredulously. "Why do you want to marry me?"

He shrugged. "I like you."

"I like you too. That's why you don't have to marry me. We've had a lot of fun, Charles. Why spoil it?"

"I didn't mean just sleeping with you. I like a lot of other things about you."

"For instance?" she asked.

He shook his head. "Women. They never change. Always snooping around for a compliment. Well, for one thing I like your honesty."

"I'm a bitch," she said.

"I didn't say you weren't. I said you were honest. And you're kind. You'd have to be to put up with an old crank like me."

"You're not so hard to take. You could have been mayor of this town if you'd wanted. You own eight theaters and fifteen restaurants that I know of. I'd say you weren't hard to take at all."

"Then marry me for my money."

"You don't know anything about me."

"The hell I don't," he said emphatically. "Your mother died four years ago in a dirty joint on the South Side. She was no good. You got yourself a job working at Donnelly's as a file clerk. You went to night school, and a year later you were working as a secretary for the law firm of Larruthers, Benson and Burns on State Street. You won a silly contest, 'Secretary of the Month' or something, and they put your picture in the paper. A week later you were modeling at Marshall Field. You were doing fine there until one day an aging millionaire stopped in to get something for his niece, and now he has you here in this hotel and is asking you to marry him. How about that?"

"You had me checked," she said with mock severity.

"Sure as hell did," he agreed cheerfully. "A man with all my money can't be too careful. I want to marry you."

"I don't love you."

"Like me?"

"Of course I do."

"Then it's all settled. I want to make you legal."

"It won't work, Charles."

He was suddenly serious. "Look at it this way, Doris. I'm alone in the world except for a sister I don't like very well. I have no one to work with or for. Money is no fun when you're alone. I want someone with me, to share the things it can buy and the good times that go with it. I've worked hard, and now for Christ's sake, I want to play awhile. With you."

"Are you trying to get me in that bed again?"

"Damn right."

"You're a great actor, Charles. It's no wonder you're rich."

"Then let's go out and get married."

She laughed. "Ask me on a full stomach. I'm starving."

Doris married Charles Dowling three weeks later, and they honeymooned in Jamaica. Doris accepted her husband's gifts and kindnesses with a wide-eyed, childish appreciation that brought a smile to Charles' face. She, in turn, gave him what he had expected, a loyalty and devotion that bore with them a love he considered a bonus.

They had been married two years when Charles came to her bedside one night and told her he was going to die.

"They told me a long time ago. I didn't want to worry you, but time is getting short now, and there are things we have to talk about."

Three years before, the doctors had found cancer in his body and had given him two or three years to live. He had tried the known medical treatments, but without letting himself believe he was going to get better. He hadn't really cared before he married Doris, but now he was reluctant to go.

"I don't suppose it was fair to you, darling," he told her. "I should have told you, I guess. Forgive me?"

"Forgive you?" she whispered. "Forgive you for being so kind and wonderful? For giving me a life I dreamed about? Charles, I told you when I married you I could never love you. I was wrong. I love you now, and I have for a long time."

She held him in her arms then, and she was holding him again on the day he died.

His sister and niece contested the will. Doris was sick of selfish and desperate people, and it was at her suggestion that the settlement was made out of court. The estate was divided three ways, but Doris received over three hundred thousand dollars. She would not be a rich woman, but she would not be a poor one either.

Before she left Chicago she rode out to the South Side on a blustery winter day when the sky was overcast and a fierce wind beat in off the lake. Snow was piled in the gutters along 63rd Street, and the drunks and rollsters were behind the signs and in the doorways out of the cold. She told the cabdriver to wait while she went into the Mt. Carmel church. It was empty at that time of day as Doris knelt for a few minutes and thanked God for letting her escape. When she left she passed an old, ragged woman stumbling down the street against the cold and dismal wind with a wine bottle under her arm.

For a moment she thought it was her mother.

When the war broke out, Doris was living in San Francisco. She had a smart apartment on Nob Hill and worked as a fashion editor on a small weekly magazine. Her life was pleasant but dull. When she remembered her husband, which was quite often, it was with gratitude and tenderness if not with longing. She was extremely popular and received frequent proposals of marriage. She treated the supplicants with a detached amusement and told all of them the same thing.

"You're very sweet to ask me, but to be perfectly honest, I don't think you can afford me. And I certainly can't afford you."

She joined the WARDS in the summer of 1942 because she felt left out of the mighty, swirling whirlpool of activity that swept around and through San Francisco. Everyone in uniform felt and looked important. They were going somewhere, doing something, heading for strange places with names foreign to the tongue. Their eyes were bright, they laughed loud and often, and they drank too much. They seemed to have a destination to go to although none of them could tell you where it was.

"Where ya headin', Mac?"

"West. How about you?"

"Tomorrow."

"Well, good luck. Buy you a drink before you shove?"

"Why not? Money's no good where we're goin'."

"What're you flyin'?"

"Torpeckers. Good Christ but I hope I lay one into a flattop."

"Well, happy landings. Let's hope we're indestructible."

101]

"I'll drink to that. Good Christ but I'm gonna give it to them bastards. Wait and see."

Doris heard and understood and pitied and admired. When the time came she knew she must go west with them. She packed her bags, closed the apartment and sailed on the *President Wilson* for Honolulu.

Standing on the deck, she watched the Golden Gate slide past. The day was cold, and the wind from the west blew briskly down the entrance to the harbor. Then they were out at sea and she turned her face west, into the driving spray, and saw on the horizon the hunched backs of the Farallons. She did not turn back again; she had left that part of her life behind.

Doris lit another cigarette and smiled at Ann. The younger girl had listened attentively.

"Well, there you have it," Doris said. "The story of my life."

Ann looked at her for a time in silence. When she spoke there was admiration in her voice.

"Doris, I think you're simply wonderful. You sound like something out of a book."

"Rags to riches? Maybe you're right."

"Lend me a million, huh?"

Doris laughed and said jokingly, "What have you got for security?"

Ann thought a moment and grinned. "I've got a secret. Promise you won't tell?"

"Cross my heart."

"Well," Ann said in a confidential whisper, "Alice Finucane is going to have a baby." She watched Doris for her reaction.

"Alice Finucane bores hell out of me," Doris said. "I resent the fact that she can have a baby, married or not."

"How can you envy her? You know she's not married."

"Because she's having a baby and I'm not."

Ann asked hesitatingly, "Can't you have any? I mean . . ."

"You're damn right I can," stated Doris. "Only I don't care to procreate without a husband."

"Well," Ann said decisively, "there's always Maxwell Winston the Third."

Doris looked at Ann, a slight frown wrinkling her forehead. "Damned if you're not right." Doris got to her feet, picking up her cigarettes.

[102

Frog Delacrois entered his office at 0800 that morning. He grunted a "good morning" to his aide and told him that he did not wish to be disturbed until Captain Balta arrived.

"A dispatch just came, sir," the aide reported. "Priority from Washington. It's on your desk."

Delacrois tore open the dispatch and a broad smile crossed his face as he read:

FROM: *Chief of Naval Operations*
TO: *Reginald Delacrois, Rear Admiral USN*
SUBJ: *Change of duty*
        Upon receipt of these orders you will consider your-self detached from your present duty and you will pro-ceed and report to Commander in Chief, Pacific Fleet, for duty involving flying as Commander Task Force 58.

There was more in the dispatch, but Delacrois had read all he wanted to know. He sat back with a sigh and folded his hands over his stomach. It had taken him almost thirty years to win them, but now they were finally his: three stars. Vice Admiral Delacrois in command of Task Force 58. Released from a desk and the confines of Oahu with the three bright silver stars on his collar to take with him into the fight.

"Thomas," he bellowed, summoning the aide. "Go over to ship's service and buy me a set of vice admiral's stars. Buy me three or four sets. Hurry it up."

"Yes *sir!*" His aide beamed. "Congratulations, Admiral."

"Pack your bags, Thomas. We'll be leaving here. And soon, I trust."

When Thomas returned with the collar insignia, Delacrois re-moved his two-star pin and fastened on the badge of his new rank. He placed the old stars carefully in the box the new ones had come in. He was admiring himself in the mirror when Sam Balta entered the office unannounced.

"Don't you ever knock, goddammit?"

"I see you're your usual jovial self this morning, Frog."

Delacrois sat down at his desk and beamed at Balta. "Sit down, Sam. Sit down. I've been too busy to have my coffee. Always grumpy before coffee." He frowned at Balta. "Incidentally, Captain, are you in the habit of addressing your superiors by their nicknames?"

103]

"Only when I'm not mad at them. I'm not mad at you this morning." He paused. "Yet," he added.

"Familiarity breeds contempt, they say. I'm not sure you ought to call me Frog anymore."

"I've been calling you that for twenty-five years."

"Ah yes," said Delacrois. "But that was before this morning. Almost anyone can refer to a rear admiral by his nickname. But a vice admiral is something entirely different."

"Vice admiral. By God, Frog." Balta reached across the desk to clasp the Admiral's hand. "By God, Frog," he repeated.

Delacrois pushed the dispatch orders to Balta. "Read 'em and weep."

Balta read the orders, and a look of genuine pleasure spread across his face. "Wonderful, Frog. Simply wonderful." He looked fondly at his friend. "You're the man for the job too."

"You may not be so happy when you learn that I intend to fly my flag aboard the *Concord*. So dust out your flag quarters, Captain. You'll be the flagship."

"Why shouldn't I be happy? The *Concord* is honored."

"I had a feeling yesterday that you weren't too pleased with me."

"That was yesterday." Balta smiled. "Today you're a vice admiral."

Delacrois handed Balta the small insignia box. "Here, Sam. Take these."

When he opened the box and saw the two stars of a rear admiral, Balta frowned. "Why me?"

"Because you'll be next. I want you to wear them when you make it. They brought me luck, and I hope they'll do as much for you."

"You have my thanks and much more. I'll keep them just in case."

"Well now," said Delacrois. "You seem in a fine humor this morning. Am I correct?"

"Never felt better."

"In that case let's talk about yesterday." The Admiral leaned forward in his chair to lend emphasis to his words. "What happened yesterday was one of the goddamndest things in the history of naval aviation. An area commander simply cannot overlook such a thing. Do you agree?"

"You're not overlooking it," Balta said equably. "You have the captain of the *Concord* in your office, and shortly you will also have

[104

the air group commander and the fighter squadron skipper. Are you all set to crucify them?"

"Should I?" the Admiral asked.

"What's to be gained by it? Exposing these men or subjecting them to punishment won't aid the war effort. Incidentally, Frog, you are now commander of Task Force 58 and the best damn pilot in your command happens to be Harry Hill. If you're going to crucify Hill maybe I'd better give you back these two stars. You may need them." Balta looked pleased with himself.

"There's something you don't know, Sam."

"There's nothing I don't know."

"As a matter of fact, there are two things you don't know. Last night Air-Sea Rescue fished the hydraulic tank from Remson's plane out of the water. It had a fifty-caliber shell hole in it."

"Oh?" murmured Balta. "So?"

"So one of that gunnery flight shot down the tow plane."

"Do the pilots know this yet?"

"Not yet."

"Then I suggest you don't tell them," stated Balta.

"Sam," said the Admiral, "for Christ's sake, one of them killed the tow pilot."

"Maybe. Maybe not. Who'll ever know? There were six pilots shooting at that target. Any one of them might have shot wild. What the hell, you can't crucify six of them. Besides, what law did they break?"

"Don't talk to me about laws. I only know they shot down their own tow plane, killed the pilot and then damn near started a civil war with Patrol Squadron 24. And Sam," the Admiral's voice was gentle, "I can find out who fired the shells that killed Remson."

"The hell you can."

"Shortly after sunrise this morning a coast guard cutter fished what was left of that target banner out of the water about sixty miles west of Barbers Point. The tow bar had torn loose so the damn thing floated. I can have that banner checked by experts, and they'll tell me who made the run that killed Remson."

"You mean check the hits? Maybe somebody didn't get any hits. He'd be the one?"

"That's right, Sam. I can do that."

"But you haven't. Why not?"

105]

"I want to give Hill and Crowley a chance. I want to hear what they have to say. Then I'll decide what to do."

"Do you have to do anything?"

"Yesterday I felt I did. Today I'm not so sure. After all, I'm not ComFairHawaii anymore. I'm Task Force 58. We'll see, Sam. But goddammit, let me handle this. Keep that tremendous mouth of yours shut."

"If you weren't three stars," Balta said, "you wouldn't dare talk to me like that."

At 1000, Admiral Delacrois sat in the high-backed chair behind his desk as Captain Balta introduced the two young officers who had just been announced.

"Admiral," said Balta, "Commander Crowley, CAG Two, and Lieutenant Commander Hill, Skipper of Fighting Two."

"Sit down, gentlemen," Delacrois said. He pushed a silver cigarette box toward them. Crowley shook his head, but Hill nodded his thanks and lit one.

"You understand why you're here?" he continued.

"Yes, sir," Crowley said quickly. "That unfortunate thing yesterday. Disgraceful, Admiral. I assure you it won't happen again. I will see that it doesn't." Crowley all but glared at Hill.

The Admiral looked at Balta, who was watching Crowley with distaste. Strange, mused Delacrois. An air group commander who doesn't fight very hard for his own people. This is not good. He looked at Hill.

"And you, Mr. Hill?"

Hill glanced at Balta before he spoke. "That's not why we're here, sir. We're here because we are responsible for what happened."

"I don't see it that way," Crowley said sharply.

Hill continued, "No matter who did what yesterday, Commander Crowley and I are in positions of command. When you command you accept the responsibility for what is done by your subordinates."

"I see," said Delacrois. Balta was grinning at him because he knew Hill had made the correct answer. "Did you shoot at that PBY, Hill?"

"Not at it, sir. If I had, it would have gone down. I don't miss targets that big. No, I didn't shoot at it, but I did shoot around it." Hill kept his eyes fixed on the Admiral's. There was no hint of confusion or embarrassment in his voice. "To be honest, Admiral, if

[106

that pilot had not turned back, I think I would have shot him down."

"Your own plane?"

"Remson was my friend and one of my boys. What would you do?"

Balta said gently, "Yes, Admiral. What would you have done?"

"I'm trying to find that out, Captain," Delacrois replied wryly. He turned to Crowley. "What would you have done, Commander?"

"I don't think it was necessary to fire at that PBY, sir. I think he would have turned back anyway."

"Perhaps he might. Perhaps he might," mused the Admiral. He took a deep breath and loosed his bombshell. "What would you say, Commander, if I told you that one of your pilots had shot down that tow plane yesterday? Had fired the shells that sent Remson into the sea and killed him."

Crowley hesitated only an instant. "I'd say it was a court-martial offense, sir."

"I already knew, Admiral," Hill interrupted in a quiet voice.

The Admiral looked at Hill in surprise. This was something he had not expected.

"How the hell did you know that?" Balta demanded.

"My boys told me after the hop."

"You mean they came and confessed?" asked Crowley. "Admitted to killing a squadron mate?"

"Confessed, horseshit," Hill said angrily. "They told me they'd made a lousy run and fired too shallow. One of them saw a piece of the undercarriage tear off."

"Which one?" asked Crowley.

"I don't remember. Three of them claimed they did it."

Hill lies well, thought the Admiral. "Which one do you think did it, Commander?" he asked Hill.

"I've no idea, sir. It might have been me. I made a lousy pass myself." Hill looked at Balta, and his voice softened. "What difference does it make? Remson is dead. Nobody wanted him that way, but he is."

"I think he has a point there, Admiral. Remember where these men are going," said Balta.

Delacrois spoke in a dry tone. "Thank you, Captain. I'll try to remember."

Crowley cleared his throat. "I think we should have a board of investigation, sir. This thing can't go unpunished."

107]

"Oh, for Christ's sake," Hill said. "Remson is gone. He died doing something he wanted to do, something he believed in. He died flying a navy plane. How many chances do we get to die for something? Most guys sit it out. Remson died the way he wanted to die. Who the hell are you, Crowley, to pass any judgments?" Hill remembered then and stopped. "My apologies, gentlemen."

"Accepted," said the Admiral. "I like the way you talk, Mr. Hill."

"Besides," Hill said, "no one will ever know whose shells hit Remson. I think it's better that way."

"Well," Delacrois glanced at Balta, "you may be wrong there, Hill. You may be wrong."

"The target banner, sir?"

"How the hell did you know about that?"

"I have friends in the Coast Guard, Admiral. They thought I ought to know. As a matter of fact," Hill smiled, "they offered to get rid of it for me."

"Well, by God," said Delacrois. "That's against regulations."

"What is?" asked Balta slyly. "You don't run the Coast Guard. They have their own admirals."

"Why wasn't I told about this?" Crowley directed his question to Hill. "I'm the air group commander, Mr. Hill."

"You have my congratulations," murmured Hill.

Delacrois watched the flush spread across Crowley's face. There is something here, he thought, that I know nothing about. I think Balta has been holding out on me. Good old Sam.

"We'll let the matter rest for the time being." The Admiral stood up, terminating the meeting. "I'll think about this and let you know what I decide. Then again, I may not let you know anything. An admiral's prerogative, eh Sam? You may go, gentlemen."

"Sam," he said as the men rose, "stay a moment, will you?" He turned to the others. "Hill, I will never approve of anyone shooting at one of my patrol planes. But," and his eyes twinkled, "you may tell the men in that flight yesterday that I admire their spirit."

After they had gone, Balta poured two cups of coffee and faced the Admiral across the desk.

"Well, Frog?"

"That Harry Hill is something. Where did you find him?"

"He belongs to you now."

"So he does. Tell me, Sam. What goes on between Hill and Crowley?"

[108

"It's a long story. Goes all the way back to Midway when I had the air group. Crowley was in my outfit. Hill was on the *Hornet.* He came aboard the night of June 2nd with a bad engine. Stayed all night on the ship and then flew with us the next day. He was there when Crowley turned his ass and ran."

"Ah," said Delacrois, "I have heard something of that. Only rumors, of course."

"Nobody knew for sure. Not even I. Crowley may have been the victim of circumstances. But somehow I can't believe it."

"We'll give him the benefit of the doubt, Sam. Until he proves otherwise."

"Of course, Admiral. Your wish is my command. How about dinner tonight?"

"Make it tomorrow night. I've got something to attend to tonight."

Balta smiled. "You've always been the ladies' delight, Frog. Is this something new?"

Delacrois shook his head. "No, Sam. I think this may be the end of something old. We shall see, old friend."

Balta got to his feet and picked up his gold-braided hat. "You're too goddam old for that sort of thing, Admiral."

"When I am too old for 'that sort of thing,' as you so quaintly put it, I will retire to the Old Sailors' Home."

"Well," Balta said from the doorway, "the Home is in Philadelphia when you decide to apply. Philadelphia, Pennsylvania. Good morning, Vice Admiral, sir."

Late afternoon is the loveliest time of day in Hawaii. The heat has dissipated itself against the mountains looming to the north of Honolulu and Pearl Harbor. The midday clouds that gather over the mountains have diffused themselves into tiny puffs of slowly drifting white cotton. The air is heavy with the scent of flowers as if the islands were all part of one gigantic bouquet.

Seated under an umbrella by the swimming pool at Fort Shafter, Vice Admiral Delacrois studied the finely modeled body of the girl seated on a striped pallet beside him.

"Thanks for coming, Frog," Doris Dowling said. "And congratulations on your promotion."

"You heard already?"

"The girls at Shafter know everything."

Delacrois smiled at Doris with warm regard. "Suppose you tell

109]

me then why you got a vice admiral all the way out here. I'd have seen you tomorrow night anyway. It's the reception for the new CO at Kaneohe."

She hesitated a moment, then spoke softly. "I won't be going, Frog. I'm afraid I won't be seeing you anywhere anymore."

He watched her, his face expressionless. He had long known this had to happen one day, and had wondered how it would affect him when it did. Now he was honestly surprised to find himself feeling only a deep gratitude toward Doris.

"It has been a long time, hasn't it?"

"Over a year." Doris smiled up at him. "And fun, Frog. All of it has been wonderful fun."

His eyes and his voice were gentle. "I don't think I ever truly appreciated you before. I never before had a mistress who had both honesty and humor. I am grateful, Doris."

She made a face. "That word 'mistress.' It makes me feel old. Call me your 'girl' or something."

He chuckled. "I knew that would prove to be the cause of my downfall sooner or later."

"What would?"

"I'd make you feel old. There are too many years between us, my dear. I always knew that. It was one reason I considered myself very fortunate to have found you and held you as long as I did."

"You're not old," she said seriously. "You'll never be old."

"Not for someone else. As a matter of fact," his eyes twinkled, "there is a new Wave senior officer aboard my command who is fifty years old and looks ninety-four. Perhaps I may seek to interest her in my charms. It is worth thinking about."

She knew he was making it easy for her. Impulsively, she reached for his hand. He smiled down at her, and she thought to herself, What a wonderful man. What a wonderful human being.

"Frog," she said huskily, "I want this to end with a laugh. I couldn't stand it if you were hurt or . . ."

"Or didn't like you anymore?" he finished.

She nodded.

"Dear Doris," he said gently, holding her hand in both of his. "Does a man curse God when he dies? No. He thanks Him for everything he has received from His hands throughout his life. He tries to put into words how grateful he is for things that were given him that he never deserved. They call these words prayers. My thanks to you

[110

for what you have so generously given me of your youth and your loveliness are my prayer to you." He shook his head. "You have only my eternal devotion and esteem. Believe me."

Doris knelt by his side, tears brimming in her eyes.

"Frog, damn you. You're making me cry."

"I feel a little like it myself," he admitted.

"Kiss me?"

He bent his head and softly kissed her lips. It was a light kiss, a breath of parting between two people who would not say good-bye because they were strong enough to preserve the relationship in an older and more lasting way. With the fleeting kiss they were lovers no more; they were friends.

"May I ask who this young man is? I presume there *is* a young man. I warn you, Doris, if you are shedding me for another old man, my wrath will assume three-star ferocity."

"He's an ensign. I'll tell you something if you promise not to tattle." Her eyes sparkled now.

"I am not in the habit of 'tattling,' as you put it."

"I'm going to marry him."

"Well," mused Delacrois, "the young man didn't waste any time."

"He doesn't know about it yet."

"I see." The Admiral nodded. "*You* have decided to marry *him*. *He* hasn't decided to marry *you*. Is that correct?"

"Not yet. But he will," Doris said smugly.

"He'd be a damn fool if he didn't. I doubt you need any help in this matter, but is there anything I can do?"

"Maybe later, Frog. I don't know yet. Maybe later you could help. Vice admirals are supposed to be able to do anything, aren't they?"

"That's what they tell me. What is the ensign's name?"

"Maxwell Winston the Third. He's in Fighting Two."

Delacrois concentrated a moment. "I seem to remember that this new ensign of yours is involved in some sort of trouble out at Barbers Point. There couldn't possibly be two Maxwell Winston the Thirds, could there?" He could not suppress a smile.

"Are you serious, Frog? Is he really in trouble?"

"Almost but not quite. I think he'll survive. In fact now that I know he's part of your plans, I'm sure he'll survive."

Doris breathed a sigh of relief. "You are a darling, Admiral." She laughed. "Maybe you could make him a commander or a captain or something."

111]

He inclined his head. "Or something."

"What was the trouble?"

"I think I'll let him tell you that. I'll be interested to know what he says."

Doris eyed him speculatively. "Why, Frog?"

"I made a judgment this morning on men I've never seen. I made it because of the impression a man named Harry Hill made on me. Do you know him?"

"You can't say anything bad about Harry Hill to me. I won't believe it."

"On the contrary. I can speak only well of him. He has a great loyalty to his men. Your Winston is one of them. I'm interested because I want to know if Winston deserves such loyalty. I hope he does."

"I know he does. You'll like him."

"Possibly," the Admiral said dryly. "Don't waste too much time, Doris. He won't be around forever, you know."

She looked at him, her face suddenly grave. "He's going out?"

Delacrois shrugged. "They all do, you know. He isn't out here for a vacation."

"Can you tell me when?"

"You know I can't," he said regretfully. "But it will be soon."

"There's so little time," she whispered, almost to herself.

"Is there ever enough time, Doris?" he asked gently. "For any of us?"

"Well," she said with sudden determination, "there's going to be enough time for me. I can be hell on wheels when I want to, Admiral."

Watching her, the determined light in her eyes, he could only envy young Winston.

"A question, if you will?" he said mildly.

"Anything."

"This Winston of yours. What is it in him you want? I know you'd settle for nothing but the best."

"You're wrong there, Frog. He's not the best. But he will be. I know it's there. I think he needs someone. Specifically, me. He's about to discard his little-boy suit and put on his long pants. He doesn't think he's ready yet, but I know different. He's sort of bewildered and scared, I think. But he's going to be all right, Frog. He's going to be all right."

[112

Delacrois got to his feet. "If he realizes his great fortune, I'm sure he'll be all right. I promise you I'll do whatever I can if the occasion should arise. I expect to be invited to the wedding."

She took his arm affectionately. "You're going to give me away. How many girls have a vice admiral give them away?"

As they walked together toward Delacrois's car Doris felt a sudden confidence that everything would turn out perfectly. She looked up at the Admiral's strong, weathered face and was aware of a sense of security in his friendship.

"You smell like an Italian pimp," Marriner said laconically. He was seated on his bunk, a beer can in his hand, watching Bates with a critical eye.

Bates wrinkled his nose. "You may be right." He was standing before the mirror examining himself in feigned admiration. He turned to Marriner. "Sure you won't come along?"

Marriner yawned. "What the hell would Ann Murphy do with the two of us?"

"It does present a problem," admitted Bates. "There's always Helen, God have mercy on her."

Marriner shook his head. "I'm going to the movie with Stepik."

"Exciting," said Bates. "I wonder whatever became of that wild-eyed hellion I knew in flight training?"

"He mellowed with age," said Marriner. "A thing you might consider."

Bates said in a disinterested tone, "Called Julie lately?"

Marriner lay back on the bed, his hands clasped behind his head. "Yeah. I tried yesterday and the day before and every goddam day when I could get a call through since I got here. She doesn't live there anymore. No one we knew knows where she went. I finally got hold of Sally Dustin. Remember her?"

"She introduced you to Julie. A skinny girl with a cavernous mouth, as I recall."

"Well, she didn't know anything either. If Sally hadn't heard, I guess nobody did. Christ, my phone bill is a hundred bucks already."

"A wife is expensive. I told you that."

Marriner took a drink from the can. "I'm worried about her, boy."

Bates scoffed. "You? You worried about somebody? Don't bullshit old Bates. You don't give a damn for anything in the world. You told me so yourself."

113]

"That was a long time ago," Marriner admitted.

Suddenly serious, Bates said, "It was, Dick. Don't worry about it. She'll be all right. I'm sure of it."

"Sure," said Marriner. "Sure she will." He sat up on the edge of the bed. "I talked to the Skipper tonight."

"So?" Bates' voice was cautious.

"He said not to worry."

"Who worried?"

Marriner chuckled. "Winston did. The poor bastard."

"You think he believed us? About us making lousy passes and all that?"

"I don't know. I hope he did. That's a lousy thing to live with. Max going with you tonight?"

"Yeah," said Bates. "I borrowed the Skipper's jeep. Come on along. You can see a movie out there with Helen."

"I prefer Stepik." Marriner laughed. "When you come right down to it, Steve is sexier than she is."

Bates nodded. "Going to call again tonight?"

Marriner inclined his head. "Yeah. I don't know who the hell I'll call, but I'll think of somebody. Goddam it, she has to be someplace. Nobody just disappears." He looked at Bates quizzically. "Do they, Batesy?"

Bates stood in the doorway. "No, Dick. Nobody just disappears."

The evening had gone well with the unembarrassed conversation between people who felt no need for constraint. They mixed martinis in the kitchen of Ann Murphy's quarters. Bates, admitting he was probably the world's greatest expert on such matters, carefully poured the drinks while the others watched with critical amusement.

"Six to one," Bates announced. "There is no other way."

Doris, catching Winston's eye, picked up her drink and walked out to the balcony. Bates and Ann watched Winston follow her.

"Your friend Doris," Bates said, "is a very lovely girl."

"Does Winston think so?"

"Unless he's blind, he does." Bates sipped his drink.

"She likes him," Ann said frankly.

"Why wouldn't she?"

"If you mean because he's rich, you're all wrong. Doris has money of her own. Plenty of it."

Bates raised his eyebrows. "I didn't know that. Sometimes I'm

[114

glad I don't have any money. I'd never know whether people wanted me or the lucre." Then he added in honesty, "Of course there are times when I wish I had all the money in the world."

"What would you do with it?" Ann laughed.

"I don't know. Give half to Marriner, I guess."

"You like him, don't you?" she said.

"I love the bastard."

"Men do that sometimes. Why?"

"I don't know," Bates said thoughtfully. "He's a helluva man. I feel alive when I'm around him. I know this. If I had my back to a wall I know goddam well Marriner would be right there with me or doing his damndest to get to me. That's what counts."

Ann looked at him tenderly. "Dear Bates," she said. "Doris was right about you, you know."

"How's that?" He smiled.

"You are so very uncomplicated."

He bent over and kissed her lightly. "Let's see what they're doing out there."

"Let's not," Ann said. "Let's leave them alone." She finished her drink and took Bates' hand. "We can go out the back way. I'm starving."

"But what about Max?"

"Max doesn't need you right now. He's got all he can handle without the benefit of your ribald witticisms."

"What are they?" Bates asked facetiously. "Okay. Let's sneak out then. I feel like a traitor."

After they had gone, Doris and Winston sat in the moonlight on the balcony. The night was warm and fragrant, and the wind rustled through the palm trees. He raised his glass in a toast.

She touched glasses. "I'm glad you're here, Max."

He placed his glass on the table. "You make it sound important." He laughed self-consciously. "I mean, you sound like you really mean it."

"I do." She held out her glass. "Pour me another, will you?"

As he poured he said, "Bates claims his martinis are known throughout the civilized world."

"Somehow I think you and your friends do most things well."

He laughed softly. "They do. I'm the weak link, I'm afraid."

"I don't believe it." Then she asked in a serious voice, "What trouble were you in out at Barbers Point, Max?"

115]

He looked at her in surprise. "How do you know about it?"

"This island is too small for secrets," she lied. "I only heard you were in some sort of trouble." She hesitated. "Don't tell me if you don't feel like it."

Watching her, Winston experienced a sudden relief.

"We were on a gunnery hop," he said slowly. "Remson was flying the tow plane. I made a lousy pass, got sucked way behind and because I didn't want to look bad in front of the others I shot anyway. I hit Remson's plane, and he had to make a water landing. He was killed in the crash." He looked at her despairingly. "I killed him, Doris. I shot Remson down."

She was very careful. "You're sure, Max? You're certain it was you?"

"I'm certain."

"What did the others say?"

"Those wonderful bastards," he mused, not answering her question.

"Did they know?" she asked.

"I told Hill I did it. I told him the whole thing. He was Remson's best friend."

"What did Hill say?"

"What did *he* say? You mean what did Hill and Marriner and Bates say. They all said the same thing. They said they had made a lousy pass too. They claimed they might have done it." He shook his head. "But I did it, Doris. I saw the piece of undercarriage fly off."

"But you didn't hide, Max. You went to Hill and told him." She covered his hand reassuringly. "Do you think Remson would have held you responsible?"

He hadn't thought about this. Now he said, "No, I don't suppose he would. He would have laughed it off, I guess." He was silent a moment. "But he can't laugh anymore, can he, Doris?"

"No. But you can, Max. Don't forget it. It took something for those others to share the blame. They must think a great deal of you."

"I don't know why," he said.

"You don't give yourself enough credit, Max. When a man like Hill stands by you, then you're in very elite company. He wouldn't bother if you weren't worth it."

He lifted her hand and kissed it. "Thank you, Doris. I think you're very good for me. I feel better now."

"Good," she laughed, "then make us some more martinis."

[116

"Are you trying to get me clobbered?" He grinned.

"You'd be surprised. I think maybe I am."

"Funny," he said in a mock-serious tone, "I was considering doing the same to you."

"Are you sure it's necessary?" Doris asked quietly.

The levity left Winston's eyes. He watched her carefully. "Are you hungry?"

She shook her head. "Not unless you are."

"Why don't we take the martinis over to your place?"

"All right. I've got cold cuts and stuff in the icebox."

He seemed uncertain. "You're sure about this?" He came to stand over her.

"Dear Max," she murmured. "Yes, I'm very sure about this."

He drew her up out of her chair. "I am too," he said. "For the first time in my life I really want something. I want to get it on my own."

He took her into his arms and kissed her. She drew back and studied him, a tiny smile on her mouth.

"You have to know this, Max. I set out to trap you tonight."

"Easy, wasn't it?" He chuckled.

They kissed again, and finally Doris sighed. "Max, you'll never get those martinis made."

Later, after Doris had changed to a quilted blue peignoir, they sat on the sofa in her apartment.

"You look like a bunny," he said.

"I don't feel like a bunny."

"No? What do you feel like?"

"Like a woman." She turned her face to his, and he brushed her lips in a fleeting kiss.

They were silent for a time. From another room music sounded from a record player. Finally she lifted her head to look at him.

"You'll be going out soon." She made it a statement, not a question.

"I know. They're getting the planes ready now."

"When, Max?"

"Who knows? When the orders come. A few days. A few weeks. Nobody knows but the admirals and the enlisted men. They know everything."

She kissed his cheek. "Are you afraid?"

He smiled. "I suppose so. I'm not sure." He thought for a moment, seeking the words to explain what he felt. "If I was going alone I

117]

think I'd fold. I doubt if any man wants to fight all alone. But when you are fighting alongside your friends, it doesn't seem so bad. If they can take it, there's no reason why I can't."

"I think," Doris said, "I will pray for your friends too. All of them."

He said nothing, but he turned her face to his and kissed her with a lingering sweetness. Her arms tightened around his neck, and she moaned gently against his lips.

They both drew back and studied each other, a question in their eyes.

"All of a sudden," he said, "you are becoming the most important thing in my life."

And this is the way love comes, she thought. Not all desire and passion but also with a sweet confusion and with a sudden absence of loneliness.

They kissed again, and her mouth parted under his. She could feel the hard muscles in his arms tightening under the tension of his need.

"Max, Max," she whispered, an urgency in her voice.

His hand fumbled for the lamp switch, and then there was only the silver splash of moonlight through the open French doors.

[118

VII

November, 1943

The 0800 position report of the Japanese Imperial First Fleet placed it at 28 degrees north latitude, 150 degrees east longitude. The fleet was making fifteen knots under a glowering sky on a course 120 magnetic. The First Fleet spread itself over half the area to be scanned by the naked eye. Three aircraft carriers, two battleships, five cruisers and a horde of destroyers and destroyer-escorts headed southeast on a mission of destruction. Two days out of Tokyo Bay and hurrying on the basis of an unreliable report that a task force had sailed recently from Pearl Harbor, destination unknown but presumed to be the central Pacific.

The Imperial First Fleet. Battle-proven and sternly proud. Secretly ashamed of the sneak attack on Pearl Harbor and angered at missing the great battle at Midway. The shame was buried under loud banzais and the anger stifled under fervent vows to represent the Emperor well and, if need be, die for his glory and for the bones of long-dead ancestors.

Mighty First Fleet. The battle-hardened veterans of China skies were here and the best of aircrew, seamen and officers. After Midway there was no more talk of American softness or vulnerability. Men with records of brave achievement were called from all outposts of the Empire and set under the command of the fiercest fighter of them all.

He stood now on the bridge of his flagship, the 22,000-ton *Akiti,* and watched with hooded eyes the tactical maneuvers of his fleet. Admiral Togyama stood only five feet three in his stocking feet and weighed one hundred and ten pounds. A tiny man, he could rise to monumental proportions through force of command.

119]

He barked an order to his Chief of Staff. There was a flat, unemotional quality to his voice, which was devoid of any hint of warmth.

"Inform the captain of the *Haraga* to maintain his position. He is four hundred yards behind the guide."

A hard, craggy face, lined from decades of war and marked by a deep hatred for anything not Japanese. He was loyal to the Emperor as long as it suited his purpose, but when he turned away he did not trouble to hide the derision in his eyes. He had lived for conquest for sixty years, and the idea of peace was repugnant to him.

Greater Prosperity for the East Asian Sphere. A jumble of meaningless words but they would serve to cover for the wars which were the destiny of all the Samurai.

The despised Americans had an appointment to keep with the First Fleet. He would seek them out and blast them out of existence. He would stand on this bridge and watch the destruction, and then perhaps he would allow himself a smile. No junior officer could remember when the Admiral had last smiled.

Togyama squinted into the freshening breeze that had sprung up during the past half hour. A small doubt was nagging at his mind, reminding him that even he could fall victim to the doubts that bedeviled other men.

This report on the task force that had been sighted leaving Pearl Harbor. It had come from a submarine patrolling fifty miles west of Kauai Island. Four large carriers had been reported. The Americans must have deployed new carriers west, carriers unknown to the General Staff in Tokyo. Togyama was not reluctant to meet the enemy head-on; in fact, it was his intention to do so. But where were they headed? His force was not large enough to divide and fan out across thousands of miles of Japanese-held territory. He had it in his mind that the American target would be one of three island complexes in the central Pacific. Which one he did not know, but as to the deployment of his fleet the decision was his alone.

He had opened his secret orders that morning, forty-eight hours out of Tokyo. He had not been surprised when he learned he had been given an unprecedented choice as to how to utilize the fleet. He understood this generosity on the part of the General Staff.

A majority of the General Staff believed an American invasion of the Marshall Islands was in the offing. Certainly the Marshalls provided the logical base for any enemy movement westward in the central Pacific. Togyama himself believed the attack would come at the

[120

bastion at Truk, for he did not believe the Americans were capable of launching an amphibious assault at this time. They, too, had suffered heavy losses at Midway and the Coral Sea, and their sea power had taken a bad beating around Guadalcanal. The memory of the night action off Savo Island brought a glint to Togyama's eyes. One Australian and three American heavy cruisers had gone down in that violent surface battle.

There was another possibility that had to be considered. The Americans could be striking at the Gilbert Islands, just south of the Marshalls. There was an airstrip at Betio Island in the Tarawa group. Thus he had the three possibilities to contend with.

He turned to his Chief of Staff. "I wish to see the air group commander in my sea cabin immediately. Tell him he need not dress."

Usually when junior officers were called to the Admiral's quarters they appeared in dress blue uniforms, for when Togyama conducted an interview it was more an audience than anything else.

His sea quarters were spartan. A small canvas cot with a table next to it to hold his books and writing materials. In a corner was a tiny shrine. Togyama believed that victory belonged to the man who fought hardest and best. However, if there were gods of battle, which he doubted, he intended to have them on his side.

When Isoku Yamota knocked with gentle deference on the Admiral's door, Togyama opened it himself, an honor not often tendered. Yamota entered, bowed stiffly and stood respectfully at attention.

The Admiral waved Yamota to a chair. He sat opposite the younger man and studied him in silence for several moments.

"I have sent for you, Yamota," the Admiral said at last, "to acquaint you with the situation and to solicit your judgment. I do you honor in this respect."

Yamota inclined his head. "I am unworthy, your Excellency."

Togyama shook his head. His cold eyes guarded any emotion he might have displayed. "No," he said, "you are not. I have a considerable respect for you, Commander. You are the greatest flier in Japanese history. You have proven yourself invincible in the air. I respect your conduct in battle and even more so, your judgment. That is why you are here."

Togyama rose and walked to a map on the side of the cabin. He faced Yamota.

"We sailed under secret orders, Commander. When I read them

121]

this morning I found I have been allowed discretion as to the employment of the First Fleet. I may move as opportunity dictates."

He moved his finger over the map, tracing the central Pacific area. "The central Pacific, Yamota. The American fleet is headed somewhere in this area." He clasped his hands behind his back and paced restlessly as he spoke. "We were hit hard at Midway and Guadalcanal. We do not have sufficient force to prepare for all contingencies. Where, in your judgment, would the enemy be heading?"

Yamota, who had already considered this, replied without hesitation. "The Marshalls, the Gilberts or Truk, your Excellency."

"We cannot cover all three. That is the problem."

"Did the sighting report mention any support shipping? Landing craft or troopships?"

Togyama shook his head. "Only the attack force. However, that may mean nothing. The amphibious force could be approaching from the north or south, away from our patrolling range. Of course," he added, "we cannot be certain that there *is* a landing force."

"What is your supposition, Excellency?" asked Yamota.

"Truk."

Yamota said respectfully, "May I disagree, sir?"

Togyama nodded. "That is why you are here."

"The Americans will attack Truk, I have no doubt. But not yet. Perhaps in a few months when they have more carriers. It would be ridiculous to attack Truk with less than twelve major carriers. The Americans, Admiral, are not ridiculous. We found that out." Yamota thought he saw a flicker of interest in the Admiral's eyes. "I am in no position to say whether they will attempt a landing, but I believe their carrier force to be heading for Kwajalein or a target somewhere in the Gilbert group. Possibly Tarawa."

Togyama studied the map. "That still leaves us with a choice. I think the Marshalls." He looked at Yamota.

"I have a plan, sir, if I may suggest one."

"You may."

Yamota approached the map. He ran his finger down the area separating the Marshall Islands from the bastion at Truk.

"If you place yourself between Truk and Kwajalein in the Marshalls, you will be able to cover any contingency in either of those places. Down south here," his finger moved down to the Gilbert group, "we can meet them with land-based aircraft."

The Admiral frowned. "Our last reports indicated less than twenty fighter planes based at Tarawa."

[122

"Sir," said Yamota, "if you will place the task force within flying distance of Betio, I suggest I fly my air group in, under cover of darkness, to the airstrip. We can park the planes under camouflage. When the Americans come, if they do, they will find a surprise waiting for them. If they attack to the north you can detach the carrier for a night run, and we can come out at dawn and rejoin the ship."

The Admiral looked at Yamota grimly. "They will roar in, expecting no air opposition. They will find nearly a hundred fighters waiting for them."

"The carriers will hit first, sir. Several days, I expect, before the assault troops land. If they do intend to land. Unless they are sneaking down from the north, we shall have the area covered for any emergency."

"When do you wish to fly in?"

"It depends. When was the American force sighted?"

"Last night."

Yamota consulted the map again. "Then we are approximately the same distance from the objectives. If we increased speed to twenty knots I believe we could launch the night of the 17th."

"There will be the problem of fuel for your planes." Togyama was talking to himself. "I can send a dispatch to Truk and have them forward a supply by the 19th. Ammunition, spare parts." He looked up at Yamota. "Your plan is acceptable, Commander. You may set about your operational plans. I will order the force to make twenty knots."

The Admiral walked to his desk and removed from a drawer a small bottle of saki. He poured two small cupfuls and handed one to Yamota.

"I understand this is to be your last war cruise, Commander."

Yamota smiled. "I have heard reports, sir. Perhaps," he shrugged, "I am too old."

"A man is never too old to fight. I think, in your case, you will do much good in the homeland. Our people need heroes, Commander. The face of this war is changing. The Americans are coming west with ships and planes produced at a far greater rate than we can hope to match. We must stiffen the spines in the homeland for what lies ahead. It will not be easy in the days to come."

"I understand, Excellency." So even the vaunted Togyama had his doubts.

The Admiral raised his glass. "Victory." Almost as an afterthought he added, "And the Emperor."

123]

VIII

November, 1943

On the morning of November 12, 1943, the submarine *Tarpon* cruised submerged at a depth of 150 feet. She was on the 23rd day of her cruise and lay approximately 800 miles northwest of Kwajalein. As the hands of the ship's clock, set in the bulkhead over the hatch in the tiny wardroom, touched 0853 the sonar operator, sweating in his cramped cubicle, suddenly clamped a hand over his earphones, pressing them tightly against his ears. He listened intently.

A few minutes later the skipper of the *Tarpon*, a cheerful young lieutenant commander with a blond beard and the improbable name of Buford Slover was standing at the periscope.

"Take her up to periscope depth," he ordered.

The *Tarpon* tilted gently and eased her nose toward the surface. With an impudent shrug she thrust the rounded tip of her periscope above the choppy waters. Buford Slover glued his right eye to the periscope and slowly swung a hundred and eighty degrees, moving the periscope in an arc.

"For Christ's sake!" he breathed. He turned to his executive officer. "For Christ's sake, Harry. Take a look."

Harry peered through the scope and straightened up to look at Slover. "My God, Bu. The whole goddam Japanese Navy is out there."

Buford nodded and returned to the periscope.

At this moment a twenty-five-year-old Japanese Navy pilot named Haraku Itomi was sitting at the controls of a Mitsubishi dive bomber in which he was flying an antisubmarine patrol. He had launched from the carrier *Akiti* three hours earlier, and he was very tired, for

[124

nothing is more monotonous than a four-hour antisub patrol. The endless searching of waters that never change can lull the most disciplined mind. Haraku shook himself awake and called the carrier to announce he was turning to begin his inbound vector toward the ship. Just then he spotted a variance in the vast sameness below him. A school of fish perhaps? He decided to investigate. At least it would serve to occupy him for a moment. Anything was better than plodding along straight and level and half asleep. He peeled over, throttled back slightly and dived toward the ocean and the rippling wake that had appeared on the choppy sea.

Buford Slover was counting the ships and noting the types to his exec.

"Three carriers, two BBs, four CLs, 10 DDs and a whole mess of escorts. Give that to Hemlen, Harry. Get it off right now."

He took another quick glance through the periscope. Then his voice roared out over the subdued murmur of the engines. "Battle stations. Make ready all torpedo tubes. Stand by to fire."

Haraku Itomi pulled out of his dive and swept over the elongated shadow that was the *Tarpon*, so low that the slipstream from his propeller threw a foam of spray onto the glass eye of Buford Slover's periscope. Haraku's heart surged. He climbed steeply even as his right hand reached out and flicked on his master arming switch, arming the five-hundred-pound bomb hanging under his port wing. He soared up and up and then wheeled over gracefully, the nose of the plane sweeping past the horizon and through an arc of sky and then down through the horizon again until it pointed at the rippled wake of Slover's periscope. He flicked on his gunsight and made a terse report to the *Akiti*.

"Swallow One. I am investigating what appears to be an enemy submarine." Suddenly he wanted more than anything heretofore in his life to sink the submarine that loomed in the bright rings of his gunsight. His altimeter was unwinding past 3500 feet.

Radioman Third Class Hemlen was sending his report across the endless miles to ComSubPac at Pearl Harbor. He had completed the address and now the message itself began to go forth! "Sighted large enemy force. Position 25 degrees north, 154 degrees east. Force consists of . . ."

It was as far as Radioman Hemlen ever got.

Haraku Itomi sped past 2000 feet vertically. He was aware that it was too late now to recover from his dive. His eyes were glued to

125]

the gunsight and the dark shadow of the *Tarpon* filled the bright rings. His bomb was armed, but there was no need to flick the release switch.

This bomb he was delivering personally.

Commander Submarine Forces Pacific was a bowlegged master tactician who had earned his stars through a meticulous devotion to duty and a thorough understanding of the problems faced by the submariner. He was deeply concerned over the welfare of every man under his command. When he received the broken message from the *Tarpon*, less than a minute had passed since Itomi's plane had sent the submarine twisting to the bottom. He knew instantly what the disrupted message meant. He cursed bitterly and decided to deliver this message himself.

Commander in Chief, Pacific Fleet, that stern, glacial man who ruled from a lonely throne, rose to greet the submariner.

"Bad news, sir," said ComSubPac, handing the message to his superior. "Young Slover. We got this much."

The stern man read the message. "You checked the position?"

"Yes, sir. Eight hundred miles northwest of the Marshalls. They didn't have time to send course or speed."

CincPacFleet got to his feet. There was a barely perceptible note of excitement in his voice.

"They're out, Tommy. They're out with their fleet." He flicked the intercom button. "Get my staff in here immediately."

He looked at his subordinate. "I'm damned sorry about your man, Tommy. But he got the job done."

"How do you know their fleet is out? We didn't get a composition report."

"We knew they had left Tokyo, but we thought they were heading down the coast and then to the Philippines. If this position report is correct, and I see no reason to doubt it, they're heading for the central Pacific. Maybe we can get them to tangle."

ComSubPac spoke carefully. "Maybe they can get at our amphibious forces too."

"I don't think so." The four-star admiral shook his head. "We've got several days to plaster Tarawa and Makin before the Marines go in. If they want a fight we can get at them before the landings."

Thirty-five minutes after Buford Slover had first sighted Togyama's force, dispatch orders went out "Top Secret" to Vice-Admiral

[126

Reginald Delacrois aboard the *Concord,* four days out of Pearl and heading southwest.

Delacrois stood with Captain Balta on the inner flag bridge. This is Admiral's country where no one comes except by call of duty or invitation. Even Balta was here only by invitation although the *Concord* was his own ship.

"They must have got wind of the landings, Sam." Delacrois spoke quietly so the others on the bridge would not hear. "But they're going to be in the dark about deploying their fleet. How the hell would they know where we're headed?"

Balta said, "The same way they got wind of the situation."

Delacrois shook his head in disagreement. "Common sense would tell them that. I mean where *exactly.* The Marshalls, Gilberts, Truk? Where would you station yourself if you were Togyama?"

"If I were Togyama," replied Balta solemnly, "I would commit hara-kiri. How would I know, Admiral? I'm only a captain." After a moment he added, "Kwajalein, I guess. I'd figure to find us at Kwajalein."

"I would too," said Delacrois. "And we're going to Tarawa. So we find them with their pants down. Plaster the atoll for two days and then head north for Togyama."

"Don't we cover the Marines?"

"Not until the 20th," the Admiral replied. "Jocko Cleary will be coming out a few days behind us with another force of light carriers to escort the amphibious ships and troop transports. We'll be able to give Togyama anything he wants."

"It would be nice," mused Balta, "if we had time to hit Wake Island or someplace so the air group could get their feet wet."

"They'll be okay, Sam. They've got Hill and Dusane and Lacy."

"They've also got Crowley," said Balta.

The Admiral appeared not to have heard Balta's remark. "We launch on the 16th."

"We'll be in position by sundown of the 15th."

"Good." The Admiral looked at Balta and smiled. "Is Barry over his peeve yet?"

"Hah!" Balta snorted. "He refers to me as Captain Iscariot."

"I don't think he really minds."

"Of course he doesn't," said Balta. "He figures he has to make some noise so people won't think he's a war-lover. Anyway, he's not flying. He's just acting exec until my new one gets to Pearl.

127]

What the hell. A man can't go to sea without an executive officer, can he?"

"He certainly can't," said Barry Wheeler, who had come up unnoticed. "Captain Iscariot, sir, I received your message to report to the flag bridge. In fact when I received your order I was writing a letter to a hotel in Miami, canceling a reservation I had anticipated using on my thirty-day leave. It appears I won't be going anywhere for some time except back and forth over the Pacific Ocean."

"I certainly agree, Commander," said Delacrois. "It seems to me almost inhuman to practically shanghai a veteran pilot like yourself. Only a coldhearted, ruthless old man would do such a thing."

"See here!" Balta protested. "Frog, you yourself suggested I—"

"I recall no such suggestion, Captain," interrupted Delacrois.

"Right here on your bridge before we sailed. You said . . ."

Delacrois smiled at Wheeler. "Barry, did you ever hear of an admiral suggesting personnel changes to a captain of a ship? It's contrary to naval custom and procedure."

"It's all right, Admiral," said Wheeler. "I suppose there ought to be *somebody* up there who knows what a good fight means."

"Goddamit," roared Balta in a voice that startled a second-class seaman just entering the bridge area with a jug of hot coffee. "Who's been trying to find a fight for over a year now? Me. That's who." Suddenly he grinned at Wheeler. "I don't need any help from wet-behind-the-ears commanders although I guess you might be of some help if things get hairy."

Wheeler bowed. "I thank you, Captain Iscariot."

"Barry," Delacrois said, "I want to talk to the squadron commanders and the CAG tonight. Have them in my cabin at 1900."

"Right, sir—1900." Wheeler saluted and moved off the bridge. The two older men watched him leave.

"You love him like a son, don't you, Sam?" Delacrois said.

"Like he was my own." Balta shook his head slightly. "You know, Frog, I really didn't want to take Barry out again."

Delacrois watched Balta closely. "You said yourself he won't fly. He's just the paper work exec."

Balta looked uncomfortable. He rammed his battered pipe into the corner of his mouth. "Yeah. I guess I said that."

"There's something you *didn't* say, Sam." Balta did not answer, and Delacrois continued. "Want me to tell you what it is?"

"Yeah, Frog. Tell me."

Delacrois leaned on the bridge counter. "I'll tell you, Sam. Barry is your insurance. And mine too, I guess." He looked sharply at Balta. "Tell me, Sam, do you really intend to let Barry go when we get back to Pearl?"

This was a question Balta had avoided asking himself because he knew the answer, and it frightened him.

Finally he said, "No, Frog. I guess I don't."

"You're afraid your air group commander will fold. You need Barry for insurance, to take over in case Crowley can't hack it. Hill is junior to Lacy and Dusane, and you can't give him the group. So Barry is your insurance and mine and every damn pilot's in the air group. Well, I guess I'd do the same if that's any consolation to you." He slapped Balta lightly on the shoulder. "Does Barry know?"

"Hell yes, he knows. He's the smartest bastard I ever met. He didn't say anything but he knows. Secretly he's glad he's along because he still considers this air group his. If anything fouls up, he wants to be here. Some boy, Barry Wheeler."

As the Admiral and the Captain talked on the bridge, several decks below on the 02 deck the air group commander tossed fitfully on his bunk. Bob Crowley did not sleep well. He had been troubled for a long time by strange, mixed-up dreams. Now his face looked drawn and haggard in the dim light of the overhead bulb in the cabin.

Bob Crowley's recurrent dream was a mixture of a boyhood memory and a nightmare which took place near the island of Midway more than a year before. It always started the same way, this dream. He was ten years old and he was wrestling in the backyard of his home in Chicago with a next-door neighbor named Bobby Anderson. They had been playing baseball, and Bobby had refused to give up his turn at bat. Crowley had grabbed Bobby and they had tumbled onto the ground, laughing and yelling. In the struggle Crowley had found himself straddling Bobby, staring down into the younger boy's laughing face. It was then that he had felt his manhood for the first time. He did not understand why it had happened or even what it was. He only knew a surging stirring in his loins, and his legs had tightened around Bobby convulsively. Bobby had stopped laughing then and struggled to his feet. For some strange reason Crowley had felt uncomfortable around Bobby from that time on. This part was actual memory.

After Midway the dream took on jumbled and incoherent additions. For over a year now Crowley had dreamed he was flying alone

129]

in a tremendous space of lonely sky. Suddenly out of a lone cloud, floating inoffensively on his starboard side, Bobby Anderson appeared, standing on the wing of a blood-red airplane. He was waving and shouting although Crowley could never catch the words. Bobby was stark naked and his body had matured since that day so long ago in Crowley's backyard. Crowley tried to see who or what was flying the plane, but somehow a misty vapor swirled around the cockpit, and he could not see through it. His dream never did resolve this mystery. Crowley flew and flew and flew but he could not get away from the blood-red plane.

Crowley knew that Bobby Anderson was trying to tell him something in the dream. He was afraid to find out what it was and yet night after night in his dream he sought desperately for the answer. Secretly he feared his failure as a man; the shame which he first experienced that morning with Bobby in the backyard had never left his mind. It had made him feel different when he compared himself to other men and had instilled in him a feeling of inferiority if not grotesqueness. More than once in his waking hours Crowley had asked himself if Bobby was trying to tell him what it was in his, Crowley's, makeup that differed in such a way that he could get a sexual stimulus from another male.

Now in his dream Crowley was pushing the throttle all the way forward to the stop and he laughed when he saw he was outdistancing the red plane. He looked out toward a great thunderhead rising majestically in the distance, and from its center emanated a great burning cross fashioned out of rays from the setting sun. He knew the cross meant something to him, perhaps an answer for his shame, and he threw the stick over and banked steeply toward the great cloud. He felt he could survive forever if he could reach that ray-crossed sanctuary. But now the red plane was closing on him and Bobby Anderson's figure was supplicating, gesturing and calling out.

"Wait for me."

Crowley was almost to the giant thunderhead, and the cross was burning brightly before his eyes when Bobby's voice changed timbre, became deeper. Commander Crowley opened his eyes in panic and heard the air group duty officer knocking on his cabin door.

He sat up, his heart thumping.

"Come in!"

The duty officer poked his head inside the room. "Just got word from the bridge, sir. Meeting in the Admiral's quarters at 1900."

[130

"Okay," mumbled Crowley. "What time is it?"

"Just 1800, sir."

Crowley got wearily to his feet and sloshed cold water on his face and arms. He surveyed himself in the mirror and decided he'd better shave before the meeting with the Admiral. He looked and was tired. These damn dreams every night. And now this combat operation coming up.

Crowley told himself he was not frightened. This was only the apprehension that every man experiences when he is about to go into combat. But he had been there before. Long months ago he had flown out with others of his own kind to contest a piece of sky. That he had failed, and had further compounded the failure with the furtive lie that had found acceptance, had only served to goad him further. Like a masochist crying out, pleading for the lash, he had come running a second time to investigate this cowardice that had made him less a man.

Now he wondered if it had been a mistake.

Marriner knocked on the door of Hill's cabin.

"Come in."

Marriner stepped into the small room. "You sent for me, Skipper?"

Hill closed a book he had been reading and smiled at Marriner.

"Sit down, Dick. Yeah, I've got a word or two for you. Have a smoke?"

After Hill had lit their cigarettes he sat back and studied Marriner. The kid was eager and not at all soft. He had an enthusiasm for flying, and he wouldn't scare worth a damn.

"Dick," Hill said, "I am about to break all hell out of a precedent."

"Well," Marriner replied gravely, "when you get to be a squadron skipper I guess you can break hell out of anything you want."

"Exactly," agreed Hill. "If I didn't have one handy to smash I suppose I'd go out and look for one."

"You want me to help?"

Hill nodded.

Marriner pursed his lips. "May I ask what this precedent is?"

"You may," Hill said. He deliberately let the younger man wait while he lit another cigarette. "I always smoke these things two at a time."

"Take your time, Commander," Marriner said.

131]

"All right then. I am giving you a division, Marriner. All your very own."

"What?" Marriner's surprise was plainly evident. "You're kidding, Skipper."

"I never kid about serious matters, and this is a serious matter. I am aware it is damn rare when a boot-assed ensign becomes a division leader. Leading four planes into combat is not usually a job for a neophyte. In fact I'm not sure it has ever been done before."

Marriner still could not accept it. "But why me, Skipper? I don't know anything about this business."

"Nobody does," Hill said mildly, "except me. I know everything about it. I am the only fighter pilot in the Navy who does."

Marriner shook his head. "I still don't get it. Why me?"

"For one thing," said Hill, "your gunnery scores. You and Anders shot the highest percentage in the air group. Two boot-assed ensigns setting a new marksmanship record." He scowled. "It is almost unbelievable."

"Why not give the division to Anders?"

"He's a little young for one thing. For another, I've got just as important a job for him."

"More important than division leader?"

"He's going to be the air group commander's wingman. I want a good gunner flying with CAG. Someone has to keep him alive to run the strikes. Strike leaders become very important to us at times. Besides, I think if Anders had to take over that CAG section in the air, he would do a good job. Anders has something going for him up there."

"He says he was born for this," Marriner said.

"And he means it and he's right. I think Anders will be great in this business."

"You still haven't told me why I get the division."

"You're growing up, Dick, whether you realize it or not. The other men look to you in the air. That's all that's important to me. On the ground you can be the world's greatest sonofabitch, but if other men will follow you in a fight, then you have what it takes to lead. It isn't always fun going in first, knowing you are responsible for the lives of the men following you. You have to grow up to accept the responsibility. I like the way you've come along since you came to me. I think you're just unsure enough of yourself to use caution and just certain enough of yourself to go in when the time

[132

is right. Anyway, it's my decision and as you say, the skipper of a squadron can do any goddam thing he pleases. I am pleased to give you this division. You will have Bates for a wingman, Winston for section leader and Stepik as number four man. That suit you?"

Marriner grinned. "Suit me? You know damn well it suits me, Skipper." He chuckled. "Wait till I tell them they'll be taking orders from me." Marriner shook his head unbelievingly.

Hill laughed and got to his feet. "Come on. Now let's go down to the ready room and listen to the intelligence officers tell how it's going to be where we're going. Always remember one thing when you're listening to an intelligence officer, Marriner. They have all sorts of interesting information, but as a rule not a goddam one of them has been where you're going or has any intention of ever going there. Remember that."

Ready Room One, the fighter ready room, was a tangled confusion of flight gear, sprawled bodies, interwoven conversations liberally sprinkled with coarse oaths and an occasional snatch of a dirty song.

Along the cluttered bulkheads assorted flight gear hung haphazardly. Flight helmets, flight jackets, Mae Wests, .45- and .38-caliber pistols and cartridge belts, parachute harnesses. Plotting boards, maps and survival gear lay strewn around on empty seats and on the deck. A large board in the front of the room was marked off in yellow lines providing spaces in which to write pertinent information for the pilots. Here appeared the day and the hour of the flight, ship's position, target position, wind information, flight personnel and mission assignment.

Now on the board, in large, carefully printed letters was the admonition:

GET THE ENEMY FIGHTERS FIRST!!!

The babble of conversation stilled as Hill yelled, "Okay, heroes. Knock it off a minute." The pilots sat back in their seats as Hill walked to the front of the room.

"An announcement, gentlemen. First, we now have a new division in this outfit. It will be number two division and will be led by Ensign Marriner." The other pilots craned to get a look at Marriner, their surprise evident in the murmur of voices that followed Hill's statement. "Bates will fly number two, Winston has the second sec-

133]

tion and Stepik flies ass-end Charlie." He smiled at Stepik. "Okay with you, Steve?"

"Certainly, Skipper," Stepik answered.

"Okay, then. In a few minutes Lieutenant Redding will be here to brief you on what we are supposed to do. Listen carefully and afterwards I'll have something to say."

Winston slid into a seat next to Stepik. "What the hell goes on, Steve? I don't want a section. I'll fly on you."

Stepik shook his head. "No, Max. The Skipper wants it this way, and so do I." He looked at Winston solemnly. "You can handle it, Max."

"I'd rather you led the section, Steve," Winston said doubtfully.

Stepik touched Winston's arm. "Listen, Max. You can't walk through this war with a crutch. None of us can. You can lead this section just as well as I can and just as well as anyone in this squadron. I'm glad to fly wing on you." He laughed and punched Winston lightly on the shoulder. "We'll give them hell, boy."

The noise ceased as Hill's voice called out, "Knock it off."

Lt. Redding, the Staff intelligence officer, was a skinny, almost cadaverous man with a sallow complexion that had seldom seen duty under the sun. He confronted the pilots with a sheaf of notes in his hand, and when he spoke his voice was flat and monotonous, almost hypnotic. Later the pilots would retain only the highlights of his speech.

Redding started off with a résumé of the situation as it now stood and moved into the nature of their mission and probable enemy opposition.

The American strategy, Redding told them, was based on the supposition that as long as the Japanese could operate from Truk, any American amphibious operations to the northward of New Guinea-New Britain were exposed to enemy naval attack unless we ourselves furnished adequate fleet support. But Truk would continue as a secure base only so long as the surrounding screen of islands remained firmly in Japanese hands.

It had therefore been decided that the Marshall Islands were to be our first main objective. However, we lacked thorough reconnaissance that would be required if our invasion was to be successful and our losses contained within acceptable limits. Land-based aircraft were needed for this extensive photographic work, but we had no airfields in range of the Marshalls, and our patrol planes could

[134

not reach them. Therefore it had been decided to initiate the offensive with an invasion of the southern flank, namely the Gilbert Islands and in particular, the island group at Tarawa. There was an airfield at Betio Island in the Tarawa group, and the other islands in the chain afforded numerous sites on which airstrips could be built quickly. In addition we would be coming from our main line of communications to the South and Southwest Pacific. These airfields would be useful as bases from which our land-based aircraft could be operated throughout the Marshalls.

Without violating security, Redding had just told the pilots where they would be going on their next cruise.

The Gilbert operation, Redding continued, was important in that our plans for it established the organization and the pattern that would be used thereafter as a basis for future operations. The American task organization contained a fast carrier task force, of which the *Concord* was the flagship; a Joint Expeditionary Force which would be sneaking in from just south of Mille Atoll in time to open the invasion of Tarawa on the 20th of November; and a logistic force which was leaving Pearl Harbor on the 17th.

Simultaneously with the attack at Tarawa, a smaller invasion force would undertake a blitz attack at Makin Island one hundred miles to the north.

As a preliminary to the invasion the carrier force would smash the island defenses at Betio, Makin and Mille Island, a Jap airfield halfway up the chain toward the Marshalls. The *Concord*'s air group would hit Tarawa. In particular, Fighting Squadron Two was responsible for the destruction of enemy aircraft in the Tarawa area.

"You will probably find little air opposition when you go in on the morning of the 16th," Redding said. He consulted his notes. "There are less than twenty-five Jap fighters reported in the area."

"Horseshit," Hill said in a loud voice.

Redding flushed. "That's what the reports say."

"Everybody on this ship may tell you," Hill said levelly, "that you will meet a handful of second-class fighter planes and fewer decent fighter pilots the morning of the 16th. Everybody except one, that is. *I* am the exception. I tell you nothing except that you had better damn well be prepared to fight against the odds. That's the only way to go into a fight. Only a jackass or someone who isn't going to be there will tell you it's going to be a pushover." He grinned at Redding. "Nothing personal, Al."

135]

"Of course not," Redding replied sourly. "It's just that I'm a jackass, that's all."

"Not your fault," Hill agreed cheerfully.

"You will comply with directives and drop your belly gas tanks before you reach the target area," Redding continued.

"Skipper," Marriner said, "may I say something?"

"You may, Marriner."

"If we launch the morning of the 16th we're going to be nearly two hundred miles from the target. It seems damn silly to drop our tanks until the last minute."

"It's in the directives," Redding said. He scowled and added deliberately, "The *Admiral's* directive."

Marriner looked questioningly at Hill. An ensign had no business contesting an admiral's directive.

"How did you know the distance from target on the 16th?" Hill asked Marriner.

"I checked our position this morning and plotted it."

Hill nodded his head. "You continue to amaze me, Marriner. You may answer Mr. Redding's statement concerning directives."

"Well," said Marriner, "the most precious thing we have on this trip is the gas in our tanks. Without it we're as useless as teats on a boar. I learned a long time ago that an airplane won't fly without gasoline. You may be the best fighter pilot in the world, but if your prop isn't turning you're not about to win a fight whether it's with a Zero or a baby in a buggy. It seems ridiculous to me to throw away gasoline on a long hop like this unless we've actually made contact with airborne enemy fighters."

Redding spoke sarcastically. "A bullet hole in that tank and you could explode, Mr. Marriner."

"That's right," agreed Marriner. "*I* could explode. Not you, Mr. Redding."

"Well put, Marriner," Hill said. He got to his feet and faced the pilots. "Whether or not the experts have decreed it is wiser and safer to drop your belly tanks before you are committed to combat, you will, as long as I lead this squadron, keep them on until the enemy has actually joined the fight. Screw the directives. If they want to burn somebody's ass for this, let them burn mine. It's callused. There's time enough to drop them when you charge your guns. If we have to fight, then at least we'll have plenty of gas left for other things." He paused a moment. "Like getting back to the ship, for

[136

instance. Or making a few lousy passes at the deck if your plane is shot up."

"Well," said Redding, "I tried."

"Our fault, Al. We're individualists." Hill spoke again to the pilots. "Mr. Marriner seems to have assimilated a great deal of practical knowledge so he will now give you all a lecture on standard fighter defensive tactics, gentlemen. I must attend a meeting with the Admiral. Listen to Marriner closely because Harry Hill has devised an admirable method to keep you alive when you are outnumbered."

Hill stopped by the door and beckoned to Cortney Anders.

"Anders, I want you to know I think you deserve a division just as much as Marriner."

Anders grinned. "I'm glad to see Dick get it, Skipper."

"I've got a job for you too, Anders. A damn important one. You're flying wing on the air group commander."

Under ordinary circumstances flying wing on the CAG was considered an honor. But Anders had heard the rumors about Crowley too. Nothing concrete. Nothing certain. Something about an afternoon at Midway a long time ago. And Crowley was a man who did not mix, who withheld himself from his men. His ability was an unknown factor.

"I'll do the best I can, sir," Anders said.

"Ride a close wing, Anders," Hill said slowly. "A very close wing. Don't let him get away from you. Not ever."

It was a strange remark from a squadron commander, but Anders had no time to question Hill because the Skipper was gone.

Stepik, Winston and Bates were congratulating Marriner.

"Do I have to call you Mr. Marriner?" Bates asked.

"Sir will do," Marriner allowed.

"You should be proud, Dick," Stepik said quietly. "It's quite an honor."

"I am, Steve. But I still don't figure it."

"Dick," Winston said, "I'd just as soon Steve led the second section. He's better up there than I am."

Marriner watched Winston, aware that this was the first time he had been called upon to make a decision that could affect other men's lives.

"No, Max," he said. "I think you'll do just fine leading that second section. You're going to be a hell of a help to me. To all of us."

"I'm sure of that too," Stepik said.

137]

Winston said very seriously, "I won't let you down, Dick. Any of you."

"The hottest division in the fleet," Bates mused. "Marriner's Marvels. How about that?"

"If you marvels will sit down," Marriner laughed, "I will get on with my lecture about the Hill Weave. As soon as I learn what it is."

The aircraft were spotted aft on the broad expanse of the *Concord*'s flight deck. Tie-down ropes led from the underside of the wings to the small steel tie-down rings set flush into the deck. Mechanics worked industriously, polishing, probing, testing. When the pilots left the flight deck in the airplanes the mechanics truly held their lives in the hollow of their hands.

Chief Petty Officer Lars Rasmussen squinted an eye in critical examination of the work of Machinist's Mate 2nd Lawrence O'Toole who was fervently polishing the side of airplane number 00. 00 was a very special aircraft. Other planes would be flown by a variety of pilots, depending on availability and the spotting of the flight deck. 00 would be flown only by the air group commander himself.

Rasmussen was a broad, powerful man, whose misshapen face showed traces of a hundred barroom fights. A dedicated man and a chief petty officer in the United States Navy. Only that and nothing more because that was all there was to life for him. There is a belief in the Navy Air Corps that the Chiefs can make or break a squadron. Rasmussen was the leading Chief in Fighting Squadron Two.

"Put a little elbow grease into it, Irish," Rasmussen told O'Toole.

"Chief," O'Toole said, "tell me something. I rub this airplane till my goddam elbow is about to fall off. Right? Now do you suppose it's gonna make this airplane fly any better? Or make the pilot any better?"

"Irish," Rasmussen said, "in this Navy we don't try to understand why we do things. We follow orders. Commander Crowley left orders that he wanted his plane shining like a baby's ass. So we are following his instructions."

Rasmussen circled the plane, regarding it with a grave disapproval. "Not bad, Irish, but I think it needs another forty minutes or so."

"You're out to bust my ass, Chief," mourned O'Toole. "I might as well have something to polish as long as I gotta scrub this miserable bastard."

[138

O'Toole picked up a dirty, smudged rag and industriously swabbed the side of the plane, leaving long streaks of grime on the otherwise shiny exterior. He stood back and regarded the plane.

"There," he exclaimed.

"Two hours and forty minutes, Irish," Rasmussen said.

Crowley was on his way to the Admiral's bridge when he passed by the island entrance and saw O'Toole and Rasmussen.

The two enlisted men saluted respectfully as Crowley approached. The air group commander looked at the side of his airplane and wiped a finger along it. He inspected his finger with a frown.

"Having trouble following orders, sailor?" he asked O'Toole.

"No, sir," O'Toole replied.

"It looks like you are to me," Crowley said.

"Sir—" Rasmussen began.

"I wasn't speaking to you, Chief," Crowley interrupted curtly.

"I been working on this bas—on this plane for two hours, sir. She'll be ready in a few minutes," O'Toole said plaintively.

"What's your name, sailor?"

"O'Toole, Machinist's Mate 2nd Class."

"Sir."

"Sir," repeated O'Toole.

"You?" Crowley asked Rasmussen.

"You know my name, sir," Rasmussen replied softly. "Rasmussen. Leading Chief, VF-2."

"Following orders has become a game with you two?" Crowley said in a hard voice.

"Following orders is our business, sir," Rasmussen said levelly.

Crowley said, "I am going to flag country. I intend to pass by here in a little while, and I expect to see both of you working on this airplane. Working seriously, not playing games, you understand. I want this airplane polished so I can see my reflection in it. Is that understood?"

Rasmussen said very carefully, "Commander, in Fighting Two the leading Chief does not polish airplanes."

Crowley flushed. "Are you arguing with me, Chief?"

"No, sir. Merely relating a squadron practice. Commander Hill's directive."

"I am the air group commander. Not Commander Hill."

"Commander Hill is my CO," Rasmussen said calmly. "He gives me my orders."

"I think you are arguing with me, Rasmussen. Consider yourself on report."

Rasmussen was aware that leading Chiefs were not put on report.

"Your prerogative, sir." Rasmussen nodded almost imperceptibly. He turned his back on Crowley, took the rag from O'Toole's hand and started to wipe down the side of the airplane.

"You're insolent, Rasmussen," Crowley said. "Damned insolent. You think I don't know the reason for your insolence?"

"Yes, sir, I think you do."

"And what is the reason, Rasmussen?"

The weathered Chief turned to face Crowley. He folded the rag neatly in his big, callused hands.

"I was on the *Yorktown* with you, sir."

Crowley's eyes flared, and he took a step toward Rasmussen. The Chief did not move.

"I wouldn't, sir," Rasmussen said. He nodded toward the island structure. "We're not alone."

"I'll break you," Crowley grated.

Rasmussen nodded. "Perhaps. But I've been there before."

"I want this plane polished like a mirror, Chief. And I want *both* of you working when I come back." Crowley wheeled toward the island.

"Jesus," breathed O'Toole, "what was that all about, Chief?"

"You wouldn't understand, Irish. Something that happened a long time ago."

"But he put you on the report. Jesus Christ, putting the leading Chief on report. It ain't done, that's all."

Rasmussen smiled at O'Toole. "It isn't important. Feel sorry for him, Irish. He's trying to pull a curtain down over a portion of his mind. But he can't do it. So feel sorry for him."

O'Toole polished industriously for about ten minutes. Then suddenly a smile creased his face, and he began to hum under his breath.

"Chief," he said disarmingly, "I got to take a leak. Okay?"

"Sure, Irish. You've worked hard all of ten minutes. Go ahead."

O'Toole hurried below to the crew's quarters and rummaged around in his foot locker until he found what he was looking for. He put it in his pocket and hurried back to the flight deck.

"Feel better?" asked Rasmussen.

"Sure, Chief. Say, I'd better climb up in that cockpit and wipe the windshield and instrument panel. Gets dirty as hell in there."

[140

O'Toole climbed up on the wing and slid back the cockpit canopy. Then he leaned down into the recesses of the cramped cockpit and fastened a rubber contraceptive to the lowest seat brace, far back in a corner.

O'Toole straightened up and muttered to himself, "Put the leading Chief on report, will he? That lousy sonofabitch."

Admiral Delacrois stood at the head of the long mahogany table in his briefing room and watched his junior officers file in; Captain Balta, the air group commander, the squadron skippers and his own intelligence people.

"Be seated, gentlemen," the Admiral said. "I intend to present you with my operational plans and at the same time to pick your brains for anything I can use in the forthcoming strike at Tarawa Atoll."

While Lieutenant Redding read the operational orders, Delacrois sat back placidly and studied the faces of his commanders. Meetings such as this were not according to customary procedure. Admirals did not consult with junior commanders before an attack. But Delacrois knew this was a new air group. He noted that the officers were listening to Redding with politeness but with no great interest. This was always the way when a man who did not have to go into battle told the men who did all about what they might find and what action was to be taken under certain circumstances. Fighting men made up their minds what to do as they went along. It was the only way. You don't ask a doctor to tell a football player how to kick a football.

Redding finished, and the Admiral said, "Now, gentlemen. This won't take long. I will make a few statements, and you will comment on them."

He looked at Commander Lacy, the dive bomber skipper. "Mr. Lacy. In detail, your targets, please?"

The dive bomber pilot was nervous. Lacy was a reserve officer who in civilian life had been a promising real estate salesman in Portland, Oregon. He believed all admirals were to be avoided at any cost.

"Any shipping to be found in the area, sir. I presume the torpedo squadron will go in first so my secondary target will more than likely be my primary. All ground installations on Betio Island. Gun positions, gun emplacements, ground storage facilities, roads, bunkers, transportation facilities and communications. Mainly, however, enemy fortifications that might impede the landings."

"Excellent, Lacy. You, Mr. Dusane?"

The torpedo skipper grinned. "Same as Lacy, sir. We hit shipping first and then cream the island."

The Admiral was aware of Crowley's displeasure. He was deliberately passing over Crowley until the end because he had to know the relationship, within the group, of the commanders and the CAG.

"Mr. Hill?"

"Fly escort to the target. Get the bombers in safely." Hill hesitated. "Admiral . . . may I make a suggestion?"

"You may," said Delacrois.

"Some people seem to think we can expect little, if any, air opposition." He glanced at Redding. "I think it's ridiculous to assume any such thing."

"Go on, Mr. Hill."

"I think we ought to have a predawn launch and send in half our fighters to clear the air."

Crowley interrupted. "There will be only twenty enemy fighters on the field."

Delacrois looked at Crowley. "I see you have read the recco reports. Very good." He glanced at Balta. "Sam?"

Balta waved gently at Hill. "I'll let Mr. Hill talk for me."

"The mission doesn't call for it," Crowley said.

"Doesn't call for what?" asked Hill.

"A predawn launch. It's just asking for trouble. How many of the new pilots have ever made a predawn rendezvous?"

Hill spoke to Delacrois, his voice earnest. "Sure it's hairy, Admiral. But sooner or later they'll have to do it anyway. They can't learn too soon. And if there are more than twenty enemy fighters at Betio, and *I* think there are, my boys will have a fighting chance. They won't get jumped, and the Japs won't be able to use the sun."

"It isn't worth it, Admiral," spoke up Redding.

Hill looked at Redding. "You going to be there, Al?"

Redding did not understand. "Be where?"

"At twenty thousand over Betio or Truk or Kwajalein or any of the others we'll be going to later on. There'll be others, you know."

"Of course I'll be there." Redding still did not comprehend.

Hill shook his head. "No. I mean will you be *there*. Will you be sitting up there with only a turning prop between you and disaster? That's what I mean." Hill's voice turned harsh. "Goddammit, don't tell me what's worth what. Or what's called for. My boys need to know everything there is to know, and they need every break I can give them. Not the next time or the time after that. This time." He turned to the Admiral. "Pardon, sir."

"Thank you for your opinion, Commander," said Delacrois.

My God, Delacrois thought, how few there are of them. The real fighters. The professionals. The men who wear the real bird of glory on their shoulders and are unaware of it. I'd trade ten dozen Reddings and as many Crowleys for one Harry Hill. I hardly know this sandy man in front of me, and yet I love him. He flies and fights in the same straightforward, methodical manner, seeking perfection in everything he does. Only a few of us will ever know his name because he speaks too well, and when you speak too well and at the same time speak only the truth you run afoul of weak men in high places who become afraid of you. When other men are afraid of you, your end is always in sight.

Where do they come from, the Harry Hills? Where does this country find them? We are fortunate to have such men, and I wish to God there was a formula we might write down, a set of exact figures that would produce all the Harry Hills we need. He'll take off from this ship and because he's in the air over the useless, barren piece of land we'll attack, because he's there men will live who otherwise might die. All of us fall far short of perfection, those who command most of all. I sometimes think no man should be given the right to command. But then where would we be? So I will issue the orders that Hill will carry out, and he will be doing it for me and for Sam Balta and for all of us. For everyone but himself because what has he got to gain? He won't obtain this precious third star to which I attach such importance. He won't make the next selection list for promotion as Sam Balta will.

He'll just do his job with no thought of reward. Even the import of what he accomplishes will be decided by men who wear clean clothing and sit in comfortable offices far from the battle. If he dies, he'll probably do it unseen and unspoken for. There's very little to urge a man beyond the call of duty, but Hill will stand up when the time arrives to be counted.

It is men like him who have made our Navy great. I wish there were more of him.

Delacrois decided it was time to consult Crowley. "You have a suggestion, perhaps, Commander?"

Crowley was seething. There was no excuse for the Admiral's

deliberately bypassing him. Would this damn thing never end? Would one mistake on a distant afternoon hound him the rest of his life?

"I doubt the wisdom of a night launch, sir," Crowley said. "I don't believe we'll find any appreciable number of enemy fighters at the target."

"If we do," Hill spoke up, "how many pilots will we lose?"

"And how many might we lose on a night launch and rendezvous?" Crowley shot back.

The Admiral turned to Balta. "How about it, Sam?"

The Captain nodded solemnly. "We might lose one or two men, sir. It *is* a calculated risk."

The Admiral spoke deliberately. "Commander Crowley, your concern for the lives of your men is commendable." He turned to Hill. "Your men, Mr. Hill. The lives of your men. How important do you consider them to be?"

Hill took a deep drag on his cigarette and studied the amber tip on the end. He tugged gently at his earlobe. Finally he said, "Sir. Men are going to die on this mission, and they're not going to die in a great battle. This won't be Midway or the Coral Sea or the Solomons. But they'll die just the same. Now," his voice grew angry, "I don't expect my men to live to become admirals, but I expect them to die, if they have to die, as the best damn fighter pilots in the United States Navy."

"Your eloquence is commendable," Crowley said sarcastically. "But as the air group commander I do not advise a predawn launch."

While Admiral Delacrois listened to the suggestions of his subordinates Captain Balta watched him with concealed mirth. Balta knew the Admiral had already made up his mind to launch in the darkness, and he also knew the Admiral had made his decisions concerning the forthcoming operation without the benefit of advice from his juniors. But Delacrois wanted the younger men, the men who would do the fighting, to feel that they had had a hand in the fashioning of the plans. A man fights better when he thinks he is carrying out his own decisions.

While the talk grew animated in flag country, darkness fell swiftly, and the ship was darkened for the night. The portholes were battened down and the blackout curtains dropped over passages and hatchways. Soon the *Concord* was nothing more than a giant shadow passing through the Pacific night.

[144

Now two things occurred simultaneously.

In the conference room Admiral Delacrois, tired of the babble of voices, decided he and Balta needed a drink. He told the assembled officers that the carrier would launch before dawn on November 16th. Then he thanked the men for their cooperation and dismissed them.

Three miles off the starboard beam of the *Concord* the prow of the Japanese submarine *Ueno* cut the night waters. The *Ueno* was homeland bound, her torpedo tubes empty after a successful foray in the central Pacific. All she could do now was observe, but that was sufficient. She had been shadowing the task force for some hours until the darkness had permitted her to surface and employ her radio. Now she was ready to set into motion the chain of events that would make American intelligence estimates of the situation one hundred and eighty degrees out of phase.

The *Ueno* dropped back, allowing the task force to move on unsuspecting. Then she sent a message in code that was in Admiral Togyama's capable hands six minutes later.

Togyama had intended launching the night of the 17th and sending his fighters into Betio. Now, with the *Ueno*'s message in his hands, he ordered his navigation officer to plot a position on the American force based on their reported direction and speed. Shortly thereafter the navigator's report indicated to him that the Americans would be in the vicinity of either the Marshalls or the Gilberts by the morning of the 16th.

He spoke impersonally to his staff. "What speed must we make to be in position near Kwajalein by the morning of the 16th?"

A few seconds later the reply came: "Twenty-seven knots, sir."

"Make it," Togyama ordered.

He moved to the plotting board and studied the area where he would wait for the Americans. When the enemy arrived he would confront them between Kwajalein and Truk, able to move wherever the situation demanded. If they attacked the Gilberts they would come in unsuspecting. And on Betio Island they would find Isoku Yamota and eighty-five of the best fighter pilots the Emperor had to offer.

IX

November, 1943

It was D-Day for Air-Group Two. General Quarters blasted at 0200, and the *Concord* came alive. All preparations for the attack had been made. All that remained now was to put them into effect. The fighters stood gassed and armed on the flight deck, while the bombers were weighted with heavy, cumbersome bombs. The mess cooks had worked all night preparing food for the next day, and now they stood wearily behind their counters waiting for the rush. The chaplains had completed their services; communion had been bestowed and confession heard, and the men had made their peace with God.

At 0215, Commander Crowley lay in his bunk and stared at the overhead. Dimly, from down the corridor, he heard the persistent creaking of a loose porthole cover. He twisted in the bunk and cursed the porthole, and even as he did so he knew he was not cursing the porthole at all. He looked at the glowing dial on his watch. His heart was thumping painfully in his chest, and he felt a cold sweat on his body. He knew he should be considering the hours ahead, the decisions he might be called upon to make, the possible alternatives if things didn't work out as planned. He should be considering rendezvous procedures and strafing tactics and ways to take advantage of the weather. He should be mentally selecting targets of opportunity because assigned targets had a habit of disappearing before the reality of an attack.

But Crowley cursed again and knew he was considering none of these things.

Crowley was wondering how he might get himself grounded.

[146

There were ways. A bad back was medically impossible to disprove. An earache might work or a twisted ankle. Such were the thoughts torturing Crowley's mind at 0215 as he swung his feet over the side of the bunk and sat there afraid, his throbbing head held between wet palms.

In Ready Room One the pilots rubbed sleep out of their eyes and climbed into their flight gear. The duty officer scribbled weather information on the blackboard, and the sound of voices was muted under the clacking of the teletype.

Hill sipped coffee and made a wry face. He was sprawled in his chair, surrounded by the younger pilots.

"Nervous?" he asked Marriner.

"A little," Marriner replied. "I felt like this on graduation day."

"Well," Hill said, "today you're graduating, sure enough."

"Skipper!" The duty officer's voice broke in. "Look at that damn teletype."

The information on the teletype screen from Combat Informations Center, CIC, brought a frown to Hill's face.

LATEST WEATHER REPORTS INDICATE LARGE THUNDERHEAD ACTIVITY EN ROUTE TARGET. TOPS ANGELS 25. EXTREME TURBULENCE.

"Well," said Hill, "that makes everything just dandy. Tops at twenty-five. What the hell are we supposed to do, go under them and come out on the target sitting on the deck like clay pigeons?"

"It isn't your worry, Hill," Crowley's voice said. The air group commander had come in unnoticed. "I'll be leading the flight. All you have to do is follow."

"Don't take us into that storm, Commander," Hill said.

"When I want your opinions, Hill, I'll ask for them," Crowley said, and, having asserted his authority, moved off.

Stepik stirred his coffee in his methodical way, and regarded the next few hours with a certain resignation. He had asked to be here, now he would make the best of it. A question came to his mind, and he spoke to Hill.

"The rendezvous, Skipper. What if we miss it? Do we chase after the rest or do we circle the ship?"

"You circle the ship," Hill replied. "But don't worry about it."

"I had the goddamndest dream last night," Anders said.

"You were going down in flames." Hill smiled because he had experienced it once himself.

"No," Anders shook his head, "I dreamed I married a rich widow I met last year at Pensacola. I was a banker in Tallahassee, and I was still in bed at twelve noon."

"That's a good dream on a night like this." Stepik smiled.

"How old was she?" asked Bates.

"Sixty-nine," Anders said. "That wasn't so good."

"Where's Max?" Marriner asked.

"He stopped at the chaplain's office," Stepik answered.

"Here he comes now," Anders said.

Winston came over to them, shrugging into his Mae West. "Any orders, Boss?" He grinned at Marriner.

"Hang on tight. That's all," Marriner suggested.

"Make your peace with the chaplain, Max?" Bates said with a laugh.

Winston was serious. "Is there anything wrong with it?"

Bates sobered at once. "No, Max. No, there's nothing wrong with it."

"Each of us gets ready in our own way," Hill said. "Me? I thought I'd get ready by drinking a cup of this abominable coffee. All it's doing is souring my kidneys."

Redding, the intelligence officer, came into the ready room to be greeted by a chorus of friendly jeers. Hill got to his feet.

"Briefing time, heroes," Hill called loudly. "Mr. Redding has the floor."

As Redding went over the pertinent data for the first hop, the predawn launch, sweaty fingers grasping slippery pencils made significant marks on the plotting boards. The marks were made diligently, with great concern, because they might easily mean the difference between life and death. A carrier is not a stationary airfield, and unless you know exactly where it is at any given time, along with its intended course and speed and the direction of the wind, you are a man in an airplane with no home to return to.

Crowley had left the ready room before the briefing began. Having made his appearance there and asserted his authority before the younger pilots, he had gone to the number three deck, below the waterline, and knocked on the flight surgeon's door.

Now Crowley lay on a table in the aviation examining room.

[148

"Say where it hurts." The flight surgeon was kneading Crowley's back which didn't hurt anyplace at all.

"Right there?" the doctor asked.

"Right there," Crowley groaned. "I don't know how the hell I twisted it, Doc."

The sonofabitch is lying, thought the flight surgeon. This bastard is red-dogging for a grounding slip. Well, he won't get one today. I guess the rumors about him are true. What a lousy, no-good sonofabitch!

He pressed down hard with his thumb just off the small of Crowley's back. Crowley jerked and let out a genuine groan of pain.

"Right there?" asked the doctor.

"Yeah," mumbled Crowley.

"Well," said the doctor straightening up and turning to a table against the wall, "we'll have to do something about that. Don't suppose you can fly with your back in that shape, eh?"

"I'd better not try, I guess. Jesus. This would have to happen on a strike day."

The doctor took a long syringe and inserted a needle.

"Especially with you being air group commander," the doctor said in a commiserating voice. He leaned over Crowley's body.

"Right there, you say?"

"Right in there, Doc."

With a deft movement the doctor inserted the needle into a muscle in Crowley's back.

"Christ!" Crowley rose up with the pain.

"That ought to do it," the doctor said.

Crowley got to his feet with a grimace of pain. He put on his shirt while the doctor scribbled on a pad of paper.

"Here!" The doctor offered him the slip of paper. "Get this prescription filled after you get back from the flight."

"But my back. I thought . . ."

"A little spasm, that's all. That shot I gave you will relieve the muscles for at least twenty-four hours. You won't have any trouble. Lucky thing you came to me right away. Now you won't miss any hops at all."

On the flight deck, Machinist's Mate 2nd Class O'Toole carefully made the cockpit ready for Commander Crowley. Number 00 was polished to a shining brilliance. O'Toole delicately reached down

149]

in the recesses of the cockpit flooring and groped until his hand touched the device he had fastened there.

"You sonofabitch," he said into the night wind, "see how this sticks you at twenty thousand feet."

On the black bridge of flag country, Admiral Delacrois and Sam Balta tried to detect the first faint glimmerings of dawn.

"I'm glad we're together on this one, Sam," Delacrois said.

"I am too, sir," Balta agreed.

"Sir, is it now? Why the formality, Sam?"

"We're fighting today. You're in command, Frog. You're on a throne today. I'm mortal enough not to want to touch it or even get too close to it." He sighed softly. "It's times like this when I wonder about the wisdom of acquiring stars."

"The sound of the bands and the marching is gone now, isn't it, Sam?" the Admiral murmured. "All the ones who waved us off with bright handkerchiefs have gone and left us to our particular brand of loneliness. No more martial music to stir the blood. But here we belong and here we'll stand. I say it again, Sam. I'm glad we're together on this."

"Frog," Balta said quietly, "those kids down there in the ready room. Do you suppose some day, many years from now, on the day they die, maybe they'll look and feel again as they do this very minute? Do you think the gods will do that for them, Frog?"

"I never doubted it," said Frog Delacrois.

In the darkness Sam Balta nodded and was satisfied.

"It's time now, Sam," Delacrois said. "Let's have 'Pilots Man Your Planes.' "

"I'll attend to it, sir." Balta moved off into the night.

The well-briefed pilots in Ready Room One jumped to their feet as the teletype screen in the front of the room flashed out the "Man Your Planes" message.

"One minute, my heroes!" Harry Hill knew he had to say something because they were young men and they were going into battle for the first time.

The pilots stopped their nervous shuffle toward the door. They turned, and Hill found himself staring down into a sea of upturned faces.

"You've all been sent halfway across the world to do a job," Hill said evenly. "You have been handed a trust. How you keep that trust is up to each one of you individually.

[150

"I expect no man to be a hero because most heroes are already dead. Stay alive as best you can within the limits that trust sets for you.

"You are better than they are! Remember this and remember to stay in two-plane sections. *Don't get caught alone.*"

Then, because he wanted them to leave with a laugh, he added, "And don't forget their eyes. They slant. When they have to look into the sun, and that's where we'll be coming from, their eyes *pucker,* and rumor has it they all go blind."

Hill was rewarded by a spattering of laughter. "Let's man the planes," he said, and the men crowded out the door into the darkened passageway that led to the flight deck.

Hill bumped into a figure just outside the ready room door. He heard Crowley's voice in the darkness. "You're loquacious, Hill. You should have been a politician."

"I wanted to give them something to take along."

"I suppose you did. But I'm leading this flight. Remember that, Hill."

"I have no choice, Crowley." Hill's voice was harsh.

"*Commander* Crowley, Mr. Hill." Crowley accentuated the rank.

"Sure, Crowley," Hill replied as he pushed past the air group commander and followed his pilots down the passageway.

The flight deck was still a pitch-black platform along which the pilots were guided by the red glare of the night lights held by the deck crewmen. They had memorized the positions of their planes from a chart in the ready room as they could not have found them in the darkness.

One by one they climbed into their cockpits. Long months of training guided their hands as they buckled themselves in, but muffled curses sounded in the night as knuckles skinned on sharp projections in the cramped cockpits. Shoulder harnesses fastened, seat belts buckled. Radio connections plugged in. The plane captain standing unseen on the wing helping as best he can.

Now they begin the long wait. Sitting alone in their cockpits in the dark they strain to hear the order to start engines. It may come in a minute, a second or an hour. How lonely can a human being get? The only crutch left consists of two hands and a headful of training. Everything is up to the individual now. Christ! This waiting is the worst of all. I wish I could take a leak. That goddam pistol is sticking in my ribs. My goddam foot is going to sleep. Jesus, it's

151]

dark. Going to be a bitch to rendezvous. Black as a witch's teat. The air smells good this morning. Wonder what it would be like out here in peacetime. Spend your vacation at Tarawa. Frolic in the surf on the sun-swept beaches of Betio.

Out of the lonely night the bullhorn roared the summons to battle! "Pilots! Start engines!!"

Flip the switches, slap the primer switch three or four times. Hold down the starter switch and listen. When she turns over a certain number of times she will catch, then shove the mixture control to auto lean. There are other ways as satisfactory but the book says this way is the best. In the dark you can't see what the hell you are doing anyway so you might as well follow the book.

With a gigantic stutter the heavy prop spins and whirls, and she is purring now, all two thousand horses of her. The plane shudders gently from the vibration of the spinning metal blade as you consult the multitude of phosphorescent dials staring at you from the instrument panel. Only a few of them have import at this particular moment. They will tell you if you are going to launch today or if you are going to sit it out on the ship, cursing your luck if you are a hero and blessing it if you are not. Watch the flutter of the oil pressure gauge and observe the climb of the cylinder head temperature. If the needle moves past 200 degrees you may be in trouble. Fuel pressure is of paramount importance because when the pressure fails there will be no gas in your cylinders and the airplane will no longer fly.

Crowley was first to be signaled forward out of the chocks. Captain Balta and Admiral Delacrois watched from the bridge as his plane swung around and headed toward the pitching bow of the flight deck. They were remembering other mornings long past.

Crowley settled in his cockpit and gave a last tug to tighten his shoulder straps. He could see nothing before him but the line of deck lights on either side of the flight deck. There was no horizon, and beyond where the lights ended there was only a black nothingness.

At 0330 the bullhorn sang out again above the thunder of the revving engines.

"Launch aircraft!"

With the order the *Concord* straightened out of her turn and plowed into the teeth of the freshening wind.

Crowley brushed the sweat out of his eyes and watched the red light out on the deck. Christ, what a morning. Now the red light began a slow circular motion, ordering Crowley to advance his throt-

[152

tle. Faster now the light swirled. Crowley advanced his throttle evenly all the way to the stop. The engine wound up, and the roar grew to a shrill, ear-splitting thunder. The prop control gauge read 2700 revolutions per minute. Crowley had to stand hard on his brakes to keep the plane from lunging down the flight deck.

When it required all the strength in his legs to hold the straining monster in leash, when the instrument panel shook violently and Crowley's hands threatened to slip off the controls, then Fly One, the man with the light, threw his arm downward in an abrupt gesture. Crowley took his feet off the brake pedals, and Number 00 leaped down the flight deck.

As the plane passed the island structure the green lights on the instrument panel were all that could be seen, and then they too were gone as the plane ran out of runway and sank off the bow into the night.

"Whatever I may think of Crowley," Balta said to the Admiral, "I will have to give him this much. He's there, and I'm not. I'm not sure that I envy him."

"But you do, Sam. You do," murmured Delacrois.

Balta said nothing, and his nod was lost in the darkness.

As Crowley passed the last deck light and felt the plane leave the ship he pulled up his gear lever, throttled back and headed out toward the rendezvous sector. Behind him the others were launching, and he switched on his navigation and running lights so the others could join up on him. He felt almost as if he were the only living thing in all the world.

At the exact moment Crowley was switching on his running lights, one hundred and eighty miles away Commander Isoku Yamota led a large force of fighter planes into a landing circle above the airstrip on Betio Island. He broke off and came into the downwind leg. He called the tower and reported his position and only now did the tower turn on the runway lights. Behind him his flight milled in the circle, broke off in divisions and followed him down. He skimmed onto the rough runway at approximately the same time that Harry Hill led Fighting Two into a close rendezvous with Air Group Commander Crowley in a sector of the sky eight miles away from Task Force 58.

Yamota was leading a group of eighty-five Zero fighter planes from the carriers *Akiti* and *Sugami*. He anticipated joining action with the enemy shortly after daybreak. Up to this point his timing had been

153]

perfect. Flying from the airstrip at Betio he would have no fuel problem, while the carrier planes could not delay too long before starting back to their ships. Estimating the enemy task force to be approximately two hundred miles out at sea, Yamota gave the Americans less than forty minutes over the target.

Commander Yamota taxied up and cut his engines. He had only one order for the officer waiting for him at the flight line.

"Get these planes refueled in half an hour. That is the maximum time allowable. With or without refueling we launch in thirty minutes."

It would take more than thirty minutes for Commander Crowley to rendezvous his air group and cover the one hundred and eighty miles of sky to meet Yamota, but Yamota had no way of knowing this.

Air Group Two had rendezvoused and vectored out on course for Tarawa just as dawn cut a slat of gray along the edge of the sky. With the first light the pilots could see a gigantic endless bank of towering purple cloud formations looming in front of them. The front was a solid mass with no visible holes in it, and it appeared about one hundred miles ahead of the group's present position.

The first radio communication of the morning came from Dick Marriner.

"Christ! Look up ahead, Charlie Leader." Since this was Strike Charlie according to the operational plan, Crowley as the leader had been designated Charlie Leader for call sign purposes.

Crowley did not acknowledge but he recognized the towering wall of cloud as another obstacle in his path this fresh fall morning.

Marriner led his division off to one side of Hill and his group of four. On his right wing Bates flew three feet off the wing tip, his teeth flashing in a grin whenever Marriner looked at him. This morning was a ball for Terrence Bates. He loved the plane and the clouds and the smell of oil and grease and the feel of the stick pressing against his hand. He would even love his enemy in a few short minutes.

Winston added a little throttle and inched forward until his plane flew even with Marriner's. When Marriner looked at him, Winston pointed up ahead at the mean-looking cloud bank. Marriner made a motion with his hands indicating he supposed they would try to climb over the clouds. Winston shrugged and dropped back into posi-

[154

tion. He turned his head and gave a thumbs-up to Stepik flying number four man.

The clouds were closer now and loomed higher in the threatening sky. Black puffs of mist jutted from their sides, and purplish menacing protuberances swelled along the steep walls. An occasional blast of lightning scarred the barrier with a streak of silver-white, and the bulbous-teated underside of the great structure reached down to the surface of the ocean itself.

Crowley had been climbing steeply, and the group had followed him. As they approached twenty-five thousand feet any but the most inexperienced eye could discern one startling fact.

They were never going to get over the top of this monstrous front.

Still Crowley kept his nose in a climb. At this altitude the air was too thin to permit smooth formation flying, and the entire formation straggled while the pilots pumped their throttles in order to maintain position.

Hill waited until the bank of thunderhead cloud was only fifteen miles ahead, then he called Crowley.

"Charlie Leader from Charlie One. Your intentions?"

Crowley's voice answered: "Maintain formation, all Charlie planes."

Hill looked behind him and assured himself all elements were in position. He consulted his plotting board, sliding it out from under the instrument panel, and decided they were eighty miles from Tarawa. If the storm covered fifty miles of area, the target should be just on its far side. To try and penetrate the forbidding front was preposterous. The planes would become separated, the pilots confused, perhaps panicky. Crowley was leading them into disaster. Hill was reaching for his mike button when Marriner's voice sang out.

"Charlie Leader from Charlie Two. These airplanes will *not* climb over the weather. That cloud bank reaches to angels forty."

Good boy, Hill murmured to himself. Now the skipper of the dive and torpedo bombers lent the weight of their experienced opinion. Still Crowley bored ahead, approaching the first outposts of the storm front.

Marriner was now flying one hundred yards to Crowley's starboard and slightly astern while Hill was in the same position on Crowley's port. What is this crazy sonofabitch going to do next? Marriner wondered. I don't intend to trust my division to the mercy of this

155]

black bastard reaching up in front of me. Even the instruments won't work in there where the winds must approach two hundred miles an hour.

Marriner was no longer watching Crowley. He was watching Hill. Marriner was responsible for the men flying on him, and he was not going to let Crowley's poor judgment kill them.

The formation droned on, and the first sweepings of rain spattered on the windshields. The sun was gone now, lost in a flat, dull expanse of gray overcast. Pillars of cloud obscured Marriner's vision, and he was forced to transfer his gaze to Crowley. He had to have someone to fly on in this sort of weather. He moved a little closer to Crowley and Anders.

Eighty miles away, Isoku Yamota roared down the Betio runway at the head of his force of Zero fighters. He veered in a wide circle to his left and started a climb toward his rendezvous to the northwest. He intended to wait for the enemy ten miles southeast of Tarawa, between them and the island.

Yamota had already decided the Americans would come in under the weather. They had no fighters capable of topping the forty-thousand-foot storm, and he doubted whether any flight commander would be stupid enough to attempt to fly through the front.

The Americans would come in on the deck, a few hundred feet over the water, expecting only a handful of Zeros to meet them. Yamota smiled as he thought of the surprise in store for the enemy when he swept down with his eighty-five fighters from the altitude advantage.

The pilots of Yamota's fighter force wore the traditional flags under their flight suits or around their heads. They were all experienced combat fliers and being familiar with the hazards of their profession they prayed to their gods and their ancestors. Commander Yamota was a Christian, and he prayed to St. Jude, the patron saint of the lost and the lonely. Briefly he wondered if some American pilot might be praying to the same saint. If so, how could the saint grant both supplications? He wondered about this for an instant and thought perhaps a coin fashioned of old truths was tossed and allowed to fall where it would. He decided that was as good a way as any.

Crowley had his eyes glued to his artificial horizon, now the most important instrument in his cockpit. The instrument contained a mini-

[156

ature airplane which always remained level with the invisible horizon and below which was a straight line. Crowley did not allow the miniature plane's wings to deviate from the straight line. It was his indication that his plane was flying with its wings level and in no danger of stalling or spinning out.

Now, with superb stubbornness, Crowley entered the body of the cloud bank, boring a hole where trespassers possessing far greater skill would not have dared to enter.

Immediately he was subjected to a wild buffeting, and his ears heard the wind scream in wild outrage. Anders, a few feet away, could barely make out Crowley's plane. Neither man had ever encountered such a storm.

Hill saw Crowley and Anders disappear into the murderous thunderhead and knew what he had to do. No radio would function within that heaving mass. He banked steeply to his left and called on his radio.

"This is Charlie One to all flight Charlie planes. Make a one-eighty. I say again. Make a one-eighty. We're not about to fight that baby."

The planes of Strike Charlie wheeled majestically and presented their tails to the storm. Unfortunately Marriner had already entered the maelstrom when Hill made his transmission, so he did not hear the order and thus kept on after the CAG.

Crowley had not been in the storm two minutes when he knew he had made a stupid blunder. He had no business in here, but now he was afraid to turn back. He did not trust himself on instruments except when he was flying with his wings level. If he made a turn his artificial horizon might tumble in the turbulence, and he would fall to his death. In his fright Crowley had forgotten his wingman, Anders, and Marriner's division.

Hill had taken over the lead and now flew a course parallel to the storm front. He intended to fly due south for nine minutes, then turn due west and fly until he reached Tarawa Atoll in such manner that it appeared off his right wing. He would continue on past the atoll for five minutes, then reverse course and come in on the target from exactly the opposite direction from that by which he had originally approached it. He turned and checked the other planes on the strike. Behind him the fighters crisscrossed over the torpedo and dive bombers. Hill could not find Marriner, and only then did he realize Marriner had followed Crowley into the storm. He fired a quick, short burst from his guns, checking their action. The other planes did the same, and the sky was briefly laced with tracers.

Then all was gray-soaked silence again except for the steady droning as the planes flew south. Hill turned west and took up his new heading. Twenty minutes later a faint line of silvery froth showed dimly through the rain curtain off the starboard bow of the formation. They passed the atoll like phantoms in the mist.

Hill's watch read 0515.

Crowley was terrified. A roll of thunder shook the sky. A split second later a jagged white ribbon of lightning emblazoned the twisted cloud mass, and Crowley cringed; the last vestige of self-control ran wetly down his leg.

At that moment the rubber which O'Toole had secreted below the seat in the cockpit of Crowley's plane succumbed to the radically reduced air pressure at 27,000 feet. It burst with a sharp noise remarkably like a lightning bolt striking a metal surface—which was exactly what O'Toole had intended.

Crowley screamed in terror.

Panic-stricken, he yanked back on the stick, an absurd maneuver even in clear weather. As it was, Crowley's plane was in a climb and flying very nearly at stalling speed. Its nose reared upward, the last few knots of flying speed were dissipated, and it stalled. The plane shuddered, its nose wobbled sluggishly, and then it started to fall off on one wing.

Marriner saw Crowley stall.

"For Christ's sake, Anders, get away from him!" he called.

Marriner started to bank away as Crowley began to spin downward, with Anders still on his wing but falling off himself. Just then Marriner and his four-plane division hit a vicious downdraft. The formation was hurled downward through the sky.

"You're on your own, Charlie Two flight," Marriner called. "Rendezvous on recovery west of the front."

It is normally possible to recover from a spin, even in foul weather. And as he fell, Marriner fleetingly recalled the words of Harry Hill. "If the bastard won't stop spinning, just let her go. If you've got the altitude she'll come out by herself."

So Marriner waited, watching his altimeter unwind. Christ, he thought, I hope the rest didn't follow us in here. That stupid bastard Crowley. Probably killed half the air group. Well, maybe when he

[158

spins into the water he'll find some justification for himself. I can't. The bastard nearly nailed me to the cross.

But Crowley did not spin all the way down. He recovered at four thousand feet in a terminal velocity dive. With trembling hands he reset his artificial horizon and took up a course that would lead him back toward his point of entry.

Marriner's plane came out of the spin at 10,000 feet. He maintained a westerly heading and broke out of the front in seven minutes. He circled slowly, waiting for his division to come out of the storm.

West of Tarawa, Hill eased his throttle forward and put on 2400 RPMs. The planes of Strike Charlie started to climb in the sky. In front of them, twenty miles away and looking in the opposite direction, Commander Yamota waited patiently for his trap to shut.

At 12,000 feet, Hill leveled off on a course 090. Ordinarily he would have elected to come out of the sun, but the storm front rose to such heights that the sun was still too low in the sky.

His watch read 0540 when Hill spoke.

"Strike Charlie from Charlie One. Torpedo bombers will push over in two minutes. Go in on the deck at max speed. Acknowledge."

Dusane's laconic voice acknowledged. Hill's mind raced ahead, probing possibilities. The bombers would draw any fighters on Betio, and Hill would be twenty seconds behind the bombers.

Two minutes later Dusane transmitted. "Pushing over."

The bombers headed for the deck.

"Move up, Charlie chickens," Hill called. "Hold in tight and stay in section as long as you can." He paused. "Good luck."

So Air Group Two flew to battle.

Winston, Bates and Stepik had found Marriner as they came out of the front. Now they came into the target area from the east, low along the water, and so it was that Marriner spotted Yamota first. He swept the sky carefully with his eyes, and saw Hill and Strike Charlie barreling across from the west. Marriner made the tallyho.

"Tallyho Strike Charlie from Charlie Two. Bogies east of the island, angels eight. A million of them."

Hill saw Yamota then, and he knew he had been right. By some alchemy or other the enemy had produced a formidable fleet of fighters. Well, so be it.

159]

Hill banked slightly and came to Yamota head-on. Yamota had not yet seen the Americans.

Marriner saw Hill coming in, and he thought, God love you, Harry Hill. You saw what we failed to see. You saved the strike and brought them here on a westerly heading, which was the only way we could have salvaged anything this morning. It remains to be seen now what we do salvage.

The distance between the forces narrowed, and still Yamota had not seen his enemy closing from his rear.

Hill was five miles away now.

"Strike Charlie. Drop belly tanks."

The cigar-shaped tanks tumbled from the bellies of the planes and twisted slowly toward the ocean below. Down on the deck, Dusane and his pilots skirted the water at masthead level. Low and fast they came, and if it ever crossed their minds that they might be decoys it was never evident from the unswerving course they flew.

Hill called the dive bombers. "Charlie hawks, go in."

The dive bombers started to peel off for position to initiate their runs.

Then down on the water a twenty-five-year-old lieutenant in Dusane's squadron lowered his eyes a moment to adjust his trim tab. His plane's nose lowered just enough to cause it to lose nine feet of altitude. This was enough. The nose hit the top of a reaching wave, and in a split second the lieutenant and his plane disintegrated in a burst of orange flame and billowing black smoke.

Six miles away Yamota saw the flame and pouring smoke. In an instant his trained mind grasped its import, and he turned to the west.

"The enemy," he announced calmly to his flight. "Dead ahead and level."

So the battle starts all even. No surprise attack and no trap to snap shut. This is the way it should always be. Great fighters do not need the odds.

Stand at ten thousand feet and watch the battle joined. Stand on a platform of cloud as the two forces collide head-on at a closing speed of 800 miles an hour. On the one hand eighty-five Zero fighters, the Emperor's best. To meet them, hurtling across the sky, sixty squat Hellcats in Navy blue.

March the banners across the ravaged sky. The Rising Sun and the Spangled Banner. The dawn came slowly this day, staining clouds and water a dull red.

The two formations clashed with a high, thin wail. The air came alive with the cracking of the fifty-calibers, and the formations dissolved into a melee.

Hill kicked hard rudder and went for Yamota head-on. They flew unswerving into their respective fires, passing within inches of each other. But when they turned to pick up the fight, other planes had intervened. The entire sky was a jumble of diving, climbing planes.

As Hill swung up and over in a high chandelle he no longer flew the airplane consciously but by feel and instinct. His eyes were never still; he looked for the leader of the Jap formation and cursed as he knew he had lost him. At the top of his chandelle he hung almost motionless in the air, his nose falling through the horizon and down as his airspeed built up and he swept down in a dive and saw a Zero swing in behind a Hellcat which was turning violently in an effort to escape. Hill glanced quickly over his shoulder to check his tail, and then ranged up behind the Zero and centered the enemy fighter in his gunsight. When the wingspan of the Zero filled his sight, Hill laughed and squeezed the firing button. He held it down in a long, sustained burst because he was dead on the Zero's tail, and when you are in that position you do not preserve ammunition.

The tracers laced out in red threads and worked a stitched pattern up the side of the Zero as Hill moved out slightly to get an angled burst. A short puff of black smoke gasped from the belly of the Zero, followed by a tongue of flame. Then there was a burst of orange, and the Zero came apart in the air. Hill eased his throttle back, moved his mixture control to auto lean and reduced his RPMs two hundred revs. He swung around, hauling back on the stick, and headed back for the fight.

Marriner and his division came into the fight from the east. They swung around a pillar of cloud and came upon the fighter pilot's dream, four Zeros in formation directly in front and below. Marriner signaled Winston to move his section out and take on the outboard two Zeros. Winston and Stepik acknowledged, then pushed over and came in on their targets. Winston opened fire first and got his man in one burst. The other Zero banked steeply to his left and Stepik followed him in a tight, almost vertical turn.

The lead Zero had split-essed out of the fight, and Marriner followed him, leaving the last enemy fighter to Bates. Marriner might have opened fire before the Zero half-looped, but for some reason he would never understand he had chosen to give the enemy an even break. If he had been a more complicated man he would have said, "I wanted to know how good I was. It is no criterion of skill to destroy a man who can't see you." Later Marriner realized that this is an admirable but foolish manner of thinking.

Marriner pulled out of his maneuver to find the Zero coming straight at him. He dropped his flaps and chopped his throttle all the way off. The flight-training manuals say that this maneuver is suicidal. Marriner knew better. As the Zero turned after passing him, Marriner had reduced his speed considerably and so was able to turn within a tight radius. Now he was behind the Zero and closing as he raised the flaps and shoved the throttle forward. He moved the pip on his gunsight ahead of the other plane, closed from the Zero's port side and opened fire with three short bursts from approximately the eight o'clock position. Tracers splattered the side of the Zero and smashed the canopy and the pilot's head in a spray of glass and blood. The Zero abruptly fell off on the left wing and began a spiraling dive completely out of control. It fell three hundred feet, and then the wings tore off and the wasted fuselage spun madly through the sky like a wounded butterfly.

Marriner pushed the stick to the left, eased on rudder, and his nose came around in time for him to see another Zero coming down on him from above, its guns winking. He knew instantly the other pilot had miscalculated his mill lead. The bullets would fall short. The Zero swept by, guns still blazing, and Marriner kicked his plane around to the right, slamming the stick to the corner and jamming on right rudder. His plane almost spun on its axis and pointed its nose down and to the right in such a manner that the enemy, completing his ineffectual run, flew directly through Marriner's gunsight from right to left. Marriner merely held the firing button down, and the Zero flew through a hail of lead. The enemy plane heaved once, rolled onto its back and exploded.

The fight was two minutes old, and Marriner had downed two planes.

Elsewhere in the sky, men were fighting for their lives. At first, in the initial excitement, they had fought in silence. Now voices cut across the sky.

"Out of that cloud, Zeke. Watch them out of that cloud."

[162

"Four o'clock low, Jack. You take the leader."

"You're out of range, Charlie Seven. Close on him."

"Watch your ass, Charlie Six. Watch your ass."

"Look out, Tom. The bastard is coming in on you."

"All right, Seven flight. Move into section, and we'll take them head-on."

"You've got him, Sy. You've got the sonofabitch."

"How do you like it up here, Tojo? Hot, ain't it?"

"Charlie Five, they are on your tail. Look out, Charlie Five."

Steve Stepik made his first kill while he was on his back. He had followed the Zero around trying to turn inside of him to get a proper mill lead. The Zero pilot was good, and the fight ranged all the way from 12,000 feet down to 1500. At that point the Jap pilot elected to employ a maneuver that had been recommended by none other than the Emperor's ace of aces, Commander Yamota.

It is a matter of record that a Zero could out-turn any American fighter made during World War II. Yamota reasoned, sensibly enough, that if a Zero completed a loop within a prescribed area of space, a Hellcat would necessarily need much more space to complete the same maneuver. Therefore if a Zero could entice a Hellcat to a low altitude and induce the Hellcat to try to follow it through a loop, it was a mathematical and aerodynamic certainty that the Hellcat would never recover from the back, or diving side, of the loop but would fly into the water or the ground in a nearly vertical dive.

When the Jap pulled up in the front side of a loop, Stepik's mind recalled Hill's warning. "Don't ever let the bastards suck you into a loop at low altitude. Follow them to the inverted position. If you can't hit them by that time, let them go. Roll out. You'll never pull out if you follow them through. Remember this and live."

Stepik followed the Zero up and up until his nose was pointing directly at the sky. He shoved on all the power he had and rolled the prop control to full RPM. Then he went past the vertical, and his nose came down out of the sky and approached the horizon. He was nearly on his back when he opened fire. The Zero was just passing the inverted position and starting down into his recovery when Stepik's bullets hit him. The Jap died upside down, which is probably as good a way as any to do it.

Stepik had lost track of Winston, and so he did not see another Zero boring in on his flank. Winston was not there to protect him, but Terrence Bates was. Bates intercepted the Zero with a full deflection shot that took off the Zero's entire tail empennage. The enemy fighter cartwheeled through the sky, tumbling end over end, and suddenly a black figure was hurled from the cockpit. It fell four hundred feet and then there was a flash of white as a parachute blossomed.

"What do you say, Steve?" Bates called. "Do we let him get away?"

Before Stepik could answer, an unidentified voice burst over the radio.

"Charlie Five. They are behind you. For Christ's sake turn, Charlie Five."

Commander Yamota was leading the three-plane section that was coming up behind Charlie Five. Yamota too regretted not finding the American leader after the initial pass. Now he swept up to Charlie Five's flight and with a meticulous display of gunnery, sprayed the American formation with a tail-end, no-deflection shot. Three planes of Charlie Five division fluttered and dropped out of the sky. The leader pushed over in a dive and lived until he reached 4,000 feet, when Yamota caught him from long range and shot away his left arm. Then Charlie Five, staring numbly at the stump where his arm had been, looked up just in time to see the ocean rushing toward him.

Yamota saluted the fallen enemy and returned to the business at hand. Pulling up into an Immelmann turn, gaining altitude and reversing direction simultaneously, he rolled out on top of the half-loop to find Winston flying directly ahead of him on a crossing course.

Winston was looking for the rest of his division and had forgotten for the moment the rule by which a fighter pilot lives: never stop looking. Thus he was taken completely by surprise when Yamota opened fire, and only the crimson tracers alerted him to his danger. He reacted instinctively, shoving the stick downward exactly as Yamota expected him to do. Yamota had already shoved on full throttle and full RPM and was closing into point-blank range.

Then Dick Marriner wheeled down from above and swung in behind Yamota. The Japanese mentally shrugged. One must destroy one or the other. What difference? He decided to let Winston get away.

No, Commander Yamota. You made your first mistake of this unholy morning. You should have made for Winston, who would have been an easier kill. Instead you elected Dick Marriner, who is your equal in the sky.

Marriner and Yamota fought a fight to be remembered, employing

[164

every maneuver in the fighter pilot's handbook. Every trick of the trade and some not yet invented. They fought from 15,000 feet down to sea level and then back again. Yamota was poised, confident, deadly in his cockpit. He had looked like this in other skies over Manchuria and China when he was a younger man. And Marriner, younger but quite as deadly, flew with the razor-sharp precision of a surgeon's blade.

Hill saw it as he circled outside the fight and spoke once over his radio.

"Charlie Two from One. I'm standing by."

"Roger," came Marriner's terse reply. "He's mine."

The two planes circled and dived, turned and climbed and rolled. They defied laws that had been written by lesser men as they dogged each other relentlessly.

The first doubt hit both men simultaneously and each was filled with a vast admiration for the other. They had run through the logbook of flying, had tried each other's mettle to the utmost, and neither had found the other wanting.

From stalling speed to terminal velocity, from sea level to 15,000 feet they had fought the best fight they knew. And the advantage never came. They fought to standstill, but ultimately the margin of victory was on the side of Dick Marriner.

Yamota ran out of ammunition.

He completed a half roll and was pulling tight in an effort to get a quick, fleeting burst at the Hellcat which already was dropping down in a steep, diving turn. But when Yamota fired his guns, nothing happened. In that moment he resigned himself. He had won sixty-seven mortal encounters in the air, and he had long ago prepared himself for the one he would lose. That he should lose because his guns were empty was a bitter thing, but this was his way of life. He regretted his inability to end the fight as a warrior should, all guns blazing as he fell down the sky. In his cockpit he shrugged and flew on a steady course. His opponent had won the day.

When Marriner saw Yamota pull his nose into firing position he braced himself, knowing he was open to a short burst. He waited and then stared as his enemy straightened out and flew off on a steady course. The realization came immediately. Out of ammo! Marriner echoed his enemy's regret. This was no way to end a fight.

He shoved his throttle forward and pulled up alongside Yamota's plane. The Japanese looked across the few feet of sky, gave a half-salute and fired an imaginary pistol with his hand. Marriner knew he had been right. He saw the other man smile and nod his head.

The bastard is telling me to go ahead and kill him. He's ready to die. Well, goddammit, I'm not ready to end this fight just yet. Not till we meet again. And somehow, some way, we will.

Hill had watched Marriner and now he called, "This is Charlie One. Want me to make the kill?"

"Negative," Marriner replied. "This one gets away."

"Roger," Hill said. He had watched the fight, and he understood.

Marriner waved a salute at Yamota and peeled away from the Zero. He was preparing to join up on Hill when he noticed his oil pressure was dropping.

"Skipper," he called, "take a look at my underside. I'm losing oil pressure."

Hill slid under Marriner's plane and inspected its belly.

"You took several hits on the underside of the engine. How low is the pressure?"

"Fifty-five and dropping," replied Marriner.

"Let me know if it doesn't stop," Hill said, "It doesn't look too bad."

Around them the vicious battle had ended as abruptly as it had started.

The combatants drew off and watched each other warily. Nervous glances swept over the gas needles and gauges in the Hellcat cockpits. In the heat of combat an insignificant thing like the amount of gas in your tanks can be forgotten. But there comes a time when it is just as important as the tail hook nestling on the underside of your tail. Now the needles were well below the halfway mark, and the task force was almost two hundred miles away.

"All Strike, Charlie chickens. Rendezvous immediately. This is Charlie One."

The Hellcats swung over from every corner of the sky, and the rendezvous began. Hill saw Marriner's division intact again as Winston, Bates and Stepik joined up.

"Charlie Two. Take your division and head for home. Don't wait for the rendezvous."

"Roger from Two," Marriner acknowledged. His division banked away toward the east.

Dusane and Lacy and their bombers had done the job well. The ground targets at Tarawa had been plastered. Gas and oil storage tanks and dumps. Hangars and grounded aircraft and runways were blasted and burned. The bunkers and gun positions had been pounded mercilessly. Eight hundred yards from shore a freighter burned fiercely on the water.

There would be other flights that day and the battle was only beginning. But the rest would be anticlimactic. Yamota had been hit severely. When he landed at Betio he learned that most targets of worth had been damaged or destroyed. There was little left for him to protect.

The vaunted First Fleet had another and a bigger fight coming up in the Marshalls, and Yamota had no intention of wasting his pilots in another battle over this worthless piece of ground. He took his surviving pilots back northwest to Togyama and the Fleet.

Hill was rendezvousing his newly christened veterans. But there were empty spaces in the four-plane divisions, for men had fallen from the sky. No fight is ever one way, for both sides always lose. It is the measure of the victor which side recovers from its losses and returns to rejoin the fray.

The calls came in to Hill as the divisions joined up.

"Charlie Three. One gone."

"Charlie Four with two."

"Charlie Six with one."

And so the tally was added in Hill's mind. He would live with it for the fifty minutes it took to fly back to the task force and then he would bury it away to be remembered when he was old and had nothing better to remember.

So the fight ended, and Air Group Two had been blooded. Each man returning alone in his cockpit had experienced his measure of fear and had gone on. There was a regret for the dead but not for the way they died. Was there a more satisfactory way? In the individual hearts was a conviction, lasting and eternal, that their mettle had been proved, the right to the badge of honor earned. It was a glory that could never be revoked.

"Sector Able on the YE," called Hill, and the hands turned the radio dials accordingly.

When the coded dot-dash came clear across the intervening space, they knew they were truly on their way home.

All that was left now was the circle above the ship, the sweeping dive into the landing circle. Then the precise pattern up the groove and the welcome sight of the landing-signal officer, paddles in hand,

167]

waving them on in, across the pitching fantail and so onto the deck and into the wires. The quick, hard, satisfactory jerk as the tail hook caught and the plane was hauled to a standstill from a speed of eighty miles an hour in a matter of seventy feet.

Air Group Two had been blooded and was winging home, course one zero zero. Destination Task Force 58.

Marriner was forty miles from Tarawa when he realized he was not going to make it. His oil pressure needle had dropped all the way down to the stop. He had only a minute or two left.

He called Winston on the radio. "Max, this is Dick. My oil pressure is gone. I'm going in."

Winston and Stepik moved up in the formation, and Bates closed in on Marriner's other wing.

"Two o'clock, fourteen miles or so, Dick. Those two small islands." Bates' voice was calm.

Marriner looked over at two o'clock. In the distance he saw two tiny islands, each about five hundred yards long and lying about a mile apart. Between the curving ends of each island a calm lagoon reflected the morning sunlight.

"They're not on the map," Winston called. "Can't tell if the Japs have them or not."

"What difference?" Marriner said. "My engine just froze." His propeller jerked to a stop as the engine ceased to function, and Marriner immediately pushed the nose over to maintain flying speed. With the engine silent he could hear the wind whistling outside the cockpit. He watched his airspeed carefully. Without power the plane could stall much more easily. He trimmed the plane to maintain a steady one hundred knots and set his course for the islands.

"We'll follow you down," Winston said.

"Check your gas," Marriner told him. "One of us in the drink is bad enough."

Winston realized he and the others had very little fuel in the tanks. "We'll wait till you get down," he called. "Then we'll get help."

"Roger, Max, but don't foul yourself up. I'll be okay."

Marriner dropped his flaps, slowing the plane further. He swung wide and pointed his nose at the island on his right, having decided to set down in the lagoon about a hundred yards offshore. He pressed the canopy ejection lever and pushed the canopy back along the track until it flew off in the slipstream. Then he tightened his shoul-

[168

der straps and seat belt and unbuckled the leg straps on his parachute. He checked his airspeed, noting it read eighty-five knots. Looking behind, he could see the other three planes on his wing, escorting him down.

The island was closer now, and he could see the coral reefs under the smooth waters of the lagoon. It appeared uninhabited.

"Going now, gang." Marriner was surprised that he felt no fear. He was suddenly very certain he could bring this water landing off safely. He eased back on the stick and the glassy water swept by as he skimmed a few feet above the surface. His airspeed had dropped further, and when the needle reached 68 knots the plane settled gently onto the water, skipped once and then plowed its nose under. Marriner felt the shoulder straps bite into his flesh as he was thrown violently forward. Even before the plane's forward momentum had stopped he had thrown off his safety belt and shrugged out of his parachute harness. The plane settled back in the water and went under almost immediately. Marriner swam out of the cockpit when he was six feet under the water.

Winston, Bates and Stepik circled low over Marriner as he swam to shore. Only when he was on the beach and waving to them did they head away.

Marriner watched the three planes fly off, and it was only then that he realized the seriousness of his predicament. The task force was more than a hundred and fifty miles away, busily engaged in fighting a war and with little or no time to worry about a single ensign stranded on an island that wasn't even on the maps. He was considering the hopelessness of the situation when he looked across the lagoon, and his heart almost stopped beating.

A small patrol craft was coming from around the curve of land at the end of the other island. Even from this distance he could make out the Rising Sun fluttering from the masthead.

Jesus Christ. Japs. And they had seen him crash-land. Marriner ran back from the shoreline into the concealment of a group of palm trees. He took his .38 from his shoulder holster, and using a handful of dry coconut shredding he dried the pistol's action and rubbed the water off the cartridges. A sense of hopelessness came over him as he watched the patrol boat nearing the island.

High in the sky Winston had been taking one last look back after plotting the position of the island on his board when he saw the Jap boat. He checked his gas gauge and bit off a curse. He knew Stepik

169]

and Bates had even less than he did. Wingmen always had to use more gas than the section or division leader they flew on.

Now Bates saw the Jap boat. "Max from Bates. There's a boat going after Marriner." Bates started to bank away.

"Hold position, Bates," Winston called. "What is your gas state?"

"Fifty-five gallons," Bates replied.

"You, Steve?"

"About the same," Stepik acknowledged.

Winston's gauge read almost seventy gallons, indicating a little more than an hour of flight time left. It was going to be close. He pressed his mike button.

"Bates. Stepik." Winston's voice suddenly held a note of authority. "Continue to the task force. I'm reading seventy gallons. I can take care of that Jap boat myself. You'll never make it back if you don't leave now. Get back to the ship and start rescue procedures."

Winston waited a moment while the wisdom of his decision became apparent to Bates and Stepik. Then Winston surprised himself.

"That's an order," he said quietly.

Stepik's voice was mild. "Okay, Max. Good luck."

"I don't like it, but I'll go along," Bates said. "We'll be back, Max, if you don't make it."

Winston banked away. "Roger," he called.

Ensign Hiro Yoshida, in command of Patrol Craft 701, had seen the American plane go into the water and had watched the pilot swim to shore. When the escorting planes left, he boarded his four-man crew and set course for the island a mile away. He left a fifth crew member ashore to radio headquarters on Kwajalein for a destroyer to come and pick up the American prisoner.

Now Yoshida approached the island cautiously. He knew the American pilots carried pistols. He was five hundred yards offshore trying to discern the American somewhere back of the fringe of palm trees that lined the beach when Maxwell Winston came in low along the water and opened fire at point-blank range. His tracers threw up columns of spray as the shells walked their way forward and into the Japanese boat. On his first pass Winston killed a petty officer in the bow, blasting his body over the side.

Marriner watched Winston's attack. Goddam it, you wild, crazy, wonderful sonofabitch. No gas and you came back anyway. This is one I owe you. Crouched behind the tangled undergrowth Marriner

[170

saw Winston pull up, reverse course and come down again. This time his shells tore a hole in the waterline of the 701, and she listed sharply over on her left side as the sea poured into her hull. One of the shells struck the helmsman and drove him back against the wheelhouse wall where he slumped to the deck, dying.

Winston read fifty-five gallons on his gas gauge and knew he had time for only one more run. He came in low again and fired until his guns were empty. He hit another crewman this time and all but demolished the sinking 701. There was nothing more he could do. He flew a last pass over the spot where Marriner crouched, waggled his wings, and set a course for the task force.

As Winston disappeared over the horizon Marriner turned his eyes back to the 701. Only a piece of the stern was still above water, but from behind it he saw two men paddle into sight in a small rubber raft. One was carrying a rifle, and the other was rowing toward Marriner with strong, even strokes of a small paddle.

Marriner squirmed back in the undergrowth, got to his feet and trotted toward the other end of the island. This promised to be a deadly game of hide-and-go-seek.

X

November, 1943

If ever, Cortney Anders promised himself, I get out of this
mother of a thunderstorm there is a thing I will do if it is the last act
of my life. I will catch that useless sonofabitch Crowley, and I will
jam those gold wings of his up his ass!

For twenty minutes Anders had wrestled his plane through the
roughest, dirtiest weather he had ever experienced. And he had done
it in a white-hot anger. Perhaps the anger had kept him alive.

In the black, wind-tossed frenzy of the storm he had called forth
every skill he possessed and then had borrowed some on credit. He
shoved on full climbing power and watched his altimeter unwind as
a downdraft hurled him toward the boiling waters below. He chopped
off the power, dropped his wheels, held the stick full forward in diving position and watched with horror as his altimeter climbed steadily
as the plane was caught in a vicious updraft. At the mercy of the
titanic wind he flew upside down, right side up, and on his side.

Sweat filled his eyes and ran down into his collar. Blood seeped
from a bitten lip, and his fingers were cramped from the deathhold
he maintained on the stick and throttle.

He wrestled with the controls, fought the rudder and cursed the
elements, and finally he felt the fury of the storm lessen. The shriek
of the wind lowered, and the beat of hail against the sides of his plane
muted to the sound of rain slapping on the windshield.

Then the darkness of the storm gave way to a lighter, grayish,
swirling mist, and finally Anders flew into sunlight and back to the
world of the living. He felt as if he had been lost in Hell.

Now he set a course which would circumvent the storm and get
him to the target. He was steadying on a westerly heading when he

[172

saw Crowley's plane below him heading southeast toward the task force.

At first the enormity of the truth eluded him. Then he understood! Why that lousy, mother-biting bastard is running away from it. So it was true, all of it. Nearly kills off the air group and maybe he succeeded for all I know. Gets me in that mother of a storm and then sneaks out and runs for home. Guys he is supposed to be leading fighting and dying all over the place, and he runs for home.

Anders pushed over, knowing his altitude advantage would give him the speed he needed to catch Crowley, who was below and slightly ahead.

Anders decided to shoot Crowley out of the sky. But as he closed on his plane something on the water below snagged a corner of his attention and perhaps saved Crowley's life.

A Jap twin-engine Betty bomber was flat-hatting along at sea-top level. It was only one mile off his starboard bow, and he could plainly make out the red meatball on its fuselage.

Lieutenant Sako Sakai had drunk a farewell toast that morning in the operations hut on Betio Island. It had been a grave moment as they raised the tiny saki cups in a gesture of understanding and sayonara. Lt. Sakai had then gone alone to a room where he had wrapped his body in a flag of the Rising Sun and had bowed respectfully before a picture of the Emperor. Then Sakai and his crew had taken off from Betio in their bomb-laden airplane to hunt out the American fleet and sink one of its major carriers, with his bombs if he could, by diving his airplane into it if all else failed.

Anders yelled into his mike, "Charlie Leader. Two o'clock on the water. On the deck. Get into it."

Crowley's plane did not deviate from its course. Obviously, Anders realized, the CAG had shut his radio off in the storm and had not turned it back on. He brought his plane down on the water and moved in behind the Betty.

Sako Sakai had no premonition of disaster. He had resolved to die for the Emperor if need be. If he did, back in the town of Sendai they would bury his flight scarf which he had sent home, and they would pay him honor as a hero who had died for the Emperor and had taken an American carrier with him when he went.

Sakai was anticipating meeting certain revered ancestors in the hereafter when Anders' first shells blasted into the flight compartment of the Betty. The sudden roar at first stupefied Sakai. He glanced at his co-pilot and gaped when he saw that one of the shells had hit the co-pilot in the neck and nearly torn his head off. The trunk slumped forward, arterial blood flooding from the neck, and Sakai had to reach out and shove the body back before it fell against the control column and sent the Betty careening into the water.

Then Sakai took evasive action. He turned hard right, pulled back on the stick and wheeled the Mitsubishi bomber into as tight a circle as it could maintain.

The abrupt maneuver threw Anders' aim off, and his shells passed behind Sakai.

It was the fierce flame of the tracers which alerted Crowley, three thousand feet above, to the spectacle of the Hellcat and the unwieldy, relatively defenseless Betty. He peeled off and roared down.

Anders swung in again and chopped off a little throttle, losing a few knots of airspeed and enabling his plane to pull in as tight a circle as the Betty. Now he inched his nose ahead of the Betty's flight path and brought his guns to bear in such manner that he could fire ahead of the enemy plane with the proper mill lead. He managed a quick burst before the Betty swung over into a tight turn in the opposite direction.

Anders' quick burst took its toll. One shell hit Sakai in the small of the back, just above his belt buckle. Sakai let out a great heaving sigh as the pain swept over him. The strength left his hands, and the Betty straightened and flew a steady course, wings level. Sakai was conscious only of the all-consuming agony which boiled in his midsection.

Anders swung in for the no-deflection kill shot. Right smack dab on his ass. No deflection and shoot dead ahead and hold the trigger down. This is Sunday-go-to-meeting time and good-bye Mr. Tojo. Yes sir. This is a bright and sunlit day, and all is well with the world. Is it not, Mr. Tojo? Ho hum and yo-de-do. Hit the trigger again, Cortney my boy. That Betty isn't going anywhere at all.

Anders' long burst filled Sakai's cockpit, but Sakai was already dead. The Betty was flying by its own trim, with a dead man's hands on the wheel. Sakai died with his eyes open, looking ahead to the doorway where his ancestors waited with his white flying scarf in their hands.

Anders did not see Crowley coming in. He was ready to fire the final burst that would consign the Betty to the water. In fact his finger was tightening on the trigger when Crowley flew directly between

[174

Anders' plane and the already doomed Betty. Crowley opened fire immediately, and the enemy plane shook as Crowley fired point-blank.

The Betty flew into the water and exploded.

Anders was filled with a disgust. Crowley had taken the kill away from him. Briefly he wondered if he shouldn't have gone ahead and fired and the hell with Crowley if he had been hit. The disgust ripened into a rage, and Anders pounded his fist on the canopy.

"Join up, Anders." Crowley's voice was buoyant.

"I will have a word with you when we land, Commander," said Anders as he moved up on Crowley's wing. Crowley said nothing, and they flew back toward the task force.

Captain Balta was the first to spot the incoming planes. He had been on the outer bridge since daylight.

"Mr. MacNamara. Get word to the Admiral that the strike planes are approaching the screen."

He watched the planes take shape over the outer screen of destroyers. He tried to count them, but it was not really necessary. The formation was appreciably smaller now than when it had flown out in the dawn's first light.

"Turn up that radio," Balta bawled to the OD on the inner bridge. Balta recognized Hill's voice as the radio blared.

"Charlie Leader from Charlie One. I am taking my division down first. We are short on fuel."

"Negative Charlie One. I will land first."

Winston's voice came over the air. "Charlie One from Two Three. I am reading empty. Request immediate landing."

"Go down first, Two Three," replied Hill.

"I said negative," came Crowley's voice.

"Go down Two Three," repeated Hill. "If Charlie Leader cuts you out of the pattern I'll shoot him down myself."

"You won't have to, Charlie One," came Anders' voice. "This is Leader Two, and I'll do it myself."

"What the hell goes on here?" It was Delacrois's angry voice. "What kind of a rat-race are we running?"

Balta nodded to the Admiral. "It's nothing, sir. A slight misunderstanding up there."

The Admiral rubbed a hand over his face as he watched the planes milling above.

175]

"They didn't all make it, Sam." He drew a long breath and expelled it slowly.

"What did you expect, sir?" Balta replied.

"I expected nothing. I merely hoped."

"You'll have other occasions to hope, Admiral."

The first division broke off, and the lead plane followed Winston up the groove. Balta watched approvingly as the planes swept in over the fantail in perfect landing passes, received their cuts and screeched into the arresting wires.

And so they came home. Tired and sweaty but triumphant, and they held up various combinations of fingers as they taxied past the island so the Admiral and the Captain could see the number of the enemy they had accounted for.

"I will want to debrief the flight leaders," said Delacrois. "As soon as they have landed."

"Of course, sir." Balta would have preferred to see them alone before the Admiral's sharp questions could pry the trouble out into the open. He watched Hill get out of his plane and speak with the young officer who had piloted the first plane to land.

Delacrois paced the bridge nervously. Balta watched him, understanding the man's dilemma. The Admiral gently hit the railing with a clenched fist and turned troubled eyes to Balta.

"Twenty Zeros never did that damage, Sam."

"We'll know soon enough. They could have got it from antiaircraft."

"Horseshit the man said," said Delacrois. "They don't shoot that well."

"Well," remarked Balta, "take it easy, Admiral. You've got a long day ahead."

"Goddammit, stop calling me Admiral."

"I remember when it was Lieutenant Delacrois. You were more relaxed then."

Delacrois smiled. "Good old Sam. Bring me back whenever I forget, will you?"

"Always have," Balta said, watching Hill and a young ensign come onto the bridge area.

"Well, Hill?" said the Admiral.

"They were waiting for us, sir. Nearly a hundred Zeros."

"How many men did you lose?"

[176

"I make it twenty-three, sir. A couple of bail-outs over Tarawa that we won't get back." Hill hesitated. "It could have been worse, sir."

"How do you mean that?" asked Balta.

"We nearly didn't make the target at all."

Delacrois frowned. "Explain that, please."

"I'd prefer to let Commander Crowley do that, sir." Hill's voice held a hint of anger.

"Skipper?" Winston said tentatively.

"I've got a man down on an island forty miles east of Tarawa, sir," Hill said.

"What kind of shape?" Delacrois spoke curtly.

Winston said, "We circled him, sir. He's okay, but we'd better get him out before the Japs get him."

Delacrois looked at Balta. "We've got no way to get him out. I can't send a destroyer all the way in. Maybe in a few days but not now. I can't chance it, Sam."

"There's a way, sir," said Hill. He looked at Balta. "There's an OS2U seaplane lashed against the overhead on the hangar deck."

"What the hell is an aircraft carrier doing with a seaplane on the hangar deck?" Delacrois's voice was incredulous. "Carriers don't use OS2Us."

"This one does," Balta said. "I brought it along just in case something like this happened. I request permission to launch the OS2U, Admiral."

"Hell yes, launch it. Now. Send it off the catapult on the hangar deck. Get that boy back here."

"I'll fly it, sir," said Hill.

"A question, sir," Winston said to Hill. "I think I ought to fly it, Skipper. I know where the island is and where Marriner went down. Besides I have a reason to get him out."

"What's the reason, Ensign?" asked Balta.

"I left him out there, sir. I want to bring him back."

"He's right," Hill said. "I'll fly the escort. How about it, Admiral?"

Delacrois nodded to Balta.

"MacNamara," Balta yelled. "Get that Kingfisher ready for a hangar deck launch."

Anders did not have his word with Crowley when they were on the deck. MacNamara was waiting for them with a summons to the

177]

bridge. The Admiral and Balta were bending over a table map of Tarawa Atoll when Crowley and Anders appeared.

"Commander," said Delacrois, "make this short. I want your summary of the action over the target."

"Due to unavoidable circumstances, sir, I did not reach the target."

The Admiral glanced at Balta, puzzled. "You didn't get to the target at all?"

"We encountered a heavy front, sir," said Crowley. "I estimated its height at twenty thousand feet and figured to climb over it. I entered the front climbing. Commander Hill evidently didn't follow my thinking and took the strike planes around another way."

The Admiral looked at Anders who said, "That front was forty thousand feet high, sir."

"Ensign Anders is new at this, Admiral. The front was half that high," Crowley insisted.

"I see." The Admiral spoke again to Anders. "Go on, young man."

"The storm got too rough, sir. We spun out at twenty-five thousand feet. I lost Commander Crowley on the recovery and didn't find him again until we were both in the clear."

"Then if Hill hadn't taken the strike around the front they all would have been loused up in there. Is that right?" The Admiral's voice was cold.

"I didn't spin out at all," Crowley said. "When I realized the turbulence was getting worse, I came around on a reciprocal heading."

"What about it?" Delacrois asked Anders.

Anders shrugged. "It could have been that way, sir."

"Why didn't you head for the target when you came out of the front, Commander?"

"I started to, sir," Crowley said. "But I spotted a Jap Betty on the water and went after it."

The Admiral glanced at Anders, who murmured, "He did like hell."

"What is your story, Ensign?" Delacrois asked him.

"I had the Betty cold," Anders said. "Commander Crowley came in at the last moment and got off a burst. I think the pilots were already dead." Anders looked at Crowley. "When I spotted the Commander first he was flying on a heading that would have taken him back to the task force."

"You didn't try to make the target?" Delacrois asked Crowley.

[178

"I was plotting my position, sir. If there was time, I intended to make for Tarawa after we got the Betty."

"After the Betty, then. You still had time to get there. What did you do?"

Anders answered in a disgusted voice. "We came back and circled the task force for a half hour, sir. Till the others came home."

"It was too late. I didn't intend to fly into the target after the attack was over with only a two-plane section, sir. It would have been foolhardy."

"Of course," muttered Delacrois. "Foolhardy."

Balta spoke up. "Did you have your gun camera on, Commander? When you shot down the Betty, I mean?"

"I did, sir."

"And you, Ensign?"

"Yes, sir. I blew half the cockpit away. The films will show it."

"Well," said the Admiral, "we'll have to wait for Hill to get back to find out what happened over the target." He turned to Crowley. "In the future, Commander, I suggest you make a more determined effort to reach the target area. However, well done on that Betty. Both of you."

After Crowley and Anders had gone, the Admiral said to Balta, "I want to see the gun camera films from both those airplanes, Sam. Something smells around here."

"Crowley."

"Not necessarily. But we'll see. I can't understand a man leading a strike force into thunderhead cloud. It's murder."

"A man can do stupid things when he's frightened, Admiral."

"Let's not judge till we know more, Sam. Give the man a break."

"But he wasn't there, Frog. He never got there. The others did the fighting, and he circled the ship, goddammit. Hill's pilot is out there on a lousy piece of island because he did the fighting. Crowley circled the ship, and I can't forget that."

"Speaking of Hill, there he goes now."

On the starboard catapult Hill's plane was winding up in a full-throated roar. The cat officer dropped his arm, and the plane leaped down the track and off the bow. Stepik followed and then Bates. From below on the hangar deck another engine roared, and then the OS2U appeared climbing from below the flight deck and arcing away into the sky. Hill and his two wingmen circled until Winston joined on them, and shortly they disappeared westward.

179]

For an hour Marriner had crouched behind the undergrowth at the far end of the island. He had seen the two Japanese come ashore in the rubber raft. At first he had thought they would separate and try to close in on him from two sides. But as the minutes lengthened he decided they were going to wait him out. Perhaps they had got word to someone and expected reinforcements. What the hell to do now? He could sit there and wait to be captured. He could try to swim for it, but there was no place to swim to. He had a pistol and they had a rifle. No odds there. They knew he was alone and had no way of getting off this lousy hunk of sand.

He listened carefully, but there was not a sound on the island. Stretching to his left was a clean sweep of sandy beach that circled the far end of the island. In front of him was a solid growth of coconut palms. The beach to his right was rock-strewn where it was not pure coral. He did not have to worry about the Japs coming from his right. He wondered briefly if his cartridges were dampened by the water and if they would fire. For the fifth time he wiped the action on his .38 with a handful of leaves. He felt reassuringly for the heavy knife on his hip.

Ensign Hiro Yoshida had lost face. The 701 had been his first command, and now it would probably be his last. He was infuriated with himself for his stupidity in leaving the camouflaged anchorage before the American planes had disappeared. He had lost three crewmen and his ship, and his disgrace would be unbearable unless he could bring back the American prisoner in chains.

He reasoned he had only to keep the American on the island until a destroyer or a seaplane could arrive from Kwajalein. This task should prove easy enough. He had a rifle, and he knew the American had only a revolver.

He ordered his crewman to keep a close watch on the right-hand side of the island while he watched the left. It was improbable the American would move before nightfall, but Yoshida had taken the last chance he was going to take that day.

Marriner had a decision to make. Was he going to wait for them to get reinforcements to come and get him? He held little hope that the task force could send a ship a hundred and fifty miles into enemy waters to get him out. At least not until after the landings, and they were four days away. He didn't have a chance in hell of hiding out

[180

here for four days. Not with those two Japs somewhere on the island.

The solution? Get rid of the two Japs. Marriner decided to wait until nightfall and make his play for the enemy.

Actually Winston in the OS2U made Marriner's decision for him. When Marriner heard the first far-off rumble of the plane engine he thought it was a Jap seaplane. But as the plane swung around over the island he recognized the familiar lines of the Kingfisher even before he saw the markings on the fuselage.

Marriner's problem abruptly became more acute. The Japs had a rifle, and the pilot of that OS2U would be a sitting duck when he set down in the lagoon.

Marriner slid his knife into the scabbard and pistol in hand moved silently into the grove of coconut palms.

Yoshida saw the OS2U too and smiled. Perhaps, he thought, he might even gain face this day. Two American pilots and an American airplane. He watched as the plane began a long gliding turn, losing altitude and heading toward the lagoon.

Marriner was halfway up the island now, crawling on his hands and knees, his pistol sweaty in his hand, his heart banging against his ribs. He had to get to the Japs before that poor bastard in the plane got himself killed.

Yoshida had taken position behind a large log. He rested the gun barrel on the log and tracked the plane down, keeping the bubbled canopy in his sights.

The noise of the plane engine allowed Marriner to get within a few feet of the Jap crewman. Yoshida with his rifle had his back to him when the crewman turned suddenly, startled as Marriner's foot crunched something on the ground. Before he had time to cry out Marriner lunged with his knife, plunging the blade into the man's stomach. Even as he felt the knife sink home Marriner twirled the Jap around and threw his arm across his throat, cutting off the incipient cry. He tightened his forearm against the Jap's windpipe and with his left hand grasped the knife hilt and struck again and again at the man's body. Then he quietly let the body slip to the ground.

Ensign Yoshida, intent on tracking Winston's approach, did not hear Marriner moving quietly behind him. Marriner, not at all certain that his gun would fire, decided to use the knife again.

Winston leveled off over the glassy water of the lagoon and set the Kingfisher down gently. He was taxiing toward the shore when Yoshida moved out from his cover and drew a bead on the defenseless pilot. He had raised the rifle to his shoulder when Marriner raced out onto the beach and dove at his knees. The two figures rolled over the sand. A knife flashed in the sun.

Marriner heard the life sigh out of Yoshida. He gave the knife a final vicious twist and got to his feet, trembling, and looked down as the Jap gave a last heave and died. Marriner turned and walked down to the water.

In the flag office the Admiral handed Captain Balta a half-filled tumbler of whiskey.

"Those two young men," Delacrois said. "I'm going to give them a medal. DFCs, I think."

"A good idea, Frog. What about Hill?"

"A good man. He saved us today. I don't think he overestimated the results. We gave them a licking, Sam. Today should clear the way for the landings on the 20th. The other carriers all but wiped out Mille Atoll. I think we'll head north of Tarawa and wait for the amphibious force."

Balta studied the glass in his hand. He wiped a bead of sweat from it and contemplated his finger carefully.

"Frog. What about Crowley?"

"Crowley?" Delacrois allowed a puzzled look to appear on his face. "What about Crowley?"

"You know damn well what about Crowley. He flunked his exam today."

"No, Sam. *Maybe* he flunked his exam today." The Admiral did not want to wrestle with the problem of Crowley now. After all, Crowley might have been telling the truth. That other pilot, what was his name? Anders? He was young, and this was his first combat mission. It was easy to get screwed up on your first mission. At least Delacrois allowed himself to believe this.

"Look, Sam. Air group commanders aren't easy to come by. Nothing on Crowley's record indicates he won't carry through. Christ, man. He's got a Navy Cross."

Yes, thought Balta, and goddam it, I gave it to him. Then, because he knew the Admiral had weightier things to live with, he laughed and said, "Okay, Frog. We'll make do with him. But I'd rather have Hill up there in front."

"So would I. But I don't think Hill would like it. He's happy where he is."

[182

"Thank God for the Hills," Balta said. "I wonder what old men like us would do without them."

"Make do with the Crowleys, I suppose."

Balta nodded, saluted and left the office. Delacrois watched him go and felt the warm glow that comes from a friendship that is cemented by long years of comradeship in a way of life that is much like a priesthood in its selectivity. His hand gently rubbed the three stars on his collar and he thanked Sam Balta silently for being what and where he was. He walked out to the bridge and gave orders to make speed for a position north of Tarawa.

Long after the flight had landed and the planes had been parked on the flight deck, the fighter ready room was still a loud mixture of young voices, curse words, waving arms and wild tales.

"I had the bastard on his back, and he was pulling through too tight. I let him go and sure enough the stupid shit did a high speed stall at twelve hundred feet and went in on his back. Burned on the water."

"We found them under a cloud at angels eight. Three of them and they must have been in primary. Didn't know their ass from third base. Scattered and ran, and we got all three."

"Did anyone see that Zero with all the flags painted all the Christ over the side of the plane? Who the hell was he?"

"Marriner fought him. Fought him to a draw."

"Jesus. What a fight that was."

"Where's Marriner? That bastard can teach me any time he feels like it."

"Hey, Marriner. How was that guy? He looked good."

"Yeah. He was good. About as good as I expect to meet."

"You get him? Did the bastard burn?"

"No. No, I didn't get him. He got away. Maybe some other day."

"Well, tough luck. Jesus. What a fight."

"How about that Crowley?"

"You can have him for my money. All two cents of it."

"Somebody said he got a Betty."

"How about it, Anders? You were flying on him. That no-show get a Betty?"

"Maybe. He shot at it anyway."

"How was it on that island, Marriner? Lonesome?"

The squadron duty officer touched Hill on the arm. "The air group commander would like to see you in his quarters, Skipper."

185]

"Thanks," Hill said. So Crowley wanted to see him. Well, he wanted to see Crowley too. Hill threaded his way through the room and stopped at the blackboard on the forward bulkhead. He took a piece of chalk and wrote in large letters:

WETTING-DOWN PARTY
HILL'S QUARTERS
1900-2030

He acknowledged the rousing cheers with a wave and headed for Crowley's quarters.

Crowley was sitting at his desk examining papers when Hill's knock sounded on the door. He looked up and said, "Come in."

Hill watched Crowley as the air group commander inspected a sheet of paper he held in his hand.

"Hill," Crowley said, "you don't seem to be able to instill discipline into your enlisted people." He put the paper down.

"You're speaking of Chief Rasmussen," Hill said softly. "I saw the report you made out on him."

"What action have you taken?"

"Not a goddam bit. Rasmussen's my leading Chief."

"Since when," Crowled asked, "are leading Chiefs exempt from charges of insolence?"

"Do you mean to tell me," Hill said slowly, "you got me up here to discuss an insubordination report on a Chief?"

"What I get you up here for is my own business," Crowley said sharply. "Watch yourself, Hill. I'm the air group commander around here."

"More's the pity," Hill said brutally.

Crowley flushed. "You're not indispensable, Hill."

"You are, I suppose. Listen, Crowley." Hill leaned his fists on the edge of Crowley's desk. "I'm sick and tired of your chicken-shit. We both know what you did today and by Christ, I've got half a mind to make an issue of it. I told my guys to shut up because I don't want to see this air group ruined before it gets started. I'll even take a chance on you to save it, and that's like betting on the Little League to beat the New York Yankees. But listen very close now, you mealy-mouthed sonofabitch. You ran today. Just like you did at Midway. I can't prove it, but then again I don't have to prove it, do I? You claimed a plane that Anders shot down, and that is about as horseshit as a man can get out here. You're a disgrace to the

[184

wings and the uniform and to the men who have to fly under you."

Crowley was on his feet, his face a stain of black, murderous rage. "I'll have you court-martialed for this!"

"You do that. You just do that. I may even demand a court. I'd like to see your face when I testify under oath and my guys testify. You'd be crucified, you useless bastard, and you know it."

Hill's words had come fast and hard. Now he took a deep breath, and the flush left his face.

"Listen, Crowley," he said almost wearily, "I'm not out to crucify you. Christ. I pity you. Your stinking failures are safe with me until such time as they threaten the well-being of any member of this air group. Then I'll blast you all over God's green acre. Stay away from me and don't lean on me. And don't try to touch any of my men."

Crowley looked at the man before him and swallowed his bitter anger and frustration.

"Tear up that goddam report on Chief Rasmussen," Hill said.

Crowley did not move. He sat and looked up at Hill, and all the hate a human mind could conceive was in his eyes.

"I said tear up that report," Hill repeated.

Crowley's voice was a barely audible whisper, a choked and strangled hiss. "I'll get you, Hill. Damn you, I'll get you."

"If somebody doesn't stop you, you're liable to get everyone in the air group," Hill said. And then because he did not really want to destroy this man he added, "For Christ's sake, Crowley. Face up to it, man. Ask for a change of orders. Tell them anything. Tell them you can't sleep or you've got asthma or your back aches. Tell them your eyes are going bad. Why drive yourself against this thing? You don't belong out here. Not leading this group. You know it and I know it, and if you don't stop pretty soon everybody on this goddam ship will know it."

"You'd like that, wouldn't you, Hill? You'd like to take over this air group." Crowley's voice shrilled, and his face twisted in anger. "Well, I'll tell you something. If anybody goes, it won't be me. You hear me? I'll be in the next promotion list for Captain, and if you think I'm going to let you or anyone like you screw me up you're all wet. And another thing. I've got a Navy Cross, and any lousy lies you start spreading about me, who the hell do you think will listen to you? Do you think you'll ever get a Navy Cross? Like hell you will. I'm the commander of this group, and I'll be the one who gives the orders. Understand?"

185]

"Oh for Christ's sake," Hill said. This bastard hasn't understood a thing I've said. He's scared and he's dangerous because any frightened man in his position is dangerous. He can destroy this air group, and he will unless somebody stops him. Who else is there but me? How did I get in the middle here? I'm thirty years old, and a third of my life has been dedicated to this service and this business of flying. There are other men with more rank on their collars who should handle this job. They caused it, and they should accept this responsibility. But no one has stepped forward so I am left with this sonofabitch.

"I told you to tear up that report," Hill said.

Crowley smiled and slowly ripped the sheet of paper in two. "I intended to tear it up anyway, Hill," Crowley said. "Rasmussen isn't really at fault after all. You're the one who's at fault. You failed to instill discipline into an enlisted man under your command. You're lousy officer material, Hill, and it will be noted on your fitness report."

"Remember what I said, Crowley. Don't lean on me or my men. I won't say anything about what happened this morning up there, and neither will Anders." Hill slowly shook his head. "But you can't beat this thing. I don't enjoy saying this to any man, Crowley, but sometimes it's the only way. You're a coward, Crowley, which is bad enough, but you've compounded it by becoming a liar to boot."

"Get out of here, God damn you. Get out of here."

"A pleasure," Hill said. He paused at the door and shook his head sadly. "You know, Crowley, I could be sorry for a man who owned up. Who admitted he was in the wrong place at the wrong time. It's no disgrace to be unable to face certain things. Most of us have experienced that at some time or another. But to hide from it for the sake of a lousy captain's eagle when you endanger the lives of other men, then it becomes damn near criminal."

Hill shut the door softly and left Crowley staring bleakly at the bare metal panels of the door. There was no sound in the room, and there was no one to watch as tears slowly flooded Crowley's cheeks.

Chief Rasmussen moved quietly through the enlisted crew quarters, diligently inspecting the bodies sprawled in the tiered bunks until he came upon Machinist's Mate 2nd O'Toole.

"O'Toole?" The still form did not move. Rasmussen leaned down and grabbed a handful of O'Toole's red hair. He raised O'Toole's head about eight inches from the pillow and abruptly rammed it back down against the iron guardrail at the head of the bunk.

[186

"Jesus!" roared O'Toole. "Oh, it's you, Chief. What the hell you doing?" He rubbed the back of his head.

Rasmussen sat on the edge of the bunk. "There's a small matter I wish to discuss with you, O'Toole."

"Yeah? Okay. What gives?"

"You know, Irish," Rasmussen began slowly, "I'm going to need another first-class mech. I think I may make you a first class despite your drinking."

"No kiddin', Chief? Hell, I don't drink no more'n the rest of the guys. Hold it better too."

"Sure you do. Like the last liberty in Pearl. It took three MPs to get you back."

"Them lousy army crumbs."

"Another little matter, Irish. Number 00, the air group commander's plane. Did you read the yellow sheet after the hop this morning?"

"Naw, Chief. I was helpin' O'Malley on number thirty-four."

"Well, it seems there is an appendage to the yellow sheet regarding unexplained engine noises that occurred at 25,000 feet. You know anything about such noises?"

A grin split O'Toole's face. "No kiddin', Chief? What noises?"

"Well," said Rasmussen, "I went to the trouble to climb up and look around the cockpit after I gave the engine a run-up and everything was working just fine. Guess what I found looking around that cockpit, Irish?"

"A turd," O'Toole said. "The crud probably crapped in his pants."

"Not at all. You may find it hard to believe this, but I found the remnants of a rubber tied to a seat brace. Now you don't suppose Commander Crowley was screwing a broad up there in that plane today, do you, Irish?"

"Well, for crissake. Now what do you know about that! How you figure Crowley got a broad up there with him?"

"It poses a question, Irish. But Commander Crowley says that whatever it was that caused the explosion, it nearly made him lose control of his airplane. This might have been serious."

"Serious? Balls. Not to a pilot who knows a goddam thing. That crud would spin out if the wind blew too hard."

Rasmussen nodded judiciously. "Perhaps. But we're not in the contraceptive business, Irish. Try to remember this."

187]

"But he put you on report, Chief. *You*. The leadin' goddam Chief."

"No. He tried to put me there. The Skipper took care of it. From the looks of him I'd say he and Crowley went round and round."

"Well, I'm not sorry, Chief. That crud had it comin'."

Rasmussen smiled. "I didn't come down here to chew you out, Irish. I came to tell you you'll be making first class in a matter of days. Don't let me down." He got to his feet and stood looking down on the younger man. "And take it easy on the air group commander."

"Jesus, Chief. I got nothin' to do with the crud. None of us guys gets the time of day from him. You wanta talk to a guy who kisses his ass, why, talk to Rathburn over there."

"Who?" Rasmussen asked.

"Rathburn. That kid over there at the table." O'Toole nodded his head in the direction of a large table set against the bulkhead where a young sailor in a T-shirt sat reading a book.

"Whoever he is," said Rasmussen, "he needs a haircut."

"He's a new mech with Bombing Two. Doubles with the ammo crew. He knows the CAG better'n anybody."

Rasmussen looked sharply at O'Toole, aware of a sudden, sly innuendo in the sailor's voice.

"How do you mean that?"

"How do I mean it?" O'Toole's voice had a hard edge. "How often you ever hear of an air group commander inviting an enlisted mech to his quarters? And givin' him *booze?*"

Rasmussen frowned. "I don't believe it."

"Well, don't take my word for it. Randall, the yeoman, went up there to deliver a message and found Rathburn drinking whiskey with the CAG."

"This sort of thing happen often?"

"Hell, yes. That Rathburn don't stand watches or nothin' else."

Rasmussen smiled. "Sounds like you're red-assed, Irish."

"Me? Naw, Chief. I don't give a good goddam what Rathburn does. Some of the other guys, though, they can't take him."

The Chief patted O'Toole's shoulder absently. "See you later, Irish. I'll let you know when you make first class." He walked slowly across the room and sat down across from Rathburn.

"Reading something good there?" Rasmussen spoke in a friendly tone. The youngster looked up.

[188

"Oh, Chief. Yeah." He laughed embarrassedly and held up the book for inspection. *"Indian Love Lyrics,"* he said. "A favorite of mine."

Rasmussen watched him closely. "I read them a long time ago. I had a favorite." He squinted his eyes in concentration. "About a girl captured by thieves, I think it was."

"Sure," said Rathburn. "That's in here. Near the back of the book, I think." He thumbed through the pages as Rasmussen got up and moved to his side, to stand peering over his shoulder.

"Here it is," Rathburn said.

Rasmussen leaned over to look at the book, and as he did so he rested his hand on the boy's naked shoulder. He pretended an interest in the poem.

"Yeah," he said. "That's the one, sure enough." He let his hand run back and forth across the boy's shoulder and neck in an almost fatherly fashion. Then he straightened up and looked down into Rathburn's eyes, praying he would not see what he did see.

Rathburn's eyes stared up at him in mute appeal. There was the hurt, scared look of a trapped animal and another thing too. A thing that shunned the light of day.

"Yeah, kid," Rasmussen said sadly. "Those are good poems." To himself he added, You poor, misguided, sick sonofabitch.

Then, because he wanted out of this mood, he said sharply, "I suggest you get a haircut, Rathburn."

The boy dropped his eyes. "Sure, Chief. Tomorrow I'll get one."

Rasmussen left the crew's quarters, afraid of what he had found there. He swore bitterly at the way of things.

"Try some more of this roast beef, Barry." The Admiral was eating with obvious good appetite, as was Sam Balta. Barry Wheeler, as junior officer present, had preserved the amenities and had thus far consumed only one rather slim slab of the succulent roast.

"You talked me into it, sir," Wheeler said, spearing a large end cut. "My compliments to your chef whoever he is."

Delacrois looked up. "Don't think I eat like this every night. Tonight's an occasion."

"Oh?" said Balta.

"A celebration." Delacrois smiled. "The air group did splendidly today. Splendidly. Or is that bad English?"

"It's marvelous English," Sam Balta said. He heaped a mound of mashed potatoes onto his plate. "Yes, Admiral, splendidly is exactly the word."

"You can thank Harry Hill," Barry Wheeler said.

"I intend to," Delacrois admitted. "With a DFC."

"He's got one," Balta said. "Give him something else."

"Okay," Delacrois agreed. "You write him up. Make it whatever you want."

"A Silver Star then," Wheeler suggested. The Admiral nodded.

"You talked further with Hill?" the Admiral asked Balta.

"No, sir. But Barry did."

"I had a drink with Harry on my way up here," Wheeler said.

"You did, eh? He have anything to say?"

Wheeler looked uncomfortable. "No, sir. Nothing special."

The Admiral wiped his mouth with a napkin and loosened his belt a notch. "Had nothing to say about Crowley?"

"No, sir," said Wheeler.

"Have you?" asked Delacrois.

Wheeler frowned. "I don't think I understand, sir."

"The hell you don't," said Delacrois. He looked at Balta, who had assumed an air of angelic innocence.

"You already know my sentiments, Admiral," said Balta.

"You feel the same way?" Delacrois asked Wheeler.

"No, sir, he does not," answered Balta.

"Goddam it, Sam. Let him answer for himself."

"Well, Admiral," Wheeler said carefully, "all I can say is that the attack apparently was successful. We beat them in the air. That's welcome news for a new air group. They measured up."

"Did Crowley, in your opinion?" The Admiral kept punching relentlessly.

Wheeler shrugged. "I'm an executive officer. I work in an office down in the wardroom area. I don't know what goes on in the sky anymore."

"Sam," Delacrois said, "will you make this young man answer me?"

"Crowley had a bad morning," Wheeler admitted. "But nothing that couldn't have happened to anyone else. He spun out in a storm. Who the hell hasn't?" Wheeler looked at Balta. "Have you, Captain Iscariot?"

"Never," Balta admitted modestly.

[190

"Did you," Delacrois asked of Wheeler, "look at the gun camera films of Crowley's kill on that Betty?"

"Yes, sir."

"And what did you think?"

Wheeler inspected the ceiling for thirty seconds before he answered. "I think that Anders shot that plane down, sir. But that does not mean that Crowley mightn't have *thought* he shot it down. Things can get confused up there, Admiral."

"I'd like to remind you," Delacrois said dryly, "that I too have been 'up there,' as you so quaintly phrase it. Plainly speaking, Commander, do you think Crowley phonied that claim?"

"I can't say, sir." Wheeler shook his head. "He could have figured he made the kill."

"And what about the storm?"

"Yes," Balta said, "what about the storm, Clarence Darrow? You want to defend this man. Tell us about the storm. By what magnificent thought processes did Crowley decide to enter that storm front when any five-year-old can tell you a Hellcat Fighter is incapable of climbing over a forty-thousand-foot weather front?"

Wheeler laughed softly. "I refuse to be baited. I'm the exec of this ship. I'm not running a critique on combat operations. Ask me an easy one."

"All right," said Balta. "We'll give Crowley his due. We've nothing definite against the man. Not yet. But I think if some people would talk we would tear the hide off that man. He frightens me."

"Nothing frightens you."

"Age," the Admiral said solemnly, "is the greatest barrier against fear. Sam Balta has an abundance of age."

"I resent that," Balta protested. "And Admiral, before we adjourn this delightful dinner, let me ask one question. Have we heard anything regarding my new exec? I know Barry is sweating to get back to the States and turn fat and useless."

Wheeler did not see the quick wink Balta gave the Admiral.

Delacrois leaned back in his chair and regarded Barry Wheeler with a genuine warmth and affection. "In a hurry, Barry?"

Wheeler grinned. "I'm ready, sir, if that's what you mean."

"Well, let's hope he shows up before the next operation. I wouldn't want you to have to go along on that one. It might get pretty rough out there. No place for a short-timer."

"You expect it to be a big one, sir?" Wheeler could not keep the

191]

excitement out of his voice. "I mean, if I thought the Captain here really needed me . . . well, I wouldn't mind. . . ."

"Oh no," interrupted Balta. "I don't need short-timers mooning around my decks when the Jap fleet is waiting out there. Get in the way, get underfoot, mess things up in general. Who needs a man in a fight who has his mind set on things like sunlit beaches, warm beds, perfumed women? Oh no, thank you."

"I can't say as I blame you, Sam," said the Admiral.

"Wait a minute, Captain," began Wheeler.

"It's all right, Barry," Balta said, breathing a deep and deceitful sigh. "Don't apologize. We realize you've had enough."

"There are plenty of billets back in the training command. Ever been stationed at Pensacola, Barry?" asked the Admiral, his eyes twinkling.

"Only as a student," Wheeler admitted.

"Well, he won't find it so bad, Sam," said Delacrois. "Except for the flies and mosquitoes. Eat your goddam ass off all year long."

"At least they won't be shooting at him back there," Balta said. "Funny how a man's nerves wear thin when people keep trying to kill him. Some last longer than others. Something in the genes, I imagine."

"Oh certainly," agreed Wheeler, "something in the genes. No doubt about it."

"Well," sighed Balta, getting to his feet, "that's the way the ball bounces." He patted Wheeler gently on the back. "You were good in your day, Barry. Pretty damn good in your day."

"I thank you for the kind words, Captain."

The Admiral ushered both men to the door. "Barry," he said as they prepared to leave, "I've been thinking."

"Aha," snorted Balta.

"While we're in Pearl," he continued, "before your relief gets here, I think maybe it would do you good to keep your hand in. You never know what kind of duty you'll draw in the States. I mean maybe you ought to get some time in the Hellcat and make some field carrier landing practice. Good training, you know. Might try a little gunnery too. Just to keep sharp, of course."

"Of course," agreed Wheeler. "Looking at you two I have a feeling I'd damn well better keep pretty damn sharp. Okay, Admiral. Captain Balta, I am sure, will get me on a flight schedule."

"Glad to." Balta grinned. "Good night, Admiral. Thanks for a delicious dinner."

[192

As Captain Balta and Barry Wheeler left the Admiral's quarters, three decks below the air group commander tossed fretfully on his bunk as he sweated out another dream.

The sudden slap of a heavy wave against the side of the ship awakened him, and he sat up, shaking his clouded head. That goddam dream again, he thought fuzzily, not even sure where he was.

Then realization came to him, and the utter hopelessness of the entire day he had lived through washed over him, and he groaned. He got up and opened his desk safe and poured a strong drink. He swallowed it neat and waited for the familiar warmth to seep into his belly and lighten the black futility that engulfed him. He lit a cigarette and splashed cold water on his face. As he dried his face vigorously with a rough towel, the thought came to him, and he acted on it. He could not pause to consider because he knew if he did he would suffer shame again, and he had had enough of it that day.

He picked up his telephone and dialed a number. A voice answered on the phone.

"Is Rathburn there?" Crowley asked.

In a moment Rathburn's voice came over the line. Crowley's hands were wet with sweat, and he found himself holding the telephone so tightly his knuckles were white.

"Rathburn?" he said. "This is Commander Crowley. I'd like to talk to you about the new armament plan we're going to put into operation. Can you come up here for a minute?"

"Certainly, sir," said the voice. Crowley wondered if he detected a contemptuous note in it. "I'll be up in ten minutes, sir," Rathburn said.

Crowley slowly replaced the telephone. Now that he had done it he felt the familiar sense of relief. The whiskey was warm in his belly, and he felt a surging in his loins. He looked in the mirror at his flushed face, rubbed some after-shave lotion on it and then combed his hair carefully. He put the whiskey bottle out on the desk and placed two glasses alongside. Then he turned down the overhead light and left the desk lamp flooding the room with a soft, intimate glow.

He heard the sound of footsteps far down the corridor, and the last thing Crowley did before his visitor arrived was check the lock on his cabin door. It worked perfectly.

Winston found Marriner and Bates in the junior officers' bunkroom eating sardines and drinking whiskey.

193]

"Hi, Max," said Bates. "Where's Steve?"

"Writing letters as usual."

"That man writes more letters than anybody I know." Bates looked askance at Marriner. "Except Marriner maybe."

"There's a difference though," said Marriner. "Steve gets answers to his."

"You hear the scuttlebutt?" Winston asked.

"Which one?" Bates asked. "There's so many goddam rumors flying around this ship a man would think he was in a girls' dormitory."

"A sub report said the Jap fleet was pulling back from the Marshalls. They aren't going to fight."

"Why should they?" Bates said. "They can't hold these stinking little islands. They'll wait for a better day."

"They've got time," said Marriner. "We've got time. Everybody in the world has time. This goddam war may last forever."

"Dick." Winston's tone was serious. "I haven't thanked you for today. That Jap had me cold."

"The hell you say," said Marriner. "You would have made out. I got to him first, that's all. Any thanks to be given around here, I'll give them to you. You silly bastard, you could have gone in the drink today trying to save my ass."

"You're both a couple of heroes," Bates murmured. "Which brings up some more scuttlebutt. You're both getting medals, I hear. It will be nice flying with real live heroes. I feel honored."

"Horseshit." Marriner grinned. "I'll let you wear it on liberty."

"Stepik ought to get one too. He saved my ass today. Seems like everyone was saving everyone else's ass all morning. This fight may go down as the greatest ass-saving aerial engagement in history." Bates chuckled to himself.

"Well, anyway," Winston said, "thanks, Dick."

"It was a day, all right," mused Marriner. "I won't forget it."

"*You* won't forget it," exclaimed Bates. "What about me? I have to sleep in the same room with a man who kills with a knife. Christ knows what I might wake up to find. Some crazy, gibbering bastard standing over my bunk with a butcher knife in his hands. I may have to put in for a transfer."

Marriner laughed. "Any idea where?"

"Yeah," answered Bates. "Fort Shafter. I may become a WARD."

[194

XI

December, 1943

Doris would never forget that morning aboard the *Concord*. Years later she would still recall the broad expanse of flight deck and the rows of bronzed young men drawn to stiff attention. The sun beat down in the December heat, and the wind burned across the hot planks.

The invited guests sat in a tiered grandstand on the forward end of the flight deck, mopping their faces with soaked handkerchiefs and wondering what madness had brought them to come to a presentation ceremony on such a damnably hot day.

Admiral Delacrois had called Doris two days after the task force had returned to Pearl Harbor.

"Have you seen your young man yet?"

"I certainly have," Doris replied. "He tells me you're quite an admiral."

"Ah," said Delacrois. "Thank him for me. Seriously, Doris. Your young man has made something of a splash in the Navy pool. He did quite a job out there. Has he told you about it?"

"All he's done is blush when I asked him. His friends told me."

"Has he told you he's up for a medal?"

"Not a word. How do you like that? What kind of medal?"

"A Distinguished Flying Cross. Day after tomorrow, and I want you there as my guest."

"Front row center?"

"You can sit on his lap if you wish."

Doris laughed. "Thanks, Frog. I'll be there. Can I bring a friend?"

"Bring all you wish. It's a day these young men may declaim but they'll never forget. I don't think you will either."

"Is he going to be up there all by himself?"

"No. That entire flight seem to have undertaken to win this war all by themselves. They're all up for an award."

"Count me in, Frog. What time?"

"Be at the Main Gate at 1000."

"In English, please."

"Ten o'clock, and you know it as well as I do."

"Frog, I'm throwing a party for the squadron. Hell. Make it the whole air group. Will you be guest of honor?"

"Three stars may dampen the young men's spirits. May I bring Sam Balta?"

"You couldn't get in without him."

"Somehow Sam makes me feel my youth again."

"I'll bet you two were something."

"You're fortunate not to have been around. I'll tell Sam we'll both be the guests of honor."

"Fine, and I'll be on your flight deck day after tomorrow."

The Admiral's aide, a fleshy young man, was standing before a microphone amidships. The Admiral stood three feet behind his aide, and even from a distance Doris could see his freshly starched white dress uniform wilting. Why did the Navy insist on dressing its officers in whites when the heat hovered around one hundred degrees? Next to Delacrois, Sam Balta perspired with as much dignity as he could muster.

"Christ sake, Frog," Balta muttered. "If you don't get this crap over with you'll have to give me a Purple Heart."

"It would go well with your face," Delacrois murmured.

The aide was reading the citation for the next award, his voice distorted by the loudspeaker into a strong nasal tone.

"Ensign Richard Marriner. Front and center."

Marriner stepped forward, turned sharply, marched with precise steps to a spot in front of the Admiral, turned abruptly left and saluted.

"For extraordinary achievement in aerial flight as a fighter pilot in Fighting Squadron Two on 16 November, 1943 . . . shot down two enemy fighters . . . on an island in the Tarawa

[196

group did attack and single-handed . . . leaving both enemy dead in order to protect the life of . . . in keeping with the highest traditions of the Naval Service."

The Admiral stepped forward and pinned the small emblem on Marriner's breast, just above the gold wings. As the clasp snapped home Delacrois felt a brief fierce envy for the young man before him. This piece of metal he had pinned on Marriner's chest was something that had been denied him because he was far past the age at which men hurtled fighter planes through the sky, far past the age at which men were over the hill in this business. As Marriner saluted and about-faced, the aide was already reading the next citation.

"Ensign Maxwell Winston. Front and center."

Winston walked tall and proud, with his shoulders stiff and his head high. He faced the Admiral almost defiantly, as if to say, "Well now, we have fooled the both of us, haven't we?"

The aide's voice droned on:

"For extraordinary achievement in aerial flight as a fighter pilot in Fighting Squadron Two on 16 November, 1943 . . . did remain behind when his fuel was critical . . . at extreme peril to himself . . . did return to his ship and launching an OS2U to return to . . . set down the plane in the lagoon of the island . . . with utmost disregard for his own personal safety . . . to deliver his squadron mate from . . ."

Delacrois looked into Winston's eyes as he pinned the medal on his chest and envied Winston. And it was in this moment on the flight deck of the *Concord* that he realized that it was not because of Doris, because Doris was part of a life he had left behind, but because he was suddenly almost ashamed of his aging body. He had the thing that all of them strove for, the three stars, but he did not have and would never again have the thing he wanted and these men alone possessed, the youth that came only once.

He offered his hand to Winston, and he meant it when he said, "Well done, Ensign."

Other men stepped forward in their turn to be decorated, and finally the ceremony ended with the ship's band playing "Anchors Aweigh." Then Balta stepped to the microphone.

197]

"All hands . . . dis . . . MISSED." The neat rows dissolved into separate groups of earnest young officers comparing notes and admiring each other's medals. Balta wiped his forehead and turned to the Admiral.

"Let's get out of this heat before I have a stroke."

Delacrois cocked an eye at the sun. "How far above the yardarm would you say that sun is?"

"Far enough," replied Balta. "I suggest we repair to my quarters and have a drink. I think that is what old men should do at a time like this."

Delacrois's eyes spotted Doris and Winston sitting on the lower tier of the grandstand. "Yes, Sam," he said. "I agree. This is no place for old men."

"I'm glad you were here, Doris," Winston said. "Maybe it seemed sort of corny to you."

"It was about the un-corniest thing I've seen in my life, Max. There's nothing corny about a hero."

He blushed. "I'm no hero, Doris. I was scared the whole time." He looked down at the medal on his breast. "Hill said something to us once. I didn't understand it then, but I do now. He said all the heroes were dead men. He was right."

"Well," Marriner's voice cut in, "you're the next best thing. You're a live almost-hero." They looked up to see Marriner and Stepik grinning down at them. Winston introduced Doris to Steve.

"Do I look any different than before?" Marriner asked solemnly.

"Only around the eyes," Doris replied with a laugh. "You've all got that grim, dedicated look around the eyes. And those uniforms! I think dress whites are beautiful but not in a hot sun. You all look like you slept in them."

"Is that any way to talk to a hero?" Marriner demanded, aggrieved. "I hear you're throwing a party for the air group."

"A party to end all parties. You'll be there?"

"You're doing this by yourself?" Marriner did not answer her question.

"All by myself." She nodded gravely. "I have two reasons for doing it. An excess of patriotism and an abundance of money."

Marriner looked at Winston and shook his head. "Max, old man. Here is a beautiful girl who also has money. You're a fool if you let

[198

her get away." Marriner was joking, yet Doris sensed the anger under the hint of laughter.

"You seem angry at someone or something," she commented bluntly.

Marriner looked at her and smiled. "I was a fool once, Doris. I guess I don't want to see my friends become fools too."

Stepik interrupted quietly. "This talk gets beyond me. A flight deck in a hot sun is no place for serious discussions. I vote we adjourn."

"Just because you're almost-heroes I have an invitation for all of you." Doris looked at her watch. "In two hours I will have a thirty-foot sloop at my disposal. If you bogus sailors will man her we can go for a tour around the island. I'm a hell of a tourmaster."

"Whose boat is it?" Winston asked.

"An old friend's," she replied. She saw the laughter in Marriner's eyes. "I have a great many friends on Oahu."

"I think it would be great," Marriner said. He turned to Stepik. "How about it, Steve?"

Stepik grinned. "I haven't much experience with sloops, but I'll give it a try." He spoke to Doris. "Would it be all right if we brought Bates and Anders along? If there's enough room, I mean?"

"Bring anyone you want," she said. "We'll load her to the gunwales."

"That is pronounced gunnels," Marriner corrected.

"Okay, Admiral." Doris laughed. "We'll meet you at the Yacht Club in two hours."

When the others had gone, Winston turned to Doris. "Dick was right, I guess." He hesitated. "I mean about me being a damn fool if I let you get away."

Doris smiled and kissed him on the cheek. "Little by little, Max, you are finding out. It's taking some doing, but I think we're making headway. Indeed I do."

They were walking slowly across the flight deck, hand in hand, when with his free hand he unfastened the medal from his breast. "What am I supposed to do with this?" he wondered aloud.

"Do you really want to know?" she asked.

He turned the cross-shaped medal over in his hand, his finger rubbing the propeller emblem engraved on the topside.

"Yes," he said. "I do."

"Then keep it near you, Max," she said. "Keep it where you can pick it up any time you doubt yourself again. It won't make you any braver, but it will be there when you wonder how good you are. If nothing else, it's a testimonial to someone else's confidence in you." She looked at him closely. "Does that make sense?"

"It does," he said slowly. "Pin it back on, will you, Doris?"

She pinned the medal back on his tunic. Then she took his face in her hands and kissed him on the mouth.

He took her hand again, and they strolled toward the aft end of the deck.

"Tell me about Marriner," she said. "Bates said he was married."

"He doesn't talk much about it. I think something happened. I don't know what."

"I like him. Stepik too. In fact, I like all your friends."

"Before the war I had no idea people like them existed." He spoke meditatively. "Marriner saved my life."

"I thought you saved his."

"That was later. When we went in on Tarawa, I lost Stepik right at the beginning. I was all alone, fat, dumb and happy, and a Jap almost got me. Marriner came out of nowhere and took the fight on himself."

She said with conviction, "You would have been all right."

"No," he said, shaking his head. "Whoever the Jap was, he was somebody special. His plane was covered with flags—you know, the kind they paint on when you shoot an enemy down. Marriner took him on, and they fought the damnedest fight anyone ever saw. Even Hill says he never saw one like it. I wouldn't have lasted twenty seconds," he admitted frankly.

"Marriner killed him?"

"No. He let him get away when the Jap's ammo gave out."

She was plainly puzzled. "That doesn't sound like a smart way to fight a war."

"I didn't understand it then myself," he said. "But I think I do now. I think Marriner didn't want to win by default. The man was too good to die because his guns were empty. Besides, I think Marriner is looking forward to meeting him again."

"Would he have given you or Marriner the same chance?"

Winston shrugged. "I don't know. I like to think so. It makes it easier to fight that way, I think." He frowned at a thought deep within

[200

him. "Easier to fight and harder to kill, if that makes any sense to you."

"Is it hard for you to kill, Max?" She asked the question tentatively.

"Not the first time," he said slowly. "After that I don't know. The first time it's only an airplane you're shooting at. When you hit it, it isn't a man burning in the sky, it's a hunk of metal. Later on you realize somebody died when you squeezed the trigger. Maybe that's why, after a fight, your right hand, the trigger hand, is damn near paralyzed from the pressure you put into it when you squeeze the trigger. Maybe you're doing it against your will and don't even know it."

"Do the rest of them feel the way you do, Max? They tell me a fighter pilot has to love what he does."

"I do. I guess they all do. Except for Stepik maybe. He's only doing what he has to do. It's a hard thing to explain. How the hell can you explain it when you look forward to fighting another man you don't know and hoping you'll kill him? If you met him on the street you might buy him a drink. Because he's in an airplane painted differently than yours and he flies under another flag, you're going to do your best to kill him. If you want to live, that is."

"I think," Doris spoke carefully, "you had better not think too much about the other man. I think you'd better remember to stay alive and learn to love this more than you do. Like Marriner or Bates or Hill."

"Well, I've made a start at it. We'll see."

She didn't want to talk any longer about the start he had made at killing so she changed the subject and said, "The party will be Christmas Eve."

"Trees and tinsel and everything but snow?"

"The whole works. The Admiral and Sam Balta are the guests of honor, whatever that means."

"They're great. Both of them." A perplexed note came into his voice. "I still don't know why the Admiral whitewashed me after Remson died. He could have crucified me."

"Why should he? You weren't at fault."

"No? Tell me who was, then?"

"Remson." She spoke flatly.

He looked at her in wonder. "How the hell do you figure that?" There was a trace of anger in his voice.

201]

"You're an idiot, Max. Remson landed that plane in the water, didn't he? No one else was at the controls. He brought it down, leveled it off, set it into the water. You didn't land that plane. He did it himself. If you want to go on blaming yourself because you're afraid to say it out loud, I'll say it for you. Remson made a mistake in judgment, a bad landing, and he died because of it. Now for heaven's sake, stop carrying a cross."

He was silent a moment. Then he looked at her and spoke slowly. "Thank you, Doris. I think you've just done me a hell of a lot of good. I also think you're a damn smart woman."

"Scheming too," she laughed, glad to be done with this mood. "Let's get the boat ready. I want to forget the war this afternoon."

He bowed to her. "This afternoon I intend to make you proud of me. There are one or two things I do better than other people. One of them is operating thirty-foot sloops. I had one when I was fourteen years old. I always knew that someday the knowledge would come in handy. Today, I am the captain, and you may be surprised at some of the orders I intend to give you."

"And if I don't obey?"

"Insubordination. Punishable by any sentence the captain decides."

"In that case, aye aye sir."

Marriner followed the graveled path down to the jetties that formed a sheltered mooring. The others were already aboard the sleek ship, stuffing food into the icebox and filling ice buckets with cans of beer.

He dropped lightly into the boat as Stepik and Bates cast off the lines. Winston was at the helm as they moved out into the stream. Watching him, Marriner caught himself thinking of Winston as he had first met him. He laughed and Winston turned from the tiller.

"Cut me in on it."

"I was just thinking, Max," Marriner mused. "Four months ago you didn't know your ass from third base and you were scared of your own shadow. Now, standing by that helm, you look like Errol Flynn as Captain Blood."

Winston nodded gravely. "I always thought I was the buccaneering type; shining sword, pillage and rape, sparkling jewels."

"Who's talking about rape?" Doris had come up from below, carrying a tray with whiskey bottles and glasses.

[202

"Winston was," Marriner told her. "I didn't know they did such things in high society."

"Somehow," Doris said, "I don't think Max ever had to rape anyone in his life."

"Meaning *I* did?" Marriner was smiling.

"Well?" Doris laughed.

The sloop had come out into the open sea now, and the bow began to smack into the waves, throwing a fine mist of spray back onto the open cockpit. Doris sank down on the cushions and threw her head back, allowing the spray to wet her face and her hair.

Leaning back, Marriner studied her face as she smiled into the rush of spray and wind with a genuine pleasure. She looked like some kind of a goddess who had come to play for a little while on a sunny afternoon. As she turned her head to look at him, the sudden change of shadow on her face brought the memory of his wife to his mind. It wasn't her features that reminded him of Julie but the quick smile that came unbidden to her lips, a trick that Julie had that had always veiled from him what she had been thinking.

"A penny, Dick," she said quietly.

"They're not worth it."

She watched him as he bent over to light her cigarette. "Can a girl get nosy? Really nosy, I mean?"

He spread his hands wide. "I'm a man with nothing to hide."

"I'm walking a tightrope, Dick. Shut me up if you want. What about your wife?"

"What about her?"

He spoke hurriedly because it disturbed him to realize how much Julie had occupied his mind for the past few months; how many times he had remembered her smile; the sudden changes in her moods; her laughter. He wondered how he could have been such a fool as to grind his heel upon the only thing that had ever meant anything to him.

"You don't have to talk about her if you'd rather not."

"I know it, Doris. Give me a minute." He laughed embarrassedly.

What can I say? That I would give anything to have it to do over again? That I know now what was the matter with me? Face it, Marriner, you stupid bastard. You got married because you wanted something to leave behind when you went to war. Everyone wants that, I guess. But they don't all get married and then refuse to acknowledge that they're scared little boys. They don't refuse to admit or

203]

realize or face the fact that they needed someone to leave behind. So now that you know what you did you also realize that you no longer have anyone either to leave behind or come home to. That poses a question: Is it tougher to have no one to leave behind or to have no one to come home to?

"I don't know where she is, Doris," he said aloud finally. "I don't know where she went or how she's feeling or if she's ill or hungry or a goddam thing." He shook his head and spoke bitterly. "I don't know a goddam thing."

"Do you want to tell me about it?" she asked softly.

"What good would it do? I butchered the whole thing and now it's too late. Christ, what she must think of me."

"If it was that bad," Doris said, "what makes you think she thinks of you at all? Maybe you're just sticking needles into yourself."

"I went to war, Doris," Marriner said, "and forgot I ever had a wife. Or at least I made myself try to forget."

"Why would a man do that?"

"A man wouldn't. A boy did."

"You're not a boy any longer."

"Who knows?" Marriner shrugged. "But it's still too late. To goddam late."

Doris shook her head. "You don't know much about women, do you, Dick?"

"I thought I did, but that was a long time ago. I don't think I know a damn thing about women."

"Well, you're making a start now. The first thing is to admit it. The second is to figure out how to get your wife back again."

"Got any suggestions?" he asked wryly. "Maybe I'll ask for a leave of absence from the war and go looking for her."

"Let me think about it," Doris said. "Maybe I can come up with something."

He studied her carefully. "Why are you so interested in helping me?"

Doris got to her feet. "Because you saved Max's life. You may have to do it again. I'm on your team, Dick."

By 1615 in the afternoon Marriner had consumed eleven cans of beer and was reasonably drunk. The others aboard the sloop were gathered in the cockpit, harmonizing in an off-key rendition of the Fighter Pilot's Lament.

[204

"All around is desolation,
Cold and silent as a tomb;
Grandma's got vaginal strictures,
Mother has a fallen womb."

Marriner, weaving slightly, climbed up on the guardrail and stood peering owlishly at Bates.

"Going someplace?" Bates asked.

"Certainly am," Marriner mumbled.

"Where?"

"Forty fathoms down," Marriner announced. "It's been nice."

Bates tossed his empty beer can over the side and fished in the ice bucket for another. "Well, good luck."

Marriner nodded solemnly and fell over backward into the water. Bates walked slowly to the side of the ship and watched Marriner's head bob to the surface twenty yards behind the sloop. Winston was jibing around to come alongside Marriner.

"Get back in the boat, you damn fool." Doris threw a life preserver to Marriner.

"I prefer to remain where I am," Marriner said and went under again.

"Can he swim?" Doris asked Bates.

"All Navy pilots can swim," announced Bates. "It's part of the flight training program. You have to stay afloat for twenty-five minutes without touching the sides of the pool."

"Well, get him out of there."

Bates said calmly, "It won't do any good. His mind's made up. I always knew he had a death-wish. So long, Dick old man. Tallyho, old fellow."

Marriner waved and went under again.

"He's going to drown." Doris' voice held a note of anxiety.

"It seems reasonable to assume that," Bates said gravely.

Marriner bobbed to the surface again and floated, his arms outspread, his head thrown back. Slowly he turned over and sank again.

"Aren't you going to do something?" Doris demanded of Bates.

"I certainly am. I'm going to open another can of beer."

The sloop was drifting alongside Marriner now. He looked up at them with a solemn expression.

"I'm going now."

205]

"It's been nice, old man," Bates said somberly. "May I have your whiskey?"

Marriner nodded. "It won't do any good to try to dissuade me. My mind is made up. This is the only way."

"The better part of valor," Winston agreed. "Shall we drag your body back or do you want to be left out here?"

"It makes no difference."

Bates sat on the gunwale and studied Marriner gravely. "You're certain this is the only way, old man?"

"I've thought it over for a long time. I see nothing ahead but lonely years. Nothing but an endless succession of medals and admirals kissing me on the cheek. I think I'd get tired of medals after a while. There are only so many medals you can get, you know. After that, what else is there?"

Bates nodded in agreement. "I never thought of it in quite that way. I see what you mean." He looked at the others. "You can see his logic, can't you? I mean, after the medals, then what?"

"Nothing," Stepik agreed judiciously. "He's better off with the sharks."

"Did someone mention sharks?" Marriner asked.

"I did," Stepik said. "The reason I mentioned them was because I just saw a fin cutting the water over there."

"Indeed," Marriner said. "You know, this water is colder than I thought. A man could catch cold in here."

"Well, Max," Bates said. "His mind is made up. We might as well go ahead and let him sink in peace. So long, old fellow. You've got guts, if I say so myself."

"I believe I'm getting a chill in here," Marriner said.

"It won't last long, old man," Bates said. "You can keep warm wrestling that shark over there."

"I didn't wear my wrestling shoes. I think I'll come aboard now."

"Don't be silly. After all this trouble? Go through with it, man. How can you face yourself if you back off now?"

"Throw me a line or something."

Bates picked up a loose coil of rope and tossed it to Marriner.

"There," Bates said.

"It isn't fastened to anything," Marriner complained. "What good is a loose rope?"

"Tie it around your neck and pull yourself out of the water," Bates said after a period of consideration.

[206

"It's not tied to anything, goddam it."

"Well, in that case tie it to that shark I see coming."

"Where?"

Bates regarded Marriner solemnly. "You're absolutely sure you want to do this? Nothing but an endless succession of medals and admirals kissing you and all that. Is that what you want? Think it over carefully. You've got plenty of time before that shark gets here. He seems to be a poor swimmer. I can swim that fast myself although he probably wrestles better than I do."

"Will you get me out of here?"

"Well," said Bates, making a line fast and tossing it to Marriner, "I will do it for Julie. You've done enough to her without making her a widow already."

The setting sun bathed the patio of the Aloha Gardens in a golden radiance. Scattered groups of khaki-clad men and brightly arrayed girls spotted the flowered grounds, and in a corner a small artificial waterfall gurgled insistently against the muted murmur of voices that welled from the garden. A long oaken table served as a bar, and on it the rows of glasses and whiskey bottles glinted under the rays of the dying sun. Two Filipino bartenders worked rapidly, sloshing the whiskey into the glasses with practiced dexterity. On a raised platform in the center of the patio, a three-piece combo lilted pleasant melodies into the laughter and babble of voices.

Doris surveyed the scene with pleasure. Christmas never seemed like Christmas in the islands, but she had decorated a large tree which stood now in a far corner of the patio, long streamers of white cotton hanging from its limbs and crowned by a glittering paste star.

As Doris listened to the flow of conversation, she was aware that the talk was always the same at these parties. Today the men talked about the recent award ceremonies aboard the *Concord,* and bantered about their individual heroic exploits. Without exception they assumed a sort of disdain for the decorations they had won, but Doris knew that each of them was trememdously proud. Those who had not won a medal would go back to battle with increased determination, promising themselves that they too would win their right to a multicolored bit of ribbon. It was a goad, an incentive to rise to the heights, to win approval in their comrades' eyes. Some of them would try too hard, and they would die before they attained glory.

When they tired of talking about their medals, about the varying

207]

degrees of their heroism, they spoke in softer voices about the thing that was of paramount importance to every one of them.

Where do we go next? What goddam island will we attack next?

They found a multitude of possibilities to consider in the vast Pacific Ocean. With solemn faces they discussed military strategy, problems of supply and logistics, of public morale and communications, the relative merits of various aircraft and shipbuilding companies back in the States, the probable location of the Japanese fleet. True, it was mostly conjecture, but talking about where they might be going gave them a sense of having a hand in their destinies. They could forget for a moment that to the Navy Department they were only brown manila folders, their names stenciled on the outside and inside a comprehensive history of their lives. The histories were unimportant. What mattered was the designator number after their name. If it was 1315 or 1310 it meant they were pilots and would more than likely do the greater part of any dying that had to be done. Another number could mean they would never see the enemy, and might not even hear a gun fired in anger.

But it made them feel a part of that dim, seldom talked about band of men who sat in paneled offices, under a great weight of gold braid, and made the final decisions. They wanted to pretend for a while because pretending was all that had been left for them. They knew other hands were already manipulating the plotting boards and fingering highly secret intelligence estimates of enemy capabilities. Somewhere to the west they all had a rendezvous to keep, and the waiting was the worst part. After a while the whiskey and the women grow tiresome, and the training flights get boring as hell. It is an entirely different thing to shoot at an enemy plane than it is to shoot at an inoffensive target banner twisting at the end of a tow rope. A target banner doesn't burn and twist downward through the sky as a testimonial to victory.

Delacrois stood with Sam Balta and Barry Wheeler. As a waiter hovered with a tray of fresh drinks, he saw Bob Crowley making his way toward them. The Admiral frowned, because he was enjoying himself and did not want to talk with Crowley. Sam Balta's uneasiness about the man had communicated itself to him. But what could you do at a party? He grabbed a drink as the waiter departed.

He lifted his glass to Balta and Wheeler. "Enjoying yourself, Sam? Barry?"

[208

"I always enjoy parties," Balta growled, eying the approaching Crowley. "Up to a point."

It was Wheeler who greeted Crowley. "Hello, Bob," he said.

Crowley nodded at Wheeler and made his respects to the two senior officers. Then he turned back to Wheeler. "I see from the flight schedule you've been taking some field carrier practice. Any special reason?"

"No," Wheeler said. "I thought I'd see how rusty I was."

"How rusty were you?"

Balta answered, directing his words to Delacrois. "I watched him. Never got a wave-off. He's better than he ever was."

Wheeler bowed to Balta in mock humility. "I am all gratitude, Captain Iscariot."

"Captain Iscariot?" Crowley asked wonderingly.

"A private joke, Bob," Wheeler explained. "Captain Balta is an inveterate jokester."

Over Crowley's shoulder Delacrois saw Doris approaching. He had been watching her on the balcony above, and experiencing the same feeling of satisfaction he had known so often before when he observed her beauty and reminded himself it belonged to him. Watching her now he experienced a sudden sense of disappointment that it was over.

"Hello, my dear," he said as she approached. "You look lovely."

"I bow to three-star rank," echoed Balta, "and I agree. You know Bob Crowley?"

Doris acknowledged the introduction to the tall, spare man with the silver leaf of a commander. She remembered a vague rumor about Midway or was it Guadalcanal? No matter. The man looked tired, drawn.

Crowley stopped a passing waiter and handed Doris a drink.

"Is everyone having a good time?" she asked brightly.

"It's important to you, isn't it, Doris?" the Admiral asked shrewdly.

"Yes, it is," she admitted, then her voice dropped and she said, so softly that only Delacrois could hear, "I want to talk to you, Frog. It's important."

He nodded. "How is Ensign Winston?"

"That's what I want to talk about later," she said.

There was incessant movement about the patio as groups formed and reformed. Marriner was sitting with Hill, Winston and Anders.

209]

Their talk was liberally animated with almost painful manipulations of hands describing intricate maneuvers in the air.

"Why do they always talk shop at parties?" Doris looked at Delacrois.

The Admiral shrugged and looked at Wheeler. "You've got an answer, Barry?"

"The good ones do it because they want to live with it. In that way they'll live longer. The poor ones do it to impress pretty girls. And to make themselves believe they're indestructible. Marriner over there," Wheeler gestured toward the table, "is reliving his fight at Tarawa. Not to show off. He's doing it because he wants to remember every move he made and every move his opponent made because they may fight again, and next time may be the last, at least for one of them."

"That's ridiculous," Doris said disbelievingly. "The chances of their meeting again are one in a million."

Wheeler laughed. "Believe me, Doris, they'll seek each other out. I can't tell you how it happens, but it does. Two men who fight like that, exhausting one another's abilities, they can't let it end that way. Somehow, some way, they'll meet again and finish it."

"That makes sense to me," Balta agreed.

"They look like little boys," said Doris.

"We're all little boys," the Admiral said gravely. "Some of us have gray hair and wrinkles and don't sleep well at night. That's the only difference."

"Not the only difference, I'm afraid," reminded Balta gently. "There is the matter of accepting the inevitable."

Delacrois nodded his head in understanding, but Doris said, "You lost me there, Captain."

Balta continued patiently. "Life ultimately ends, my dear, in an inevitable defeat. You never win. Never. As the years pile up you find yourself drawing nearer to confrontation with that defeat. When you accept it and no longer fear it, then you have ceased to be a little boy. You are then very close to the secret of contentment if not happiness."

"I didn't realize you were so profound, Sam," Delacrois said.

"Only under the influence of whiskey." Balta smiled and took Wheeler firmly by the arm. "I must borrow this young man for a time, Admiral."

[210

Doris and the Admiral watched Balta and Wheeler become lost in the crowd around the bar.

"I like Captain Balta, Frog," Doris said. "There's something very real about him. Something very secure."

Delacrois glanced at her with a smile. "You're growing up, Doris."

"It's about time, I expect. Frog, now may I talk to you?"

He nodded. "Would you like to sit at a table?"

"Let's walk."

They strolled slowly through the crowded patio, the Admiral pausing now and then to acknowledge a greeting.

"You do enjoy these parties with your boys, don't you, Frog?"

"They make me remember other times, and that's not always a good thing," Delacrois replied. "Sometimes it can take you back too far." He offered Doris a cigarette.

"And," he continued, as he held a match to the cigarette, "it isn't wise to become too attached. It's much easier to send them off the flight deck if they're only faces and names, and nothing more than that."

"Let's sit up there on the balcony," she suggested.

After they were seated, Delacrois studied Doris.

"You have a problem?" he asked.

"I'm not sure I should burden you with it."

He smiled and covered her hand with his. "I would be hurt if you had turned to someone else." After a moment he added, "Does that surprise you?"

"No," she said in a choked voice. "You're pretty wonderful, Frog."

"There are those who will dispute that," he said jokingly. When she did not speak, he asked, "The problem has to do with young Winston?"

She nodded, and he noticed a faint flush on her face. "Go on," he urged.

"Frog," Doris said, "I think I'm pregnant."

"Ah," murmured the Admiral.

"I'm not sure. Not yet."

"Well," he said, "it isn't the end of the world. It has happened before to other girls." He paused for a moment. "Winston, of course."

"There's only been one other. You know that."

He chuckled. "To be honest I would be pleased to delude myself into thinking it was the work of these aging loins. Does Winston know?"

211]

She shook her head. "No. Listen to me, Frog. I did this on purpose. You understand that? I got pregnant on purpose."

"Others have before you, my dear. Don't make it sound so damning."

"But it wasn't really fair."

He smiled. "Maybe not. Most women aren't when it comes to getting something they want. God protect us from women with a mission. I often think this war would be over in a matter of weeks if we let the possessive women of the world take over the fighting." He was silent a moment as he considered what Doris had told him. "You're sorry now?" He put it as a question.

"I think I made a damn fool mistake. I love Winston, Frog, and maybe I've ruined the whole thing. If he married me I'd never know for sure whether he loved me, felt sorry for me, or thought he had to do it."

Delacrois nodded his head in agreement. "You have something there. But the damage, if there is damage, is already done. What remains is to discover a practical solution."

"I could have an abortion."

He glanced at her sharply. "Is that what you want?"

"It's the last thing I want."

"Then put it out of your mind." He was silent for a matter of seconds, then he said, "Do you think Winston is in love with you?"

"I *think* so. But how can I be sure? Do these fliers of yours really know what they want? They're in the middle of a war and many of them aren't going to live to see the end of it. They know that. What does that do to your sense of values? They go out on that carrier and every night they lie there and wonder if they'll be around tomorrow night at the same time or if they'll be dead. Christ, Frog, how can anyone think clearly under a pressure like that?"

"You make it sound worse than it is, Doris. They get used to it just as fighting men everywhere get used to it. After a while it becomes a matter of rationalization. And they all rationalize in exactly the same way. They figure the man in the next bunk or the next chair is going to die tomorrow. The poor bastard, they think, he's going to get it tomorrow. They never think of themselves because if they did that for any length of time they wouldn't be worth a damn to themselves or anyone else. In fact, a great many of them would simply refuse to go into the fight. It's happened before to

[212

brave men. One morning they simply say to themselves, Well, today is the day I'm going to get it, and so they decide they won't go out that day. It's as simple as that. And I can't blame them. It isn't cowardice. It only becomes cowardice when it happens too often."

"Well, it all means the same thing to me as far as Max is concerned. He may think he loves me and wants to spend the rest of his life with me merely because he's out in the middle of nowhere, and I happen to be passingly attractive."

"I think," agreed Delacrois wryly, "we might concede that point."

"So there we are," Doris said with an attempt at levity. "I don't know what to do next."

"You might relax," Delacrois suggested. "You're not even certain yet. Why not wait until we return from the next cruise? It won't be a long one. By that time you'll know for sure."

"How long will you be gone? Or is that top secret?"

"A matter of two or three weeks. Not longer."

"Is it going to be bad?"

"I think not. I think this will be a breather for something worse."

"I could hate this war," she said.

"Without it you'd still be a San Francisco matron."

"I was never a matron anywhere, and you know damn well I wasn't."

He chuckled. "Have you seen a doctor yet?"

"No. I'm only a little overdue, but I feel sure of it." She brightened perceptibly. "I could be wrong though. All this trouble for nothing."

"Trouble?" said Delacrois. "There's no trouble here. Winston should be honored you've chosen him. The means you employed weren't necessarily recommended by the Christian League, but at least you regret them now. You know, Doris," the Admiral spoke cautiously, "there are certain codes skirted in Navy Regulations that would enable me to order him to marry you if you're pregnant."

"That would be a hell of a way to get married! From . . . Commander Task Force 58; to . . . Ensign Maxwell Winston; subject . . . marriage, orders to engage in. Besides, you forget another thing that Winston might come upon."

"You mean our . . . relationship?"

She nodded. "It would really throw a rod into the works if he knew about that."

Delacrois said contemplatively, "Somehow I don't think your Max

213]

would be affected too much by that. Perhaps I'm giving the young man excessive credit. But you're not giving yourself enough. Christ, Doris, you can have any man on the island."

"Not pregnant, I can't. Besides, I don't want any man on the island. I want Maxwell Winston the Third, and I don't even care about those numbers on the end of his name."

The Admiral smiled. "That may be. But from the other side of the coin, how does he feel about your background, your family? You know he comes from quite a family, a family where ancestors are more important than the people you have to live with." He shook his head. "I sometimes wonder why certain people attach so much importance to the dead. I should imagine one box of bones is much like another, no matter the pomp and circumstance attending the laying away."

"I told him about me. Skipping a few incidentals here and there."

"What did he say?"

She giggled. "He looked like he swallowed a bowl of alum."

The Admiral rose to his feet. "Well, try not to worry about this. I'm sure it will all work out for the best. And just for the record, I would have been the proudest man on the island if it had been me."

"They'd have court-martialed you."

"They don't court-martial vice admirals. Are you sure you don't want me to put a little pressure on the young man?"

"Goddam it, Frog. I don't want him to pity me or marry me because he's afraid of a black mark on his qualification jacket. I wouldn't want to think he could be forced that way. As a matter of fact I think he might tell you to go to hell and think what that would do to my pride and your three-star austerity."

"The idea chills me." Delacrois helped Doris to her feet. "We'd better be getting back to your party. People will talk."

She laughed gaily. "You and I were never a great secret on the island."

Delacrois watched Doris move back among her guests, and then he turned and approached Hill and Winston at the bar.

"May I join you, Commander?" he asked Hill.

"Our pleasure, sir. What will you have?"

"Whiskey will do. Just a glass of whiskey."

The Admiral accepted a drink. "Was I interrupting anything?" he asked Hill.

[214

"No, sir," Hill answered. "I was just philosophizing with Winston here."

"Continue, by all means," the Admiral said.

"Well, sir, I was mentioning to Winston that I thought it would be a pretty nice gesture on God's part if he sort of took a special interest in these young men standing around here getting drunk. I thought it would be nice if He would just allow them to always be exactly the way they are now. No lines on their faces, no diminishing of their eagerness and innocence. I think that would be pretty damn nice of God."

"Captain Balta expressed the same opinion not long ago."

Hill suddenly became serious. "Admiral," he said quietly, "you were ComFairHawaii before you got the task force. There was an incident a couple of months ago that sort of left us hanging in mid-air, if you know what I mean."

"You're speaking about the Remson incident?" The Admiral deliberately made his voice impersonal.

"Yes, sir," said Hill. "Is it closed, Admiral?"

"Do you mean is it forgotten?"

"I suppose that's what I mean, sir."

"No, Commander," Delacrois said, "it has not been forgotten. But it has been shelved temporarily." The Admiral glanced at Winston. "I think I should tell you something concerning that morning that you do not know. We recovered the target banner and checked the results of the gunnery hop."

Carefully, Hill said, "May I ask what the results were, sir?"

"They have not been made public. Perhaps they never will be."

"I'm not sure I understand, Admiral." Behind Hill's courteous formality there was a hint of anger.

"And I'm not sure it's necessary that you do, Commander." Delacrois allowed the vestige of a smile to play on his lips. "Let me put it this way. The men involved on that hop have distinguished themselves in combat." Again he spoke to Hill but his eyes were on Winston. "I have no wish to discipline heroes. Unless one of the parties concerned on that flight should do something that might make me think he doesn't deserve leniency, why, I think that report might well disappear forever. Now if you gentlemen will excuse me, I see Captain Balta looking slightly confused over there. He usually feels lost at parties."

215]

As the Admiral left, Hill whistled softly. "Now what," he said to Winston, "do you suppose that old bastard was talking about?"

"It sounded like he was warning somebody about something."

"Well," Hill said, "tomorrow I'll sober up and think about it."

Delacrois joined Sam Balta and Barry Wheeler at the end of the bar.

"You look pretty damn smug about something," Balta said.

"All admirals look smug. It's part of the job."

"Well, thank God captains can look as pissed-off as they please. From the looks on Hill's and Winston's faces, I would say you'd just said something of import to them."

"I was talking about the Remson incident," Delacrois said.

"I meant to talk to you about that," said Balta. "Are you wiping it clean?"

Delacrois clucked disapprovingly. "That would be against regulations, Sam."

"I would take it as a favor if you did."

The Admiral grinned. "You know it's not customary to ask admirals to whitewash charges such as this. People might talk."

Balta turned his head and watched Doris as she laughed with a group of attentive young pilots. His eyes danced as he said to Delacrois, "Well, Frog, it's possible people might talk about a great many things. Fortunately, most of them never do. We are all lucky in one way or another."

"I love you, Sam," said the Admiral, "and I admire you more than any man I know. Let me put it this way. In the manner of a gardener I have planted a seed this evening. It will nurture, expand and grow and all will be well with the world. I doubt if you have to worry anymore about the Remson incident."

Balta regarded his long-time friend with a penetrating glance. By God, old Frog is up to something. I don't know what it is or how it involves Doris and Winston, but I have a feeling I'll learn the answer before too long.

"I'll sleep better tonight for that," he said aloud.

"You sleep better than any man I know," Delacrois said. "Let's have another drink. Barry?"

The three men drank and listened to the conversation surrounding them. Most of the men had congregated at the bar, and the vivid talk of flying men filled the night.

[216

"I'll never use an Immelmann in a dogfight. They've got you by the balls when you roll out."

"You stick to that, boy. Never use an Immelmann. Your life expectancy will be about two minutes."

"Remember this. The day of the Lufbery Circle is gone. Planes are too fast, and they'll make high-sides on you and pick you off one by one, and you'll never bring a gun to bear."

"Speaking of bears, you see that new broad working at the PX? She looks like one."

"I hear we've got a new fighter on the boards at Grumman. The F8F. They say it can out-turn a Zero."

"Balls. Not a goddam thing can out-turn a Zero, and that's from experience."

"Listen to von Richtofen."

"The tension is getting to them, Sam," Delacrois said. "They're trying too hard. They're tired of waiting."

"So am I, Frog. When do we go out?"

"Soon, Sam. Soon," Delacrois murmured.

"Well," said Balta, "my aging bones tire easily. I think I'll make my respects to Doris and head back to the ship."

They headed across the room to where Doris was holding hands with Winston and listening to Marriner who was sitting with them, demonstrating some aerial maneuver by an almost impossible juxtaposition of his hands.

"Doris," the Admiral said as they approached, "we must be leaving. It was most enjoyable." He turned to Winston. "I hope, young man, you realize how fortunate you are. Let me commend you on your excellent taste and judgment."

"Admiral," Balta sighed, "this isn't an awards ceremony. You can step off the soapbox."

XII

January, 1944

The days of the New Year came, bringing a sudden stirring of activity throughout the island. The portents at first were no more ominous than the faint ripplings on the water that herald a hurricane, no more significant than the rustling of a sea wind through a super-structure.

On the long strip of runway that split Ford Island, airplanes landed with a squeal of brakes, their gas tanks empty after the long haul across the waters from Moffett Field, Los Alamitos and North Island. Gold-braided men, serious and hard-eyed, disembarked carrying brown briefcases attached securely to their wrists by chains and handcuffs. They were pale, as though long denied the sun in the confines of the Pentagon.

In the officers' clubs men of high rank began to gather in quiet groups and speak in low voices. They drank sparingly, and always at the entrance to the rooms in which they sat there stood two large Shore Patrolmen, .45's holstered at their sides. The eyes of the officers were alternately troubled and exultant as they consulted the contents of the brown briefcases.

In the bars where the enlisted men gathered to cram some measure of enjoyment into the night before the curfew sounded, strangers appeared. They came unobtrusively, and they said very little. They stood for long hours listening and when, occasionally, a youngster would speak of something he had heard—only a rumor of course, concerning this or that—the strangers would gently tap him on the shoulder, and escort him from the premises. After a while it became obvious that it was best not to speak of matters of rumor.

[218

On a lonely, flower-strewn road high above Pearl Harbor there stands a promontory, a jutting of land where the hillside has fallen away or eroded through the years, which hangs out over the hillside, affording a magnificent view of the Harbor. Every Tuesday at sundown one Camaro Kodake would stand on the platform of land and record the activity in Pearl Harbor for later transmission by hidden wireless to Imperial Headquarters in Tokyo. On an afternoon in early January he had just lowered his high-powered field glasses, a present from his father on his graduation from the Imperial Naval Academy, when he sensed the presence of intruders. He turned to face three hard-visaged men in the uniform of United States Marines. Camaro dropped his field glasses and stupidly went for a .38 Smith and Wesson which he carried in a shoulder holster. By the time his pistol had cleared his holster he was already dead, five slugs from the strangers' .45's embedded in his chest. He died facing the Emperor because that is the way he fell as the powerful slugs smashed into his body.

Along the stately corridors of the buildings over which flew the starred flags of the admirals, the conference rooms were filled late into the night. Junior duty officers and Waves assigned to secretarial duties wondered at the communications officers who passed in and out of the conference rooms, always flanked by two heavily armed guards. Mess stewards carrying urns of hot coffee were stopped at the door and relieved of their burdens by Marine sentries. Sometimes, as the door opened, a quick glance into the room was possible, but all that could be seen was an assortment of graying old men, blouses discarded and shirts open at the neck, sitting around a table under a heavy blanket of cigarette smoke, talking quietly over untidy arrays of papers scattered over the table.

Observant citizens of western Oahu noticed a surprising increase in aerial activity in the area near Barbers Point. From sunrise to sunrise they could hear the incessant droning of the engines, and on clear days they might sometimes hear, from far out at sea, the faint but unmistakable stutter of machine guns and the thump of heavy bombs.

Along the docks at Pearl Harbor and Ford Island men worked through the hot day and the cool night. The heavy cranes swung the articles of armament over the rail and down into the holds. Food and clothing, ammunition and bombs, toothpaste and shaving

219]

gear, ice cream and medicine and more bombs and fifty-calibers and thirty-calibers and twenty-millimeters and forty-millimeters and all the rest of the vast supply of war. The men worked hard because they sensed the urgency and responded with everything they had.

Now and then the tall, spare, gray-haired man himself would wander through the maze of confusion on the decks. The workers stopped a moment under the level scrutiny of his eyes and then bent again to the task with renewed endeavor. He was The Man, the leader who sat away and above, and who, as far as they were concerned, held the entire war in his two hands. They would never talk to him, never touch him, but he belonged to them, all of him, four stars and all. His name was Nimitz.

In the communications offices the telegraph keys chattered endlessly. Tired young men flexed cramped fingers and consulted worn code books. Orders flashed across oceans and mountains. Trains moved thousands of miles away and airplanes lifted off runways, their engines straining under the increased load factors. Ships slipped their moorings in the quiet darkness of midnight and like ghostly black shadows glided westward, their decks crammed with the articles of war. Past the Aloha Tower, where once the bright passenger cruisers gaily docked to the nostalgic strains of "Aloha Oe," the grim, gray and camouflaged ships of war cut their silent paths through the water and slipped dockside to await off-loading of their cargoes.

The Island hostesses gazed with dismay at the empty seats at their dinner tables, bereft of the usual eligible officers. At the Officers' Club liquor store on Ford Island, the manager called for extra help as the waiting line stretched out of sight two hundred yards away. The bottles would be tenderly conveyed to cabins on the carriers, there to be stowed with loving fondness in the desk safes, row on row of whiskey and gin and Scotch and rum. Those who did not indulge in drink would barter their allotment for outrageous prices. One hundred dollars for a bottle of rye. One hundred fifty. On the last day before shoving off, perhaps two hundred. Money is of little use to a man in the sky a thousand miles from nowhere. Whiskey can be consumed after returning to the ship. And another thing: money would be left on the accounting books in the ship's office to be forwarded to the next of kin should that be necessary. But whiskey would be left to a buddy or a roommate, and thus seemed the most logical investment of all.

Certain private secretaries and enlisted yeomen and Waves, all

[220

cleared meticulously for "top secret" information, began typing the strange hieroglyphics of task force components.

Then the young men with the wings began to pass words of quiet conjecture among themselves. Since they would do the fighting, they assumed it was proper to try to arrive at a conclusion as to the exact place where they might die. Talking about their destination gave them a sense of belonging, of having had a hand in the determination of their destinies.

Kwajalein? Where the hell is it? The Marshalls? And *what* the hell is it?

Guam? What the Christ do we want with Guam? Unless somebody wants to study mosquitoes.

Don't suppose we could be going all the way? To the Homeland?

Well, if we are, please count me out. I'll wait here till you get back. I didn't lose a thing that far away, and I don't think I'll make the trip, thank you.

How about Saipan?

Sounds like a Chinese dinner.

I keep thinking Truk.

Well, stop thinking it. If you don't, I'll disinherit you. If we ever go to Truk I think I'll have to admit I'm a coward.

The older men, with eagles and stars, came along with wise eyes and lies on their lips. No, we have no idea what is up. Routine as far as we know. They wore smiles and lied and lied, and the young men who would fight and die did not believe them—not worth a damn.

At night aboard the carriers the young men would sit long hours at their desks composing letters about which they all joked. No one ever admitted he thought about his own frailty. Each, within his own mind, was indestructible. But what the hell. A man *could* get hurt. He might fall up a tree or something.

They were universally amazed at the difficulty they encountered when they finally attempted to set down on paper the things they felt. "Dear Mom" suddenly appeared to be an entirely inadequate salutation.

Finally they wrote the stilted phrases that could not disguise the truth, wrote them secretly and alone, sealed the envelope and consigned it to the safe until a day should come when someone else would have to inventory their effects. (Of course it was utterly ridiculous to assume this would ever happen.) When they

221]

finally locked the safe and spun the dial, they had locked away a very secret part of themselves.

The tempo on the island increased, and some of the pilots grew puzzled and uneasy as the long days dragged. A torpedo pilot reported at the Ford Island club that his mechanic knew a yeoman in the flag office who said that orders were being cut for an attack on an island named Palau. Where the hell was it? Another man heard from a college buddy who was an intelligence officer on the *Ardennes* that they sure as hell were going to Saipan.

The rumors were sifted, weighed and sorted and finally out of the conglomeration a strain of truth began to show. It was a faint, amorphous thing at first because the pilots did not want to believe it and so forced the realization to the back of their minds.

A supply officer who had been called to Admiral Delacrois's office to report on the readiness state of certain vital supplies, had chanced to observe a map spread out on a table in the office. There had been only one mark on the map, a heavy purple circle drawn around a single island group in the far central Pacific.

Well, for Christ's sake, where was it?

Truk!

The name itself had a death-doom sound, foreboding as a midnight shadow on a graveyard wall. To the men of the fleet it brought forth the crawling fear of the unknown. It was a place known only by circles on a map, a latitude and longitude delineation, by the passing tongue of a long-range reconnaissance pilot who had seen it from twenty thousand feet. It was a far-off, whispered place, painted to awesome images by fables and ignorance. But these assured a great, sprawling, unbelievably powerful bastion, an unassailable fortress from which the enemy could thumb their noses at the naval powers of the universe. A stronghold so powerful and impregnable it had never been spoken of as a target except in jest.

The name whispered in awe, for years military men of the West had argued among themselves concerning the fortifications the Japanese might have built on the high-cliffed islands lying inside the protective and encircling coral reef. For years Truk had been the Gibraltar of the other side of the world.

Now all that was known for sure was that Truk was the hub of the Japanese South Seas empire. Vast, formidable, a shadowy promise of death and destruction.

[222

Fuck Truk, the pilots laughed, because we will never go there. There is only a one-way road to the bastard and no place to make a U-turn. They laughed again and again because it is much easier to expel laughter than it is to swallow fear.

Truk.

The rumor persisted and gradually nourished itself into the truth, and so they set themselves against it as best they could.

Truk.

One time or another every man faces adversity's chilling wind. One man will flee from it and like an unresisting kite, fall to the ground. Another sets himself against the wind, and that which would destroy lifts him as readily to the heights. We are not measured, the young men reminded themselves, by the trials we meet. Only by those we overcome.

Fuck Truk—and the words became more a curse than a joke. Out in the gunnery areas the pilots spent long hours in the air perfecting their shooting techniques. Ten percent hits were no longer good enough. Try for twenty-five. Fifty. On the bombing targets at Molokai and Maui the enlisted men who tallied the scores as the pilots dropped their water-filled bombs, and fired the blazing rockets at the painted circles on the ground, recorded in amazement the scores that heretofore would have astounded them. Ten foot average. Eight foot average. Jesus Christ, the bastard had eight bull's-eyes.

High in the sky over Honolulu the twisted contrails streamed as the fighter pilots practiced their trade. The snarling whine of laboring engines heralded the dogfights that went on continuously during the daylight hours. There would be no time to practice when the battle was joined.

So in the days of the New Year the young men argued and spoke heatedly, and their nerves grew taut with waiting. The tempo of activity increased steadily until it seemed the entire island was a fused bomb waiting for the detonator. Tempers thinned, and the fleet seemed to stir restlessly at anchor. Junior officers cursed their superiors, and the superiors cursed the flag rank.

"So it will be Truk," Sam Balta said to Frog Delacrois as they sat having coffee in the Admiral's cabin, while outside the myriad sounds of in-port activity filled the morning air.

"It will," Delacrois agreed.

From the comfort of a heavy leather chair, Balta watched the

Admiral as he scanned the papers for Operation Password, the code name given to Task Force 58's upcoming attack. As the Admiral read, a small smile shaped on his lips.

"Something funny about this?" Balta asked dryly.

Delacrois sat back in his chair. He regarded Balta without seeing him. "I suppose so, in a way. Know what these orders read?"

"They say, 'Go to Truk.' Ridiculous," Balta said and snorted.

Delacrois leaned forward in his chair. "They say, 'You will seek out the enemy fleet and destroy it. You will then attack the naval complex at Truk Harbor and deliver such damage as is practicable before withdrawing on or by the 18th of February.' Now isn't that a lovely set of orders?"

"Well. One thing anyway. Things couldn't get any worse."

"They're only giving me four carriers."

"What do you want? The whole fleet?"

"Goddam it, yes."

"Stop all the crap, Frog. You're as excited about this as a schoolboy with his first piece of ass. This is what you wanted, isn't it?"

"I could use some more carriers."

"And I," said Balta, "could use some more teeth. But I don't have any more."

Delacrois suddenly grinned with schoolboy pleasure. "Goddam it, Sam, we're finally going after them. We're going right into their goddam backyard."

"Will the *Concord* have the honor of carrying the flag?"

"I wouldn't ride another ship."

"You know," Balta said in mock seriousness, "there are rumors of a suicide corps being formed in Japan. Kamikazes, they call themselves. If they come after us, they'll go for the flagship first. I'm not sure I want you aboard the *Concord*."

Delacrois smiled. "Well, you can be sure of one thing. At least you will die in the best of company. Mine."

"That certainly is something to help me sleep well at night."

"Sam," the Admiral said, his voice suddenly serious, "we've got a lot to do and not very much time to do it in."

"Have we at least got time to qualify the air group in night carrier landings?"

"No. I'd like to be able to, but it's more important they finish the gunnery and dive bombing."

[224

"Right with you, Bat Two," Hill called cheerily. "A black sonofa-bitch it is."

"How do you want to go in, Bat Leader?" Dusane's voice was calm.

"Right into the middle of them. Get what we can on the first pass. Then you'll have to take over fighter direction."

"Right you are. Here we go."

The three-plane formation smashed at the heart of the enemy bomber force. Coming out of the dark night completely undetected, they opened fire at the silhouettes of the Bettys milling in their own flare lights.

Just before they reached firing range, Hill called Anders. "Move out, Cort. You're on your own. Shoot to beat hell."

Anders was still in a slight bank, easing away from Hill, when he saw the guns of Hill's plane erupt. Quickly he straightened his wings and pressed his trigger even before he had time to take a bearing on an enemy plane. His tracers were already blazing across the sky when he saw a two-plane section of the bombers wheeling in front of him. He jerked the stick quickly to the right, swerving his fire in the direction of the enemy, and he saw his tracers licking at the night and fall-ing short of the enemy planes. Good, he thought, they should look like they're short. Even as he thought that, both the Jap planes burst into gigantic fireballs of flame and multicolored smoke and fell out of the sky. Anders banked hard to his left, and a shadow filled his gunsight. Since he was still firing at the planes he had already de-stroyed, the shadow passed directly into his line of fire, and another ball of twisting flame fell toward the water below.

Hill's voice came to him. "Bat One. Reverse course. They're run-ning for home."

"This is Bat Two," came Dusane's voice. "They're heading out on vector 295. I say again 295."

Anders reversed his heading and took up 295, pushing his throttle to the stop and rolling on 2500 RPMs. He watched his airspeed build, as he came down to 1500 feet. He was away from the Jap flares now, and the night was again black as the inside of a coffin. Then he spotted Hill's exhaust less than a mile directly ahead of and slightly above him. He rolled on a few more RPMs and trimmed his plane, trying to get every knot of speed out of it. He drew closer to the ex-haust and just as he was about to swing out and come up on Hill's wing he saw more exhaust flames flickering on ahead.

257]

He had missed Hill and come up behind a straggler in the Jap formation. He called Hill on the radio.

"Bat Leader from One. I'm right behind the bastards. A slew of them. Watch for my tracers."

He opened fire from directly behind the straggler, and the bomber turned on its side and fell off on a wing, its entire tail surface blown away. Anders flew right through the debris and closed on the rest of the formation.

"I saw you." Hill's voice was laughing. "I'm coming up behind you now."

"Better hurry, Skipper. There won't be any left."

Now Anders eased off power and steadied his speed to equal that of the enemy. The plane he had just destroyed had not burned in the air, and he must have killed the radio operator. The rest of the bastards didn't even know he was here. He grinned in the darkness of his cockpit.

This time when he opened fire he sprayed his tracers in a wide, sweeping arc across the space of sky in which he estimated the enemy planes would be, keeping his finger tight on the firing trigger, kicking his rudders alternately and holding his wings level.

He got two kills this time, both flamers, and then he saw Hill over to his left, all guns blazing, and more planes were falling and burning.

Christ. How many were they getting tonight?

On the bridge of the *Concord* Delacrois and Balta listened to the excited voice of the CIC officer coming in over the ship's intercom.

"Good God, Admiral. They're shooting down the whole damn Jap air force."

Delacrois flicked the intercom switch. "How many kills?"

"Sir," the voice replied in a wondering tone, "we can't even count them. According to this radar screen they've already shot down seven."

"Seven." Delacrois turned to Balta and slapped him on the back. "For God's sake, Sam. They're doing a job."

Miles away the Jap formation split, half turning starboard, and half turning port. Hill saw the exhaust flames separating and called Anders.

"Take the port, Cort." He chuckled at the rhyme.

Hill turned hard, firing as he did so, and although he hit only one Betty, smashing the engine housing and causing an explosion, he

[258

killed two. The resultant blast of flame enveloped a second Betty and two of them went down together. Hill had to yank savagely on the stick to avoid the flaming debris, and when he brought his nose around again the exhaust flames had vanished.

"Jupiter Base," he called. "I've lost the bogies. Do you have weather out here?"

It was Dusane who answered. "Affirmative, Bat Leader. A line squall or something like it due west of us about fifteen miles."

"This is Jupiter," called the *Concord*. "No line squall. Weather up to fifteen thousand moving our way."

The hell with it, thought Anders. He was hard on the tail of the formation he had followed. He had lost distance when they turned abruptly, had been sucked behind because in the darkness he could not fly precise formation. But Dusane had given him a new vector, and now he was closing again.

The weather front was before him, but it was only a blacker patch against the already ebony curtain of the night. He was not sure where it began or how high it went, and he decided to press for a kill until the exhaust flames in his sights disappeared.

He noticed the first tracings of mist on his windshield when he turned his gunsight lights full bright, and then he knew there was no time for closing. He pulled his nose up far above the nearest enemy exhaust flame and let his finger press full down on the trigger. When he saw the tracers arcing out he sprayed right and left, left and right. He was close enough to see the spurt of flame where a shell hit a gas or oil line, and as he banked away to avoid running up onto his enemy, he saw another plane light the misty sky in an explosion. Then he had turned and his back was to the Bettys disappearing into the storm.

He sagged low in his seat and wiped the sweat from his forehead. Unconsciously he reached out and kicked both gun chargers and then felt in the darkness and switched off his gun switches. He turned off the gunsight he wouldn't need any more that night.

It was so goddam dark and he was so tired. He laughed aloud in the cockpit because suddenly it came to him that he and Hill and Dusane had just done something that had never been done before. They had come out from a carrier at night, attacked a heavy enemy formation and all but destroyed it. For Christ's sake, how many did they get? His mind tried to remember the kills.

Seven, ten, twelve. Well, damn it, he had known he was good, and he had proved it to himself. He stretched his arms out in front of him and grinned up at the night sky.

Delacrois and Balta watched the "bat" team land. All they could see from the blacked-out bridge were the landing lights of the planes sweeping down on the starboard side of the ship and then breaking off far ahead of the carrier to come around on the downwind leg. The lights were tiny against the vastness of the night, but they were all that could be seen except the truck lights of the motionless screening men-of-war.

"God damn," Delacrois said softly, "hairiest operation anywhere and any time, and what a magnificent thing they made of it."

Now the landing-signal officer had raised his lighted paddles and Hill was coming up the groove, seeing nothing in the night but those two slender wands. He came around and the wands remained horizontal, indicating his pass up to this point was satisfactory; they lowered slightly into an inverted V, meaning he was a little low; he eased back on the stick, and the wands raised to the horizontal; he came almost around to a position aligned with the deck, and now he could discern the deck lights, visible only from directly astern. The right-hand wand moved up and down in a rapid fashion; he was coming too fast. He eased back on the throttle and held the nose level with back pressure on the stick until the wand came back to the horizontal and remained there. His eyes flicked downward for an instant, and he saw the airspeed needle quivering exactly at a perfect eighty knots; and so he came roaring over the fantail in the dark, saw one wand blink out and the other sweep across in a throat-cutting gesture, and cut his throttle all the way back and held the stick in his lap and waited for the breathless rush forward and then the tug of the wire and the jerk of the shoulder straps.

Harry Hill had come home.

The Admiral had broken out a bottle of ancient brandy when he debriefed Hill and Anders. In quiet, unemotional tones the two young men had related their experiences of the evening. To Delacrois and Balta it was an amazing thing that two ordinary human beings could shoot down a dozen enemy planes between them in the course of one fight. But Hill seemed to take it as a matter of course, while Anders, who looked as if he ought to be in high school, seemed lost in a reverie, his mind a million miles from a three-star admiral's bridge.

[260

Actually Anders was wondering if he should have gone into that storm after the remaining Bettys.

After the younger men had gone, Delacrois looked at Balta and sighed. "God, Sam. They take it so easily." The Admiral beckoned to his navigator.

"It's time to stop fooling around and set a straight course for our objective. I want the force to be in position for launch by 0400 on the 16th. Not more than two hundred and fifty miles from Truk."

The navigator consulted his chart and looked up. "If we set a direct course sir, that'd be morning after tomorrow, Admiral. We can be in position by 0200."

The Admiral nodded, dismissing the navigator, and spoke to Balta again.

"We'll double the antisub patrols tomorrow."

"As you say, sir."

"You're going to start that 'sir' business again?"

"I was thinking," Balta smiled, "the first flight into Truk. It could get rough."

"Of course it could. What the hell can I do about it?"

"Nothing," Balta said softly. "Except to be sure Hill is on the first fighter sweep."

"He will be," grunted Delacrois. "I already had my mind made up."

"I thought so," Balta said. "You're learning, sir. Three stars and all, you're learning."

"And you," said Delacrois, "are impertinent. If I had less important matters to consider I'd probably court-martial you. As it is, I wonder how that B-17 is making out. It would be a lovely thing, Sam, if we could catch the bastards with their pants down taking a leak."

The B-17 *Easy Victor* was not doing well. Her departure had been delayed almost a full day. Three hundred miles from her base she had developed trouble in the number three engine and had to turn back. Despite the attention lavished upon her, it was almost nine o'clock at night on February 15th when she became airborne again. It was not destined that Admiral Delacrois should find the Japanese Fleet within the confines of Truk Harbor.

261]

The Mitsubishi bomber from Truk was one hundred miles out at sea on a course that would converge at midnight on February 15th with Task Force 58's plotted positions as reported by the survivors of the night-flying planes which had maintained contact with it. The Japanese pilot was concerned however. His plane did not have the range for this type of flight. If the Americans had changed course, he did not have the fuel to conduct a thorough search of a wide expanse of ocean in order to find them and determine their whereabouts and their goal, especially at night. The pilot checked his navigation data, and after rapid and expert calculations added three inches of manifold pressure to his engines, and manipulated his propeller controls to give another one hundred and fifty revolutions to his props. Thus he insured he would arrive at his expected rendezvous area forty minutes early. The forty minutes would allow him to search an additional sector to the north and so, in the final analysis, Admiral Togyama would have time to land his air groups on the fields at Truk while he took his fleet itself westward to await another day when he would be better prepared to meet the American fleet. But Togyama did not leave behind a token force. He left four air groups of the most experienced Japanese pilots headed by Commander Isoku Yamota.

As Task Force 58 steamed silently through the Pacific night, Chief Rasmussen lay on his bunk in the Chief's quarters. He wondered if he had done a foolish thing.

Mech O'Toole had called him that night at 2200 to tell him that Rathburn had been summoned to Commander Crowley's quarters. Rasmussen had pondered, and hard, as to whether he should follow the young seaman to the CAG's quarters.

In the end he did not go and now as he sought sleep he tried to convince himself it had been because tomorrow he would lay this whole unwholesome mess into Harry Hill's lap. It was too much for an enlisted man. Christ, wasn't it trouble enough to fight a war?

XIV

February 16, 1944

The battle? The first raid on Truk?

Well, it is in the books, impersonally with all the dates and facts and specifics. The history of the two days is told in a minimum of words. Such is the way of the chroniclers of minor engagements, and because Togyama chose not to fight, this was minor.

But see the raid for what it was. The first plunge into the middle of the forbidden land. A lunge against the strongest outpost of the Japanese Empire.

The second meeting between the pilots of Task Force 58 and the battle-hardened veterans of the First Fleet. The 16th and 17th of February, 1944, were days never to be forgotten. When Togyama withdrew, undefeated, waiting to fight again, the pilots had only each other to fight and it proved enough for both sides.

Never wave the flag, they say. The teachers say it and the wise men say it and the editors say it, but goddam it, until they have been there let them shut up. Task Force 58 did not say it.

Task Force 58 said, Fuck Truk, here we come. Some of us are afraid and some of us are brave, some are strong and some are weak, but goddam you, Togyama and your First Fleet, here we come.

Isoku Yamota felt that the sky he flew in was his own. He took his group and four others into the air from the First Fleet, and flew them to Truk Harbor and scattered them about the myriad airfields in the complex. He could not win this fight, not without the capital ships. But since his fleet was not going to fight, he would do as much as he could with his air groups. In the back of his mind was a faint hope and a prayer that he would meet the one man in all the world who most wanted to meet him too.

263]

General Quarters sounded at 0430, blasting enlisted men and officers out of their bunks and onto the cold steel decks in the first hint of dawning. Twenty-eight hundred men answered the summons in a wild scramble of pounding feet and muffled curses.

In Ready One the first fighter sweep had been called thirty minutes before GQ. Breakfast was served to the first strike long before the others ate, and this presented a question. For when Hill told the mess steward he wanted only coffee and a roll, Marriner looked at him askance.

"Skipper, in case you don't know it, they're serving steaks this morning. I'll say it again. Steaks."

"A dangerous luxury," Hill said. "I don't advise it."

"Any time," said Bates, "I can eat a steak for breakfast instead of powdered milk, I'd be a damn fool to turn it down."

"Some pilots," said Hill, "like to eat before they fly. Others do not. Always remember there are no toilets in the sky, and it is foolhardy to hang your ass over the side of a fighter plane going three hundred miles an hour. A man I know tried it once at a training field in Texas. He unbuckled his parachute, then he hung his rear end out into the slipstream."

"Dead no doubt," said Bates, preparing to cut his steak.

"No," Hill replied. "He lived to tell about it. He was lucky because he fell out at nine thousand feet and had time to rebuckle his chute. It opened at one hundred feet and he broke both legs and several vertebrae which certainly is better than disintegrating."

"I'm not so sure I'm hungry after all," Bates confessed.

"Boy," Marriner said to the steward, "I believe I'll just have coffee and a roll."

Breakfast finished, the pilots repaired to Ready One and donned night-vision goggles which helped to adjust their eyes to darkness and which all pilots launching before dawn wore for thirty minutes before takeoff.

Stepik was the standby pilot on the fighter sweep, the extra man who stood by in case a scheduled plane should be unable to launch. It was a thankless assignment, especially at 0500 in the morning. And because the duty officer had lent six pairs of the night-vision goggles to the dive bomber squadron in an unguarded moment of generosity, Stepik was without the goggles this morning. It did not really matter since standby pilots rarely launched on a hop as important as this one. A pilot would do almost anything, even try to

[264

take off on one magneto, rather than miss the first attack on Truk. So Stepik did not worry about his lack of night-vision glasses.

The minutes before a strike are precious minutes which a man lives within himself. Stepik and Winston sat side by side in a comfortable silence. They had lived together now for six months, and Stepik had watched Winston grow from a frightened kid to a hell of a fighter pilot. Stepik allowed a smile to ease the strong line of his mouth.

Winston turned his head. "What's so funny?"

"I was just thinking, Max. About all of us. You and me and Dick and Bates and Cort. How much has gone under the bridge since we wandered out here six months ago."

"It doesn't seem that long, does it?"

"Time goes fast out here, Max. You'll be getting married soon. Cort will get a Navy Cross for that business the other night. Marriner's shown signs of becoming the greatest fighter pilot since Hill. Bates will always be Bates, and I can't say anything better about him." Stepik laughed softly. "All of us have done pretty well when you consider that eighteen months ago we were living in a different world."

"We sure as hell were," Winston agreed. "You know, Steve, I think each of us has helped the others in some way. I can't put my finger on it, but I know it's there."

"Well," Stepik said, "we've managed to stay alive together, and I can't think of a better measure to go by."

"When it's over, Steve, when we're finished, what will you do then? It's none of my business, I guess, but you never say anything. Not even about your wife."

Stepik closed his eyes and found that he actually wanted to talk about his wife, here, now, in this ready room just before a battle. He wanted to tell Winston about their love and his hopes and his dreams.

"We've been married four years, and every year has been better than the one before. I don't know what it is we have between us, but I don't think many others have it. I know that to me she's all there is in the world. She is so good she doesn't believe that everyone on earth isn't exactly like her. And if she believed it she'd shrug and smile, and then forget it. I don't suppose I can ever give her the things she deserves. But whatever I become she'll make me because without her I'm nothing. I often wonder what I did before I met her. I'm sure that if someone chopped my leg off she'd feel it ten thousand miles from here. If she stopped loving me this minute, it would make no difference in the way I feel. I could no more stop loving her than I could hold my breath and die. And one other thing, Max. As long as I know she's somewhere in this world, breathing the same air and watching the same sun and moon and stars as I do, then I'm a happy man, and a happy man can't be beaten." Stepik smiled. "I think one day you'll feel like this about Doris if you don't already." He looked up at the front of the room as the sound of the teletype alerted the pilots slouching in their seats.

The words slowly marched across the screen, as the men watched them intently.

"Pilots Man Your Planes."

Removing the night goggles the men filed from the ready room into the dark passageway that led to the flight deck. Stepik found himself in a black void and had to hold his hands against the bulkhead to guide himself. He felt a fresh breeze on his face as Hill opened the hatch leading to the small ladder that led from the catwalk to the deck itself. Stepik followed the sound of whispered voices until his hands grasped the rungs on the ladder.

Outside the flight deck was pitch black and Stepik could make out neither the island structure, the horizon nor the sky itself. The planes for the launch were spotted forward, while on the aft end of the ship, mechanics were in the cockpits of the torpedo and dive bombers, running up the engines in preparation for a later launch.

The scheduled pilots, their eyes accustomed to the night after thirty minutes of adaptation, could see the outlines of the airplanes clearly and made their way forward. Stepik, whose plane was spotted farther aft since it was doubtful that he would have to launch, waited a moment for his eyes to compensate for the sudden change from light into darkness.

Nearby, a third-class machinist's mate named Sanders was having trouble in the cockpit of one of the SBD dive bombers. For ten minutes the engine had thwarted all his efforts to get it started until finally Sanders had flooded it by a too strenuous application of the primer. Now after waiting three minutes for the flood of gas to subside, he was ready to try again for one last time. If the bastard wouldn't turn over now, Sanders was resigned to downing the plane and sending it back to the hangar deck where he would have to work half the day to fix it. He bent his head over into the cockpit to check the bat-

[266

tery and generator switches, and so he did not see Steve Stepik who, having decided his eyes were as adapted as they were going to get within the time allowable, had started for his plane. In the blackness Stepik did not distinguish the shape of another plane between him and the spot on the deck where he thought his Hellcat to be.

Sanders pressed the starter button, and the propeller started to turn very slowly just as Steve Stepik walked within the radius of its arc. The great slab of steel wheeled majestically through the air and crashed into Stepik's shoulder, just at the point where the arm joins the torso.

Stepik felt no pain at all. For an instant a shadow seemed to loom above him out of the night. Then it was as if a great pump had sucked all the wind from his lungs. He gasped at a dull heaviness that seemed to be weighting his shoulder. For a moment he thought he had walked headlong into a parked airplane, but as he started to curse his clumsiness he felt himself falling and then the excruciating agony hit him, a river of molten pain sloshing down over his shoulder and arm. He made an effort to get to his feet, but he could not move. He tried to roll over, and the pain again washed over him in a sickening wave that made him retch.

In the cockpit, Sanders swore as the prop jerked to a halt. It had turned over three times, but the engine had not caught. She would have to go below to overhaul. Sanders turned off the switches and was starting to climb out of the cockpit when he heard a sound that he could not quite put a name to.

Admiral Delacrois and Captain Balta were on the outer bridge when a white-faced medical corpsman arrived. ·

"What happened down there?" Delacrois demanded.

"One of the pilots walked into a prop, sir. We've taken him down to sick bay."

"Who was it?"

"I don't know, sir. The standby pilot, they said."

Balta consulted the flight schedule. "That would make it Stepik." He turned to the corpsman. "Is he dead?"

"Not yet, sir. His arm is pretty bad though. Doc Mulloy . . . I mean Commander Mulloy has him now."

Balta nodded in dismissal and turned to the Admiral. "There aren't enough goddam ways to kill them off in this war. We have to

267]

walk them around a black flight deck in the middle of a sea of turning props. Is there anything else we can think of to lower the odds? Goddam it."

"Do you have a better way to manage things, Sam?" Delacrois's voice was gentle. "If you do, I'm willing to listen."

He was interrupted as the air officer spoke over the deck bullhorn. "Strike able planes, start engines."

Crowley, as air group commander, moved into position first. With the wands of Fly One to guide him, he hit his left brake hard and swung his plane around to face down the flight deck. The red arc of the launching officer began to whip in a rapid, circular motion. Crowley pushed full throttle forward, and his engine wound up in an ear-shattering scream. Suddenly the red arc stopped, hesitated, then dropped toward the deck as Fly One gave him the "go-ahead."

Crowley nodded and released his brakes. Even as he cleared the end of the flight deck another plane was moving into launching position. One after another the planes received the fallen wand and swept into the night, their navigation lights gleaming on the tips of their wings as they soared off the bow into the enveloping blackness. Each man in each plane had undergone an abrupt transformation. He was a fighter pilot in a fighter plane on a fighter mission. He had even lost the individuality of his own name. Now he was nothing but a call-sign and a number.

On the darkened outer bridge Balta turned to the Admiral from watching the dimming lights as they circled to rendezvous.

"I'll be going down to sick bay, Admiral," he said. "There's nothing I can do down there, but I'd like to look in on the boy."

Because there was nothing else to say, Delacrois said, "You do that, Sam. Tell Mulloy he can have anything or anyone he wants."

As the first saffron promise of dawn played on the horizon, one hundred miles away to the west, the Mitsubishi pilot from Truk faced a serious problem. Hours earlier he had reached the area where he had expected to contact the American task force. But he had been totally unable to find any trace of its presence. For hours now he had searched in every direction, flying over the empty sea. Now he had another problem for his fuel level was dangerously low and within a half hour at most he would have to turn and begin his inward vector back toward Truk. He wondered if, in this half hour, he should stretch his northward leg another fifty or sixty miles. It seemed useless since the Americans would only have set course in that direction if they aimed at the Truk bastion itself, an impossible goal. He consulted his how-goes-it chart, a record which many aviators consider quite as important as the wings on their airplanes, and learned that he had enough fuel left to essay the added distance. Yet it was not just a matter of fuel; when Admiral Togyama issued an order, he expected to have it carried out. With a resigned sigh the Japanese pilot set his course northward, stretched in the cockpit of the Mitsubishi and sat back to watch the beauty of a Pacific sunrise. It would, he mused, be another hour or two before his wife would wake to a new day, and he consoled himself with the thought that this was his last mission before returning to the homeland.

The entire task force strike had rendezvoused in the dark and climbed steadily for altitude. They raced the daylight into the sky, climbing to twenty thousand feet and finding the sunlight as they steadied on a vector for the target. Now they reduced power settings to save fuel and settled down for the long haul to the target area.

Sam Balta entered sick bay to observe Stepik lying on a table covered with a sheet. My God, he thought, is there this much blood in all the world? Stepik's shirt had been cut away and lay wadded against the wall, a soggy, red and black mass. Mulloy, the ship's doctor, had his back to Balta as he bent over the still body. Two corpsmen stood by the table. In all the room there was only the muffled sound of Mulloy's hands manipulating some instrument against Stepik's flesh. Balta closed the door gently and stood there, holding his breath, afraid even the noise of breathing might disturb Mulloy's concentration.

Finally, when he could hold his breath no longer, he expelled it in a long sigh. Mulloy heard and twisted his head. He nodded to Balta. "Come up, if you wish, Captain. This is part of war you fly-boys never bother to watch. Come up."

Balta moved forward beside Mulloy. He looked down at the still form. "My God," he whispered, "is there any blood left in him?"

"Perhaps enough," Mulloy said. "The body fights back. He's in shock now, and his blood is moving much slower and so there will be less of it on your well-scrubbed decks. Give me the knife, Benson."

"His arm?" asked Balta. He could see the shark-belly whiteness

269]

of Stepik's hand against the darker grayish hue of the fingernails. He kept his eyes averted from the bloodied, mangled mass of splintered bone and convoluted muscles and meat that seemed to be stuck haphazardly onto the end of Stepik's shoulder.

"I will cut," Mulloy answered shortly. "I will cut because it may save his life. It also may not, and in that case he'll be buried tomorrow with only one arm. I doubt if he'll care much one way or the other."

While he spoke, Mulloy's fingers were working deftly finishing what the propeller blade had begun.

Mulloy reached for a small bone-saw, and Balta tried to shut his ears against the grating of the saw. Mulloy grunted once, and as he straightened up one of the corpsmen moved from the table bearing an object in his hands. Balta looked at it and swallowed as he left the operating room.

Margaret Stepik screamed and sat up in her bedroom. She rubbed her right shoulder which ached intolerably and tried to remember the dream that had been terrifying her when the pain had awakened her. Along the sleep-fogged rim of her consciousness there was a haunting premonition of disaster. She shivered before the unnamed dread and fell back on her pillow to murmur a prayer for her husband a half a world away.

The Mitsubishi bomber had reached a position within a relatively few miles of the point at which it would have to turn ninety degrees to port and commence the long inbound journey back to Truk if it was to arrive with any fuel in its tanks. But for these last few minutes the plane continued on a northerly heading, on a course which, unknown to the pilot, would bisect the westward course of Task Force 58 in exactly thirteen minutes. The pilot observed a layer of low-level clouds directly ahead of him and pulled back gently on the control column. The Betty quickly climbed the two thousand feet necessary to clear the cloud cover. But the additional altitude announced the bomber's presence in the vivid morning sky.

In the radar plotting room of the *Concord* a young ensign sat before the screen, half asleep after two hours of following the endless circling of the radar beam around the circumference of the dimly lighted dial. Suddenly he was jolted to attention by the appearance

[270

of a foreign blip on the screen. Friendly planes were under orders to continually display their IFF signal, a radio signal actuated by a switch in the cockpit that made a special blip and thus identified the plane concerned as a friend. The *Concord* CIC officer now knew that an enemy plane was approaching the force and could not fail to spot it. He called the Strike Able leader.

"Strike Able from Jupiter. Bogey closing on the screen. He is thirty miles from you, eleven o'clock. If he makes a sighting they will be waiting for you at target."

Receiving the transmission Crowley realized that the enemy might be alerted to the attack and so have time to launch their aircraft and be waiting when Strike Able came into Truk. He looked behind him and saw an armada of more than two hundred airplanes. It still could not smother the fear that came to him.

The voice from the *Concord* came again. "Bogey angels eight."

Hill called Crowley. "Red Leader from Red One. Suggest you send a section out to get him."

"Detach one of yours, Red One," Crowley replied.

Hill saw Marriner's division flying off his wing and decided to detach them to splash the bogey.

"Red Two," he called, "detach and intercept. Come in to the target later if you have time."

Marriner tapped his head in reply to Hill's order and banked over and away from the formation. He called the *Concord*.

"Jupiter from Red Two. Ready for vector."

"Vector two-five-five," came the answer. "Buster."

This last order indicated to Marriner that he was to employ full power to get to the enemy as quickly as possible.

As the CIC on the *Concord* directed Marriner's division to the bogey, the Mitsubishi pilot had already spotted the trailings on the water that betokened ships-of-the-line. His radio operator was sending the information to Truk, and Isoku Yamota was already preparing to take to the air at the head of his fighter armada. The Americans would not come in undetected today.

Marriner spotted the Betty first, a small speck of shadow on the water far below.

"Tallyho from Red Two. Low on the water. Ten o'clock nine miles." As he pushed over he called Winston, leading the second section, "Max, move out and we'll bracket the bastard."

271]

The Americans came in behind the Jap plane, two planes on either side, prepared to make the attack regardless of which way the enemy turned. Marriner opened fire first, and his shells hit the Mitsubishi near the nose section, miraculously missing the propellers. Marriner saw a chunk of fuselage tear away in the wind. Then the Jap turned hard port and directly into Winston's guns. Winston turned with him, holding his mill lead and watching his tracers work up the side of the plane and into the cockpit. The bomber nosed over and went into the water almost vertically.

But the damage had been done, Truk had been alerted, and Yamota steamed west, away from Task Force 58, at flank speed.

Strike Able was coming in with the sun at their backs, but it would be two hours yet before the sun would be high enough to do them any good.

Crowley was just pushing forward on his stick, preparing to lose altitude, when Hill's voice came to him.

"Red Leader. Negative. Maintain altitude." Hill knew that all they had to beat the odds was their altitude.

Crowley held his nose down, and Hill called again. "What the Christ are you doing, Red Leader?"

The entire American formation was now strung out across the sky as pilots firewalled their throttles and rolled on RPMs, seeking to hold formation even though Christ knew where the strike leader was taking them.

Hill finally realized what Crowley had in mind. The CAG was going down on the water to try and take advantage from the rising sun. To Hill this was unbelievable. If they came in on the water, they might well lose every goddam plane on the strike. He called Crowley again, his voice hard and angry.

"Red Leader. You can't go in on the water. They'll clobber us."

Crowley held his plane in a dive and passed fifteen thousand feet. Now Hill called the entire strike. "All Strike Able planes. Hold your altitude." To himself he thought, This maniac in front will kill us all.

The massive formation leveled off and went in to Truk at fifteen thousand feet, leaving Crowley to swear bitterly and climb back to his position at the front of the flight.

Back on the *Concord* the knowledge that an enemy snooper had been splashed within sighting distance of the task force set off a flurry

[272

of speculation. The word flew from messengers to gun captains to flight mechanics.

"The bastards are waiting for us."

"How the hell do you know?"

"They splashed a snooper a few miles out."

"Bullshit. How the hell would they know we're coming?"

"I'm no admiral. They'll be there though. Hundreds of the bastards."

"Jesus," a corpsman on the *Concord* said, "those bastards are flyin' into a trap."

"They get flight pay, don't they?" a mechanic answered.

"You want to change places with them?"

He got no answer.

Men in exposed areas donned their steel combat helmets and manned their duty stations looking like a swarm of hooded devils from a medieval nightmare. Cooks and bakers clambered into forty-millimeter mounts and mess stewards manned twenty-millimeter cannon. A considerable portion of American fighting strength in the Pacific became acutely aware of the threat posed by that blip on the screen that had been splashed by Red Two.

Fifty miles separated Strike Able and Isoku Yamota's Zeros when the Americans caught their first glimpse of Truk. Through their windshields the pilots at first saw only a smudge on the horizon. They tightened their seat belts, checked their gun switches and set their gunsights up full bright. When they looked out of their cockpits again the smudge on the horizon had taken form, had separated into lumpy shadows on the water. Another five miles and they could see the steep-walled, cliffed islands within the encircling silver band that was Truk's coral reef.

Then they were there.

They came over Truk at fifteen thousand feet. Fighting Two arrived first, banging into Truk at four hundred miles an hour, whistling a scream of warning to Yamota and his Zeros hovering over Dublon Island. Hearts quickened and fingers tensed on the triggers long before the first tallyho was raised.

They came in over the slim line of coral in the early morning sun, most of them only twelve months or so away from a schoolbook or the June prom. They held tight formation as they came into Truk, and the shadows of their planes mottled the sea within the atoll.

273]

Only fifteen miles separated Strike Able and Yamota's Zeros now, yet neither side had seen the other. High in the sky early morning light is faulty, and men straining too hard sometimes miss a target altogether. Yamota knew the Americans were coming, for he had received contact reports continually from his ground radar. But he had elected to fight within the confines of the harbor itself so that the antiaircraft batteries on the islands would lend their weight to his attack.

Hill probed the sky in front of him, and so he was the first to sight the enemy. At first it was only the quick glinting of the sun on the polished wing of a fighter. Then Hill's eyes picked them out.

Hill waited a short moment for Crowley to make the tallyho. Then when Crowley failed to act, Hill judged his position, then called, "Tallyho. Eleven o'clock ten miles. The whole goddam Jap air force. Let's hit them."

The two forces came together head-on. But Crowley, at the last moment, turned hard port, and so it was Hill who led Task Force 58 into the fight. He and Yamota came at each other nose-on, and neither man wavered. They opened fire simultaneously, flying down the paths of their own tracers until they winged past each other, separated by no more than a few feet. Hill had taken a hit somewhere in his starboard wing, and Yamota noticed a slight fluctuation in his oil pressure.

No matter, Yamota thought, I am fighting over my own land, and when the oil is gone I can land on any of several airfields. That man in the Hellcat is good. He never made a move to divert his flight path. They are dangerous, the ones who will fly down your throat. Yet they are the best, the stubborn ones. Yamota turned back to the fight. He felt a confidence in this morning's work. To fight over your own territory is a wonderful thing, because you have a confidence that the enemy does not have. In combat in the sky, confidence is a great asset to a fighter pilot.

Yamota returned to the fight unaware that his confidence would be tested by Dick Marriner who at this moment was still fifty miles away, heading toward the target under full power.

Hill swung his plane into a wingover roll and as he did so, he felt the vibration in his starboard wing. He looked out and could see the shredding of the leading edge where Yamota's bullet had entered. Goddam, he thought, the bastard must have hit something inside

[274

there. The wing fluttered but sustained the flow of air as Hill straightened his plane out again.

Hill might have beaten Yamota had it not been for the flutter in his starboard wing. As it was, he fought Yamota all over the sky until Yamota scored another burst in his starboard wing. Hill had just come around after sucking Yamota into an inverted position, but when he pointed his nose down, where he expected Yamota to be recovering from his upside-down position, he found his opponent had outguessed him after all. Yamota, applying hard forward stick while on his back, had actually climbed in the inverted position, so that when Hill looked below, Yamota came from above and hit him again in the wing section. This time Hill felt the wing shudder, and the stick banged violently in his hand. Goddam, he thought, the bastard hit me good.

Crowley had come into the fight with trepidation. After Hill had led the formation into the first encounter Crowley had swung wide and entered the fight from the starboard side. He came in fast, leaving his wingman, Anders, fifty yards behind. This suited Anders perfectly because he had no inclination to fight by Crowley's side in such an engagement. Anders watched Crowley barrel into the melee, then he swung over and up, trying to climb two or three thousand feet so he would meet the enemy with an altitude advantage. It took Anders one minute to climb twenty-five hundred feet, and when he had, his airspeed had dropped off to one hundred knots. He came out of his climb just as a Zero opened fire at him. Anders grinned in his cockpit because his speed disadvantage would win this one for him. Easily now, his slow speed allowing him to turn quickly inside his opponent, he brought his guns to bear and opened fire, and the Zero disappeared in a mass of debris. Anders continued hard in his turn, rolled over onto his back and screamed down into the fight.

Desperate to avoid his opponent's fire, Harry Hill put his plane into too tight a turn. Instantly his damaged wing faltered under the strain and he tumbled off on one wing in a semi-spin, a half-stalled condition. Yamota was on him like a hungry tiger. Hill managed to kick hard rudder and shove the stick all the way to the corner of the right side of his cockpit, but now he knew he couldn't beat this man, not with his ruined wing. His eyes swept the sky, looking for a way out of his dilemma.

In desperation he headed for the cloud bank that hovered over Dublon Island.

As Yamota turned to follow him, Marriner and Winston sped to the scene from the east, late for the fight but not too late to get in their licks.

Yamota closed on Hill from the rear, his throttle all the way forward, his eyes peering through his gunsight as he measured Hill for the kill.

This is not the way to kill, he thought. Not when your opponent is wounded, his wing shattered and his plane unable to defend itself. But it goes this way sometimes. I would let this man go, but what then would I have to go on, in other fights? You can't let all your beaten enemies go. This man is good, but his plane is beaten, and so he can at least die knowing it was his plane that faltered and not himself. Yamota closed within fifty yards of Hill, just as Hill slid into the cloud bank over Dublon Island.

Yamota smiled because he knew his enemy would have to come out. A man can't fly in a cloud bank forever. Not when his carrier is two hundred and fifty miles away. He circled around the cloud bank and took up a vigil at its base.

One moment Hill was flying in bright sunlight, and the next he was immersed in the milky nothingness of the cloud. He flew straight ahead, and soon he was in murky blackness, flying on instruments as the air grew rough and shook his plane relentlessly.

Marriner wasted no time. He put his sights on a Zero, scored a hit with a two-second burst and watched the Zero tumble burning through the sky. Winston had sheared off and taken on another Zero, and they were wheeling in tight circles, each trying to get inside the other's radius of turn, when Marriner, coming to Winston's aid, saw Yamota against the cloud base where Hill had taken refuge. He swung in that direction.

Harry Hill cursed. He was not in the habit of losing. He circled carefully in the cloud, flying blind, knowing his fuel would not allow him to stay in there forever.

Marriner saw the speck that was Yamota against the cloud base and threw a quick glance at Winston. Winston was holding his own, so Marriner defied the rule book that forbade breaking up the two-plane teams and went for Yamota.

[276

Crowley had done nothing. He had skirted the fringes of the violent fighting until now he saw a single Japanese plane flying along the base of a cloud. He had no way of knowing it was Isoku Yamota who was more than a match for two of him. So he went after the lone plane, at the same time that Dick Marriner was closing from the opposite direction.

And as Crowley and Marriner headed for his opponent, Harry Hill decided the time had come to take his chances and flew his plane out from the pillar of cloud into the sunlight. He had only a moment to adjust his eyes to the light, for Yamota gave him no more time. He pounced from above. He might have preferred a more even fight, but he was a fighter pilot and he did what he had to do.

So he wheeled in on Hill from the rear, narrowing the distance between the two planes. Hill's plane loomed ever larger in Yamota's gunsight rings. In a few seconds his shells would be hitting Hill's plane, violently buffeting it in the sky.

Marriner arrived just in time to see Crowley swing his plane into position behind Yamota. Good, he thought. He's got that Jap bastard cold. Then as he flashed by on a reciprocal course Marriner glimpsed Hill's number on the side of his battered plane.

Crowley was within extreme firing distance of Yamota now and directly behind him, but Crowley did not fire. He watched as the Zero filled his gunsight, and still he didn't fire. His eyes were squeezed almost shut, and his finger was slippery on the trigger. Dimly, far back in his mind, there lurked a fear that if he fired now the enemy would turn on him in anger. It was ridiculous and illogical, but Crowley was past lucid thought. So he closed on Yamota without firing a round. Crowley was letting Harry Hill die.

Marriner flashed past on a reciprocal heading.

"God damn it," Marriner's voice yelled. "Open fire. Open fire."

Marriner swept up in a tight reversal and started back down again, but he was far out of range. Only Crowley could save Hill, and Crowley did not do it.

Crowley's finger was loose now on the trigger. He felt like a spectator sitting in a hundred-dollar seat at ringside. He was dimly aware that what he was doing was wrong, but he could do nothing as his mind and muscles refused to function.

Harry Hill knew he could do nothing more. Through his rear-view mirror he had seen Crowley's plane swing in behind the Zero and for a second had thought he was saved. But he wasn't, and he

277]

knew it now. Yamota's slugs slammed through his fuselage, and he banged the stick over to the right, twisting the plane around. He saw the Zero turn with him, and then Yamota's shells tore into the side of the cockpit and ruined Hill's body between the neck and the waist. Hill doubled over in the cockpit, and blood sprayed from his mouth onto the instrument panel. His body pushed against the stick, and the plane nosed over in a steep dive.

Yamota knew the kill had been made, and he turned away to take on the Hellcat behind him. Crowley continued to fly on blindly, not making even a token pass at Yamota.

But now Marriner was sweeping down on Yamota's tail, all guns firing. Yamota heard the sounds of the shells before he saw the Hellcat and instinctively rolled over and pulled into a split-S. Marriner was with him all the way, rage welling in him.

Hill knew he was going to die. In his acceptance of the fact resignation mingled with regret. Well, I always expected this only now that it's come I realize I am not quite ready to go. I would like to kill that bastard in the Hellcat who was behind the Jap and never did a damn thing. I saw him there just before my body fell apart. Hill made an effort to focus his eyes, and saw his altimeter needle unwind past three thousand feet.

Three thousand feet to live. Over the roaring of the wounded engine Hill's mind groped at the memories that crowded his dying brain.

The pain was filling him now, rising up to his throat and into his mouth. Well, Christ, it has been a good go, and I've had all the best of it. The fighting was not quite finished yet, but I suppose others will carry on for me. I hope they get that sonofabitch who shot me.

The altimeter needle swept past one thousand feet, and Harry Hill knew he had only seconds left.

With a superhuman effort he pushed himself upright and looked down the nose of his plane at the onrushing ocean.

A half mile away from the place where Hill died, Marriner and Yamota went at it a second time. Some time during the fight the knowledge came to Yamota that he had again found the man he had fought over Tarawa. Perhaps it was his excellence in avoiding the clever traps Yamota set for him, traps that had worked successfully in a hundred other skies. Whatever it was, Yamota knew he had found his man again. Marriner had recognized his foe when, after his first firing burst, the Japanese executed a half-roll and a snap

[278

from the inverted position. Then too, no two Japanese pilots could possibly have had that enormous number of flags decorating their planes.

This time Marriner felt no inclination to spare his opponent. He had seen Yamota kill Harry Hill, and was grimly determined to kill him in turn. So they fought again as they had at Tarawa, all over the sky in the greatest exhibition of fighting and flying that the other fliers who saw them had ever witnessed. There were opportunities for other pilots, one side or the other, to slide in and try for a kill on one of the two men, but none tried it. They left the two alone, and that is as it had to be.

First Yamota took the advantage, then Marriner wrested it away from him. There are only so many maneuvers that an airplane can perform and the two men employed every one known. Neither could best the other, and so they fought doggedly, waiting for the first mistake, the slightest error in judgment.

But there was to be no victory this time. For the second time in as many encounters, the two pilots were destined to fly away from each other with the question still unresolved as to which of them was the master.

As in their first encounter, it was a matter of ammunition on Yamota's part but to this was added the question of Marriner's fuel supply. Yamota had expended most of his ammunition in his kill of Hill. Marriner had two hundred and fifty miles to fly back to his ship, and as his gas needle reached below the quarter tank mark, he knew he would have to postpone a decision in this fight a second time.

Marriner was behind Yamota, striving to get on his tail and within firing range, when Yamota waggled his wings and banked his Zero sharply and headed for the airstrip on Dublon Island. Marriner started to follow him, but then he looked at his gas gauge again and considered the foolhardiness of following his opponent low over the deck across an enemy airstrip. Every gun on the island would have him boresighted. Anger flashed through him that this second fight had to end in a stalemate.

Yamota, watching through his rearview mirror, saw the Hellcat peel away and reverse course. Another time, he thought. Another time, and we will settle this. I have no way of knowing for certain that you are the man I met at Tarawa and who spared my life, and yet I am certain you are. Perhaps it is the way your plane refused

279]

to be decoyed or the manner in which you hold your own with me in a tight turn, which the engineers have told me is an aerodynamic impossibility. They said the Hellcat could not possibly stay with the Zero in a high-g turn, yet you have done it and confounded me every time I thought I had you. You are the best I have encountered, and so I know you are the man from Tarawa. Well, for the second time I am out of ammunition, and you must be short of fuel, so both of us must say 'Until next time.' And there will be a next time because I am sure that the two of us cannot go on living in contested skies. Sayonara.

Marriner climbed toward the rendezvous sector east of Eten Island, and heard Crowley's voice.

"All Strike Able planes. Rendezvous in sector X-ray immediately. Angels ten."

Three minutes later Winston slid alongside Marriner and held up two fingers to signify two kills. Marriner nodded his head. He looked around the sky and saw Bates climbing from below to join them.

It took Strike Able forty-six minutes to fly back to Task Force 58, and for half that time Marriner tried to convince himself that Crowley had had some excuse for not opening fire on the Jap that had killed Hill. But he could not convince himself, and with the formation almost within sight of the task force he seriously entertained the idea of shooting Crowley down in cold blood.

He gave his plane a bit more throttle and pulled his division forward alongside of Crowley and Anders.

"Red Leader," he called, "fire your guns."

Crowley turned his head. "What the hell are you talking about?"

Marriner jockeyed his plane in closer to Crowley's until the two planes were flying almost wing tip to wing tip.

"I said fire your guns. I want to see if they work."

"What goes, Dick?" Anders called Marriner.

"Hill's dead," Marriner replied. "Crowley was behind the Jap that got him. I want to know if his guns are jammed or not."

There was a silence, and then Anders said, "Better fire your guns, Red Leader."

Crowley flew along straight and level.

Marriner dropped back and slid in behind Crowley. "You've only got a few seconds to fire those guns," he called.

[280

"I can get him from this side," Anders' voice said.

"Don't leave me out of this." It was Winston.

"Me either," Bates cut in as he pulled out to the side from Marriner.

"If we all fire together they'll have to hang us all," Anders said, and there was no laughter in his voice.

Crowley realized that he was face to face with death. "God no," he cried into his mike, "my guns are jammed. They jammed."

"All right," Marriner called. "Give him the doubt. For the time being, anyway." Crowley might be telling the truth. Guns jammed easily at high altitude. But Marriner shook his head because he still was not convinced.

On the bridge of the *Concord*, Delacrois and Balta heard the radio transmissions of the inbound strike.

"It seems your pilots are raising hell with each other again. Christ, Sam, this has to stop." Then he realized that Balta had a drawn look around his eyes.

"Hill?" Delacrois asked softly.

Balta nodded slowly. "I don't think Hill is coming back. I think he missed, finally." Balta's voice broke.

"Well," the Admiral said and stopped. He wanted to say more, but there was nothing more to say.

Balta turned to Delacrois, and now there was scorn in his voice. "From the conversation up there I take it that Crowley's guns jammed at a time when he might have saved Hill. That's par for the course with Crowley. He hasn't been on time yet." Balta turned away so the Admiral would not see the tears of anger in his eyes.

"I'll want to speak to the men on that hop. Crowley and the division leaders. As soon as they land." The Admiral spoke flatly, carefully keeping emotion out of his voice.

Balta and Delacrois moved to the aft end of the bridge. The incoming strike was overhead now, and the first divisions were breaking off and diving for the landing circle. Crowley's section came around first and swept into the wires. Behind them Marriner and his division came, answering the landing signals with precise application of rudder and stick, sailing up the groove nose-high and steady at eighty knots. Over the fantail and, receiving the cut, into the arresting gear. One by one they taxied forward and shut down their engines on the port elevator.

281]

Delacrois and Balta saw Marriner climb out of his airplane and walk over to Crowley. He jabbed a finger in the Commander's chest.

"Your guns, Commander?"

"Listen, Ensign . . ." Crowley began.

Marriner ignored him and turned to his mechanic. "O'Toole, I want you to check the guns on this airplane. I want to know if they're jammed."

"Won't take a second, sir," O'Toole replied brightly. He jumped up on the port wing and started to pry open the gun covers.

"What do you think you're doing?" Crowley demanded angrily.

"Trying to find out if you killed Harry Hill," Marriner said in a flat voice.

He was interrupted as Hill's mechanic approached and saluted.

"Commander Hill, sir?" the man asked respectfully, only his eyes betraying the fact that he already knew the answer to his half-voiced inquiry.

"Commander Hill," Marriner said levelly, "has gone away. You may tell the other men he has gone away. Not dead, you understand. Just gone away."

The man snapped a salute. "Of course, sir. And may I say, sir, we all hope he has not gone too far."

The man walked away, and Marriner turned to Winston. "Remember that, Max. It was worth more than all the medals Hill ever got."

"Sir," O'Toole called from the wing. "There's nothing wrong with these mothers at all. Only a few rounds gone and no jam at all."

"Let's go to the bridge, Commander," Marriner said wearily. "I think you have a right to be there when I report this." Then suddenly his voice shook in anger. "You lousy, two-bit sonofabitch. Why did you let Hill die?" He put his hand on Crowley's shoulder and shoved him toward the island. "Go, you bastard," he said. "Go ahead or by Christ, I'll kill you right here on the flight deck."

But when Marriner had blurted out his accusation to Captain Balta, it was Admiral Delacrois who answered, and the hard edge of authority was in his voice.

"Slow down, young man," he said to Marriner. "Ensigns don't go around accusing air group commanders. Remember this." He turned bleak eyes on Crowley. "You say your guns jammed?"

"Yes, sir," Crowley said. "I was closing on the Jap that got Hill and I couldn't get them to fire. Not a damn round."

[282

"Were they jammed when you landed aboard?" Balta asked.

"No, sir. I tried clearing them all the way back. They must have cleared before I landed."

"And you," Delacrois spoke to Marriner.

"I came around a cloud, Admiral, and saw the Commander's plane behind the Jap. I was close enough to see his number. The Jap was directly astern of Hill." Marriner shook his head. "Hill only had one chance, sir." He looked directly at Crowley. "And that was Commander Crowley coming up on the Jap's tail. The Commander never opened fire."

"In the same situation, Ensign," Delacrois said to Marriner, "if you had been in Commander Crowley's shoes, what would you have done?"

Unhesitatingly Marriner answered, "I'd have rammed the bastard, Admiral."

Delacrois and Balta exchanged glances. "Then," said Delacrois, "you are blaming the air group commander for Hill's death because he didn't deliberately ram his airplane into the enemy's. Is that right?"

Marriner thought a moment. "Not exactly, sir. I don't think the Commander's guns were jammed. I think he froze at the controls." Marriner looked at Crowley steadily. "And I don't want to fly under a man like that."

Delacrois smashed his fist down on the edge of the table. "Goddammit, *I* will make the decisions around here. *I* will decide who flies with whom. Ensigns are not running this fleet. I am. And I goddam well do not want any more shenanigans in the sky where ensigns are going to shoot an air group commander down because they think his guns weren't jammed. I never heard of such a goddam thing."

"Ensign Marriner is still very young," Crowley said. "He hasn't been in combat too long. He has made a bad mistake. I was doing the best I could under the circumstances."

"Hill's dead," Marriner said. "Nothing is going to change that. I may only be an ensign but goddam it, sir, I know when a man is trying to charge his guns. If the Commander was trying to get his guns working he would have been kicking the charging buttons and his plane would have been skidding all over the sky. When I passed him, his plane was flying straight and level."

"That is little enough to go on, Ensign," Delacrois said.

283]

Marriner sighed. "You're right, sir. Maybe I was mistaken." What the hell, he thought, Crowley may have been trying. Maybe I'm just too pissed off because Hill died. Maybe I'm wrong and Crowley is okay. But I don't think so. He looked at the Admiral. "I could be wrong, sir. But Hill is dead, and somehow I can't accept that it had to happen."

"You'll learn after a while," said Crowley, "that these things do happen. Let's forget it, Marriner."

The Admiral was looking at Balta as he said, "Yes, let's forget it. There's enough to do without fighting with each other." Then, remembering he was a three-star admiral and not just an ordinary man, he bellowed, "And that is an order, gentlemen. You are dismissed."

As the junior officers left, Balta turned to Delacrois. "Well, Frog, that is one way," he said. "When you don't know what to do just shout. A three-star shout scares almost anyone."

As Marriner and Crowley left the flag area Winston was waiting for them. But an enlisted man approached and touched Winston on the arm.

"You're wanted below in sick bay, sir."

"Sick bay?" Winston was puzzled.

"Yes, sir," the seaman said. "Ensign Stepik has asked for you."

"Stepik," said Winston. "What about Stepik?"

"He walked into a prop on the launch this morning," the seaman said.

"Oh Christ," Winston breathed. "How bad is it?"

"They took his arm off, sir. He asked for you."

Winston tried to disbelieve this. He did not want to think of Stepik with an arm shorn off at the shoulder. Stepik was the strong, reliable pillar upon which a man could lean when he had to, an indestructible source of strength when strength was needed. He was the image a man creates in his own mind of himself as he ought to be. Winston did not want to consider Stepik as a torn and ravaged cripple. Yet it was a measure of his own maturity that he said merely:

"Thank you for coming for me. I'll go to him now."

Stepik lay on his bed in sick bay and gazed at the metal-gray overhead through morphine-dimmed eyes. A great lassitude possessed him, but he had almost recovered from the first shock that had swept over him when he realized he no longer had a right arm. He had

[284

stared at the empty pajama sleeve for several minutes while the chilling realization wormed its way into his mind.

Finally, as with all things, he had accepted the new state of affairs with which he would have to live for the rest of his life.

At a sound, Stepik lowered his eyes and recognized Winston standing in the doorway. Winston shut the door softly and sat down by the bedside. Stepik essayed a smile.

"I've only got a minute, Max," he whispered. "They gave me a shot of something. I'll sleep soon."

"Sure you will," Winston said. "I'll be here when you wake up."

Stepik nodded drowsily. "That's good. Wouldn't want to wake up alone. Stand by, Max. Good old Max."

Winston tried to keep his eyes away from the bandaged shoulder and the unhealthy color which showed under Stepik's pajama top near the neckline.

He felt a great tenderness well in him as he looked at his friend's face, and for the first time in his life he truly understood the sense of responsibility that came with an admission of indebtedness to and love for another man. He wanted to reach out and clasp Stepik by the hand, but Stepik no longer had a hand on that side.

"Things will be all right, Steve. You'll see. They'll be just fine."

"Have to figure out about Margaret," Stepik murmured sleepily, his mind reaching into another time and place. "Have to figure out how to take care of my wife. Can't let her suffer because I've lost an arm. Other ways of making a living, I suppose. Got to find one. There'll be a way. I'll look until I find it."

Winston did not speak because he knew Stepik was almost asleep. His hand gently patted the wounded man's leg. You have already found it, Stepik my friend, he thought. I won't speak to you about it now, but some day soon we'll have a talk. I need you alongside me. And you need me. Can there be a better bond between two men? Fortunately or unfortunately I have an extremely wealthy father and mother, and I have business enterprises which will fall into my lap whether I want them or not. I have been told a great deal of responsibility will be mine some day, and I'll need you with me to help carry the load. Our futures are intertwined, and I think they have been for a very long time. My Doris and your Margaret can watch us grow old together, and some day we will sit, old men in the twilight of our lives, and talk as old men will about these days we

285]

are living through. So sleep now, my good friend. I have made one of the basic decisions of my life and you're stuck with it.

Three hours later when Commander Mulloy came into sick bay he found Winston asleep by Stepik's bedside, his hand resting protectively on Stepik's good arm and his head lying on the edge of the bed.

When Task Force 58 turned back from Truk on the night of February 17, 1944, the bastion's mythical power had been blasted. Truk had been nothing more this time than the staging area for Yamota's fighters. Togyama had elected not to fight, and thus the crucial encounter would have to wait until the checkerboard of war shaped up and Togyama and Delacrois would clash four months later in a battle that would determine the course of history.

So the raid at Truk went on the records as a battle of fighter planes. By the end of the second day two hundred and four Japanese fighters had been blasted out of the sky, and almost every American pilot in the sky could be counted a hero. Fighting Two shot down ninety-seven planes, yet they considered it a sad score when balanced against the loss of Harry Hill. But you always lose something in a battle, even when you win.

So the forbidden had been met, and proved to be only a place where brave men died. Some died laughing and others crying, but one and all died fighting bravely until the end.

Years after they would talk of the Truk raid, and even would learn to smile about it. It was fearsome only until we got there. After that it was only another battle, and we were in the fighting business. It scared ten thousand men until we met it but we won. And when all is said and done, there is only one thing that matters to fighters: whether they won or lost.

"We won this one, Barry," Balta said, "but we didn't prove anything. I think Togyama made a hell of a mistake not coming out to fight. Next time we'll be stronger than we are now."

The two men were sitting in the Captain's sea cabin. Wheeler had a speculative gleam in his eye.

"You didn't ask me up here to tell me we won the fight. I already know that. I think you've got something else on your mind, Captain."

"Well," Balta admitted, "as a matter of fact, I do." He looked at Wheeler seriously. "Barry, I'm going to ask a favor of you."

Wheeler sighed. "I knew it. I've already decided to say yes."

[286

Balta smiled. "You'll stay on as exec then? For the rest of the cruise?"

"How long will the cruise last?"

"I'll be relieved the end of June."

"Then I'll hang around till then. But, goddam it Sam, no longer than that. Is it a deal?"

"It's a deal. Keep your hand in when we get back to Pearl. I want you on the flight schedule as often as possible. With Hill gone we may need you."

"Don't start in on Crowley again. Christ sake, anybody's guns can jam."

"I know it. That's why I'm giving him the benefit of the doubt. But I'm glad you're staying, Barry."

"Of course you are. I'm the best exec you ever had." Wheeler grinned. "We heading straight for Pearl?"

"A quick stop at Majuro and then all the way to Pearl. We'll be home by the end of the month."

"Pearl Harbor is not my idea of home!" Wheeler got to his feet. "If you'll excuse me I'll go below and try to write my wife and explain to her why I let you talk me into staying out in a war almost a year longer than I had to." He shook his head. "It'll take some explaining."

"Tell her you're striking for another Navy Cross."

Wheeler made an obscene gesture as he left the cabin.

287]

XV

April, 1944

Admiral Delacrois had erred in predicting the cruise would be a short one. On the way back to Pearl from the Truk raid Task Force 58 received orders to return to the new anchorage at Majuro Lagoon in the Marshall-Gilberts. There the fleet had lain at anchor through steaming days while the pilots fretted and swore at the heat. There was damn little to do lying at anchor in Majuro Lagoon. You can get brown by lying on the flight deck in the sun if you don't mind searing your backside on the boiling hot planks of the deck. You can write letters, but that palls after a short time. The whiskey runs out, and the weather gets hotter and all you can see is the surrounding, deserted atoll and the long line of ships stretching away into the distance. You can watch a movie on the hangar deck at night, but after you've seen the same movie three or four times it becomes easier to sit on the fo'c'sle deck and watch the incredibly clear sky and try to think of the day when the war will be over.

The days dragged and the nights crawled, and the heat became more intolerable, and finally one day they were called to the ready room to begin briefings on a group of islands far to the westward.

The Carolines.

On March 30, 1944, Task Force 58 drew the stinger in the tail of the Carolines, a small island complex named Palau. It was strictly a battle of the carrier planes. Togyama had put into Singapore and was again not available to contest the sky or the ocean. The fighter planes from Task Force 58 spent two days sweeping the complex, although after four hours of the first day there was nothing much left to sweep.

Fighting Squadron Two, temporarily led by the executive officer,

[288

a full lieutenant named Larson, went in first. Marriner shot down his eleventh airplane, and Anders got his fifteenth, making him the leading ace in the fleet.

When Delacrois saw that Palau offered nothing more in the way of targets to be destroyed he withdrew, stopping on the way out to detach the majority of the fleet to Majuro. The *Concord* and her escort however proceeded back to Pearl Harbor where the ship would undergo an engine overhaul and where Delacrois would confer with the man on the mountain regarding a gigantic operation soon to take place. The raid on Palau received considerable publicity if for no other reason than Palau happened to be farther westward than Tokyo itself. This in itself meant nothing, but it was heartening to the civilians who did not know that it meant nothing. So although Delacrois had hoped to catch Togyama at Palau and failed, the attack served a purpose nevertheless.

Back in Oahu there was a stirring in the air. Where not long before there had been a sense of indecision, now a feeling of expectancy that the United States would soon do something monumental to prove to the world that she was all she claimed to be hung in the air.

The Marshall-Gilberts had been taken, Truk had been smashed, and the fleet had sailed unchallenged west of Tokyo itself. How had this come about? A short time ago Americans had worried that the Japanese would be clambering ashore on Hawaiian beaches. Barbed wire was still strung along Waikiki and near Diamond Head. But now the scene of combat had moved so far west that even the remembrance of the threat seemed ridiculous. How could we ever have entertained a thought of defeat? There had been no reason for it, thanks to those eager young men who pass through here, laughing and boisterous, getting drunk on our lawns and making passes at our daughters. But then they vanish, and when we hear of them again it is in reports from somewhere far to the west of battles they have won. We are lucky to have them.

Pearl Harbor has changed this early spring. The berths are empty now as the great ships anchor at Majuro in the Marshalls. It is only a lagoon, but it provides a haven for the rapidly growing fleet that would soon cast its shadow over an entire ocean.

The *Concord* sailed past the nets to find the citizens of Oahu waiting to welcome her, waiting to acclaim her men. But the pilots were tired of talking about where they had been and what they had done.

289]

They laughed and did not answer the ever-present questioners, asking instead who was going to win the pennant this year.

They were tired of war. Perhaps it was because they knew they would be going back again and again. For Christ's sake would it never end? They were growing perceptibly older, far sooner than they should. Someday they would ask themselves, how the hell did I grow so old in a matter of a few months?

The word of what Task Force 58 had done, the things that had happened, had preceded it. Hostesses talked about it, and it was spoken of in the inns where the natives gathered. Task Force 58, they said, the enemy can never stop them. This is a fleet that has come to stay. It is led by a man called Delacrois, and he cannot be beaten. He has fifteen carriers, they said, maybe more, and cruisers and battleships and destroyers. He will win the war.

The pilots heard the stories and laughed because they knew that if anyone won the war, it would be they. But the people talked and always one question was uppermost in their minds. Where would the next battle be? Everyone knew it would be a big one. For weeks the troops had been moving through along with the amphibious ships and the supply ships. A landing somewhere?

The pilots shrugged their shoulders and said we'll all have to wait and see.

Down in the harbor the LSTs came and the LCTs and the LCIs. The tankers and the refrigerator ships and the tenders. The harbor filled again with the commerce of war but not with the men-of-war. These lay at Majuro and waited.

The pilots of the *Concord* moved off the ship and billeted at Barbers Point. Through the April days they flew and again through the nights. Gunnery and bombing and navigation and night-carrier landings on the field. Practice, practice, practice. This is a gift of grace, these few April days away from the war, so use them as best you can. You won't have time to practice a goddam thing where you're going.

It had been almost the middle of April when the *Concord* returned to Pearl Harbor, and Doris was more than four months pregnant. But she carried her baby well, the thickening at her waist barely noticeable. Winston had no trouble with official permission, and he had to hide a smile at the Admiral's almost obvious impatience. Winston knew Doris was pregnant, the Admiral and Sam Balta knew it, the

[290

squadron knew it and in fact almost everyone on the island seemed to know it. Winston didn't give a damn. He considered himself the luckiest bastard in the fleet, a belief in which his squadron mates concurred.

"You'll be best man tomorrow, Dick?" Winston asked Marriner.

Marriner was surprised. "Why me?"

"Two reasons," Winston answered honestly. "Stepik's up at Aiea Hospital for one. Second, you saved my ass. How about it?"

"Sure, Max." A thought came to Marriner. "Christ. Do I have to put on whites and wear a sword?"

Winston laughed and shook his head. "Because of certain circumstances with which we are all familiar it's going to be a quiet affair. At the station chapel. After the wedding there'll be a reception at the club. Nothing big. Just the squadron and the Old Man."

"Who's maid of honor?" Marriner tried to put the question casually, as if he didn't give a damn.

"Julie."

"Oh."

"You called her yet?"

"No. Not yet. I'm still trying to think of what I want to say."

Winston smiled. "You'll think of it."

Marriner hesitated a moment. "Max. Have you called your folks yet?"

Winston nodded. "Last night."

"So?"

"So my mother nearly fainted. Dad laughed and wished me luck. Said it was about time." Max shook his head in wonder. "All those years and I never really knew my father."

"Everything's all right then?"

"Mother will come around." Winston shrugged. "But if she doesn't it's too damn bad. This is the way it's going to be." He frowned at Marriner. "Christ, Dick. Can you imagine what Doris would be up against if they'd kept us out there indefinitely? All alone back here and four or five months pregnant."

"She's a hell of a girl. You're a lucky sonofabitch, Max."

"I know it," Winston admitted. "And now I have a suggestion for you. Go to a telephone and call Julie. Don't be a damn fool."

Marriner nodded. He walked down the corridor to the BOQ lounge and dialed Julie's number. As her voice answered he found his hand was sweating on the receiver.

291]

"Hello, Julie? This is Dick."

"Hello, Dick." Her voice was completely impersonal.

"How are you?" he asked, taking a deep breath.

"I'm fine, Dick," she said. "I hear you did wonderful things out there. Congratulations."

"Well, thanks."

"I'm sorry about Harry Hill."

Suddenly the nervousness was gone as he remembered Hill. Balls, he thought. I'm nervous and sweating over a girl, and Hill is at the bottom of the ocean. What the hell goes on here?

"Julie. How about dinner tonight?"

She hesitated only a moment. "I'm sorry, Dick. I can't tonight. I have a date."

He waited for the anger, but it didn't come. He only said, "Oh? May I ask with whom?"

"Bob Crowley."

Again there was no anger, for the memory of Hill still lingered.

"That's too bad," he said.

"I don't understand." Her voice was puzzled.

"Crowley's a worthless sonofabitch." He was speaking to Julie, but he was watching Hill somewhere in the distance.

There was a silence on the other end of the line. "Why do you say that?" Julie said at last.

Because Crowley killed Hill, he thought. But aloud he said, "Forget it, Julie. It doesn't make a damn bit of difference anymore."

She misunderstood him. "You felt that way before, Dick," she said.

"No," he said. "I wasn't talking about you and me. I was thinking of Hill. It's too late for him." What the hell, he thought, she doesn't know what I'm talking about. If that sad sonofabitch Crowley is what she wants, then the hell with it.

"I'm sorry about tonight, Dick," she said. "But I think it's just as well this way."

"Sure," he said wearily. "Sure it is, Julie. Just as well this way. I'm sorry I bothered you."

"You didn't bother me, Dick."

"Good night, Julie. I'll see you." And before she could answer he hung up the phone. He stood quietly and studied his hand and could find no trace of sweat there now. He looked out the window at the cloud-tipped mountains back of the airfield and tried to understand

[292

what had just happened to him. He felt no anger toward Julie. He asked himself if he felt resignation or regret, and he had to admit to himself that he did not.

Then what the hell had happened? He had lost Julie, and somehow it didn't mean a damn thing, and back of it all somewhere was the memory of Harry Hill. He loved Julie, of that he had no doubt. Then why didn't the knowledge that she was through with him bring forth the usual pettish anger and recriminations? What did Hill have to do with it? Hill had gone forever.

The knowledge came to him slowly, and then as he understood he nodded his head. He had another love.

Somewhere out across the ocean a man was waiting for him, a man with rows of American flags painted on his airplane, a man who had killed Harry Hill. The thing with Julie would work out or would not work out, but now in the middle of a war was no place to worry about it. He had a rendezvous to keep for Harry Hill, a meeting in some distant sky with a man whose name he did not know. He had given the man back his life once, and in return the man had killed Hill. So in a direct way Marriner felt responsible for Hill's death. He would never again be so forgiving in the sky.

"What's so funny?" He looked up to find Winston studying him.

"Funny?"

"You're standing there with a grin on your face staring out the window."

Marriner chuckled. "Just thinking things out, I guess, Max."

"You call Julie?"

"Yeah," Marriner said slowly, "I called her. She's going out with Crowley." He shrugged.

Winston watched him closely. "You don't seem pissed off."

"I'm not." Marriner smiled. "It surprises me too. What the hell, Max, I think I'm growing up."

"You're confusing hell out of me."

"Look. I have no claim on Julie. I put my name on her and she has every right to take it off if she wants. Tomorrow I'll tell her she can have her divorce. She can get it right here. When the war is over maybe I'll try again." He hesitated a moment. "Right now, Max, I don't have time to sweat it out."

"She's still in love with you, Dick."

Marriner frowned. "How do you know?" he demanded.

"Doris. She knows about these things. She said Julie's still hurt.

That's all. Don't let her get away, Dick. Not if she's important to you."

"For Christ's sake, of course she is. But I've got something I have to do first."

Winston offered him a cigarette. His eyes searched Marriner's face. "The man who got Hill?"

"Max, you're getting so goddam smart you begin to frighten me. Did Doris do this to you?"

"It'll work out, Dick. Everything will work out."

"Sure. Now let's go up to the hospital and see Steve. If they'll let us in."

"I called. We can see him. Bates is getting a jeep now."

"Ensigns don't get jeeps. They walk."

Winston laughed. "Captain Balta gave him his. Bates ought to go into politics after the war. He'd end up President."

Stepik's face was almost as white as the pillow against which he lay. There was another patient in the room, a long rubber tube disappearing down his nostril and into his stomach.

"Everything okay, Steve?" asked Winston.

"Sure," Stepik answered, closing his eyes momentarily. "Everything is just great."

"How does an ensign rate a private room? Or semiprivate?" Bates wondered.

Stepik looked at him steadily. "Just lose an arm, Terry. That's all."

Bates was unperturbed. "It could be worse, Steve. Christ, you've got another one left, haven't you? What's with the guy next door?"

"Peritonitis," Stepik said. "He isn't going to make it."

"See what we mean?" Marriner said. "Things could be a lot worse. You're going to be all right."

Winston stood by the bedside and looked down at his friend. He felt a sudden, fierce protectiveness toward Stepik. He looked so goddam helpless lying there, pale as a sheet, the lines of pain still etched deep around his mouth. There were beads of sweat on Stepik's forehead, and Winston took out a handkerchief and gently wiped them away. Stepik smiled.

"Thanks, Max."

"Wish you could be there tomorrow, Steve," Winston said. "It won't seem right without you."

Stepik nodded. "I'll be thinking of you. Both of you."

[294

"Have you written Margaret yet?" Winston asked.

Stepik shook his head. "I don't know what to tell her."

"Tell her?" said Bates in a loud voice. "For Christ's sake, tell her you lost an arm. What the hell's an arm?"

"You can't play football with one arm. That's the way I make my living." Stepik's voice was almost too low to be heard.

"You don't need two arms to run a sporting goods firm," Winston said.

"I don't have one of those," Stepik smiled.

"I do," said Winston. It was only a little lie, he thought, because I'll have one before he finds out about it.

Stepik was watching him closely. "Meaning what?"

"Meaning you're going to run it. I was fooling around with it when the war started. Going broke in a hurry too. You can handle it better than I ever could, Steve. You'll have to move to New York, though."

What a magnificent liar, Marriner thought. Aloud he said, "Who the hell wouldn't want to get out of Pittsburgh anyway?"

"Bad for the lungs in Pittsburgh," said Bates. "Smoke all over the goddam place. Everybody coughs in Pittsburgh."

"Write Margaret, Steve." Winston rested his hand on Stepik's good shoulder. "Tell her what happened. Tell her everything is going to be fine. Tell her you'll be moving to New York before long. In fact the hell with writing her. Call her on the phone."

Stepik blinked back tears as he looked at his three friends.

"You bastards make it tough on a man."

"Tell you what," said Bates seriously, "I'll buy my first pair of shoulder pads from you."

"I put in an order right now for a set of golf clubs and a gross of golf balls. I'm hell on losing golf balls." Marriner spoke in the manner of a man much concerned about his golf game.

Stepik frowned up at Winston. "You're serious about this?"

"Never more serious about anything in my life," Winston said.

"Are you doubting our integrity, Ensign?" Bates looked solemnly at Stepik. "Tell you what I'll do. On the way out I'll make the arrangements for your call to Pittsburgh." He thought a moment. "They do have telephones in Pittsburgh, don't they?"

Stepik nodded, the tears streaming unashamedly down his cheeks.

"For Christ's sake, stop crying," said Marriner. "A little pain won't kill you. You're supposed to be an All-American."

"You bastards," Stepik said in a choked voice.

295]

"Well," Bates said, "we'd better be going. This guy is going to cry all afternoon, and I can't stand cry-babies. A little pain and he goes all to pieces."

"Just get yourself well again. Doris and I will stop in after the wedding tomorrow," Winston said, and smiled.

"The honeymoon?" Stepik asked.

"We're going over to the Big Island. Kona Inn."

"Ah," Stepik nodded, "Kona Inn. It sounds wonderful."

"Crowley, the bastard, turned down his request for leave." Bates grimaced distastefully.

"I don't think he really wanted to," Winston said. "Crowley lives by the book."

"A hell of a book," Marriner said. "But Captain Balta signed the papers anyway. Max has seven days' leave, the lucky bastard."

Stepik nodded and closed his eyes wearily. "Good luck, Max. Good luck to you both."

"We'll see you tomorrow, Steve," Winston said quietly, but Stepik was already asleep.

Doris Dowling and Maxwell Winston III were married in the Barbers Point chapel at 1530 on the afternoon of April 17, 1944. Even as the chaplain read the service the roar of engines shook the frail clapboard building as a flight of Hellcats left the runway and barreled overhead. Admiral Delacrois gave the bride away, feeling with considerable regret that he was handing away the last vestige of his youth.

"You handled that well, Frog," Balta murmured as he returned to his pew.

"I was saying good-bye to something," Delacrois said softly.

Balta sighed. "I know. It comes to all of us."

Marriner was only dimly aware of the chaplain intoning the words of the service. He watched a ray of sunlight stream through the high window behind the altar, and he remembered it had been raining that day in Chicago when he and Julie had stood before the justice of peace in that musty office on the North Shore. The man had been short and dumpy, and his collar had been wilted and sweat-stained. His fee had been five dollars, but Marriner had given him twenty because he was embarrassed that Julie had to be married in such a setting.

They had not considered marriage for any length of time. Mar-

[296

riner's pockets had been filled with money, and they had felt the strong attraction that could spring up between two attractive people. For three days they had laughed continuously, pausing only now and then for a moment of seriousness.

The day it rained they had been sitting in a small bar on Howard Avenue drinking rum and Cokes. It had been warm there, a fire blazing, and they had watched the pelting rain splatter against the window. A jukebox in the corner was playing, and softly Marriner had sung along.

He had looked up to find her watching him, a hint of tears in her eyes.

"Hey now," he had said, "no time for tears. We're supposed to be happy."

She had shaken her head, laughing lightly. "I am happy. Terribly happy. Only," she had looked at him again, "that song is so sad. So damn sad because it's about all of you who are going so far away. What do you think of? All of you. What do you think of when it's almost time to leave?"

"We don't think," he had answered. "We play. We drink and sing and if we're terribly lucky we find a girl like you to play and drink with. When it's time to go it isn't so bad because none of us goes alone. I don't think too many could make it if we did. But then I want to go, alone or not. Don't ask me why. Anyway," he had taken her hand, "all this crap has nothing to do with your tears. No more tears?"

"You'll be great, Dick," she had whispered. "Don't ever doubt it."

He had looked down at her hand, resting trustingly within his own, and then he had leaned across the table and kissed her on the mouth, feeling the softness of her lips. Her hand had tightened on his, and when he had drawn back her eyes had been large.

"Julie," he had said slowly, "will you marry me? Now. Today."

She had bowed her head. Her hand had tightened again on his. When she had looked at him again her eyes had been misty.

"Why, Dick? You don't have to marry me. I'll go with you any-way." Thus simply and honestly had she offered herself to him.

"No," he had said almost angrily, "that's not what I want. I want to get married. Today. To you."

"But why?"

"What if I said I loved you?"

297]

"It wouldn't be true."

"Maybe," he had said honestly. "I'm not sure. But I don't want it the other way. I want to get married. Right now."

"Without love, Dick?" Her voice had been tender.

"I didn't say that. I said I didn't know for sure. Who the hell knows anything for sure anymore? But I think I love you, Julie. Do you? Could you love me?" His voice had been low.

"I do." Doris spoke clearly, and her voice carried back in the chapel. Marriner turned to look at Julie and was surprised to find her regarding him, the slightest of smiles on her lips. Was she too thinking of a rainy day in Chicago?

The chaplain continued. "And you, Maxwell Winston, do you take this woman . . ."

The morning Dick had left had been raw and wind-swept, with a gale tearing in from Lake Michigan, bending the trees and swirling the rubbish in the gutters. He had not wakened Julie because he had not wanted to say good-bye. He had left her there in bed, her long hair spread out over the pillow and her face very soft in the faint light. He had bent and kissed her lightly, tasting the sweetness of her lips for a last time. Then he had picked up his bag and had gone.

He took a cab down to the train station, enjoying the wind that threw a fine spray of mist over Lake Shore Drive. He opened the taxi window and let the spray beat against his face as he watched the angry whitecaps pound against the breakwaters. He was suddenly lonely on this gray early morning, and he thought of Julie sleeping in the apartment. He wanted, for a moment, to order the driver to turn around and go back, but then he remembered what he was and where he was going. As the tall buildings of the Loop appeared out of the swirling mist he remembered when he had felt like this before. On the first morning he had left for college. It had been homesickness then. What was it now?

They passed Navy Pier and a few miles offshore he thought he caught a last glimpse of the *Wolverine,* the training carrier on which he had made his qualification landings. There was a desolate look on the Chicago streets at this early hour. Briefly, he wondered if he ought to call Julie before the train left. Then he thought, The hell with it. It's done now, I've gone, why make it any tougher than it is? Christ, a hell of a morning to go to war. And all alone. Yet not really alone. A few miles away a girl wears my name now, so I am

[298

not really alone this morning. Someone cares. When he considered this he was surprised to realize it meant a great deal to him. Because a girl wore his name and cared, it was easier to move through the dawn grayness toward something far away which awaited him. He looked down at the gold wings on his uniform and suddenly decided there was one last thing to do, a thing he had forgotten.

When the cab drew up before the dirty, soot-stained terminal on Dearborn Street, Marriner got out and spoke to the driver.

"You want to make twenty bucks, Mac?"

"Hell yes, I want to make twenty bucks."

Marriner unpinned the gold wings from his uniform and handed them to the driver.

"Remember where you picked me up? 2521 Crandon?"

"Sure I remember. My stand is two blocks from there."

"Well, take these wings there. Apartment two. The name is Marriner. A girl will answer. Give her the wings and tell her I forgot. Okay?"

The driver smiled. "Okay, Mac. But who forgot?"

"Dick. Tell her Dick forgot. Tell her to keep them and wear them so she won't forget."

But it had not been Julie who forgot. The loneliness left him after he boarded the train. There were other men, and women too, heading west on the Chief, and when, the second night out, a woman asked him if he would like to have a drink in her compartment he did not think of Julie at all when he said . . .

"I do." Winston's voice brought Marriner back, and he found he was staring into Julie's eyes. Did she still have the wings? Did she remember how glorious it had been for the short time before he left? Or was it all just a painful memory that shamed her and brought the tears again? Julie, he said to himself, I wish it was a rainy morning in Chicago again, and I was a homesick kid heading out to a war. Ah Christ, how I butchered this thing.

"Then I now pronounce you man and wife." The chaplain offered his hand to Winston.

Outside the chapel Marriner put a restraining hand on Julie's arm. "I'd like to talk to you later, Julie. At the reception. It won't take long."

Julie nodded. "All right, Dick. Where were you in there?"

He frowned. "What?"

"You were a million miles away during the service."

299]

His face was expressionless. "Not a million miles, Julie. I was in Chicago on a rainy morning."

"I thought so," she said. "I was too."

"Come along, Ensign." It was Admiral Delacrois's voice. His long, sleek limousine had drawn up to the curb, and an enlisted driver was holding the door.

"I'll talk to you later, Julie," Marriner said.

Doris sat at the dressing table in the powder room off the Senior Officers' Lounge, and carefully applied her lipstick.

"What time does your plane leave?" Julie asked from her side.

"Any time I want." Doris smiled into the mirror. "We're using the Admiral's plane. Not bad, huh?"

"I'm happy for you, Doris," Julie said. "Happy for both of you. And I envy you too."

Doris swung around to face her friend. "Julie," she said contemplatively and stopped, searching for the words she wanted. "Don't let Dick get away, Julie. There isn't much time, and it would be wrong to lose him. I know this."

"I never had him, Doris," Julie said softly.

"Yes, you did. And you have him now even if you don't think so. Max knows it, and I know it. There are one or two things you ought to know, Julie."

"I don't think they could make any difference anymore."

"Don't be an ass." Doris' voice was harsh. "He's willing to do anything to get you back. But he hasn't got the time now, and if you insist on playing hard to get you're going to lose him altogether."

"I came without him. I can go back without him." Julie spoke defiantly.

"Do you really want to, Julie?"

When the other girl did not answer, Doris turned back to the mirror. She watched Julie's reflection in the glass for a moment.

"Whatever it is you expect him to do, he won't do it now, Julie. Not until he finishes a job he's set for himself."

"I don't expect him to do anything. Why should he?" Julie said. Then the import of Doris' words registered. "What job?" she asked.

"He thinks he's responsible for Harry Hill's death." Doris spoke the words bluntly.

There was amazement in Julie's voice. "That's ridiculous."

"No," Doris said. "There's a man out there. A Jap. He killed Hill."

[300

She turned again to face Julie. "Dick beat him once, but he let him live. He gave him his life, and then the man killed Hill. Now Dick has to find this man again. Max says he will. He has to."

"Maybe someone else will find him first."

"Maybe. But Max doesn't think so. He says Dick is the only man out here who can beat this man now that Hill is gone. They've fought twice now, and it's become something of a legend in the fleet." Doris rose to her feet. "So if he doesn't act the contrite lover right now, there's a reason for it. This thing means more to him than living. You and I probably can't understand it, but we can try. He was a good kid when you married him, Julie. He's a good man now. There's a hell of a difference. You'll have to grow up too now if you expect to keep up with him. I think you want to. And remember where he's going and what he has to do."

Julie said nothing and after a minute Doris continued. "Send him away if that's what you feel you have to do, but for heaven's sake don't flaunt Crowley in front of him. He doesn't deserve it. No matter what he's done."

Julie shook her head in puzzlement. "I don't know, Doris. I just don't know."

"Then I'm sorry for you," Doris said gently, "because I think it will be too late when you do know." She studied Julie's wistful face, and wondered if she had spoken out of turn about Crowley. Her own happiness gave her no reason to be harsh and flat in her judgments. But she could not believe Julie's interest in this unpopular, suspect and lost man could be motivated by anything but loneliness and a feeble desire to make Dick jealous. Julie seldom spoke of Crowley, and while Doris knew this could be a bad sign, since Julie kept herself to herself, she had long since decided that whatever there had been between them back in the States was of no lasting import. But these were no thoughts for a wedding day. Abruptly she smiled brightly. "That's enough serious discussion. Let's go drink champagne and listen to their war stories."

It was improbable that the hallowed halls of the Senior Officers' Club, normally reserved for captains and higher rank, had ever echoed to so many junior officers' voices. Admiral Delacrois had undertaken to hold the reception personally. Two white-jacketed waiters circulated constantly among the guests, carrying trays filled with champagne glasses brimming with the sparkling wine. Laughter rose above the many-keyed hum of conversation.

301]

Marriner and Winston were standing with glasses of champagne in their hands when they saw Doris and Julie enter. Winston raised his glass in a silent toast as Doris saw them and started across the room. "Don't butcher this, Dick," he said quietly to Marriner.

"I think I already have," Marriner murmured as the girls came up to them.

A waiter passed and Marriner handed the girls fresh drinks. He raised his glass to Doris.

"*Salud,* Mrs. Winston. May your years of happiness be endless."

Doris made a gesture of salute in return. The wine was chilled and very dry.

"You know what this maniac did?" Winston made the statement casually. "He called every air force base on the island and made appointments to meet their top pilots at twenty thousand feet for a dogfight. A real eager beaver."

"Have you been winning them?" Julie asked.

"So far," Marriner answered shortly.

"Remember something, Dick." Doris smiled at his stern expression. "You can overtrain in some things."

"Perhaps." Marriner shrugged. "A soldier doesn't go to battle with a rusty gun."

"And he doesn't refuse champagne either. Here." Winston handed him a drink and raised his own glass. "Short war," he said.

Doris took Winston's arm. "You'll excuse an old married couple while they speak to their guests?" She smiled at Marriner. "Don't look so grim, Dick. In fact you both look like you're waiting for the bell to ring for the last round."

"They go well together," Marriner said as Doris and Winston moved away.

"Doris told me about Harry Hill," Julie said, shaking her head. "You mustn't feel that way, Dick."

He shrugged. A waiter passed, and he handed Julie a fresh drink.

"You've changed, Dick." Her voice was faintly puzzled.

He chuckled. "I'm sober, if that's what you mean."

"No," she said. "That's not what I mean. You've stopped laughing at the world, I think."

"No. I haven't stopped laughing. But now I wait for something funny to happen."

"You never did before."

[302

He sighed. "There's a lot of things I never did before. I count them at night when I go to sleep. I was a damn fool. Julie," he said, "you can have your divorce. Get it right out here if you want to. I'm not going to contest it or stand in your way. Any grounds you decide on is okay with me."

"Dick, I . . ."

"It wasn't much of a marriage, was it?" He spoke hurriedly because he did not want to draw pity in her reply. Pity was for other men, not Dick Marriner. Then he saw Crowley approaching. He smiled. "Here comes your friend," he said and there was no rancor in his tone. He nodded to Crowley.

"Evening, Commander," he said levelly.

"Am I interrupting something?" Crowley asked, obviously ill at ease.

"Not a thing, Commander," Marriner said easily. "I was just leaving." He nodded to Julie. "Maybe some other rainy day in Chicago, Julie. Maybe then."

He touched Winston lightly on the arm as he neared the exit. "I'll be shoving off, Max. Have a wonderful time at Kona."

Doris looked across the room to where Julie stood watching them. "Julie?" she asked Marriner.

"She'll get her divorce out here," he said. "I'll give her no trouble."

"For a man as smart as you are in the air," Winston said, "you're pretty damn stupid on the ground." He shook his head. "No offense meant, Dick."

"And none taken." Marriner smiled. "I'll see you two in seven days. Give 'em hell at Kona."

Once Marriner had left, Julie turned to find Crowley watching her, a frown on his face.

"Is something wrong, Bob?" she asked.

"You know the answer to that better than I do," he said. "Are you still remembering Chicago?"

Julie did not understand. "I forgot Chicago a long time ago, Bob," she said. "It's all over with Dick and me."

Crowley could not keep the bitterness out of his voice. "That isn't what I meant. There has to be some reason you keep seeing me. I'm beginning to think it's pity. I don't like pity, Julie."

303]

"I haven't thought about it that way, Bob," Julie said slowly as understanding came to her. She hesitated and then said, "And what if it were pity? All of us need some of it at one time or another."

Crowley laughed with no trace of humor in his voice. "So all this ever was was friendship. Buddy-buddy."

Julie spoke, her voice tenser now. "If that's not enough, I'm sorry."

"No," Crowley said, "you're not sorry. Sorry for me maybe because of what happened. But not sorry because all we have is friendship." His voice was harsh. "What . . . happened in Chicago . . . it won't happen again, Julie. I know it won't."

"I know it too, Bob," she said. "There won't be an opportunity."

Crowley spoke as though to himself. "You offer friendship because you're sorry for me. Sorry for a failure in me. Well, Christ, there must be someone who has more to offer than that." He looked at Julie without seeing her. "Well, I damn well know where to find more than friendship and less than sorrow."

Doris and Winston did not return to Oahu until the 27th of April. During that time Marriner did not see or call Julie. Instead he put her in the back of his mind and set out to fly around the clock. He fought every type of Army fighter plane on the island, meeting them above Barbers Point and Hickam and Ewa and over the small, numbered landing strips that dotted the island. They met at sea level and at twenty thousand feet, at dawn and at dusk when the sun was already below the western horizon. In the dark of night he was out again, flying night field carrier landing practice. He logged ten hours a day in his plane, and honed himself to a fine edge. In the skies over Oahu, Marriner tempered his abilities and skills, striving relentlessly toward one goal.

Invincibility.

A P-47 pilot returned to his base and told of the maniac he had fought over Ewa. A P-51 pilot landed and spoke in amazement of a Hellcat that had beaten him at fifteen thousand feet over the valley. It was unheard of. A Hellcat couldn't get near a P-51. But this one had. "He was all over the sky. I never brought my guns to bear."

A flight of four Lightnings, returning from gunnery practice, were attacked by a single Hellcat, and in the ensuing melee the Hellcat beat all four of the P-38s. Not only beat them, but frightened one new 2nd lieutenant half to death.

"The bastard sat ten feet behind my tail. Just sat there. Never

[304

moved out of the slot. He may as well have been glued on my ass. I never shook him. Finally he just waved and flew away. Christ, but he was good."

One afternoon the P-47s, tired of being beaten in the sky, arranged a reception committee for the lone Hellcat. Eight of the Army's best pilots joined at twenty thousand feet over Ewa and waited for him. He kept the rendezvous alone. One by one the Thunderbolts took him on. In a matter of forty-five minutes Marriner had decisively clobbered all eight. That night the P-47 pilots called Barbers Point to get the name of the man who had beaten them. The next day Marriner became an honorary member of Army Air Force Fighter Squadron 76.

At night, when he wasn't practicing carrier landings, he flew instrument and navigation hops. While the other pilots sat around the Officers' Club bar, drinking and hazarding guesses concerning the next operation, Marriner was up in the clear night sky. He rigged a canvas shield that blacked out all outside visual contact, leaving him alone in his cockpit with his instrument panel and enabling him to fly instruments under actual conditions. He flew round-robin navigation hops on instruments, plotting a course to Kauai, Molokai, Maui and back to Barbers Point.

When, late at night, he shrugged out of his flight suit and returned to the BOQ, it was to fall into bed exhausted. But he did not sleep well. He dreamed of a man in a multiflagged airplane. Sometimes he also saw Hill twisting downward toward the water, stricken and dying. Then he would see the Zero filling his gunsights and his tracers pouring out, and often he would awake and his right hand would be clenched in a half-fist, the fingers taut around an imaginary trigger. One night he dreamed the Zero was on his tail, and he heard the *thunk* of shells hitting his aft section. Bates woke him up as he was screaming, "No. No, goddam it. No!"

Julie was not gone from his mind, but he had thrust her memory back where it did not interfere with what he had to do. If he thought of her it was only for a fleeting moment, and then the regret would come again, even though momentarily.

And now, while Marriner polished his skills and probed the deepest recesses of his capabilities, the pale men came again. They still carried the brown briefcases attached to their wrists and their eyes were still harried. And once again the lights burned long into the night in the paneled offices of the high command.

305]

Admiral Frog Delacrois watched impassively as the gray-thatched four-star admiral ran his eye over the papers before him on his desk. Strange, thought Delacrois, how the man never ages. The weight of this entire Pacific command is on his shoulders, and yet his eyes are as clear as a boy's. He has learned the secret of command, the way to bear its insurmountable weight. I hope I have learned it as well.

The patient man raised his eyes to Delacrois. "The *Concord* will be ready to sail by the middle of the month." It was not a question.

Delacrois nodded. "Yes, sir. We can shove off any time after the 10th."

The four-star Admiral nodded, and his eyes returned to the papers he held in his hand. "Your orders haven't been cut yet, but I can tell you what's in store for you." He took his glasses off and pinched the bridge of his nose.

"I think I know, sir."

The man smiled. "Go ahead then."

"Saipan and the Jap First Fleet."

The man nodded. "In that order." He rose to his feet and walked to a large wall map studded with multicolored pins. He pointed to an area in the Far East.

"Togyama has left Singapore. He's somewhere in the waters between the Philippines and Borneo. We'll find him. He's waiting there, waiting to come out and fight."

"I hope so, sir," Delacrois said flatly.

"There is a difference between waiting defensively and waiting aggressively. Togyama is waiting aggressively. He knows we are coming, and he knows *where* we are coming. Togyama is anything but a fool. He knows we will hit Saipan first."

"Do we have a composition of his forces, sir?"

"He left Singapore with nine carriers. When he knows we are on our way he'll pull in every unit he can find. But right now he has nine carriers, and his pilots are good. Damn good."

"The best they have left, sir. You're right, sir. Togyama will come out this time."

"And this time we'll finish him. Don't let him get away, Frog. Not if you have to chase him all the way back to Tokyo."

"He won't get away, sir."

"D-Day on Saipan is June 15th. You can leave Majuro at your discretion, but be in position to cover the landings by D-minus three.

[306

We've got eleven subs heading for Philippine waters now. You'll have your position reports long before Togyama can get there." The man paused a moment. "You know what this landing means, don't you, Frog?"

"Yes, sir. If Jap bombers can fly from Tokyo to Saipan, then our bombers can fly from Saipan to Tokyo. We'll be able to move into their backyard now."

"You're going to have the biggest naval command in history, Frog. I'm giving you every carrier I've got out here. You've got two jobs to do. Keep the air clear for the landings, and then find Togyama and destroy him. He may not want to fight so badly once he knows the size of your task force. If he doesn't, if he turns and runs, you've got to go after him. *You've got to catch him this time.*" The man never raised his voice, but the emphasis on his words was plainly evident.

"I doubt he'll run, sir. He's been waiting a long time for this too. His morale is high, and his men know that now is the time for them to fight back. Now or never. We'll meet them." Delacrois spoke with a simple conviction.

The four-star Admiral leaned back in his heavily upholstered chair. He rubbed a knuckle along his nose. "I understand there was a wedding last week."

"Er . . . yes, sir. I gave the bride away."

There was a hint of amusement in the patient man's eyes. "That was very kind of you, Frog. Kind indeed. I thank you for the invitation. I was tied up in a conference." He waved vaguely at the papers before him.

Delacrois rose to his feet. "I'll let my pilots fly till the 5th of May, sir. Then the planes will go in for final overhaul. I'll move out around the 13th."

"Not superstitious, Frog?"

"Not a damn bit, sir."

"All right then. I'll have your orders cut. You'll fly your flag on the *Concord*?"

"I will, sir. Captain Balta and I are old friends."

"I know." The man hesitated a moment. "You can tell Balta his stars are in the works." He picked up some papers from the desk and lowered his glance. "When he comes back from Saipan."

Delacrois grinned with pleasure. "Thank you, sir. I'll tell him."

The newly married Winstons moved into a beach bungalow near Barbers Point. It was only a temporary thing since once Winston left, Doris would move back to Fort Shafter. Her replacement from the States would not arrive for a month, and Doris planned to continue her duties until then. In the meantime, as activity increased around Pearl Harbor, the Winston bungalow became the center of Fighting Squadron Two's off-duty hours.

"How about a picnic tomorrow?" Doris asked Dick Marriner one evening.

"Why not?"

"I didn't know if you could tear yourself away from your airplane."

Marriner laughed. "There aren't any airplanes. They've gone into final overhaul."

Doris' smile faded. "Oh? You're leaving soon?"

He shrugged. "Nobody knows exactly when." He put his hands on her shoulders. "But it won't be long, Doris. You knew that. Make it easy for Max if you can."

She forced a smile. "Don't worry, Dick. No tears." She looked across the room to where her husband was mixing martinis for Bates and Anders. "Take care of him, Dick. Take care of him for me."

"You're damn right I will," Marriner said.

She looked at him again. "Julie's coming tomorrow."

"Oh?" He frowned at her. "I haven't called her since the wedding."

"I know. She felt badly about it."

"Does she know I'm coming?"

"Of course."

"Great," Marriner said. "We can play it light and easy. Old friends from Chicago." He shook his head in disgust. "Crap."

Winston approached with a pitcher of martinis.

"How are things at the squadron?" he asked Marriner as he filled his glass.

"How the hell would I know? I've been up in the air all week."

"You've been up in the air all your life," Bates said, joining them.

"Where did Anders go?"

"I sent him out for more gin," Bates said.

"Going to be drunk out tonight?" Marriner asked.

"Why not?" Bates shrugged. "The planes are down, and we've only got a few nights left." There was an uncomfortable silence.

[308

"Well," Max said slowly, "a few nights are better than no nights at all." He looked at Marriner. "All set for tomorrow?"

"Sure you want company?"

Max slid his arm around Doris. "My wife is indulging in all sorts of machinations. She thinks she can bring you and Julie together." He studied Marriner in silence. "Perhaps she can."

Marriner said nothing. Then a slow smile broke over his face. "There's a chance, I suppose. About as much chance as I'd have of walking up the Empire State Building with a trolley car on my back."

"You don't know Doris," Max said.

Marriner looked at her with approval. "You're wrong, Max. I do know Doris. I've told you before what a lucky bastard you are. I reaffirm it."

Doris laughed. "You're spoiling me." She kissed Winston on the cheek. When she turned to Marriner her eyes were unnaturally bright. "Well, if we've only got a few nights left, let's raise a little hell."

The day began well. Julie had taken a cab from Fort Shafter and was already preparing lunch when Marriner arrived. He placed the two bottles of wine he had brought on the table and watched her silently until she straightened up from her task and brushed a strand of hair back from her forehead.

"Thanks for all the phone calls," she said.

"I wasn't certain you wanted me to call," he said and went off to join Max in making a production out of packing ice around the wine bottles. Then he walked over to the food hamper and surreptitiously picked out a piece of chicken.

"Put it back, Ensign." Julie spoke severely.

"Christ," he mumbled. "It's only a piece of chicken. You'd think we were married or something." He put the chicken back.

"Yes, you would, wouldn't you?" Doris agreed innocently.

"Who cooked the chicken?" he asked.

"Julie," answered Doris.

Marriner frowned at Julie. "You never told me you could cook."

"You never gave me a chance. All we did was drink and eat at restaurants."

"We did a few other things too," Marriner said shortly.

"I do believe Julie's blushing," Winston observed. "It becomes her."

309]

Julie smiled as she buckled the strap on the hamper. "It's just a heat flush from bending over a hot stove." She surveyed the kitchen. "Well, we've got everything. Let's go."

"Have you got an umbrella?" Marriner asked her.

"What the hell do you need an umbrella for?" Winston asked. "It's not going to rain. You crazy or something?"

Marriner kept his eyes on Julie. "I don't know. It might. It rained the last time I was in Chicago."

Julie explained to Doris. "It was raining the morning Dick left. I woke up and he was gone, and the rain was pounding on the window. I'll never forget it."

"Well, it won't rain today so the hell with an umbrella." Winston picked up the ice bucket. "Come on, let's play."

Outside in the driveway was a covered carryall which Winston had borrowed from the motor pool at Barbers Point and an open jeep which Marriner had taken from the squadron.

"Let's take both cars, Max," Marriner suggested. "I can drop Julie off at Shafter on the way back. You won't have to go out of your way."

"Stop making excuses for Christ's sake." Winston grinned. "You're old enough to drive your own jeep if you want to." He looked at Julie. "You'll want to ride with us, won't you, Julie?" he asked facetiously.

"You are a bastard, Winston," Marriner commented.

Julie climbed into the jeep. "We'll follow you," she called to Max.

They drove past Barbers Point heading north and soon were beyond the residential districts and heading up toward the mountains. The paved road gave way to a rutted gravel path, and then they were climbing a steep hill, the engine of the jeep laboring under the pull. Verdant foliage surrounded them as they crested the hill, and then they were gazing down on a quiet valley where a small stream played fitfully over glistening rocks and the smell of gardenia and frangipani came to them on the soft air.

"It's beautiful, Dick." Julie's voice was hushed.

"It ought to be a million miles from Barbers Point. Listen, Julie." Marriner leaned forward, his head cocked. He covered Julie's hand with his own. "For the first time I can't hear the airplanes. Not a damn one."

She did not remove her hand, as she watched him carefully. "Can you forget them for today, Dick?"

[310

Marriner turned the key in the ignition and the engine died. He turned to look at her. "I can forget them for today, Julie. . . . Julie, have you gone ahead with the divorce?"

"No," she said almost inaudibly. "Not yet."

"I see. Well, we won't discuss it today. Okay? Today is for fun." To himself he wondered when there would be other days like this.

"Come on, you two." Winston's voice hailed them from far below on the valley floor.

Hours later when the shadows had lengthened, and the heat of noon had given way to a softly scented coolness, they lay, pleasantly exhausted, on blankets beneath a great tree. They had eaten and drunk well. Now they felt a comfortable lassitude, a sense of well-being that came very near to happiness.

"This has been one hell of a day," Marriner murmured. He rested against the tree, Julie's head pillowed in his lap. Nearby, Doris and Max stretched out on a blanket, her head on his shoulder and his arm around her.

"I wish it would never end," Doris said drowsily. "Why do all good things have to end?"

Max softly caressed Doris' cheek. "They don't, darling. Sometimes they're interrupted though. That's all that's happening. We'll be interrupted a little while."

"Damn good thinking, Max," Marriner said. He looked down to find Julie staring up at him. "You're a hell of a fine cook," he said. "You'll make some guy a great wife. Why don't you get married?"

There was a silence. Then she said quietly, "I am married."

"You ought to stay that way."

"Hear hear," Doris said.

"You're not supposed to be listening," Marriner said lazily.

"What are you doing?" Max did not open his eyes.

"Making a pass at Miss Simmons," Marriner replied.

"I thought her name was Marriner," Max drawled. He leaned over and kissed Doris.

"It was," Marriner said. "She changed it."

Doris lay comfortably within Winston's arm. "I think Marriner is a prettier name than Simmons. Why would she want to change?"

"Crazy, I guess," Marriner said.

"A crazy, mixed-up kid all right," Max agreed.

311]

Marriner turned his head. "Max," he said, "stop that. It's indecent."

"Hell," said Winston, fondling Doris' breast, "I'm an old married man. You ought to try it."

"I don't think Doris would let me." Marriner yawned.

Doris could not suppress a giggle. "You two are nutty."

"Of course we're nutty," Marriner agreed. "Why else would we be running all over the Pacific Ocean shooting at people we don't know?"

They were silent for a time, each taken up with unspoken thoughts. It was as if they were in another world far removed from the blast of engines and the stutter of fifty-calibers. Yet not too far away planes sat, waiting to go pounding down the Barbers Point runways. Far to the westward the great fleet lay waiting in Majuro Lagoon. And still farther west a hard-eyed Togyama cruised Philippine waters waiting for Task Force 58 to appear.

"Max?" Doris' voice was a whisper.

"Yeah?"

"How long before you go?"

Max hesitated before he answered. "A few days. Forget it now. We'll think about it later."

"I think about it all the time." Doris kissed him.

Winston smiled lazily. "We ought to be going home soon. I have plans for you tonight."

Doris kissed him again, this time on the ear. "Mmmmm. Sounds interesting."

"If you two don't stop it," Marriner said, "I'm going to get horny."

"Go ahead," Winston said.

Marriner abruptly bent down and kissed Julie on the mouth. She did not move, but her lips trembled beneath his.

"I just kissed Miss Simmons," Marriner explained. "I get more response kissing the side of my airplane."

"You do that often?" Max asked. "Kiss the side of your airplane I mean."

"Only when I'm horny."

Marriner reached for the half-filled wine bottle. He tilted it and took a long swallow. "Want some?" he asked Julie.

She shook her head, staring up at him.

"How long will you be gone, Dick?" she asked.

He lifted his shoulders. "Who knows? Not too long I think. We've

[312

been out here going on nine months. The tour should be over before too long."

"Then what?"

"I don't know. Back to the States to instructor duty probably. Miami or Jacksonville maybe."

"Is that what you want?"

"No. I suppose I'll come back again. It isn't over yet."

"You've done your part. Let someone else take over."

He brushed a strand of hair back from her forehead. "Where does my part end?" he asked. "You can't say that on such and such a day Dick Marriner completed his part in the war. On such and such a day he had fought so many hours, therefore he was finished with it. It isn't that easy. You were right, Julie, I have changed. When I think of the guy who left you that morning in Chicago it seems like he was someone I knew once a long time ago." He paused a moment. "Incidentally, did that cabdriver bring the wings to you that morning?"

"He brought them." Her voice was a sigh. "I cried all day."

"I was going to call you from the station. Then I thought, what the hell was there left to say?"

"You could have said you loved me."

He exhaled softly through his teeth. "I didn't know. I didn't know anything then."

"And now?"

"And now I know. I do love you, Julie. Now that it's too late." He shook his head in disgust. "Julie, this past week. There was a reason I didn't call."

She raised a hand and brushed a finger lightly across his lips.

"I know," she said. "Everyone knows."

"What the hell."

She smiled up at him. "Army pilots come to Shafter too. They're all talking about the maniac from Barbers Point. Besides, Doris told me. Will you find him, Dick? The man who killed Hill."

"I'll find him," Marriner said. "If he's there, I'll find him. I have to." He spoke from a simple conviction.

Half playfully Doris admonished Winston, "And you keep your big nose out of it when he does."

"Don't worry," Winston said. "I happen to be a coward. Dick does my fighting for me."

"Some coward," Marriner said. "Some coward at Tarawa. I'd still be wandering around that island, Max."

313]

"You owed me twenty dollars," Winston said. "I had to get you out."

But Marriner did not want to talk anymore about the war and what he had to do.

"I think it's time to go," he said, shifting Julie's head and rising to his feet. "We don't want to tire Maxwell Winston the Fourth's mother too much."

They put the remnants of the picnic back into the hamper, rolled up the blankets, and loaded the gear into the back of Winston's carryall.

"I'll take Julie back to Shafter," Marriner said.

"It's been a wonderful day, Doris," Julie said. "I'll call you tomorrow."

"Take the turn just before the Main Gate," Max said to Marriner. "You'll come out on the highway to Shafter." He clapped him on the shoulder. "See you at the squadron tomorrow."

Marriner waited until the carryall had disappeared down the road in a cloud of dust. He made no move to start the engine but sat with his arms resting on the wheel.

"I wish we'd done more of this, Julie."

She nodded her head. "I do too, Dick." She paused a fraction of a second. "Now."

"Well," he said, starting the engine. "It's too late now. Goddam it, why am I always too late." It was a statement, not a question.

They sat there in silence for several minutes as the sun slipped lower and finally dipped below the crest of the hill. Marriner reached in the back of the jeep and placed his flight jacket around Julie's shoulders. As he did so he saw she was crying.

"Hey there," he said. "Cut that out."

She shook her head, angry at herself. "Can't a girl cry if she wants to?"

"Not after a day like this. Crying is for funerals or weddings. Not today."

"Okay," she said. She dabbed at her eyes with a handkerchief. "It's all over now."

He put the jeep in gear and drove slowly up the hill, leaving dust swirls in their wake. He looked over at her and smiled.

"It didn't rain today."

"I'll always think of you when it rains, Dick." She spoke simply, frankly.

[314

"You do that, Julie," he said. "You be sure and do that."

They were silent as Marriner drove down the dirt road and turned left on the paved highway that led past Barbers Point. He came to a halt at a stop sign near the Main Gate just as a flight of four Hellcats left the runway and roared directly overhead. Julie watched him as his eyes followed the planes until they were lost from sight. Only then did he look at her.

"It was good getting away from the planes for a day," he said. "I never realized they made so goddam much noise."

"But you're back now and somehow I'm sorry."

They turned left again and headed down the main highway to Fort Shafter. It was dusk now, and in the rapidly gathering darkness the city of Honolulu stretched before them.

He breathed a sigh of regret as he drew up in front of Julie's apartment. The drive had been altogether too short.

"Unfortunately, we're home. Or you're home rather." He turned in the seat to face her. "Thanks for a wonderful time, Julie. It will be something to remember after we leave." He did not want to sound maudlin so he shook his head, laughing. "Christ, I didn't mean to sound like that."

He got out of the jeep and came around to help her out. "I'll walk you to the door," he said.

Julie let her breath out slowly in a long extended exhalation, as if some ponderous weight had been lifted from her mind.

"Do you want to come in for a drink?" she asked softly.

Marriner's surprise was evident. "Why sure. Hell yes, I'll come in for a drink."

Julie unlocked the door and stood aside as Marriner entered. She flicked on the lights and gestured at the bar against the wall.

"Help yourself," she said quietly. "I'll be right back."

She disappeared into the bedroom, as Marriner got out the ice and mixed a highball. He turned on the radio and manipulated the dial until the soft strains of a Hawaiian orchestra filled the room. Contented, he sat back on the divan and closed his eyes. Christ, he thought, this is living. I wonder if the day will come when this sort of thing will be part of everyday existence. To come home every night to this and never go to bed at night wondering if you'll be around in twenty-four hours to go to bed again. To get up in the morning after a night without dreams, without nightmares, to kiss your wife knowing that that night you'll still be around to kiss her on the lips again.

315]

To be able to turn your back to the sun and not worry that someone is hiding in it waiting to sweep down behind you. To hear a simple thing like the backfire of a car without remembering the stutter of the fifty-calibers and the deadly *thunk* as the shells hit your plane. Ah Christ, but that is for another time and another life and very probably for another man.

He looked at his watch. Twenty minutes had passed, and his glass was empty. He made another drink and called to Julie.

"Hey in there. You all right?"

"I'll be out in a minute." Julie's voice was muted.

"Well, hurry it up. I've got to beat that curfew back to Barbers Point."

He looked up at the sound of a door opening. Julie stood framed in the doorway under the soft light from a wall lamp. She wore a blue housecoat and her hair cascaded to her shoulders. Marriner drew in his breath sharply.

"Make me a drink, Dick," she said.

He started to put ice into a glass as she came across the room and stood beside him. His eyes widened and slowly he put the glass down.

Over her left breast she wore his gold wings.

"The wings, Julie," he managed to say. "You're wearing the wings."

"They were never very far from me. Never." Her eyes were misty, and there was a catch in her voice.

He let his hands fall to his side. Slowly he said, "Does this mean what I hope it means? I don't want to make a mistake again."

"That was another Dick Marriner. This one doesn't make mistakes. That's what he tells me." A smile played at the corner of her mouth.

He put his hands on her shoulders. "My God," was all he could find to say as she came into his arms.

"Dick, Dick, Dick," she whispered. "My big, strong, dumb, sweet darling."

He kissed her with a great tenderness, holding her face cupped in his hands. He felt her lips tremble and then they parted under his. Her arms crept around his neck and tightened, and he felt a stirring in his loins as she pressed against him.

"The curfew, Dick," she whispered. "Don't worry about it tonight."

He kissed her again and felt her breasts against his chest, and the

[316

pounding of her heart. He buried his head in her hair, savoring its fragrance.

His hands moved gently, unfastening the belt of her housecoat. Then he slid both hands inside the garment, and felt the smoothness of her back as he pulled her against him. She could not control a quick gasp as his hands moved over her breasts and down her legs, seeking and searching with a tender insistence. She moaned softly in his ear. Marriner picked her up and carried her into the bedroom.

Much later that night he awoke to hear the soft, rhythmic sound of Julie's breathing. He propped himself on an elbow and looked down at his wife, sleeping with a childlike innocence. He felt a great love well within him as she smiled in her sleep.

He leaned over and kissed her lightly on the mouth. She turned to him, reaching up her arms.

"Darling," she murmured drowsily.

"Julie, listen," he said. "Listen, Julie."

Outside, rain was falling.

XVI

June, 1944

At first light on May 14, 1944, Admiral Frog Delacrois stood beside Sam Balta on the bridge as Balta conned the *Concord* out of Pearl Harbor. The sun was still below the eastern horizon, and the two men were bundled in heavy flight jackets against the morning's chill.

"Once again, Sam," Delacrois murmured. "And this is the last time together."

"Your words have the ring of doom this morning, Frog," Balta said with a smile. "We're indestructible. I have decided so."

"That's not what I meant. I have something to tell you."

"What's the matter?" Balta asked. "Did I forget to shave this morning?"

"It's something more important than your whiskers." The Admiral grinned at Balta. "You're getting your stars, Sam."

Balta frowned for a moment and then he whistled softly. "Well, goddam," he said.

Delacrois put a hand on his friend's shoulder. "They'll be waiting for you after this operation. Congratulations, Sam. You deserve them."

"Two stars, by God."

"You'll find they'll bring a lot of headaches, my friend. And heartaches too."

"Well, Frog," Balta offered his hand, "when they come I'll remember how you handled them and try to do as well."

They shook hands in silence. Then Balta turned to the Officer of the Deck.

"Make twenty knots for Majuro."

[318

"Aye aye, sir," came the reply.

They walked forward on the outer bridge, and stood facing the bow, allowing the fine mist of spray borne on the freshening wind to whip at their faces.

"Sam," Delacrois said, "what about your fighter squadron? Did you get a replacement for Hill?"

"No, sir. I'm letting Larson keep them. There wasn't anyone available at Pearl. Larson can handle it now that the others know what the hell they're doing."

"Know what they're doing?" The Admiral chuckled. "You've got two of the top aces in the fleet. Anders and Marriner."

"I won't have anybody worth a damn left," Balta grumbled, "if they don't stop running off and getting married. Jesus Christ. The middle of a war, and all they can think about is what's between their legs."

Delacrois laughed. "They're young, Sam. The sap flows just like it did in us a long time ago."

"Not so goddam long ago. Christ, they get a wife and the first thing you know they're in a dogfight someplace and thinking of a girl back home, and the next thing they've got bullets all over the cockpit, and unless they're damn lucky they're dead. This is going to be a tough one, Frog. Even for those like Anders and Marriner. They'll need everything they've got and then a prayer besides."

"Tough? Yes, it's going to be tough. Togyama will come out, unless I'm greatly mistaken. He'll come out roaring too. He's got the only pilots left in Japan who are worth a damn. He and I have been heading for this ever since this war began. He can't wait any longer and neither can I."

Morale was even higher among the men of the Japanese First Fleet than Delacrois had imagined. For two weeks they had waited in the waters between the southern Philippines and Borneo, for Togyama wanted to be certain the American fleet was not going to pay a return visit to Palau.

On May 16th the fleet assembled in the anchorage at Tawi Tawi, north of Borneo. Togyama had all but swept the seas clean to accumulate the strongest attack force yet gathered by the Empire. He had nine aircraft carriers, five battleships, twelve heavy cruisers and four divisions of destroyers.

Eleven days later, May 27th, reports reached Togyama that the

319]

Americans had invested Biak. He stared at the report with expressionless eyes. He had guessed Palau, but it had been Biak. So. The American carrier fleet was conspicuously absent at Biak. Togyama sent out a search for Task Force 58.

It was June 6th when his reconnaissance reported back. Majuro was filled to overflowing with the mightiest array of naval power ever seen.

Togyama smiled grimly to himself. He turned his cold eyes on his Chief of Staff.

"I want twenty-four-hour surveillance of that fleet. Stage out of Truk at night."

Back across the Pacific the recco planes flew, touching down in the Carolines and the Marshalls in the dark of night.

But this time when they arrived over Majuro the lagoon was empty except for two supply ships and a seaplane tender.

Now Togyama knew. Certainty had replaced conjecture. He had known the Americans would come after Saipan and Guam and Tinian, but he had not completely convinced himself that the time was now. He rendezvoused his fleet again off Guimaras Island in the Philippine archipelago.

It was June 15th, and twenty thousand Americans were ashore on Saipan when Togyama finally weighed anchor and headed east. He set his speed in accordance with the top speed of his slowest man-of-war. The First Fleet boiled eastward primed for a fight.

Frog Delacrois had sailed out of Majuro Lagoon at the head of his Task Force 58 on June 6, 1944. Within seven days the central Pacific was scored by converging columns of ships constituting the greatest aggregation of sea power in the world.

Task Force 58 took up its position on June 12th, covering an area westward of the Marianas, eagerly waiting for Togyama. But he would be late. He would not arrive on the scene until the 18th. Even then he would be too far to the west to attack the American fleet effectively.

On June 18th at 2230 hours the telephone rang in the Chief's quarters on the *Concord* where Chief Rasmussen was lying in his bunk.

"Telephone, Rasmussen," a voice called. He rolled out of the bunk and crossed to the wall phone on the aft bulkhead.

[320

"Rasmussen here."

"Chief? O'Toole." O'Toole's voice was excited.

"What's wrong, Irish?" he asked.

"I might have somethin' again."

"Oh?"

"It's Rathburn."

Rasmussen was immediately alert. "Let's have it."

"Climbed outa the sack again at this goddam hour of night. Prettied himself up, combed his hair and poured that junk all over himself. I heard him on the phone just before all this. I dunno who the hell it was. But crissake, Chief, where would a guy be goin' all whored up at this time of night? Anyway, I thought I'd letcha know. You ain't got enough to do around this ship. Come to think of it, maybe Rathburn was goin' to the CAG office. Seems funny though."

"Well," said Rasmussen, "let's hope he did. Thanks, Irish. Go to bed now."

Rasmussen took his hat, a flashlight and a wire full of keys from his locker and climbed the ladder to the abovedecks.

Three decks above, the air group office was deserted, one dim lamp burning over one of the desks. Rasmussen walked quietly down the passageway and stopped outside a door. He stood there for thirty seconds, and later he would wonder whether he had really expected to hear anything from inside. Then he opened the door and looked into the empty office. The desks were clean, paper work neatly stacked. It was obvious the CAG office had been shut down for the night. The sickness was growing in Rasmussen as he closed the door and made for a ladder that would take him to officers' country.

Arriving at the deck on which the CAG's cabin was located, Rasmussen walked silently down the passageway, his heart pounding in his chest. At first, as he approached Crowley's cabin, he could hear only the drumming rumble of the ship's engines and somewhere far off the distant clacking of a typewriter. And because this thing he was about to do was so distasteful to him, he sought some means of delaying it. The only thing that came to his mind was to look at his watch. He did so and never remembered later what time it had been.

Slowly, deliberately, he reached up and slid his fingers over the top of the bulkhead where it ended four inches below the ceiling. Without a sound, he pulled himself up until his eyes were level with the opening and then he looked down.

321]

When he finally lowered himself gently back to the deck, his eyes were bleak. He stood there unmoving, breathing slowly, until his heart resumed a steady beat. Then he moved quietly up the passageway, leaving behind him the darkened room and the muted voices.

Barry Wheeler was fishing in his pocket for his cabin key, and so he did not see Chief Rasmussen standing in the shadows against the bulkhead. Only when he put the key into the lock did Rasmussen step forward into the light.

"Sir?"

Wheeler turned, surprised. "Rasmussen. What are you doing up here?"

"A word, sir. It's important."

Rasmussen's voice was grave. Wheeler opened the door. "Come on in, Chief."

Wheeler shut the door. He knew Rasmussen well as a man steeped in the tradition that had made him, never doubting any part of it, content to live within the boundaries of the life he had chosen.

"Sit down, Chief." Wheeler walked to a small portable icebox lying in a corner of the room. "Coke?" he asked Rasmussen.

"No thank you, sir."

Wheeler opened his Coke and took a chair facing Rasmussen. "Okay, Chief. Sit down and tell me what's the trouble."

Rasmussen drew a deep breath and sat on the edge of a chair. He twisted his battered cap in his big, blunt hands and leaned forward as he groped for the difficult words.

Wheeler studied the heavy-set man. There was something here that went beyond ordinary squadron troubles. Wheeler had never known Rasmussen to be ill at ease or to evince such an obvious nervousness. "If something is bothering you, you came to the right place," he said.

"I know it, sir." Rasmussen wet his lips and spoke. "There is a problem here, sir. A problem that's too big for me by far."

Wheeler started to smile until he saw the expression in the Chief's eyes. "I've never known anything to be too big for you before, Chief. Spit it out then."

Rasmussen squeezed his eyes shut, as though he were in torment. "You know my record, sir." It was a statement, not a question.

"I do," Wheeler agreed.

"Then you know I've given my life to this Navy. Knowing that,

[322

you'll realize that if there was any way I could handle this myself, I would. But I can't. And so because this Navy and the men in it mean more to me than anything in this world, I've come to you."

Wheeler said nothing. He waited for Rasmussen to continue.

"Sir," Rasmussen spoke hurriedly now, the words pouring out, "Commander Crowley is in his cabin with an enlisted man. There is an article of war dealing with the matter, but I don't know right now what it is. It deals with"—he spat the word out—"sodomy."

At first the Chief's words only puzzled Wheeler. Then under Rasmussen's level gaze Wheeler suddenly awoke to the immensity of the accusation. For a moment he could say nothing as he struggled to accept the idea.

"For Christ's sake, Chief. Do you know what you're saying?"

"I know, sir. I don't know if I'm doing the right thing by the book, but I had to tell someone. It was too much for me."

Wheeler rubbed a hand across his forehead. "You're certain of this?"

"I'd give my life to disbelieve it, sir."

"You saw it?" Wheeler was still incredulous.

"Ten minutes ago, sir." Rasmussen rose to his feet. "Perhaps I'm a coward. But you have it now, sir. How you handle it is your business. There's one other thing I'd leave with you, sir."

Wheeler found it hard to tear his eyes away from a spot on the floor. When he did look up he saw Rasmussen holding a heavy key ring out to him.

"If you have any doubts, sir, the key to Commander Crowley's cabin is on this ring. I borrowed it from a master-at-arms."

Wheeler accepted the key ring reluctantly. He stared at it and then he said, "This took a hell of a lot of guts, Chief."

"Well, sir, whatever I've done, I'm finished with it now. Good night, sir."

Rasmussen slapped his cap on his head, saluted quickly and left the cabin, leaving Wheeler to stare at the key ring in his hand.

Wheeler stood silently for some time, then he sighed, turned out the overhead light and left the cabin. He made his way quickly to Crowley's cabin, and when he arrived immediately pushed the key into the lock and opened the door. He flicked on the light and at once heard the startled voices on the bunk.

For a minute there was silence. Then Wheeler spoke heavily. "You," he said to Rathburn. "Get the hell out of here."

323]

Rathburn paused only to climb hurriedly into his dungarees and grab the rest of his clothes before plunging through the door.

After Rathburn had gone, Crowley donned his shorts in silence as Wheeler slumped at the desk, his head in his hands. Wheeler's eyes fastened on a picture on the desk, a framed snapshot of Crowley standing at attention while an admiral pinned a Navy Cross on his chest. Slowly Wheeler reached out, tossed the picture on the deck and stepped on it viciously. Crowley said nothing.

"You know something, Crowley?" Wheeler said, still not looking at the other man. "I can't even hate you. I can only pity you." He leaned down, picked up the snapshot from the floor and handed it to him.

"Keep this. It is all you'll ever have of glory."

Crowley fell into a chair and sat with his arms resting on his knees. His hands were clenched so tightly that the knuckles showed white. "Didn't you ever make a mistake?" he asked plaintively.

"Yes," Wheeler said. "I've made my share. But never when it would hurt another man. You've disgraced all of us, Crowley. I pity you, but I can't find any way to justify what you've done. That's the way I feel."

"One mistake. And you'd crucify me for this?"

A look of incredulity passed over Wheeler's face. "You can call this a *mistake?* That's all?"

"Have you a better word?"

Wheeler spoke wearily. "You've been making mistakes all your life. Unfortunately you never got caught before. It might have saved all of us a great deal of anguish."

"I'm begging you. You know what this can lead to?"

Wheeler bowed his head. He could feel a dull ache in the back of his neck. He said, "What do you suggest I do about this?"

"Suppose I ask to be relieved as air group commander? Ask for other orders?" There was hope in Crowley's voice.

"No," Wheeler said, shaking his head. "It's got to be better than that. I won't pass you off on another group."

"I'll resign. That's it. I'll resign my commission. Will that do it?"

"What will you tell them? People don't go around resigning from a war."

"I can go to the flight surgeon. Tell him the whole story. It can be kept quiet. Combat fatigue or something."

"I don't know, Crowley," Wheeler said. "I just don't know. I'll

[324

have to think about it." He paused a moment. "All right. Go ahead and write a letter tonight to the flight surgeon. Tell him everything. I'll want to see it in the morning. Then we'll see what we'll do."

"Can I finish this operation? There would be talk."

Talk! thought Wheeler bitterly. But maybe Crowley has the best way out of this. It's a terrible thing to say, but it would be better if he had the guts to go out and get himself killed. If he died fighting it would be the best answer of all.

"I don't know about that either. Perhaps. Write the letter and we'll see about it tomorrow." He got to his feet, only to pause at the door. "But first tell me why," he demanded. "Tell me why you did it. What in Christ's sweet name were you thinking of? In wartime. Aboard a man-of-war. On the way into combat. Why, Crowley?"

Crowley spoke hesitantly at first, then the words came faster and faster until they tumbled from his mouth as if in fear they would not be spoken.

"You're strong," he said accusingly. "I'm not. You never had to walk the edge of a sharp knife. You never had to swallow and gag on your fear that you might fall off. You don't dream at night either. I dream one dream every goddam night of my life. I live with it, I'm possessed by it. Have you ever been lonely, Wheeler? Loneliness can drive a man to anything. Maybe someday you'll understand this. Things that seem sordid to you can seem beautiful to a man who's always been lonely. After a while you get so you even grab at shadows just to have something to hold on to. Finally you realize there are other people in the world just like you, just as lonely. They're the only ones who understand. So where else can you turn? All you want is not to be alone anymore. Is that too much for a man to ask? Just not to be alone?"

Dear God, thought Wheeler. Aloud he said, "Ah, Crowley. You poor, lost sonofabitch. I'd help you if I could. But there's nothing I can do. You blame your failure on your loneliness. That's no crutch because I'll tell you something, Crowley. Every goddam one of us is alone in this world. It's all a question of how you conduct yourself in this loneliness, and that's the heart of your failure. You cry out in your wilderness, but you've never fought back. Now it's too late." He looked down on Crowley's bent head, and when the man did not speak he continued: "I'll see you in the morning. I have to think about this. Write the letter tonight." As he opened the door he said, "I'm sorry, Crowley. Truly sorry."

325]

Barry Wheeler did not get a chance to speak with Crowley the next morning. At 0950 the *Concord*'s Radar Plot reported enemy aircraft detected all over the radar screen. A large group was orbiting one hundred miles west of the task force at 30,000 feet.

Delacrois himself grabbed the mike and bellowed the "Hey Rube" signal to all airborne fighters to rally around the force. And he gave Sam Balta the order to "Scramble the fighters."

Thus started the battle that would go down in history as "The Marianas Turkey Shoot."

General Quarters blared and across the screens in the ready rooms the words marched: ALL PILOTS MAN YOUR PLANES SCRAMBLE. SCRAMBLE. SCRAMBLE.

When a "Scramble" is sounded a pilot takes the first plane he can find instead of following the more orderly normal procedures. So now the pilots ran to the flight deck and jumped into the first planes available and launched in the shortest possible time without regard for flight plan, rendezvous or anything else.

Delacrois and Balta watched the planes go. "Where did they come from, Frog?" Balta asked. "Togyama isn't within launching range. We have a report from a sub, the *Cavalla* I think, putting him six hundred miles west."

"Same thing he did at Tarawa," said Delacrois. "He flew them in one way to Guam. Refueled them over night and will fight them off Guam until he gets close enough to take them back aboard."

Delacrois was nearly right. Togyama had launched *half* his air groups for Guam. But he had held half of them aboard his ships since he was not yet certain that facilities at Guam could handle all his planes. Besides, a position report from one of his scout planes had placed the American fleet two hundred miles southeast of where it actually was. Togyama thought Delacrois was withdrawing to replenish. The Japanese admiral had no way of knowing that his scout plane had been in the process of sending a correction to its report when it had been shot down by a Combat Air Patrol from the *Ardennes*.

Now the American fighters strung out across the sky for forty miles as they firewalled throttles and headed for the enemy. Marriner, Anders, Winston, and Bates had been among the first launched, and had flown off together and so constituted a four-plane division ten seconds after they left the deck. Now Marriner, in the lead, suddenly swore as his windshield streaked with a film of oil. He looked down

[326

at his oil pressure gauge. It had dropped several pounds. He raised his seat to enable him to look out the top of the windshield where the oil film was thinner.

"Jehovah One Three," he called Winston. "I've got an oil leak. If I can't go in, take the division."

"Roger," Winston acknowledged.

Marriner was midway between Guam and the task force when he knew he was not going to make Guam. His pressure had dropped another five pounds, and the oil film was thicker on the windshield.

Disgustedly, he called Winston. "Max. I'm not going to make it. You take over." He tapped his head and pointed to Winston. Then he banked away and headed back for the force where he would circle uselessly until the decks were cleared to take him aboard. As he came out of his turn and took up a reciprocal heading he radioed the *Concord*.

"Jehovah Base," Marriner called. "I have an oil leak and am returning to base."

"This is Jehovah Base. Unidentified bogies coming in your direction." The voice from the *Concord* was unemotional.

"Roger," Marriner answered. He turned the plane on its side and began a circle, scanning every corner of the sky. God damn it, he thought, they're coming and I've got a lousy oil leak. He pressed his mike button and called Winston. "Jehovah One Three. This is One. Better get back here. We've got business coming in."

"Coming, Dick," Winston replied.

Marriner was in a wide turn looking straight down at the water when he saw planes flash across a patch of low-hanging cloud, silhouetting themselves against it.

"Tallyho from Jehovah One," he radioed. "Thirty or more bogies below. Look like Judy bombers. On vector for Jehovah. Am attacking."

"Go get 'em," said the calm voice from the *Concord*.

Marriner kicked his charging buttons and flicked on his gunsight. Then he peeled off, at the same time taking a last look back over his shoulder. His heart skipped a beat as he saw three planes diving on him. Christ, they had fighters with them. He was about to throw his stick hard port and kick himself into a dive when Winston's voice came to him.

"Right behind you, Dick," Winston said.

Marriner led them down for the kill. "Move out to the starboard,

327]

Max," he called. "You and Bates bracket on that side." With Anders on his wing he moved ahead to a position even with the lead plane of the enemy formation and about fifteen hundred feet above them. Then he waited until Winston and Bates assumed a similar position on the other side of the formation. Now the Judys had no place to go. They couldn't get away.

Now Marriner initiated the attack, waggling his wings at Anders and beginning a high side run. Fighting a wave of bombers like this was far different from a dogfight. One sought to assume position and make gunnery runs on them, picking them off like tin cans sitting on a fence. Marriner put his plane into a bank and turned one hundred eighty degrees. Just as he reached a reciprocal heading from the enemy he turned ninety degrees toward them and began to slide in from above and slightly behind. When he was halfway through his run Winston began his from the opposite side. Thus no matter in which direction the enemy turned they would have to face the shells from a Hellcat. The lead Judy elected to turn into Marriner.

"On their ass, Max," Marriner called as he opened fire.

The lead Judy had turned only twenty-five degrees when Marriner's fire caught it. The shells hit at the wing root, and the Judy spun off in flames. The port wing went first and then the tail assembly. The Judy looked like a broken toy tumbling through the sky.

As Marriner flashed past the enemy and pulled up to regain his altitude, Winston opened fire from directly behind the enemy formation. He sprayed the rear of the formation from directly astern and knocked down two planes. The first was hit in the canopy which shattered in a spray of bloody glass. The shells curved down into the engine and a plume of black oil smoke swirled out of the cowling. The Judy rolled over on its back and dove straight into the ocean. The second plane simply exploded.

Now the Judys turned wildly away, trying to get Winston off their tail. But they turned straight into Anders, who had lengthened his run, coming in from far astern and thus had a longer period of time in which to fire. He opened up while still out of range, arcing his tracers high over the enemy and allowing them to fall into the formation. Then as he closed from the rear he lowered his sights until he had the pip resting on the canopy of a Judy. He never took his finger off the trigger, and he shot down three planes on his first pass.

Bates had just started his run when he saw a Judy veer away from the formation. He aborted his run, swept down on the lone Judy and snapped off a two-second thirty-degree deflection shot. He hit the

[328

propeller, and the Judy's engine tore itself loose from the airplane. The fuselage and the engine raced each other into the water.

"Assume bracket position," Marriner called, and the other planes pulled back up to resume the bracket. Marriner had no intention of giving the enemy time to get away.

"Jehovah Base from Jehovah One," Marriner called. "We've got them bracketed. Splash seven up to now. There are three heading your way." Then he watched as the Jap leader pushed over and led his formation into a steep glide.

"Full balls," Marriner called as he shoved his throttle forward. With their altitude advantage the Hellcats dove steeper than the Judys and thus picked up speed more rapidly. Marriner realized that the Japs were trying to get to the task force before the Hellcats could come to them again. Fifteen miles away the Americans could see the first faint outlines of the ships and the sharper trailings on the water denoting the wakes of the heavier men-of-war.

"Jehovah Base," Marriner called. "We are coming in behind them about fifteen miles out. Hold your fire." He looked behind him and saw Winston, Anders and Bates hanging in close, a few yards away. "Jehovah One planes. We'll come on their ass. Line abreast. We've got to take them."

As he spoke he came within range and opened fire. A moment later Winston opened up. Then Anders. Then Bates. All four Hellcats rode directly down behind the Judys with all six guns blazing. As they closed in they had to retard throttle to keep from overrunning their targets. One Judy fell. Then another. Then two more.

Anders especially was wreaking havoc on the enemy. Relentlessly he pressed his attack home until he was firing from a range of thirty yards. A Judy exploded and took the plane flying on its wing with it. Anders flew through the flaming debris and never stopped firing. Two Judys banked suddenly to port and left the formation in a vertical turn. Marriner cut inside of them, and they turned back into the formation just as Winston caught them with a deflection shot. The landing gear of the lead Judy suddenly fell to the extended position, and the plane cartwheeled through the air, shredding itself to a wingless fuselage.

Ten miles from the task force the Japs began to separate like a herd of nervous cattle. One Judy tried to lead a string of the bombers out of the formation.

"Herd that bastard back in here, Bates," Marriner called.

Bates peeled over and came at the Judys, and they turned back to

329]

the formation. Marriner slid behind them and clamped down on his trigger until two enemy planes blew up and spiraled toward the water, trailing great, gushing plumes of black and red smoke.

"Get the leaders," Marriner ordered.

He pushed over and dove five hundred feet, picking up airspeed which enabled him to pull up his nose and climb up at the enemy formation from below. He came up at the belly of the Jap leader and opened fire while he was standing on his tail, his nose pointing almost straight up and in a nearly stalled position. He felt the plane shudder, on the edge of a spin, but just as he fell off on his right wing he saw the underside of the lead Jap plane split apart and burst into yellow flames.

"You got him, Dick!" Anders' voice was triumphant.

Five miles from the force the remaining Japs, leaderless now, started a turn to the left, swinging away from the direct vector to their target. The Hellcats pounced on them again, aware that the Judys were trying to assume position to come at the fleet out of the sun.

Now Marriner came up from below again. He came climbing, knowing he would spin again but not before he had fired a six-second burst. He took the second plane holding his pip on the underside of the wing root. His shells flew up and hit a five-hundred-pound bomb on the Judy's wing. The bomb detonated with a tremendous explosion. The planes on either side of the exploding Judy shuddered in the air and fell toward the water, their controls useless.

"Goddammit," Marriner called, "we don't have time to whittle at them. Bust up that formation."

He came out of his spin in a dive, hauled back on his stick and started up into a loop, knowing the time they had to scatter the Jap bomber flight was running out. He came up in the first half of his loop and reached a vertical position directly below the enemy formation. He held his attitude and flew through the middle of the Judy flight going almost straight up. He missed three enemy planes by a matter of ten feet. The Jap pilots had no choice. They reacted instinctively and wheeled their planes out of the formation. The other Hellcats were waiting, aware of what Marriner was trying to do. Now as the formation scattered, the Americans each took a section of it and bore in relentlessly. The Judys were no longer a single entity but merely individual aircraft spread all over the sky. So all across the sky the Judys fell, one by one, battered, flaming, torn to pieces. Two of them collided racing for the sanctuary of a lone cloud forma-

[330

tion south of the task force. Only one division of four succeeded in mounting an attack on the force but not one of them got past the outer screen of destroyers. The fleet sailed over the burning wreckage.

"They're turning back," Bates yelled into his mike. "What's left of them."

"Permission to go after them, Dick?" Anders requested.

"Go ahead, Cort," Marriner answered. "I can't. My oil pressure is fluctuating badly. I'll circle the ship."

"Come on, Bates," Anders called as he took out after the fleeing Judys.

"Wait for me." Winston joined up on them, and the three planes disappeared to the northwest.

Marriner called the *Concord*. "Jehovah Base from Jehovah One. Will circle the ship. Am requesting immediate Charlie. Oil pressure fluctuating badly."

"Roger Jehovah One," replied the voice from the *Concord*. "Good work up there."

"What goes over the target?" Marriner asked.

"A turkey shoot, Jehovah One. We caught them over Guam."

Damn, Marriner thought, and I missed it. For a moment he had forgotten his score for the day. His division had downed at least twenty of the attacking enemy force.

Frog Delacrois, Sam Balta and Barry Wheeler watched the planes come home. Bob Crowley came down first sweeping low into the landing circle. It was a moment of triumph, but while the Admiral and Captain Balta were exultant, Barry Wheeler was deeply troubled. He realized now that Crowley would not take the way out that had been offered to him. When the "Scramble" call had sounded that morning Wheeler had momentarily considered grounding the CAG. But then he had decided this was the opportunity to allow Crowley an honorable death in combat. Crowley had refused the offer, and now there was nothing left for Wheeler to do but his duty, repugnant to him as it was.

Delacrois spoke to Balta, a note of admiration in his voice. "My God, Sam. That division up there that stopped the Judys. Jehovah One. Who was it?"

Balta had already consulted his operations officer. "Ensigns Marriner, Winston, Anders and Bates," he answered.

"Well," said the Admiral, "that confirms my thinking. Those four aren't ordinary ensigns."

"I counted at least fifteen," Balta said.

"More than that," Wheeler added.

"Sam," Delacrois said. "I want Navy Crosses for the four of them. They saved the task force."

"It will be taken care of, sir," answered Balta.

The planes were coming aboard now, and as each pilot taxied forward out of the arresting gear and passed the island structure, he looked up at the bridge where the Admiral stood, and held up a hand with a number of fingers extended, indicating the number of the enemy he had shot down. Some held up two hands because five fingers were not enough.

"Jesus," Balta said quietly, "they really clobbered them." His face split in a wide grin, and he clapped Wheeler on the back. "How about that, Barry?"

Wheeler nodded, but his face was solemn. "A hell of a job. Sam," he looked at the Captain, "I'll want to talk to you tonight. A personal matter."

"Make it tomorrow morning, Barry," Balta said. "We'll be going over reports and writing intelligence estimates tonight."

"In the morning then," said Wheeler.

The Marianas Turkey Shoot comprised the first day of the Battle of the Philippine Sea. After the first day the Japanese had lost a total of 402 aircraft of which 366 were downed in aerial battle. Nineteen more were destroyed on the ground at Guam, while the task force's antiaircraft guns accounted for seventeen.

Admiral Togyama had only 102 aircraft left after the battle, but he did not admit defeat. He started westward during the night, intending to replenish and return to the attack. But Delacrois was after him like a wolf on the fold. Through the night of June 19-20 the air was filled with the voices of American reconnaissance pilots tracking the First Fleet. At dawn on the 20th Togyama took aboard 85 fighter planes that had been hidden in revetments on Guam. If he could find time to rendezvous with his supply train and replenish his strength he intended to return eastward, smash the American fleet and destroy the supply ships lying off Saipan. Reports from Tokyo indicated a support force of eleven small carriers was coming at flank speed to his aid.

But time was running out for Admiral Togyama.

[332

XVII

June 20, 1944

Crowley had waited twenty minutes before he answered the summons to Barry Wheeler's office.

He had been sleeping fitfully when the messenger had come at 0730 with orders to report to the executive officer's cabin. He had nodded and dismissed the man.

The nightmare which had been troubling him in his sleep was the same nightmare which had tormented him for so long. Again he had tried to pierce the strange cloud that concealed the cockpit of the plane on which Bobby Anderson stood. Again Bobby had been calling something to him in his dream, but this time it seemed as if he had been about to understand the dim voice. Then the sharp rapping on the door had awakened him to face the distasteful day. He had sat on the edge of his bunk, smoking a cigarette, trying to postpone the inevitable meeting with Wheeler. Finally he had risen wearily to his feet, dressed and left for the executive officer's cabin.

Now Wheeler sat behind his desk and watched Crowley as the man tried to appear at ease. Wheeler did not like what he was about to do. He got to his feet and walked across the office to a porthole. After a moment he turned to face Crowley.

"You wrote the letter?"

"Yes, sir," Crowley answered. He took an envelope from his hip pocket and handed it to Wheeler. Wheeler stood and stared at the envelope, then tossed it on the desk.

"You wrote the whole thing down?"

"You can read it," said Crowley.

"I don't want to read it," Wheeler said.

"Then what are you going to do with it?"

"Show it to Captain Balta." He tried to make Crowley understand. "There's nothing else I can do, Crowley."

"Christ." There had been a moment, Crowley thought, when I almost thought I might live this down. Yesterday, after I led the attack on Guam, I hoped that it might be forgiven or forgotten. But it is still here on my back, and now it will never go away. Aloud he said, "There's got to be another way, Barry."

"Don't call me Barry. No, there isn't any other way. I thought about it all night."

"Christ," Crowley repeated, torment in his voice.

"You had a chance yesterday," Wheeler said. "You could have washed it clean yesterday, and I would have gone along."

"Chance? What chance did I ever have?" Crowley still did no understand.

"I let you lead the attack yesterday. Good men died out there, Crowley. Better men than you. You could have gone with them and left something besides shame on your name."

"You mean kill myself?" Crowley's tone was unbelieving.

"I mean you could have taken one of them with you." Wheeler shrugged. "Perhaps I expected too much of you."

"Could you do it?" Crowley asked. "Ask yourself that."

"I don't know," Wheeler replied. "I hope so."

Crowley was silent, staring at the desk. Finally he raised his head. "And now?"

"Now it's out of my hands. It's too much for me. I'll give the letter to Captain Balta."

"Does it make any difference who crucifies me? One man is as good at it as another."

"Crucifies you?" Wheeler paused to consider this. "Perhaps you're right. But do you think I enjoy this? Enjoy watching a man go down? A man I liked once? No, Crowley. I don't enjoy it. It makes me sick."

"Then tear the letter up and ground me for something else."

Wheeler could not help but feel pity at the hopelessness in Crowley's eyes. He wanted to end this thing.

"Listen to me, Crowley," he said, trying to keep his voice gentle. "Try to understand. This isn't something I can whitewash. Something I can keep to myself. There's an enlisted man who already knows. Maybe more than one. I don't think they'll talk. But it isn't

[334

something that's just between the two of us. Even if it was I still couldn't help you. But this I will do. I'll do my best to see you don't get a court-martial, and I think we can keep this between a few high-ranking officers. Perhaps you can survive after all." Wheeler did not believe his own words, but he wanted to give Crowley something to hold on to.

With an obvious effort, Crowley said, "What about Rathburn?"

"He'll be dealt with in good time."

"I see," Crowley said. With a terrible finality he realized there was little left for him to say. "This thing then," he said brokenly, "it has to be done this way?" It was his last plea.

"Unless you can suggest a better way. You know regulations as well as I do."

"No. I guess not," Crowley said, his voice dead. "Leaving me by myself alone again. I guess that's as bad as anything you can do." He rose to his feet and waited for Wheeler to speak.

"You're relieved of duty, Crowley. You will confine yourself to your quarters for the time being."

"Is that all, sir?" Crowley stood at attention.

"That's all, Crowley."

"Sir," Crowley spoke softly. "Harry Hill told me once that he wished he could offer me his hand. That was a long time ago. Perhaps it might have made a difference if he had. Could you bring yourself to offer me yours?"

Wheeler watched the other man carefully. Then slowly he offered his hand. "If it will help you in any way, Crowley."

Wheeler sat motionless for several minutes after Crowley had gone. Then, reluctantly, he opened the letter the former air group commander had written.

Wheeler sat across the desk from Captain Balta in the Captain's quarters and regarded the older man as he read Crowley's letter. Admiral Delacrois had read it first, then wordlessly handed it to Balta. The Admiral had said nothing and now stood silently, looking out the porthole.

When Balta finished reading he raised disbelieving eyes.

"It's true, sir," Wheeler said. "All of it."

Balta scanned the letter again. "What action have you taken?"

"I relieved Crowley of duty and confined him to quarters."

"Keep him there," Balta said harshly. "I don't want to see him

335]

until we're back in port. I want this kept quiet until then." After a moment he said, "How did Crowley react?"

"Christ, Admiral," Wheeler said, "I really don't know. I think he feels sorry for himself because the whole world is against him. I don't know. I pity the bastard."

"He's a disgrace to all of us," Balta said roughly. "Don't waste any pity on him!"

"How did you find out, Barry?" asked Delacrois.

Wheeler hesitated. "An enlisted man, sir. I'd rather leave him out of it, unless you're going to court-martial Crowley. Then he'll have to be a witness."

"Court-martial Crowley?" The Admiral frowned. "Good God, we can't court-martial the man. The whole dirty story would come out."

"Well, you've got to do something with him," Balta observed.

"I will," said Delacrois. "I'll think of something."

Wheeler rose to his feet and stood looking down at Balta. He took a cigarette from a pack on the desk and lit it before he spoke.

"Sam," Wheeler said mildly, "I'll take your air group."

Balta glanced quickly at the Admiral and a smile broke over his face. "Good, Barry. Damn good."

"I don't want it, but I'll take it. And I'm giving it back when this operation is over. Okay?"

Delacrois laughed softly. "Sam's getting his stars when this is over. He won't need an air group anymore."

Wheeler was obviously delighted. "God damn, Sam. Congratulations."

"Accepted." Balta grinned. "I'll be needing some good men on my staff when the stars come through. How about it?"

"Let's talk about it when we get back," Wheeler said. "I don't trust captains anymore." He smiled. "But then I never did," he added.

The pilot of the TBF torpedo bomber from Torpedo Two was named Sonnenberg. He was flying a two hundred and fifty mile sector search in his clumsy Avenger, and he was more than a little pissed off. He looked at his watch, then swore heartily at the blazing sun. 1430. The heat burned through the glass top of his cockpit, scorching the back of his neck. Sonnenberg had intended to shortcut his patrol by about twenty-five miles. Visibility was so good he could

[336

see the remainder of the distance so what was the use in flying out there where any damn fool could see there was nothing but water.

He was getting ready to reverse his course while still twenty miles from the end of his search when he was rudely interrupted. Commander Isoku Yamota, leading eight Zero fighters on a combat air patrol from the *Akiti,* was flying at eighteen thousand feet when he spotted the TBF. Yamota immediately pushed over and began to lose altitude. He did not take his eyes from the tiny speck moving against the gray background of ocean.

Sonnenberg was starting his turn when his rear gunner called a tallyho on Yamota's fighters.

"Tallyho. Enemy fighters. Coming down at four o'clock. Eight of them."

God damn, Sonnenberg muttered to himself, simultaneously searching the sky for a suitable place to hide. There proved to be an insufficiency of such places. The nearest he could find was a heavy isolated rain cloud, eight miles ahead of him. He barreled for the sanctuary of cloud as Yamota changed course to intercept. But Sonnenberg won the race and disappeared into the dirty cloud just as Yamota ranged up within firing distance.

Yamota ordered his flight to bracket the cloud from its middle up to the towering crest. He reasoned that only a fool or a man bereft of his sanity would attempt to escape by diving low on the water. The TBF would stand no chance whatsoever against his fighters at low altitude. The Avenger pilot's only hope for survival lay in plotting his escape at altitude or in trying to outwait Yamota. If he had fuel enough he could stay in the cloud until the Zeros were forced to return to their carrier.

Yamota's reasoning was in line with accepted aerial tactics under such circumstances for he was not a man prone to make mistakes of judgment in the sky. Or mistakes of any kind for that matter. But in this instance Yamota misjudged.

Sonnenberg flew on instruments in the cloud turbulence while he surveyed his situation. He found very little cause for gaiety. It was not enough that he had to wrestle this recalcitrant sonofabitch all over the sky with only the help of two goddam tiny needles on his panel. It wasn't enough they had sent him away out here to Christ and gone all alone in a clumsy TBF. Now he had to get jammed up in this mother of a cloud with no way to get out unless he wanted to

337]

dogfight with eight of the Emperor's best. He decided to poke his nose out and see what the score was.

Sonnenberg flew three hundred yards out of the cloud and saw Yamota and his wingman peeling off above him. He darted back into his sanctuary but not before his trained eyes had picked up trailings on the water where Togyama's First Fleet steamed. Now he had another problem.

Sonnenberg was a young man who lived with his responsibilities and who possessed a sincere conviction that every man who wore wings had an obligation to them. He realized that it was of the utmost importance that he report accurately the position and composition of the enemy fleet.

He called his rear gunner and his radar man. "Did you guys see what I saw?"

The radar man answered. "The Jap fleet, Skipper. The whole goddam fleet."

"You understand what we have to do, Tim?"

"I do," replied Tim. "I must say it petrifies me."

"How about you, Sid?"

"Sure, Skipper. We gotta get a make on 'em."

Sonnenberg wanted to give them another chance. "We might make it by outwaiting them."

"Not a chance, Skipper," said Tim. "We got a position report and a tally to make."

"Check your guns," Sonnenberg ordered. Then he reached down and picked his chart board out of the map case. He fastened it to his thigh and slid a clean piece of paper on it. He placed a newly sharpened pencil in the slot on the board. While he did this he calculated the odds on his ever getting back to Mike Lyman's bar in Hollywood. They seemed astronomical.

"All set back here, Skipper." Sid's voice was untroubled.

"Okay then," Sonnenberg said. "We'll just have to make a dive bomber out of this tub for a little while. Until we hit the deck. Then we'll make a racer out of her for a little while. After that, if we're still in the air, we'll make an attempt at a new altitude record for the TBF. Finally, we'll try to set a new endurance record by remaining airborne until we get back home. That is all we have to do."

"Well," said Tim, "if that's all that's necessary, I think I'll recommend myself for the DSC."

[338

"When we get down on the water," said Sonnenberg, "make a tally on those ships. Get it right. I figure I'll be too busy to count."

"Roger, Skipper."

Sonnenberg started a gentle turn on the instruments. "I will now circle this bastard around and around inside this cloud, losing altitude until we come out at the base. That way the slant-eyed bastards won't see us until we're in our dive. We may even get away with this if we're lucky."

He took a chain with a St. Jude medal on it from around his neck and placed it on a knob jutting from his instrument panel. Patron saint of hopeless cases, he thought. Jesus, how hopeless do you have to get before you qualify?

"Here we go," he called to his rear seat men. The heavy cloud began to thin, and the TBF eased out of cover.

The Avenger wheeled over as Sonnenberg pushed forward on the stick and dove steeply for the ocean far below. He had come out directly under the center of the cloud base and so was obscured from the vision of Yamota and his fighters. It was not until the TBF had been sighted by a lookout on one of Togyama's escort destroyers that Yamota's flight was alerted by a radio call. By that time the Avenger was at four thousand feet, paralleling the Japanese task force from a distance of two miles. The rear seat gunner was noting on his knee pad the course, speed and composition of the fleet while the radar operator plotted an exact fix on their position, rapidly noting the latitude and longitude of the interception.

Now Yamota and his Zeros stormed down from above and fell in behind Sonnenberg.

The TBF had a red line marked on its airspeed indicator, a marking devised to warn the pilot that any speed in excess of that designated by the red line would in all probability result in the wings and tail empennage being torn off the airplane. Since an airplane will not fly without wings and a tail empennage, the men in the TBF were living on borrowed time, for the airspeed needle was twenty-five knots past the red line and still moving upwards. The entire fuselage of the plane shuddered in protest at the winds screaming along its sides. The control column quivered in Sonnenberg's hands, and the racing engine howled a complaint at this unconscionable demand.

The Avenger flashed along only a few feet above the water. The Zeros were closing slowly from the rear, and Sonnenberg estimated

339]

his chances of reaching a cloud formation several miles ahead. They were, he decided, about the same as his chances of someday becoming Chief of Naval Operations.

It was past three o'clock, 1500, when Commander Yamota finally reached extreme range and opened fire on the TBF from directly astern. The heavy torpedo bomber had flown at a speed never intended by its designers.

By this time Sonnenberg was only two miles from the cloud formation he so earnestly sought, and Yamota knew he had only a fragment of time in which to make his kill. He raised the pip on his gunsight to a point two inches above the nose of the TBF. This, he was aware, was a ridiculous manner in which to attempt to shoot down an enemy, but it was the only manner which had been left to him. Sonnenberg was one mile from the cloud when Yamota pressed his firing button, and the wings of his Zero vomited shells across the sky.

All but one of Yamota's shells fell short of the target, but the one that did not caught the Avenger just as she was in the process of being swallowed by altocumulus cloud. The shell cut sharply through the fuselage of the torpedo bomber, passed through the radar man-radio operator's shoulder and hit the radio apparatus, causing considerable damage to that priceless gear.

It took Sid, the rear seat gunner, ten minutes to get the radio man in suitable physical shape to prop him up by the damaged radio apparatus. Tim bled profusely and cursed more profusely, but in the end he set about repairing the gear as best he could, a task which he miraculously accomplished in a half hour while the bomber circled in the cloud. Yamota bracketed the cloud until his fuel supply dictated a return to base so that Sonnenberg had to stay in the cloud for almost thirty minutes, waiting for the Zeros to leave. Now he raced for home, knowing how important it was he establish radio contact with the fleet and report his sighting. Unfortunately Yamota's shell had so damaged the radio equipment that he would have to be within a hundred miles of Task Force 58 to make a clear contact.

Thus it was just after four o'clock in the afternoon, 1600 Navy time, when Sonnenberg finally sent his radio report of the sighting and position of the Japanese First Fleet.

It was 1610 when they brought the message to Admiral Delacrois. Past decisions flashed across his mind as he digested in an instant the import of Sonnenberg's message.

[340

He spoke to his Chief of Staff. "Increase our speed to twenty-five knots. Ask Captain Balta and the staff to report to the bridge immediately."

He walked to the outer bridge and breathed deeply of the salt air. Unconsciously his eyes probed the eastern horizon for the first sign of dusk, although it was still three hours until nightfall. Across the expanse of the task force the sun danced against the waves, and from somewhere below, Delacrois could hear the strains of a harmonica.

The sound of footsteps on the catwalk drew his attention, and he turned to see Balta and several staff members coming out of the gangway.

"Hurry, if you please, gentlemen. We haven't much time," Delacrois said.

A few minutes later the navigation officer straightened up from a table on which lay a large map of the central Pacific. He had drawn his lines and made his calculations, and now he spoke with the dismal knowledge of his computations straining his voice. He had no wish to pronounce sentence.

"Well, there it is, sir. By the time we launch they'll be three hundred miles away. Six hundred round trip."

"And with a fight in the middle of it," Balta added.

"There is something you should remember, gentlemen." Delacrois spoke frankly. "Togyama is heading away from us. I don't believe he is running. He is trying to replenish before he takes up the fight again. If we are to get him we'll have to go after him now. Tomorrow he may be away from us. If he can replenish and come back he might well get through to the supply ships at Saipan. Consider this before I ask your opinions."

Thus did Delacrois put the question to the tight little group standing somberly around the table. Each, in his own mind, was weighing the situation, performing mental arithmetic. The pilots would have to fly to extreme range at an hour of the day that would preclude their returning before the black Pacific night had swallowed the task force. They would be weary when they reached the enemy and infinitely more so when they got home. The gas situation would be critical, the gauge needles resting on EMPTY.

It was a matter of sending men out to fight with only a token chance of their coming back safely. Such odds are not conducive to

341]

high morale, neither for the men who will obey the decisions nor for the men who make them.

But Togyama would be away by morning, and when he came back he would pose a threat to the helpless transport and supply ships at Saipan.

Delacrois was searching for a way out. "Have you," he asked the navigator, "taken into consideration our closing speed toward the enemy?"

"I have, sir."

Balta managed to keep all feeling from his voice. "They'll have to fly at least six hundred miles, sir. With a fight or without it. Many of them won't come back."

"I know," said Delacrois. "But it may be worth it."

Balta pressed on relentlessly. "Even those who make it back. Where will they be? Out of gas and over a task force they can't see. It will be long after nightfall, Admiral."

A captain on Delacrois's staff reminded quietly, "And most of them have never come aboard a carrier at night, sir."

Delacrois pinched the bridge of his nose. In this moment he was terribly aware of the weight of command resting squarely on his shoulders.

His eyes passed over the faces of his subordinates. "But Togyama will come back again if we don't get him now. I'm responsible for the safety of those ships at Saipan. I know where Togyama is and I think I know what he's up to. So I can't take into consideration all that you gentlemen have said." He paused to look again at the map. "The only question is this. Can we launch, reach the enemy and inflict sufficient damage to warrant the attack at this hour and at this distance?"

One by one the men with him nodded. In the back of their minds they could hear the refrain of an old ballad the fighter pilots sang.

> Don't send my son to fighters,
>   The dying mother said;
> Don't give my boy an F6F,
>   I'd rather see him dead.

Well, there would be dead ones somewhere after this day's work. "How many planes?" Balta asked.

[342

"Two hundred," answered Delacrois. "Two hundred on Strike Able. We will only launch the one."

Two hundred fly out, he thought, how many will fly back? God help me, I can do nothing else.

"There'll be no time for briefing," Balta said.

"Launch them and give them target information in the air. Every minute of daylight helps." Delacrois turned to the navigator. "Get it ready."

"There are," Balta spoke almost to himself, "entirely too few minutes of daylight available." Then, in an attempt to ease the burden he knew Delacrois bore, he said, "It'll be all right, Admiral. In other circumstances I'd hesitate to launch at this hour. But there's a difference here. A difference that sheds an unusual light on the situation."

"And this difference, Sam?" Delacrois asked.

"The difference is that these men wear Navy wings, Admiral. And that makes all the difference in the world."

"Let's hope so, Sam," Delacrois replied.

Unfortunately it takes time for orders to disseminate throughout a task force. So precious minutes of daylight were wasted while the orders were relayed to task group commanders, to ships' captains, to air officers, to squadron commanders via yeomen who beat out the summonses on the teletype keys.

Then the pilots finally read the "Scramble" on the teletype screens and raced for their cockpits not entirely ignorant of their mission. To most of them it seemed a goddam fool thing to do, launching planes so goddam late in the afternoon. Holy Christ. You don't suppose they'll keep us up there till we have to come aboard in the dark? Nights out here are darker than a witch's teat, and night landings are only for guys with cat eyes anyway.

It was four-thirty, 1630, when Barry Wheeler roared down the deck of the *Concord* and soared off the bow of the flight deck. After him thundered the other brave young men who were going out to a fight in which every conceivable odd was against them. Although they had not as yet received target information from the *Concord,* there was not a man flying who did not know that Togyama's First Fleet lay far off over the western horizon at extreme range.

It was nearly five o'clock when Wheeler finally had Strike Able rendezvoused and vectored out toward the target. On the bridge of the *Concord,* Admiral Delacrois and Captain Balta watched the planes disappear into a lowering sun. Over the radio they could hear the pilots' voices wondering at the target information that had been sent to them after the launch.

"Did you get what I got?" one voice said. The voice was requesting confirmation that his plotting board deductions did not indicate that he had lost his mind. Throughout the armada of planes the pilots shook their heads in disbelief at the figures they arrived at after plotting positions.

"It won't get on my board," another voice answered in amazement. This meant that penciled vector lines extended beyond the boundaries of the plotting board.

A third voice spoke quietly. "There seems little sense working this out both ways." He meant there would be no return trip.

Throughout Strike Able other pilots were thinking the same thing.

Barry Wheeler led Strike Able as he had led many other strikes before this. Only now Cortney Anders flew on his right wing and Dick Marriner's division held steady position twenty yards off his port quarter. Looking back over his shoulder, Wheeler could see the other planes in the formation stretched out over ten miles of sky. He throttled back, leaned his mixture down and waited for the rest to catch up.

For two hours in the late afternoon of June 20, 1944, Wheeler led his men through the sky. They climbed to altitude, and when they changed blowers the engines missed for several seconds and they could hear the wind whistling along the sides of the cockpits. Two hours watching the horizon and the sea below it and sweeping the sky with eyes that were never still.

Lean and hungry for battle they came. Trusting to nothing but their own skill and the bullets in their guns. Old war cries sounded in their brains. Hey Rube. Tallyho. Go get 'em.

Their hard-boned faces burned by Pacific suns, they wore khaki shirts and helmets and pistols holstered around their shoulders. They wore the yellow jackets named for a liberally endowed film star, and they hoped to Christ the air bottles worked because they knew that some of them would be in the drink tonight.

Lone-flying men in a lonely sky, flying toward a destiny of which they knew but little. Knowing no other life than this and wishing no other.

The sky is a school where each hour of each long day is a final

[344

examination and the sharks wait to correct the papers. No easy deaths here but no prolonged ones either. A school conducted over merciless waters with nowhere but home for a man to land.

For two hours of the dying afternoon Barry Wheeler led the men of Task Force 58 toward Togyama and the First Fleet. Their hearts grew more troubled as the minutes passed away never to return again, and the needles on the gas gauges trembled toward the halfway mark.

Ahead the sea stretched toward the western sky now shading under the influence of late afternoon clouds. Pastel shadings of salmon, pink, lemon, splashed by somber reds where the shadows played. As the sun moved closer to the horizon it had lost its copper heat, and the shadows of the clouds lengthened on the water like angular, solid islands unmapped by man.

Wheeler was caressing his gas gauge with his eyes, as were two hundred other pilots of Strike Able, when Commander Yamota led one hundred fighters from the decks of the First Fleet. Togyama would have preferred to fight on the morrow. His loses over Guam had not yet been remedied, and support carriers would be on the scene the next day. But Togyama had no choice. His radar plot had announced the presence of the American air fleet, and he knew he must fight. He also knew the odds rested with him. His scout planes had accurately reported the position of Task Force 58, and he wondered how the American admirals could be so stupid as to launch a strike at this hour of the day and from such a prohibitive distance when his fleet was steadily steaming away from the attacking planes. His orders to Yamota had been succinct.

"Intercept them as far out as you can. Make them fight every inch of the way in. Make them waste their gasoline." He ordered an increase in speed, thus adding a few precious miles the Americans would have to fly.

The sun was only inches above the horizon when Barry Wheeler made his tallyho.

"Tallyho from Jehovah Leader. Eleven o'clock on the water. Thirty miles."

Other eyes picked them up. Countless slender trailings on the water, more enemy ships than any of them had seen before. Wheeler glanced at his watch. 6:40 P.M.

They bunched up then, added inches of throttle and closed up into sections and divisions. Eyes patrolled every visible inch of sky.

345]

Feet punched at charging buttons and hands twisted rheostats on gunsight panels. The belly gas tanks had long ago been discarded.

An amber haze, shot now with the deep purple of evening, lay across the western horizon when Wheeler called, "TBFs and SBDs, prepare to attack."

The dive bombers and torpedo bombers separated from the armada and inched downward, swinging slightly off course to assume position for their attack.

Marriner felt an exultation surge through him as he leaned forward and flipped on his gun switches. Here then, he thought, is the justification for it all. To look forward eagerly to the battle with no anger churning in his mind to deflect a precise mill lead or cause his hand to quiver on the stick. To come to the fight soberly, washed clean of hate and emotion. He looked behind him at Bates and Winston and gave them a thumbs-up.

Winston grinned at himself in the rearview mirror. He could afford to grin now because his fear had left him long ago. Once, a lifetime ago it seemed, fear had been a living thing, eating at the back of his mind. But that had been before he had tasted war, and now he charged his guns with a feeling of anticipation.

And so they came, the men of Task Force 58, thundering across the sky eager for the fight.

Commander Yamota and his Zeros were there to give it to them!

Twenty miles from the surface ships, Yamota swept down hawk-like, and it was Marriner who spotted him first, a faint speck against the background of multicolored sky.

"Tallyho bogies dead ahead. Four miles."

Two hundred minds concurred, this is it, as the formations closed.

Wheeler saw the Zeros coming in yet he kept one eye on the torpedo and dive bombers pushing over now into the initial stage of their attack. Yamota had made his first mistake that day with Sonnenberg. Now he made his second. He rolled to his right and assumed an intercept course for the dive bombers. Wheeler had been wishing fervently for him to make exactly this maneuver, and he slapped his stick hard left and swung his nose around and ahead of Yamota's formation. Quickly he rolled on full prop power and shoved the throttle forward. Marriner was with him all the way, and together they streaked downward for a spot directly between the lumbering bombers and the oncoming Zeros.

[346

Wheeler and Marriner knew they had to break up the enemy formation and knock the Jap fighters off the tails of the bombers. They were still out of range when they opened fire, but they held their triggers down and flew up the paths of their tracers until the range closed and the Japanese pilots' aim was disrupted by the red tracers flashing across their flight path. Wheeler and Marriner, followed by the rest of the Hellcats, rammed full into Yamota's flight, plane missing plane by a hairsbreadth and men looked from one cockpit into another in a split second of time, and thus came to know their enemy first hand.

Yamota turned into the American formation and immediately pulled back on his stick, throwing the Zero into a steep climb so that Marriner, coming down behind Wheeler, almost collided head-on with him. Both pilots turned to their respective rights and passed so close that Marriner could clearly see the multitude of flags painted just under the cockpit on the Zero's fuselage.

For a split second Marriner seemed to hang motionless as the enemy plane slowly drifted by. Then it was gone, and with a curse Marriner pulled into an Immelmann turn, a soaring half-loop with a roll-out on top, and reversed his directions.

There can't be two of them painted like that, he thought to himself. This is my man, mine and mine alone, and today we will fight this one to the finish. Hear this, Harry Hill, wherever you are. I've found him.

As Marriner looked for the man who had killed Hill, another Zero came down behind him and opened fire. The tracers slammed into his port wing, and he threw the plane into a tight turn in the same direction, wheeling tightly into his enemy to throw the tracers behind him. Another Hellcat barreled past on the tail of the Zero, and Winston, grinning in his cockpit, fired and saw his bullets tear a wing off the Zero. The enemy spun once in the air, like a broken top, and then fell earthward trailing a plume of ugly black smoke.

Wheeler got his first plane as he was coming out of the bottom half of a loop. He had lost his target at the top, the Zero rolling away from him, but on recovery his sights had filled with another Zero coming out of a half roll at the top of a chandelle.

Now who the hell ever taught that bastard to chandelle in a dogfight? Wheeler wondered, as he fired and the burst straddled the entire length of the Zero, washing away the cockpit and the tail as-

347]

sembly. As Wheeler turned away he caught a brief glimpse of the cockpit seat, still intact, tumbling through the air with the body of the pilot still strapped into it.

Yamota had turned and come back to the fight. Secure in the knowledge of his own past victories, a practiced fighter in the air, he picked the first American he saw, and this was the third mistake Yamota made that day. He had chosen Dick Marriner.

Marriner smiled when he saw his adversary climbing to meet him. Somehow he had known it would be this way, and men who have been in combat know that this is not an extraordinary thing. All the calculated odds go up in smoke when men fight to the death in the sky. There may be one hundred or five hundred planes milling in the fight, but if two men are destined to meet they will meet.

I would like him to know the man he is fighting, Marriner thought. I would like him to know we have met before, and this fight is only the continuation of something that started at Tarawa. Maybe he does know, that man in the other cockpit, but still I wish I could call across to him and tell him to fight well today because this time there will be no mercy. He killed Harry Hill, and today he dies. Then Marriner slammed the stick hard left and joined with Yamota.

Seventeen men burned out in the first three minutes of the battle. Seventeen men in Hellcats and Zeros fell, and the water below churned where they hit. The din of battle rose into a screaming crescendo, and like maddened animals the blunt-nosed fighters weaved and twisted across and up and under the clouds.

There was no room for cowards that day. No room at all. Men of vastly contrasting beliefs, worlds apart in temperament, heritage and tradition, fought with a dogged gallantry that defied description. Men in Zeros prayed to their ancestors, and men in Hellcats prayed to their Christian God, but prayers ran second to teamwork in the fight above Togyama's First Fleet. The Americans held their two-plane sections as long as they could while the Zeros scattered and fought singly and alone, and this made the difference. As the melee progressed, more Zeros than Hellcats fell toward the water below.

Barry Wheeler and his men had erected a wall of planes between Yamota and the bombers. And now Dusane took his torpedo planes down low on the deck and bored in on Togyama's ships while from altitude, Lacy and his dive bombers came down like screeching falcons. Lacy himself was hit in the latter part of his dive, a forty-millimeter shell from a gun mount on the carrier *Sugami* blast-

[348

ing past his engine and into the cockpit and through Lacy's chest. He had only a moment for deliberation. Then Lacy carried his two 500-pound bombs all the way to his target. He was smiling as he held the pip of his sight on the center of the *Sugami*'s flight deck, and when the white deck-dividing line filled his windshield he shut his eyes for a second and died in a great mushrooming ball of purple flame.

Dusane, coming low along the water, saw the havoc created when Lacy hit. For a moment tears stung his eyes. He and Lacy had been roommates all through flight training. God damn, he swore, just before he called his flight.

"Jehovah turkeys," Dusane said, "we're going all the way in." A moment's pause. "All of us."

Now Togyama's fleet opened fire at the torpedo planes. Even the battleships joined in, and Dusane had to run a gauntlet of steel 3000 yards thick before he could get behind the range of the guns. After that he would have only machine gun fire to worry about.

Can ordinary men live through 3000 yards of hot steel? The men of Torpedo Two didn't know, but they were finding out. Holding formation steadily, they bored ahead.

Bates became a hero almost unintentionally. He had fastened himself securely to the tail of a Zero at twelve thousand feet. The enemy had endeavored mightily to shake him, but Bates had clung with the tenacity of a terrier. They had fought through eleven thousand feet of the sky before Bates scored a hit and made his kill, sending the Zero flaming into the water.

As he wheeled around the smoking debris he saw Dusane's torpeckers coming in against the guns of the Japanese fleet. He realized with consternation that the plodding turkeys had 3000 yards to go through the concentrated fire of battleships, cruisers and destroyers.

Tracers from the enemy fleet thickened the air until it seemed there could be no room for the airplanes. Thousands of red-hot gun barrels fired furiously at the oncoming bombers, near misses throwing towering columns of water into the air.

Dusane was jinking now, swerving his plane from side to side in an effort to throw the Jap gunners off. Behind him the others were doing the same, dodging the waterspouts, skimming the tops of the waves and drawing ever nearer to the mouths of the enemy guns.

Bates flew above, his eyes widening in admiration. They would

349]

never make it. Not across that solid expanse of lethal metal. Dusane and his pilots were flying to certain death.

Shit, thought Bates, they haven't got a chance in hell.

Then it was that Bates made his move. Dusane and the others of Torpedo Two who had already consigned themselves to oblivion would never forget what they saw in the waning light of that day.

Bates made a transmission before he went. "Jehovah turkeys. Hold on. I'll give them something to think about."

Then Bates banked around in a turn, straightened out and swept low on the water directly down the line of the enemy ships. Broadside to them he came, exposing himself to the concentrated fire of the First Fleet. Instinctively the enemy gunners followed him with their fire, swinging their guns along his flight path and affording a brief respite to Dusane and his men coming in on them.

Bates heard the flat splatterings as his plane was battered by the Japanese fire. It was, he thought, as if he were flying through all the hellfire in the Pacific. He could see the tracers coming at him from the flashing gun barrels, in a gentle arc, then disappearing just before they reached him. They seemed to be passing under his plane, but he knew he was being hit. His plane shook, and the stick vibrated in his hand. He heard a voice shout in his earphones.

"Jesus Christ. Look at that crazy, wonderful sonofabitch."

Crazy is right, thought Bates, as a direct hit threw him almost onto his back. He wrestled the plane upright just as he flew through a giant column of spray. When his windshield cleared he could see the end of the line of Japanese ships. It seemed to be a hundred miles away.

Somehow Bates did not go down under the terrible barrage though his plane was blackened and its white markings were burned away, though his engine coughed with a cold that would never be cured, and the tattered remnants of his wing flapped testily in the rushing wind.

He passed the line of ships, and before the enemy could retrain their guns the torpedo bombers were in range and had sent their gleaming, deadly fish tumbling into the water before they pulled up and away. All along the line of the enemy the fish struck home in a varied pattern of explosions, smoke and billowing fire.

Bates turned back to the fight as soon as he was in the clear. He fired a short burst from his guns. His plane was shot to hell, but there was nothing wrong with the six fifty-calibers in his wings.

[350

Wheeler, Anders and Winston had eight Zeros cornered in a lonely section of the sky. The issue might have been considered in doubt until Bates joined in. Now it was two against one, and that evened things up. Winston was on his back when he saw Bates whip up from below and hit a Zero with a belly burst while hanging on his prop, his plane pointing almost straight up in the air. Winston laughed aloud into his mike.

"Welcome to the party. I doubt if you can maintain that position much longer."

"God damn," Bates' voice sounded surprised as he fell off into a spin.

A Zero moved down on Bates, helpless in the spin, but Winston rolled over and came down on it. Centering his sights, he fired a three-second, no-deflection shot, and the Zero came apart in the air.

Bates returned the compliment. "We're even, Max boy."

Wheeler, fighting with all the skill he possessed, was holding his own against three of the enemy by a meticulous application of every trick he had learned through the years. He dropped flaps when it might have been considered suicidal to do so, he chopped throttle and booted rudder and once he even dropped his landing gear. A Zero had overtaken him too rapidly, which was what Wheeler had intended, but as he retracted his gear a short burst from the enemy found him. Wheeler heard a solid *thunk* as a shell lodged somewhere in his undercarriage. It seemed at the time an insignificant thing, but for Wheeler it held considerable importance.

The sky was a variegated, changing pattern; the protesting engines whining on the last spin and the dizzying swirl as the sea revolved and loomed closer, and it was all there and the only thing left in the world but the last muttered curse; it was Bates and Marriner, Anders and Winston and Wheeler and all the others so far from home, splitting the sky asunder with the fury of their fight; it was Dusane herding the remnants of his torpedo bombers into a group and starting the long flight homeward. Dusane had lived and his bombers had gas tanks large enough to afford the measure of security that the Hellcats were denied.

Above the main body of the fight two lone aircraft defied most of the rules written in the fighter pilot's handbook. Yamota and Marriner had renewed their battle. Years later men who had watched the fight with only fleeting glances would still talk about it when flying men gathered.

351]

It was a duel of the masters. They fought in the sky near a cloud bank, but neither man had a thought for sanctuary. Joyously they tested each other's mettle, and joyously each admitted to himself that he had met his equal.

First one, then the other held the advantage as they wrote new pages in the book of aerial combat. Maneuvers never devised before nor attempted since evolved from their steady, competent hands as their planes performed far beyond the limits of design.

Having employed every guile and talent he possessed, Yamota decided to employ the most ancient fraud of all. This man opposing me, he thought, can only be the man I have met twice before. No one has ever fought me like this except him. Again I will say he is the best flier I have ever met. I doubt there can be two of them. I wish I might have known him and called him friend. We could fight up here all day but for the diminishing gas supply and the darkness closing in. But it will not do to end this fight in a stalemate. It is unworthy of either of us. I have tried everything I know except the oldest trick of all. Perhaps he is so adept at this business that in his confidence he will disregard the subtle warning of his mind. I will give this fight five more minutes, and then I will put an end to it.

In his own cockpit, Marriner's thoughts were lucid, unemotional. This fight will end soon, he said to himself. Listen to me, whatever your name is in that other plane. I am going to kill you now. Not with hate, in fact with no passion at all. I will kill you for two reasons; you are the enemy and you killed Harry Hill. I broke a law once and let you live. But not again.

And finally it was Yamota, feeling now for the first time the weight of his years and the heavy memory of a hundred other fights in as many skies over other lands and other seas, who made the final play. He had chosen his time carefully and with great diligence because his life would depend on his timing and his estimate of his opponent.

Yamota pushed over at five thousand feet with Marriner on his tail but out of firing range. As the Zero shrilled earthward the Hellcat followed, narrowing the distance now because its greater weight meant greater diving speed. Yamota watched his enemy in his rearview mirror, meticulously calculating exact distances. He saw the other plane coming on, drawing closer behind him, and he felt a respect bordering on veneration for his opponent, and for just an instant of time he regretted what he had to do. The moment passed

[352

however, and he once again was all that he had ever been. A fighter pilot duty bound.

Yamota eased out of his dive at one hundred feet and flew straight and level, allowing Marriner to come within firing range. His practiced eye measured carefully, and when he judged his enemy to be some nine hundred feet away he suddenly jerked back on his stick, and the nose of the Zero swept up into the first half of a loop.

Marriner had been ready to fire when Yamota started his maneuver. Into Marriner's mind came an immediate and accurate appraisal of Yamota's intentions.

He's trying to make me follow him through the loop. We're far too low, and he knows it and he wants me to come after him down the backside with insufficient altitude to recover, so I'll fly headlong into the ocean. Well, I have a surprise in store for my opponent which I sincerely believe will have fatal results.

Into the darkening skies the nose of the Zero climbed until Yamota was on his back, still watching the plane behind him in his mirror. He saw the American climb past the vertical and pull his nose on through so that now both planes were inverted with Marriner on the Zero's tail.

Yamota smiled a little sadly as the Zero swept down in the last half of the loop. The American would fly into the sea now. There was no other way.

But Yamota had made his fourth mistake of the day—it would cost him his life. He had not fully appreciated the skill of his enemy. For Dick Marriner had one trick left to play. He was still upside down when he reached out with his left hand and moved his landing gear and flap handles to the "down" position. The wheel-well doors opened, and the landing gear started to extend as Marriner eased back on his stick, the nose fell through, and the Hellcat began the final half of the loop.

When Marriner dropped his landing gear and flaps he ruined the smooth flow of air over the body of his plane, thus creating a drag effect that would allow him to complete his loop with far less loss of altitude than would ordinarily be required. His airspeed indicator did not build rapidly during the vertical part of his recovery, and because of this he eased out of his dive and behind Yamota when the Zero pilot was expecting him to fly into the ocean vertically.

Marriner opened fire as he came level. He fired a long, sustained

353]

burst with only a few degrees of deflection, and the majority of his shells found the target. Eighty fifty-caliber shells pounded into Yamota's Zero, shaking it and working a stitchwork pattern along the sides and into the engine housing. Three of the shells found Yamota himself. One hit him in the right arm, another in the right leg, while the last one tore into and through his right side.

With the awful onslaught of the pain, Yamota immediately turned hard starboard and firewalled his throttle. He could no longer see clearly through his pain-rocketed eyes, and he knew he was no longer capable of continuing the fight. He headed for the nearby bank of cloud, a man alone and beaten, his insides torn and bleeding.

This time Marriner followed, all guns blazing, for there are laws that fighting men live by which can be broken once only. Mercy is a quality to be praised, to be sung of in songs and mentioned softly in prayer, but it is not too often allowed in the high places where men fly and die. Marriner had granted Yamota amnesty once; it was written that he must not do it again.

Yamota made it to the cloud bank, but he was mortally wounded. Part of his starboard wing was shot away, and the wind screamed through the holes in his shattered cockpit canopy, tearing brutally at the raw edges of his wounds. He flew with his broken right arm and used his left to hold against the gaping wound in his side. He did this unconsciously because his brain was a boiling mass of agony, and only the trained instincts of the years guided him in the murky depths of the cloud.

For a moment he flew in a clear area between two outcroppings of the cloud and with a great effort he turned his head and saw dimly the last threshing efforts of the First Fleet as it went down under the attacks of the American bombers. As he flew back into the cloud bank Yamota admitted to himself that in all probability he was going to die. Yet because he had no wish to die alone, his bones far from his homeland, he turned his plane to a heading that would intercept the support carrier force racing to help Togyama. He remembered faintly a briefing officer on the *Akiti* mentioning that the support force was more than two hundred miles northwest, coming at flank speed. Yamota was not at all sure he could come aboard a carrier, damaged as he was, but he would try, if for no other reason than that his comrades might honor his bones.

Yamota had no way of knowing that the support force had turned

[354

back when the reports of the First Fleet's catastrophe had reached it.

The dusk had deepened to a murky darkness when the combatants drew apart. For this is the way fights end. One moment the sky is a wild place and the next as silent as a cathedral.

The voices were weary as they sounded out of the darkness.

"All Jehovah planes. Rendezvous. Time to go home."

"No gas to rendezvous," called a worried voice.

"Then head out in section or division. Course is zero nine five."

Three hundred miles of threatening darkness lay ahead, and the gas needles pointed far below the halfway mark. The towering clouds that always came with the Pacific night barred their way, blanking out the horizon, giving them no reference by which to fly their planes.

Barry Wheeler led them back through the long night. Navigation and running lights were switched on, and all about the sky the tiny needles of light announced to the pilots that there were other men around them fighting the same sick apprehension, praying to the same God and watching the inexorable downward sweep of the gas gauge needles.

They were all of the survivors, one hundred twenty-five of the two hundred who flew so bravely forth, and individually they had small hope of ever putting the arresting hook into the gear again. All light was gone now, and in the manner of the ominous Pacific nightfall far-off intermittent flashes of angry lightning lashed red scarrings on the black curtain that faced their oil-spattered windshields.

They bored ahead with magnificent disdain for the odds against them, sweat-soaked in their khaki shirts, their oily cockpits filled with the metallic odor of cooling gun barrels. Away from the flogged First Fleet with the knowledge of victory and of duty well done which is an admirable thing but does not offer means for survival on a black night, exhausted to the very marrow of the bone and striving to see a blacked-out fleet under the distant horizon which itself was not there.

When Isoku Yamota selected his course to intercept the support force he did so by the last faint crimson smudging of light on the western horizon where the sun had gone. His compass had been ruined by the same shell from Marriner's guns that had damaged his midsection so horribly. A wave of pain and nausea swept over

355]

Yamota, and he screamed aloud and bent over in the cockpit to ease the spasm. He could not raise his head while the anguish persisted, and so he was unaware that his plane slowly effected a one hundred and eighty degree turn, reversing his course. When finally he was able to lift his head again, the sky before him was no different than any other piece of the dark night, and so Yamota, unknowing, was flying out on a reciprocal of the course that he thought would take him to safety. In itself, Yamota's spasm of agony was an unimportant thing to anyone except the flier himself. But his reversal of course would prove significant indeed to Task Force 58, somewhere out in the blackness.

It was thus that Strike Able came back. They were strung out to hell and gone over the sky, clusters of tiny pinpoints of light moving steadily eastward. There was little conversation over the air because there was nothing left to say. They had a long way to go, and the needles on the gas gauges crept ever closer toward EMPTY. So they watched the needles, caught up in a hypnosis of a sort, and they swallowed hard, and the only words that passed their lips were soft-spoken and meant to be heard only by themselves and their God.

> Our Father, Who art in Heaven. . . .
> Bless me, Father, for I have sinned. . . .
> Hail Mary, full of grace. . . .

One and all, they prayed, some in fear and some without it. There were no atheists in Strike Able on the night of June 20, 1944.

Then Wheeler spoke out across the sky. "This is Jehovah Leader. I make it a hundred and twenty miles. Then we're home."

But Wheeler knew his chances of reaching safety that night were slim indeed. There were two factors that had occupied his mind during the return flight. For one thing, his gas needle would soon be touching EMPTY. For a second, he had attempted to open his cockpit canopy to allow a stream of fresh air into the cramped quarters. The canopy would not budge an inch. Only then did Wheeler remember the solid *thunk* as the enemy shell had hit his undercarriage. The shell had come up through the cockpit and had jammed the track along which the canopy slid. He had a chance left, but it was a slight one. It depended on the extent of the damage the enemy bullet had committed when it entered the area of his wheel-wells. That damage would dictate Wheeler's future.

[356

XVIII

June 20, 1944

The clock on Crowley's desk read 8:30 P.M. when he lit his last cigarette, crushed the empty pack and threw it expertly across the room into the wastebasket. He had been lying on his bunk ever since he heard the last plane of Strike Able thunder down the deck. The bullhorn voice of the air officer had come to him faintly from the flight deck.

"Respot the deck for landing." Unconsciously he had nodded his head in agreement. Good practice, respotting immediately after takeoff. You never knew when somebody would return for an emergency landing.

For almost four hours Crowley had been savoring a deep jubilation that had been churning somewhere within him. At times his shoulders shook as the utter hilarity of the thing overcame him. Then he would open his mouth and roll across his bunk as he hugged his sides in an attempt to control the almost insane, silent laughter.

Four hours can be an immeasurably long period of a man's life under a given set of circumstances. Crowley had spent them walking along the passageway of his years. It was a long, narrow corridor, and it was exactly thirty-four steps long, one for each year he had lived. For every year there was a cell set aside, facing on the corridor. On his journey he had looked into the cells, and a history of sorts had been written on the damp walls. He tried to create an image of the man who had lived in the cells, but the vision was dimmed by time and by memories that crowded together and jumbled themselves into one cell or another until all the years ran together into one fantastically hilarious confusion of truths and lies.

357]

There had been, and Crowley thought about this now as he sat on the edge of his bunk with the laughter threatening to engulf him again, one cell which opened on a wide, sunlit, flower-bedecked patio from which he could see down a long stretch of brightly paved highway. It seemed to Crowley that when he had tried to enter the patio Bobby Anderson barred the way, pointing an accusing finger back in the direction from which he had come. He had not investigated the sunlit patio or what lay beyond but had returned to the dismal passageway again.

In this fashion Crowley had visited each individual cell and his glee had increased until he laughed so hard that tears filled his eyes and his sides ached. Then he heard a voice outside in the corridor.

"Strike Able is a hundred miles out. Poor bastards."

Crowley frowned and wondered if Strike Able should have something to do with him. The words had a ring of familiarity but his mind was too tired to pursue the subject further. He shook his head as he suddenly remembered the reason for his mirth. The ease with which he had duped all of them, every one of them, the smart bastards. They thought they had him beaten, and now he would show them up for what they were. Just a bunch of ignorant slobs wearing those goddam gold wings and so covered with braid they could hardly move. He threw his head back and let his laughter peal out against the overhead in a long bellow.

He went to the door and locked it. He spent considerable time tidying up the room and making his desk immaculate. The despoiled picture of the admiral pinning a Navy Cross on his breast he studied for a period of time, and then he held a match to it, letting it burn to ashes in the wastebasket. He dialed the combination on his safe and without removing anything from it, left the safe door swinging open.

Then he walked to the washbasin and stared at himself intently in the mirror over it. Finally he spoke to himself in the mirror, and now there was no trace of laughter in his face.

"I'm sorry," he said aloud to himself.

Crowley plugged the drain in the washbasin and ran boiling hot water into it until it was full. He reached into the cabinet and fumbled among his shaving gear and pulled out a razor blade. Gingerly, he tested the sharpness against the edge of his thumb. He suddenly plunged his right hand and wrist into the basin of hot water, grimacing with the pain. Looking down he could see his hand under the water, seemingly branching off at a ridiculous angle from his wrist under the refraction of the light. When the pain had eased he withdrew his hand and wiped it with a towel. Next he drew a chair from the desk up to the basin and seated himself on it.

Grasping the razor blade in his left hand, he drew it slowly and surely across his right wrist, pressing down hard enough to insure a deep, satisfactory cut. Before the arterial blood could spurt he thrust the injured hand back into the hot water. The water immediately clouded as his heart pumped the errant blood in a torrent.

He felt no great pain, only a stinging sensation where the razor had done its work. With his left hand he unplugged the drain and let most of the blood and water run out before he plugged it again.

Crowley tried to laugh, but this time the laughter would not come. This surprised him and caused him to wonder. He realized dimly that it was late now, too late for anything. He suddenly wished he had remembered to turn off the overhead light. Too late even for that. The urge to laugh ebbed lower, and soon it was gone completely.

He was weaker now, and he shut his eyes and saw again and for the last time, a fragment of his dream. This time there was only the blood-red Hellcat appearing out of the sky and heading for him on a collision course. He could not move, and as the plane bore down on him, the swirl of vapor around the cockpit thinned and then cleared, and as the plane swept past in silent thunder he could see himself at the controls. And now, at the end of his life, Crowley realized that all his life he had fled not from others, but from himself.

He opened his eyes and saw that his blood was filling the basin to overflowing. He activated the stopper again, and this time he was aware of the tremendous effort it took to move his hand. He decided he would get to his feet and turn off the overhead light, but he could not make his legs function, and he sank back into the chair.

Suddenly he was sorry, terribly sorry. Sorry for himself and for all the men he had failed, and for the warped desire that had stained his life. He could not pray for them now, but he could murmur a plea for their forgiveness.

His eyes had closed now, and he used all of the strength that was left to him to open them again. In the last minutes of his existence he honestly sought an answer to the fiasco that had been his life. The knowledge came to him too late that there are some things in living which can find no answer and no escape.

He had a few seconds left when a thought came to him. He raised his left hand with a great effort and fumbled with the gold wings pinned on his shirt. He was dying in dishonor. There was no reason to dishonor also the wings by which other men lived. His hand was still fumbling with the clasp on the wings when his head slowly sank onto the basin's rim, and his left hand dropped to his side.

The only sound in the room then was the seeping of Crowley's blood through the overflow drain in the basin. It was 9:00 P.M., and all else was silence under a faint call sounding from the flight deck.

"Strike Able sixty miles out."

Chief Rasmussen left his quarters at 2100. He had been troubled ever since the news had spread through the ship that Commander Wheeler was taking over the air group. Now Wheeler was leading Strike Able, and chances were even that he would not be coming back. Rasmussen knew nothing of Wheeler's talk with Balta and the Admiral, and so he thought that Crowley's disgrace would go down with Wheeler. This, he knew, he could not tolerate.

When he had convinced himself that there was no answer except the one he had tried to shun, he put on his cap, walked to the fo'c'sle deck and knocked on the door of Commander Crowley's cabin. He waited several seconds and then knocked again. He could see a light burning against the overhead within the cabin. He knocked again, and when there was no answer he tried the door. Finding it locked he fished in his pocket for the key which Wheeler had returned to him. He knew that what he was doing was grounds for a court-martial, but he felt himself impelled forward by something he could not name. He unlocked the door.

Rasmussen hesitated on the threshold as he pushed open the door.

"Commander?" he called softly.

He listened and heard nothing. As he stepped into the room he was aware of the sound of water oozing down a drain somewhere in the cabin.

Five minutes later, after Rasmussen had cleaned the quarters, the blacked-out fo'c'sle deck was violated for a moment as the hatch opened and closed. Then Rasmussen quickly and silently carried the body of the air group commander to the rail and with a stifled grunt lifted it over the wire railing and let it slide from his arms and tumble into the swiftly passing sea. Rasmussen stood there in the

[360

dark after Crowley had gone and spoke to the twenty-five years of his life that had been spent under the Blue and Gold.

Well, I hope I have done right. I'm not sure. But the way Crowley did it wasn't right. Not with a furtive razor blade behind a locked door. There are better ways to die, and this way the possibility will always exist that Crowley fell over the side. It's preposterous, but men can believe anything if they want to badly enough. Well, I've done what I had to do. There's only Rathburn remaining, and I'll handle that in my own time.

Then, perhaps out of twenty-five years of habit, Rasmussen saluted the uncomplaining sea that passed along the sides of the *Concord*.

The planes of Strike Able were fifty miles from the task force when they began to fall. At random through the sky laboring engines suddenly coughed, sputtered once or twice, and quit as the props began to windmill. There was no sense in pumping the pressure lever because there was no gasoline left to pump. The pilots reacted in accord with their individual acceptance of their fate.

A section leader called to his wingman. "I'm sputtering, Zeke. I'm going in while I've got a little gas left and can control this bastard. So long, pal."

"So long hell. I'll go in with you. We can hold hands."

A hoarse voice shouted, "Jocko. Jocko. You're losing altitude."

There was a chuckle in the voice that answered. "My gas has gone AWOL. I am obliged to leave now."

All across the sky the voices matter-of-factly discussed the predicament. All of them knew there was no way out of this and that by no alchemy could their gas tanks be filled or the blackness of the night be dispelled.

A pilot agreed with his wingman as to the preferability of a parachute jump to a landing on the rough waters of the invisible ocean.

"I say let's abdicate these sonsabitches. That ocean's as black as an elephant's asshole."

"I agree. We'll jump. Get in here close, and we'll go out together."

"Roger. I hope to Christ the guy who packed this chute knew what he was doing."

"Well, if he didn't, I'll get you a new one. Let's go."

A voice spoke out. "That's it for me, Bobo. Reading empty and

361]

the prop's windmilling. Starting down now. Happy Fourth of July."

"Fourth of July, horseshit. It's too lonesome up here. I'm coming for the ride."

"Okay then. Set her up at seventy knots and hold her there. We'll have to fumble around to find the goddam ocean."

Next, a gruff voice. "Mrs. Baker's son is going swimming. Jack, how far is it to the nearest land?"

His wingman answered, "Two hundred and forty miles to Saipan."

"I'm not altogether sure I can swim that far. Here we go."

With no horizon visible in the night to guide them they had only their artificial horizons and their airspeed indicators with which to effect a landing on the water. They slowed the planes up as much as possible and then held the airspeed steady and waited for the first jarring bounce as the belly of the plane hit the water. After that there was nothing more they could do to insure their survival. It was not much of a chance, but it was the best they had with no power left under their cowlings.

Those whose engines were still functioning used every trick they had ever learned to conserve the precious fuel. Ever since the planes had left the scene of action the mixture controls had been leaned back until the engines sputtered in protest and then inched forward only a fraction to accommodate the reluctant carburetors. Now propeller controls were manipulated in such fashion that the unwieldy props turned over so slowly the pilots could almost delude themselves that they were counting the revolutions. Throttles were left untouched unless in emergency because any movement of the throttle increased the consumption of gasoline and decreased the chances for survival.

In the sky that night the pilots of Strike Able suddenly decided they wanted to live forever.

Shortly after 9:00 P.M. Terrence Bates had gone as far as he was going to go. When the realization was firmed in his mind, after the engine hacked and spit and finally stopped altogether, Bates admitted to himself that he had known for an hour that he was not going to make it back to the task force. When he had made his run down the line of enemy ships his plane had taken a beating that ordinarily would have sent it into the ocean immediately. His oil pressure had been dropping steadily, and the entire engine mounting rattled around like a skeleton on a tin roof. So when he finally started

[362

the long glide into the blackness he called Marriner, and his voice was almost cheerful.

"Dick, this is Batesy. This is as far as I go tonight unless this engine can accommodate itself to functioning on pure air. I'm going down. You and Max and Cort split my whiskey."

"I'll come with you," Marriner offered, and he did not think at all that he was doing a courageous thing.

"Negative," replied Bates. "You're almost home now. Just plot my position and see they come looking for me tomorrow. I can swim just so long."

Marriner watched over the side of his cockpit at Bates' lights until the other plane lost itself in the murk below.

"Good luck, Batesy," Marriner whispered into his mike.

Bates' voice came lightly back to them. "This is not a matter of luck. It is a matter of skill, and I'm the most skillful sonofabitch in Task Force 58." A pause, then, "Good night, gentlemen."

Ah, Bates. You will refuse to go under. This is still a game to you, and landing at night in a wrecked airplane with only the seat of your pants to guide you just lends a flavor to the thing. You will set your plane down on the unfriendly sea and you will go down in the cockpit, but you will be fighting and so will free yourself before the last breath is expended. You will not forget to drag your parachute pack with you, and so you will spend a wet night, quietly floating around the ocean, munching candy bars and whistling Irish tunes. In the dawn you will beat off some inquisitive sharks with your shoe, and then you will sight the destroyer booming at you from over the horizon. Death is unacceptable to you, Terrence Bates, and it is a pity that such is not the case with every other man up there tonight.

On board the *Concord,* Admiral Delacrois stood alone on the blacked-out outer bridge. The decision he would shortly be called upon to make was compounded by reports of Japanese submarines in the area. Out of the night Captain Balta approached him and laid a hand on his shoulder.

"I think you are earning that third star you wear tonight, Frog." Balta's voice was understanding, but he knew that no man in the world could share the terrible responsibility which belonged this night to Admiral Frog Delacrois alone.

"They're lost, Sam," Delacrois said softly. "Tired and wounded

363]

and lost out there in the night, and some of those planes even carry dead men in them." He shook his head. "They won the fight for us, and now they've come all the way back to find out they're little better off now than when they started home. Running out of gas and nowhere to land in the dark. Christ, but they must be afraid up there. They must be."

"I would be," Balta said.

They both looked up as a voice came over the bridge radio.

"Jehovah Base from Jehovah Nine. Can you give me a vector? Hello any base. Any base. Where am I, please? Can anyone tell me where I am?"

"God damn it," muttered Delacrois.

"Frog," said Balta, aware of the thoughts that were running through the Admiral's mind. "There are Jap submarines around tonight and there's also a chance the Japs followed our planes back from the fight. The book says you have two things going for you. Radio silence and the protection of darkness."

Delacrois nodded. "And yet there are a couple of hundred men out there, most of whom will die if I follow established procedure."

Balta knew he had to be blunt. "Dying is something we all face in a war."

"It isn't an easy thing, Sam."

"That's why they give certain men three stars, Frog. Because they're supposed to find answers to questions like these. Have you found yours?"

"Almost," Delacrois said. "These men fought well for me today, in as difficult a combat situation as I have ever encountered. Their conduct was nothing short of magnificent. I intend to recommend every man for a decoration."

"Well," said Balta, "they'll be of little use to them tonight."

Delacrois might not have heard. "But are the lives of two hundred men worth risking this entire force? On a scale of values, what is the weight of two hundred lives more or less? Can you tell me?"

"I've run out of answers tonight, Admiral."

"A handful of men on one side and an entire force on the other. A ridiculous comparison in any event." He turned to the hatch leading to the inner bridge. "Let's go inside."

Flag Plot was strangely quiet as the Admiral and Balta entered. A staff enlisted man brought two cups of coffee. Finally Delacrois turned his eyes to his duty officer.

[364

"Henderson," he said. "Send this signal to all the ships in the force."

Every man on the bridge held his breath. They had moved back from the Admiral, almost as if they wanted him to be completely alone, isolated, in this decision. Delacrois's eyes fastened on Balta as he spoke, as if warning the younger man of the perils of command. "Turn on every goddam light in this force," his voice rang out. "I don't mean the running lights or the navigation lights or the identification lights. I mean the searchlights, the biggest and brightest we have. I want them on full balls, and I want to see them light this place up like it was Coney Island on the Fourth of July. Get going."

Admiral Delacrois had decided to gamble his fleet against the lives of the gallant men he had sent out on so deadly a mission, so heroically achieved.

And so, for the first time under a combat sky, the lights went on.

The homing pilots saw the lights at first with disbelief. They blinked bloodshot, weary eyes, and then they shouted with joy.

"Christ," yelled a voice. "He turned the lights on. He turned the goddam lights on." The pilot might have referred to God or he might have referred to Admiral Delacrois. In that moment, to the pilots of Strike Able, they were one and the same.

"Times Square in the Pacific."

"Grauman's Chinese Theater. *Yeeeoooowww!*"

"All Jehovah planes from Jehovah Base. Check your guns. I say again, check your guns for safe."

So the switches were flipped and the handles turned on the charging-safe knobs because it is contrary to procedure to come aboard a carrier with charged guns.

Aboard the ships the men had gone wild with joy when the lights came on. They danced and hugged each other on the decks and blessed the giant searchlights and the colorful star-shells that burst all over the sky. Every unit of the task force tried to get into the act, tried to lift a welcoming hand to the weary men who had fought their fight for them.

If all was well aboard the ships, it was far from well in Barry Wheeler's cockpit. Wheeler was staring in consternation at a small dial on the far left side of his cockpit instrument panel. It was a gauge that held two small windows in it and was designed to indicate to the pilot whether his landing gear was up or down. When the gear was retracted the windows were void of any marking. When the gear was down and in landing posture the windows showed panels of diagonal stripes. It was the right, or starboard panel, that indicated a faulty landing gear on Wheeler's plane. The other panel indicated the port gear was down and locked. As Wheeler stared at the empty panel in the gauge he felt a cold chill run down his spine.

In itself a faulty landing gear is an inconsequential thing. A man can land on a carrier without one and although he will not effect an admirable landing and will without doubt make a wreck of his airplane, he will normally survive. It is not too dangerous a feat. Or he can land in the water. This has been done with no serious after-effects although not too often at night. There is a third possibility, and this one Wheeler would probably have elected because of the black night, the lack of insufficient fuel and the fact that the men he had led to battle had to get aboard before their gas gave out. He would have bailed out because he knew if he crash-landed on the deck with one gear fouled up he would delay landing procedures for at least twenty minutes, during which time many of the planes would run out of gas and go into the drink.

But Wheeler could not bail out, and thus his problem became a deadly one. He could not land aboard the carrier. Therefore he must land in the ocean. And because the shell that had struck the canopy track prevented him from either opening or jettisoning his cockpit canopy, Wheeler, sentenced irrevocably to a night landing in the water, would be unable to get out of his plane.

When Admiral Delacrois turned on the lights he saved his Strike Able. He also startled Isoku Yamota out of a half-dream in which he was walking up a flower-bedecked lane in Niigata, a bouquet of roses in his hand. From the back of the house Yamota could hear his son's happy laughter.

Yamota had not followed the returning planes of Strike Able. He still thought he was flying an intercept course for the Japanese support column. The pain was more severe now although it did not well up quite so often. When it did come he gagged on the agony and held his hand against the gaping wound in his side. The instrument panel of the Zero was only a hazy block before his eyes and in reality the plane had flown itself, trimmed up by his expert hands before the pain of his wounds had taken away a part of his mind.

[366

Now ahead of him in the distance he saw the great, searching blaze of bright white lights splitting the darkness. He smiled faintly and nodded his head to acknowledge the honor his comrades were affording him.

So very kind of them, he thought. To violate directives and turn on the lights because they know I am wounded and lost. I will land soon and they will stop this terrible burning in my stomach and perhaps someone will wipe away this sour taste of blood in my mouth. It will be difficult to land with this pain and the glare of the lights together. I will fly once low over the lights on the deck, and they will dim them or turn them away from my direction. I will come down now. They are ten or fifteen miles away, and I must enter the landing circle in a prescribed altitude and pattern so they know I am a friendly plane and not the enemy.

Yamota eased the stick slightly forward, even this gentle movement causing a great wave of agony to sweep through his body. He was at fifteen thousand feet and a little more than twenty miles from Task Force 58 when he started to lose altitude. As the airspeed built up the voice of his little son sounded again in the play yard behind his house in Niigata. Yamota forgot his pain and reached out his arms as the laughing little boy bounded down the walk to greet him.

Wheeler called Marriner on the radio. "Dick, this is Barry. How do you read?"

"Loud and clear, Jehovah Leader," Marriner replied.

"Two One from Leader." Wheeler continued, "Break off and enter the landing circle. You will be first to land. I am having difficulty with my landing gear. I will circle and try to get it down."

"A suggestion, sir?" Marriner asked a question.

"Go ahead, Two One."

"If you can't get it down, bail out. Don't try a water landing with a half-extended gear. Just a suggestion, sir."

Wheeler smiled in the privacy of his cockpit because he appreciated Marriner's concern and also because he knew he would not have time to accept many more suggestions in his lifetime.

"Thank you, Dick," Wheeler said. "Go ahead now and good luck to you."

He watched the lights of Marriner's plane break away, followed

367]

by those marking Winston and Anders, then he climbed above the landing planes and circled the force and began his final struggle for survival.

There are certain things that can be done to coax a reluctant landing gear down. There is an emergency hydraulic system to force pressure through the lines and lower the gear when the other system has failed. There is a possibility that strenuous up-and-down pressure on the gear-activating handle may jar the gear loose. There is the chance that a rapid dive and an abrupt pull-up will employ centrifugal force to throw the gear out of the wheel-well into a fully extended position. There is also an air bottle, fired by pulling on a handle situated near the floor of the cockpit, which when all else fails will usually blow the gear down. Unless, of course, someone has shot a heavy-caliber shell into the wheel-well in such a manner that it has smashed the entire mechanism beyond repair.

While Wheeler fought his peculiar fight, Marriner led Strike Able down and into the landing circle. Marriner landed first aboard the *Concord,* and after him came the others in a succession so rapid that the deck handling crews barely got one plane out of the arresting gear before another was coming over the ramp, taking a cut from landing signal officer and pounding down onto the deck.

Mustering all the skill any of them had ever assimilated, the pilots dropped out of the night, past the arced wands of the signal officer and into the wires, their hands sweaty on the sticks and a weary exuberance in their hearts and bodies. Drawn-faced and a million years old, they looked up at the inimical sky as the lonely miles and the endless hours converged on them in a bitter memory.

Winston and Anders came out of the ebony wash of night and into the blinding glare of the lights. Winston led Anders around the groove and into the final turn, chopping throttle and easing pressure off the stick until the wires caught the tail hook and the plane jerked to a halt. He looked back as he taxied forward and saw Anders make it safely home.

Out on the dark sea, as far as the eye could see and then beyond that, winking lights announced the presence of the more fortunate of the pilots who had gone down. They were in their small rubber rafts or floating in their life jackets, and they called for succor in their plight by means of the tiny flashlights they wore pinned to the front of their life jackets.

But they were the lucky ones. Far back along the road they had

[368

carved through the sky the night winds echoed the last tallyho of the men whose luck had run thin and running so, had left them to die under the remorseless sea. The restless waters allowed no monument where they went under, and the only sermons their torn bodies would ever receive would come from the seabirds on their lonely patrol.

Barry Wheeler lost his fight by minutes.

Wheeler was at eight thousand feet over the task force, vainly trying to shake his starboard gear into the extended position. He had tried everything in the book and then had invented a few things on his own. His gas needle rested firmly on EMPTY when he heard Sam Balta's voice reach out to him on the radio.

"Jehovah Leader from Jehovah Base. Do you read?"

Wheeler's voice was calm and steady as it came to Balta and Delacrois, standing together by the radio in the bridge area.

"Jehovah Leader here. I hear you five by five, Sam."

A smile of relief passed over Balta's face. "Jehovah Leader. What is your position and state?"

"I am angels eight over you," Wheeler replied. "My state is empty and my starboard gear will not extend. Things are not happy up here."

Balta turned to Delacrois, an urgency in his voice. "Are all the planes aboard?"

The Admiral's operations officer answered. "Not yet, sir. Almost, though. Some of ours went aboard the *Ardennes*."

"Barry," Balta spoke into the mike, "bring it in. The hell with the landing gear. Our planes are just about aboard. The deck will be ready and clear. Do you receive?"

"It's no go, Sam." Wheeler's voice was weary.

"Listen, goddammit," Balta yelled into the mike. "There are no more planes to come aboard. A deck crash won't hurt a damn thing. We're waiting for you. Bring it in."

"That's not what I meant." Wheeler's voice was level. "I just ran out of gas. A dead engine, Sam."

Balta groaned and looked with dismay at Delacrois. The Admiral took the mike from Balta's hand.

"This is Jehovah. Are you going to bail out?"

"No, sir," Wheeler answered slowly. "I'm not going to bail out." There was a smile in his voice then. "Although I would like to."

369]

"Well, ride her down then if you want. But I would advise a bail-out."

"My canopy is jammed. It won't move. I took a shell along the track."

A scowl came over the Admiral's face. "Jesus Christ!" he said, almost to himself. "A dead stick and a jammed canopy and a fouled landing gear. All at night. Jesus Christ." It was a prayer more than a curse.

Balta grabbed the mike again. "Barry," he shouted. "Listen. Your gun. Take your gun and try to shoot away the jammed track. Maybe you can blast it off."

They could hear Wheeler's sigh over the radio. "Sam, for the first time in a hundred missions I didn't wear a gun. I didn't have one. Remember? I was your exec until a few hours ago."

"Oh Christ," Balta said, and he was truly speaking to God now. Trapped up there in that tiny cockpit so alone no one in all the world can get near him. Trapped in there and going down dead stick with a jammed landing gear that will sure as hell flip him over on his back when he hits the water, and then he will have to die screaming and pounding with his fists against that goddam canopy as he goes foot by foot all the way down to the bottom of the ocean. Dear God, nobody deserves to die like this. Not a Barry Wheeler who lived in sunlight and with honor, and should not die like a rat trapped in a sinking ship.

Wheeler's voice came in again. "I am at angels five now. Have her set up at seventy knots. Nothing now but to wait."

"Barry." Balta's voice was strained. "When you go in, try to get loose of the parachute harness. Lean back and get your feet against the canopy if you can. Then kick it out."

This time they heard Wheeler chuckle. "Sam. I am not a contortionist. Maybe the shock on landing will free the canopy."

In the bridge they looked at each other and found only a dismal knowledge in each other's eyes. Delacrois shook his head sadly and walked away, leaving Balta alone because he knew Balta was a man standing at a graveside with his heart in his hand.

"I am passing angels four." There was a pause. "Sam. A favor if you will. Little Barry. I know you'll do what needs to be done."

Tears were streaming down Balta's cheeks as he answered. "Yes, Barry, I'll do whatever there is that needs doing. And for Betty, too."

[370

A voice sounded faintly from the flight deck. "No more planes in the landing circle. That must be the last of them."

He is dying well, thought Balta. Much better than I could ever manage. And in the hardest way of all. I've known men to lose their minds under circumstances less trying than this. There'll be a need for me to watch after his wife and boy. It won't be an obligation but an honor.

"Passing angels three now. I will land next to a DD. There is always a chance. Ask them to monitor my landing."

The operations officer passed the word to the rear escort destroyer to stand by for Wheeler's landing. The lights of Wheeler's plane were visible now, alone in the sky, circling slowly aft of the force.

War would be an easy thing, Delacrois thought to himself, if it encompassed only dead men and torn and ruined bodies. Dead men are already past all pity. They are probably better off than the rest of us. But in watching a man die like this, bravely, when death is a choking mouthful of water and you cannot get away, when it sits there staring at you, when war comes to this, I guess every man has had a bellyful. Christ, but this man is handling it well. I guess they were right. It's not where or the means by which you die. It's how you die that counts and will be remembered. Wheeler could not be doing it better. But there is another thing that counts. It counts very much, and it is the company in which you die. Tonight Wheeler is dying in very select company. If it were not for the brutal style incident to his dying, I could almost envy him.

"Two thousand feet now," said Wheeler's level voice. "This will be my last transmission." His voice hesitated a moment. "Directions are in my safe, Sam. One last thing. It's been a good go. All of it. There are no regrets on that score. A little early, maybe. Anyway Sam, thanks for everything. This is Jehovah Leader. Out." Then there was only the static coming through the loudspeaker and crackling into the silence on the bridge.

In his cockpit Wheeler did what little he could under the circumstances. He adjusted his shoulder straps as tight as possible. He had long since pumped his flaps down by hand. He would at least hit the water at the slowest possible speed for his configuration.

He unbuckled his parachute harness and slipped out of it, insuring a maximum of freedom when he went in. He kicked his boots off and that was all there was for him to do now as he watched his al-

371]

timeter unwind past one thousand feet. His airspeed was steady on seventy knots, the nose of the plane was high, his rate of descent about four hundred and fifty feet per minute. He swung the nose a little to the right to line up on a parallel course with the rear escort destroyer which had moved out from the force.

In the quiet bridge of the *Concord,* Balta clenched his fists while the tears streamed unashamedly down the tight, drawn lines of his face. He turned to Delacrois who stood beside him, sympathy in his eyes.

"I think he would want me to watch this," Balta said.

"I agree," said Delacrois, and the two men walked out to the bridge catwalk.

Wheeler strained against the shoulder harness and gripped the stick tightly as the lights of the destroyer escort loomed brighter on his right side. Under the bright lights of the task force he could see the black water heaving as his nose came down to it. He lifted his nose higher. Then higher. He had dropped his tail hook, and now he could feel it dragging through the water. He lifted the nose a little bit higher, and from the corners of his eyes he could see the water almost level with him now, almost swelling along the side of the plane. He exerted the last bit of back pressure on the stick, and then the plane stalled, shuddered once very lightly, and tumbled four feet into the ocean.

He saw the spray against the windshield, and then he felt himself lifted up and over, and the plane settled on its back, and Wheeler, in his cockpit, was under the water. The utter darkness lent him a superhuman strength as he hammered against the cockpit canopy. He felt a sudden motion, and with a horror he knew the plane was going under, port wing first. When the extended landing gear had blasted into the water it had caused the nose to dig deeper as the plane catapulted onto its back. Because of this, the plane had lost the buoyancy it might have maintained had the somersault resulted in a purely flat upside-down position.

Wheeler knew this, but he had no more time to consider it. At any rate, it was no longer important. Wheeler was fifteen feet under the surface when the water started to enter the cockpit. There was no more hope anywhere in the world for Barry Wheeler, and in this moment he proved the only real criterion of a hero. Any man can be brave when there are other men around to praise him and to hand him accolades. The only true hero is the man who can be utterly

[372

courageous when he is all alone, and there are no more laurels to be handed out.

Wheeler was thirty feet down, and the water was coming past his chest when he smiled to himself in the darkness. Just as the water swirled past his chin he took his last breath. As he did so he saw a dim flashing of light far above him through the black water, and he knew the lights from the destroyer escort were searching for him.

It's too late for that, he thought. I might as well get this over with.

Then he opened his mouth and let his soul go forth.

Two minutes later a voice from the escort destroyer announced to the flag bridge, "The plane went over on its back and sank immediately. The pilot did not get out. We kept a light on the plane all the way and do not recommend continuation of the search. There can be no survivor."

Balta heard the transmission from where he stood in the night. He felt completely helpless, and far back in his mind there was a bitterness at the way of things. He wanted to call out across the water to the place where Barry Wheeler had died. The thinking brought back to him the faces of other men he had known who had gone away from him with a laugh and a gallant word, but the faces would not focus clearly. He knew that never again would he be privileged with a friendship like Barry Wheeler's. But now, like everything that was made of flesh and blood, Wheeler was gone on a trip that he had to make alone.

Isoku Yamota circled slowly, losing altitude, dimly aware that he must enter the landing pattern at an altitude of exactly fifteen hundred feet and at an entry angle of exactly forty-five degrees. These were standard recognition precautions for the Japanese fleet and were so ingrained in Yamota's brain that they pronounced themselves even above the pain that swelled through his body.

At fifteen hundred feet he added throttle to maintain that altitude and lowered his landing gear. He was seven miles away from the largest and most brilliant shaft of light when he made his entry into the landing pattern, keeping always to an exact fifteen hundred feet. Another spasm of pain hit him now, and he groaned against the side of the cockpit.

The lights were blinding him, and he squinted against the harsh glare, feeling a distant anger because someone did not realize that the lights were causing him trouble. He was well within the pattern

373]

now and began to lose more altitude to assume his position for his carrier pass.

Yamota's plane was picked up early enough by all the radar screens in the task force, but it occasioned no undue alarm. Many of the returning planes had had their IFF identification gear shot out during the fighting and so appeared on the screens as ordinary blips. The radar plotters surmised, reasonably enough, that Yamota's plane was a late arrival from Strike Able.

Balta, standing alone on the catwalk, heard the voice of a plotter from the radar screen of destroyers.

"Jehovah from Watchdog. Latecomer in pattern. Seven miles out. Wheels down and heading for Jehovah Base."

So Yamota passed over the outer edge of the defending screen, a passing shadow in the night. No gun in the force swiveled or tracked the Zero, and on the *Concord* the landing signal officer ran back to his platform and prepared to take the new arrival aboard.

Balta saw the lights of the Zero when they were three miles away. It did not register on his grief-stricken mind that the plane was ridiculously out of position for any kind of a carrier landing pass.

Yamota took his bearing on the blazing light that emanated from the searchlight situated on the highest bridge of the island structure of the *Concord,* between a forty-millimeter gun mount and a catwalk leading around the smokestack. He was smiling through the pain in relief when he passed over the inner screen only two miles from the carrier. Soon tender hands would help him from his cockpit and lay him gently on his own bed in the bedroom overlooking the garden in Niigata. Admiral Togyama and Yamota's little son would come and stand by the bedside while he fought this awful screaming in his belly. The roaring of his engine dimmed in his ears now, and he smelled flowers in his cockpit. He shut his eyes against the sickness in his stomach.

Balta was roused from his reverie as Yamota passed over the battleship screen a mile away. That bastard is crazy, he thought. He'll never make a pass coming from that direction. He's going to miss the groove altogether.

Yamota opened his eyes and the great searchlight blazed directly into them. Only it wasn't a searchlight any longer. It was the sun in Niigata on a summer morning, and he was calling to his wife.

The Zero was five hundred yards from the *Concord* when Sam

[374

Balta realized it was going to hit the ship. Simultaneously he heard a frantic radio call from the battleship screen.

"Jehovah Base. Jehovah Base. That's a Zero heading for you! A Zero!"

With a hoarse curse Balta started to run for the entrance to the inner bridge. He had traveled about ten of the twenty yards necessary when he knew with a fatal certainty that he was not going to make it. He stopped abruptly, put his hands on the railing and stared into the night at the lights hurtling toward him.

Yamota smiled at the last as his wife appeared in the doorway of the cottage, her face alight with beauty and wonder and tenderness. He came toward her to take her in his arms. Her smiling face was fresh and smelled of roses.

Yamota opened his eyes, and his wife's figure was still there, her arms outstretched to him. He laughed and hurried as he came to her.

Isoku Yamota flew directly into Sam Balta's eyes.

When the Zero hit it exploded in a paralyzing gush of purple flame and sparking debris. A mushrooming billow of dirty black smoke covered the entire island structure. A burning wheel strut hurtled through the air and crashed into the airplanes parked at the bow. It severed the wing panel of a Hellcat and dipped its blaze into the sloshing gasoline tank. There was a puff of smoke and then a grumble that grew suddenly into a great roar, and the entire forward portion of the flight deck went up in a tremendous vortex of swirling yellow flame.

Frog Delacrois had been standing alone at one of the forward portholes, watching the deck crews spotting the landed aircraft. He was considering the order to douse the lights in the task force when the transmission had come from the battleship concerning the Zero. He had just turned to go to Balta when Yamota flew into the island structure.

Then, quite suddenly, there was no sky outside Delacrois's porthole. No sky at all.

Later Delacrois would remember the thought that flashed through his mind as he felt himself lifted and hurled back against the bulkhead to land in a dazed and bleeding heap on the bridge deck. It was as if all the elements had turned on man himself, and the whole universe had gone crazy. A second wave of pressure followed, and the Admiral was lifted as if by some supernatural hand and thrown like

375]

a rag doll against the plotting table. A blue flash streaked across his eyes, and then a choking black cloud blossomed around him and filled his lungs. He struggled to get to his feet while far away he heard a voice bawling.

"Damage control. Damage control. Fire in the island structure."

He staggered to his feet and groped toward the door. Suddenly a section of the bulkhead buckled and knocked him to his knees.

"Here, sir," a strained voice shouted in his ear. He felt strong hands lift him. The voice bellowed again, "Below, Admiral. We've got to get below."

From somewhere in the smoke another voice said, "We've shifted to steering aft. Let's get the hell out of here."

Delacrois would remember the smell of fresh air as he stumbled out of the island and onto the flight deck. He tried to raise his eyes to the sky, but he could not manage because his eyes remained glued to what remained of Sam Balta.

No one would have been able to recognize Balta had it not been for the silver eagles on the collar of the blackened and bloodstained shirt. Delacrois forced himself to bend over and stare into what had been Balta's face.

It was a miracle of sorts that anything at all was left of Balta. Delacrois knelt and started to take the blackened form into his arms. He had only touched the dead man when a hand gently pulled him away and someone draped a sheet over the mangled body.

The same voice spoke to Delacrois. "Let's get down to the wardroom, sir. Damage control will have the fire smothered in a little while."

The Admiral's throat was raw, and when he spoke it was in a harsh rasp. "Did it get below?"

At first the other man did not understand. Tears streamed down Delacrois's face, but he himself never knew if they were tears for Sam Balta or from the smoke and heat on the deck.

"No, sir," the man said. "The damage is confined to the island and the flight deck. Nothing down below. Come along, sir."

Chief Rasmussen was manning a fire hose in the flames when he saw Rathburn's body. It came to him that Rathburn had been servicing the bombers when the Jap plane hit. He cleared a path through the flames with his hose and knelt by Rathburn. A chunk of metal, probably from one of the burning planes, had taken Rathburn across

[376

the stomach, laying open the entire lower abdomen. Rathburn had died in screaming agony, his face contorted out of shape. Rasmussen felt a stir of pity. He knew then that the matter of Crowley was closed for all time.

Later Rasmussen would remember the many things as the night wore on. Much later, after the long years, when the time came to sit in the warming sun and build fanciful tales out of the memories that had dimmed to the point where no one really cared if the truth was embellished by the dispensation granted to old age, he would still remember.

It was Sandusky with his eyes burned black from the flash-flame that sprang like a wicked snake from the underside of an SBD. And it was O'Toole with his eyes not burned black at all because they were hanging down on his cheeks. And Thayer and Cormier standing steady in the heat of the blaze, gasoline running in a stream three yards away, and calling, "Stand and fight it. Stand and fight it, you sonsabitches."

It was a pile of dead stacked like winter logs against the gun mounts and Admiral Delacrois trying to tear away from the restraining hands of his aides and grab a hose and turn it on the roaring inferno. It was Marriner as he went back again and again always to emerge from the smoke and flame dragging the body of a shipmate. It was Winston, the blood running into his eyes from a gash on his forehead, lugging the wildly snapping hose to where he stood and fought the onflowing gasoline to a stand-off. And it was Marriner and Winston together, yelling like madmen and putting their shoulders to the hot tail assembly of a fiercely burning Hellcat and shoving the plane off the bow and into the ocean. It was Anders walking steadily into the flames, cold, icy cold because this was just another battle to him.

It was the raw heroism which emerged from ordinary men who heretofore had possessed no heroism in their makeup whatsoever. A baker trying to save a steward and the two of them blown over the side together and going down into the sea as brothers. The baker was a boy named Andrews from Seattle. He was white. The steward was a boy named Lincoln from Martinsburg, West Virginia. He was black. Under the water there was no difference between them at all.

Finally it was over, and the smoking debris lay dirty under the rising sun. Men wiped the grime from their faces and turned to breathe deeply of the clean morning air. Within themselves they knew a great

377]

pride, and all of them, the seamen and the mechs and the ordnance-men, the tailors and the radiomen and the gunners, all of them shared the blessed camaraderie that comes only to men who have fought side by side with other men.

Later it was Admiral Delacrois down in the wardroom and looking three thousand years old, sipping black coffee, his eyes as bleak as the frozen wastes under the Northern Star at night. And it was Rasmussen, standing respectfully at attention and mouthing his lie magnificently.

"Admiral, sir. I thought it best to report when I could. I was coming off the port catwalk when the enemy plane hit. I saw Commander Crowley fighting the blaze, sir. He was in the middle of it, fighting like hell, when a Hellcat blew. He went over the side, sir." Rasmussen paused and for a moment wondered at the look in Delacrois's eyes. "I thought you should know, sir."

The Admiral sipped his coffee. Finally he said, "Thank you, Chief. Thank you very much."

Delacrois rubbed bloodshot and tired eyes. He looked at his aide almost apologetically.

"I think we will hold burial services at 0700. I think that would be a good hour."

And that too Rasmussen would remember. The rows of canvas-wrapped bodies, each under a flag and lying so still and silent on the port elevator's edge. The ship's company drawn to rigid attention, all of them straight and proud.

The drums sounded under the bark of the rifles, and the hands snapped in salute as the shrouded bodies slid from under the flags, tumbled for only a moment through the sea spray and then disappeared beneath the waves.

[378

XIX

July, 1944

The *Concord* and her escorts came out of the western sea at first light. The gray dawn limned the gaunt ships against the lifting night clouds behind them. They came with the scars showing boldly on the blackened metal and the blood dried black on the twisted steel.

Past Kauai with all flags flying and the water glistening on the sharp prows. They came into line proudly beneath the colors that whipped defiantly under a clearing sky. Eyes that had looked down contested corridors of cloud narrowed again but only against the wind and the salt spray. The *Concord*, the Lady C of Task Force 58, steaming back again, fifty-three days departed and due to pass the nets at Pearl at 0900.

At 0830 the order rang out, "Reduce speed to ten knots."

"Aye aye, sir. Turns for ten knots," came the automatic response.

The crew lined the rails, straining to see what they would see again and again until finally they turned their backs on the westward lands and headed homeward for the last time. They wore their dress white uniforms because the *Concord* was coming into Pearl at flight deck parade, twenty-four hundred men standing at attention to honor the ship which had borne them to victory.

Four miles to the nets now and the snake-slow worming up the channel. Ashore the people watched them come, and eyes widened and lips murmured at the mangled steel.

"My God. How many died there?"

"Three hundred, they say."

At 0850 a new order: "Make turns for five knots. Prepare to enter nets."

Admiral Delacrois wanted solitude and he got it. Alone on the outer bridge he watched the sun reflect off the water, and looked

379]

back on thirty years of service and did not find them wanting. The *Concord* was five hundred yards from the nets when he raised his eyes heavenward. Well, Sir, I brought them back. Slightly bent and worn a little thin around the edges, but we're nearly in the nets now, and so I guess my job is finished here.

"Entering the nets," the cry rang out behind him.

It is a thing I wonder about at times. When the body bows with the years, when the muscles stiffen and the hair turns white, when the brain is tired after too many decisions, why is it then and only then that they finally accept the man and warrant him wise enough to go to battle under command? It is too heavy a weight for aged shoulders. Always the old men lead, and this should not be. Let the young men who fight do the leading. They are there in the arena, and theirs should be the right of leadership. Leave old men alone with their memories because that is all they have, and it should be good enough for them.

"Well, we're back again," Marriner said. "And lucky to be here."

They stood on the bow and watched the shoreline as the *Concord* inched her way toward the last bend in the stream.

"You guys hear the scuttlebutt?" asked Bates.

"Yeah," said Marriner. "The air group is going home."

"Well, don't sound so gloomy about it," Bates said.

Winston regarded Marriner with a shrewd glance. "You're not still thinking about the man who got Hill?"

"No," replied Marriner. "He's gone. I didn't see him die, but I know he's dead. Don't ask me how I know because I couldn't answer you. But I know he's gone, and that part is finished now. I did what I had to do."

"And now?" Anders asked.

Marriner looked at the boyish face and frowned. "How about you, Cort? What now for you?"

Anders laughed. "I asked first."

Marriner turned to Winston. "You, Max?"

Winston shook his head slowly. "I don't know."

"Batesy?"

"I don't know. I may stay out here a while longer." He hesitated a moment. "Then again I may just take a hot bath."

"You and Max have wives," Anders said thoughtfully. "Responsibilities. You have to go home."

Winston glanced at Marriner. "Got an answer to that one, Dick?"

[380

Marriner nodded his head. "Yes, I think so. I think I've got more reason to stay out here than either Cort or Batesy. I've got a reason now for fighting. More than I had before. I guess I'll go out again. It isn't over yet, and Christ knows when it will be. They'll be needing guys who have been there. Julie will understand. She can stay here on Oahu and wait for me. When it's over, we'll go home together."

Winston pursed his lips in concentration. "Well, in that case I see only one course of action open to me. I can't leave you out here alone and unprotected, you know. You might get hurt." An idea suddenly came to Winston. "What the hell. We can't wear these wings forever. Maybe we can find some way of making a living in civilian life together."

Marriner laughed, warmed by these expressions of friendship. "With all your money, Max, I don't doubt we'd do all right. Batesy? Cort?"

"I'll fly your wing, Dick," Anders said quietly.

"Well," Bates said, "I had expectations of leading a division of my own. However, I consent to fly tail-end Charlie if Winston will promise to stop thinking about Doris all the time and concentrate on keeping me alive. I have no intention of getting clobbered at this late stage of the game."

They stood and grinned at each other, aware that something had grown within them that would last all their lives, the love of one strong man for another.

"The girls meeting you?" Bates asked.

"No," Winston replied. "They're waiting at my place."

"Ah," Bates said knowingly. He turned to Anders. "Cort, how the hell can two guys get so horny in only fifty-three days? I'm not horny. Are you?"

"Not a bit," said Anders. "Well, maybe a little bit."

"You two are invited for dinner," Winston laughed. "Tomorrow night."

"Oh?" Bates said innocently. "I thought we'd drop by tonight for a while."

"You do and you get clobbered," Winston said.

"How long will the ship be in for repairs?" Anders asked.

"Sixty days, I heard," said Marriner. "Maybe a little less."

"Well, that gives us time for some leave. Gives you time for a honeymoon, Dick."

"Yeah, Max. I think Julie would like that. She'd like that very much. Kona Inn maybe."

381]

"Why don't we all go?" Bates inquired innocently.

"Because you'll be in sick bay with a busted head if you don't shut up," said Winston.

"Well, let's get in line. They'll be calling flight deck parade in a minute."

"After we dock," said Winston, "let's drop by Aiea and see Steve."

"Good idea, Max," Marriner agreed. "That's what we'll do. We'll go by and see Steve on the way to your house. Julie and Doris will wait a little while longer for us."

The *Concord*, her superstructure twisted like a burnt skeleton along her deck, came to the last bend in the stream. On her flight deck a voice burst through the bullhorn, and the men came to rigid attention until the voice called, "Parade rest."

Chief Rasmussen stood forward near the bow rail, lost in reflection. This is all there is for me, he thought, and I am content to have it that way. For a while there I wondered if I had done a good or evil thing. Now I know, and it no longer worries me. This cruise is over but only till the next one. This week or next week or next month, it's all the same to me because here I belong, and here I will stay until they wrap me in a canvas sack and slide me from under Old Glory.

They were coming hard on the graveyard of the *Arizona*, and so he turned his head to the formation behind him and barked in a flat voice, "Atten . . . HUT."

There were no bright garlands, no band to greet them. Scattered groups of men watched them come, and in their eyes admiration mingled with wonder as the *Concord* inched around the bend in the harbor stream and made her way slowly, majestically, toward her berth.

There was an ache in Delacrois's throat.

Well, it is over now, Sam. We took them out, and we took them back. You said to me once that you hoped someday, just before they died, the gods would touch these young men lightly and leave them eternal youth. I remember your words now because we've come back again, and most of the young men are still young and will be for a time to come. Perhaps they'll never grow old. We took them west, Sam, and they met their God in a new dimension. I'm sorry we could not bring them all back, but it is to our credit that we brought them back at all. So forget it, Sam.

That grizzled Chief told me Crowley died well, but I saw something in his eyes. I believe he lied, but in doing so he allowed me an easy way out. I will award Crowley a medal which is probably a travesty on the other men. But this can be said for Crowley at any rate, at least he was there and he died. Others did not die, including me, and so Crowley did more in that respect than I did. Let him have his medal. It won't help his soul, but it will brighten his memory.

The *Concord* was nudged into the dock by a tug nosing gently at her bow. The anchor detail stood ready on the starboard fo'c'sle deck, the heavy lines in their hands.

A voice sounded from below. "Pass over the lines. Make ready to drop anchor."

Well, we're docking now, Sam. I wish you were here. I hear the creaking of the ship's joints and the sound of voices from the dock. But I hear something else too. Remember, Sam, the football games at the Academy? Remember how, long hours after the game was over, we could still hear the cheers of the crowd ringing in our ears? Well, I hear something now over and above the sounds of the ship docking. I hear a call ring down the sky, a call sounded by all the men who lived and went down under the gold wings. It's a tallyho, Sam, maybe the last tallyho I will ever hear. It grows fainter now, and soon it will be gone.

Down on the deck Marriner and Winston looked up at the bridge where the Admiral stood alone. They saw him wave to them.

"A good old bastard," Winston said.

"I don't believe," Marriner said, "that any of us will ever know what a good old bastard he really is."

"I will," said Bates. "Every time I remember those goddam lights going on."

"I wonder," Anders said meditatively, "if the Admiral is as puzzled as I am?"

"About what?" asked Bates.

"Well," said Anders, "look at it this way. We're going back out there again, all of us. Hill is dead and Remson and Wheeler and Balta and a lot of others. What did we buy with the last year? We're going back again and all of them are dead, and what did we buy with it all?"

For a minute no one spoke. Then Marriner said, "I think I can tell you, Cort. We bought time and space, that's what we bought. Hill and the rest died because we needed time and space. Time to get our carriers out here and our pilots trained. When we got here a year or so ago we had a handful of ships and less than a handful of pilots. Now we've got so many carriers they spread over half the

383]

goddam ocean. We needed the time, and so we bought it with Hill and Remson and Wheeler and the rest. And we needed space. Pearl is in the backwash of the war now. We have the Marshalls and the Gilberts, the Marianas and in the next few weeks or months we'll have a lot of other places closer to Japan. Before the year is out we'll be hitting the Philippines and after that the Jap homeland. We needed the stops along the way that belonged to the enemy, and some of us had to die to get them. More of us will die before it's over, but we've come a hell of a long way since we reported to Barbers Point eleven months ago. It's going to be easier now because we fought this last battle at Saipan. They say we broke the back of Jap carrier aviation, and I believe them. Their good pilots are used up, and so now when we go back we'll be fighting their second string." Suddenly Marriner chuckled and slapped Anders on the back. "I don't doubt you'll wind up this war as the Navy's ranking ace."

"If you don't," Anders said.

"I don't want to," Marriner said. "All I want is to live through it and come back to Julie and raise a bunch of kids who'll probably want to become Army pilots, damn them."

The bullhorn sounded. "Liberty will commence as soon as the gangway is clear."

Delacrois smiled as he saw the young men looking up at him. Goddam it, Sam. They're so young and eager. Well, it's almost time for me to go now, Sam. I see the Aloha Tower over there and it brings a picture to my mind. Some day, when all this is finished and the luxury liner rounds Diamond Head, when the wind comes down off the Pali bearing the smell of leis and the strains of a hula band, will any of us still remember then and perhaps hear the sound of Task Force 58 rocketing over the oceanway under a great echoing in the sky?

Tallyho. Tallyho. Tallyho.

Will we hear the cries ringing down the sky until the last tallyho has been sounded and when the score has been added and the last Jap flag is painted on the side of a cockpit, what of the young men then? For this I know; heroes disappear when wars are finished.

Delacrois watched the four fliers move down the gangway and walk down the dock, proud and strong, and his lips moved in a whisper of good luck to all the young men and to all the old men too, whose names moved away into memory.

[384